**"Help me," Megan whispered.
"Help me find out the truth."**

"Goddamn it," Cole whispered through clenched teeth. "I showed you the truth. It sucks, and it's awful, but there's nothing else to do." He brushed her hair back from her face and cradled her cheek in his palm. Unable to resist touching her. Torturing himself with the silky grain of her skin under his fingers.

"I can't accept that, Cole. I won't. My brother's all I have. I'll never believe he killed Evangeline Gordon. And if I let him die without doing everything I can to prove you wrong, I'll never forgive myself."

So brave. He wondered what it felt like to be loved like that.

How would it feel to be loved like that by *her*. He'd almost had it once. Had been so close he could taste it.

Her mouth was mere inches from his, plump, succulent. Megan's cheeks flooded with heat, and when he looked in her eyes, he saw it again, that flash of awareness that told him he wasn't the only one here with unresolved feelings.

Get up, get out of here, and stop torturing yourself with this.

But he couldn't resist. He bent his head the last few inches and tasted her soft g

BEG *for* MERCY

Jami Alden

FOREVER

NEW YORK   BOSTON

This book is a work of fiction. Names, characters, places, and incidents are the product of the author's imagination or are used fictitiously. Any resemblance to actual events, locales, or persons, living or dead, is coincidental.

Copyright © 2011 by Jami Alden
Excerpt from *Hide from Evil* copyright © 2011 by Jami Alden
All rights reserved. Except as permitted under the U.S. Copyright Act of 1976, no part of this publication may be reproduced, distributed, or transmitted in any form or by any means, or stored in a database or retrieval system, without the prior written permission of the publisher.

Book design by Giorgetta Bell McRee

Forever
Hachette Book Group
237 Park Avenue
New York, NY 10017
Visit our website at www.HachetteBookGroup.com.

Forever is an imprint of Grand Central Publishing.
The Forever name and logo is a trademark of Hachette Book Group, Inc.

The publisher is not responsible for websites (or their content) that are not owned by the publisher.

Printed in the United States of America

First Printing: June 2011

10 9 8 7 6 5 4 3 2 1

To the SSRWA
Monica, who, when I pitched her the idea, told me,
"This is it!" May you wear your Brainy Smurf shirt
with pride. You ARE always right.
Nyree, who brainstormed the idea on that long ago hike
at the dish. Without you, there would be no Book 2!

And to Gajus for everything, but especially for keeping
two small boys occupied while I hunkered over my
AlphaSmart in the cabin loft.

Acknowledgments

In the crazy world of publishing, an author needs all the help she can get. I am incredibly lucky to have amazing people who support me. This book wouldn't have been possible without my writer friends who cheer me on and help rescue me from any corners I may have written myself into. So thanks as always to the SF lunch brigade—Barbara Freethy, Carol Culver, Tracy Grant, Anne Mallory, Penelope Williamson, Veronica Wolff, Poppy Reiffin, and of course Monica McCarty and Bella Andre. I also owe an especially huge thanks to Kim Whalen, agent extraordinaire, for her support, encouragement, and especially her fervent, "I LOVE this," after she read the first hundred pages of this book.

BEG *for*
MERCY

Chapter 1

It wasn't quite over yet, but Megan Flynn was 99 percent sure this was going to go down as one of the best days of her life.

And judging from the molten look Cole Williams was giving her across her tiny kitchen table, her perfect day was about to glide seamlessly into a perfect night.

"That was amazing," he said, leaning back in his chair, relaxed after a day spent on the water, followed by a home-cooked meal of fresh-caught local salmon accompanied by a bottle of Columbia Valley Pinot Noir. His plate was so clean he might have licked it, and Megan felt a ridiculous spurt of feminine pride in having provided a meal he'd so obviously enjoyed.

Megan traced the edge of her wineglass with her finger and gave him a sly smile. "So maybe next time you make salmon you'll listen to me and not cook it down to a fine dust?"

Cole laughed and leaned across the table to refill her wineglass. "My mom always said you had to cook it enough to kill the bacteria." He set the bottle down and took her free hand in his, his thumb tracing slow circles in the sensitive hollow of her palm.

Megan took a swallow of wine and smiled. "Since you grew up in a landlocked state, I'll let you off the hook. But from now on, leave the seafood to us natives. Deal?"

"Deal. I'll grill the steaks; you do the fish."

Megan tried not to let herself get too carried away with fantasies of a lifetime of quiet dinners like this and wiped what she knew was a completely moony look off her face.

But it was impossible for her not to get carried away with Cole, all smoldering and intense across the table from her. With his dark eyes, dark skin, and bold, almost craggy features, Cole was a little too rough to be classically handsome. But when his full lips pulled into that sexy smile, Megan felt like she was going to melt into a puddle and spill right off her chair.

He pushed back from the table and kept hold of her hand as he walked the few steps to the couch. He settled against the cushions and she sank down next to him, her legs folded under her short skirt.

The short, flowered halter dress was completely inappropriate for a day out on Puget Sound on Cole's boat. Even in early June, the temperature out on the water didn't get much above sixty degrees. But when she'd gotten dressed that morning, she'd chosen the dress as a key part of her mission.

Namely, to finally break through Detective Cole Williams's ironclad control.

Up until tonight, every date with the broodingly sexy detective had ended the same. With a kiss. Then more kisses that started with soft pecks and worked their way up to deep, wet, tongue-sliding, lip-sucking, blood-boiling kisses. Kisses that got Megan hotter than she'd ever been with any other man.

But no matter how hot she got, he never pushed it past hot kisses and light caresses, leaving her humming and thrumming with unsatisfied desire.

She was done with taking it slow. She wanted Cole, she wanted him now, and judging from the way his dark gaze kept straying down to the curves of her breasts swelling over the neckline of her dress, he was finally done too.

He tucked a lock of her hair behind her ear. "I missed you these last couple of weeks."

He looked a little worn around the edges, and for good reason. Cole was a homicide detective for the Seattle PD, and his latest case had him working such long hours that she'd hardly seen him.

"You sound a little surprised by that."

"I am," Cole replied, then held up a hand at her look of mock offense. "I didn't mean it like that."

"Then how did you mean it, smooth talker?" Megan gave him a playful swat on the leg that left her hand resting on the top of his thigh.

The lines around Cole's deep-set eyes crinkled with his sheepish grin. "Usually when I'm head down in a case, I'm totally focused. I forget to eat, forget to sleep, everything." He leaned in closer, close enough she could feel his warm, wine-scented breath tease her lips. "But I couldn't forget about you."

"I missed you too," Megan whispered right before his mouth covered hers. She parted her lips willingly, eager for the heat, the taste of him as his tongue thrust in. Pushing her back against the cushions, he licked, sucked, nipped, until Megan was clutching at him, practically shaking with need.

Please let tonight be the night.

As though he heard her silent plea, his kiss turned fierce and demanding. There was something different in his touch, in the way he kissed her. Like he was starving and she was the most delicious thing on earth.

Megan struggled to catch her breath as he pushed her back onto the couch. She'd known there was passion simmering under that stony cop surface, but nothing had prepared her for this.

Megan slid her hand up Cole's back, dragging the hem of his T-shirt from the waistband of his jeans. She purred in pleasure at the feel of his hot, smooth skin, the sound swallowed up by a sleek thrust of his tongue against hers. She traced her fingers up the hard slabs of muscle, her mouth moving eagerly under his as she sought to drink in every touch, every taste.

Cole pulled the strap off the other shoulder and tugged the bodice of her dress down to her waist. His groan of satisfaction rumbled through her core, sending a pulse of heat between her legs. He held himself still above her, muscles quivering as his hot, dark eyes locked on her naked breasts. Her nipples were hard, aching and tingling, begging for his touch.

A vivid flush rode his sharp cheekbones. His mouth was kiss swollen, his lips parted as his breath came in hot pants. "Jesus Christ," he said in a low, strained voice. "I've been thinking about this from the second I laid eyes on you, and even then... You're so goddamn gorgeous I don't know how I kept my hands off you this long."

He tugged his T-shirt the rest of the way over his head. Megan was treated to a glimpse of a wide, defined chest and rippling six-pack dusted with fine dark hair before he settled himself back on top of her. She let out an "ooh" at the first brush of skin on skin, a little surprised not to see sparks flying from where their bodies touched. He settled between her thighs, letting her feel the rock-hard ridge of his erection straining at the fly of his pants, leaving no doubt as to how much he wanted her. He kissed her again, his tongue thrusting in deep, lazy strokes that had her aching and shifting against him in an agony of need.

Megan kissed him back with everything she had, her heart twisting in her chest with the knowledge that sex with Cole was going to be amazing. Momentous.

Sex with Cole would change everything.

But that was okay. Because she was in love with Cole Williams. It had taken some convincing on her part to get him here, but she was pretty sure he was on his way to being in love with her too.

As scary as the idea of love was, Megan knew that with Cole by her side, everything would be okay.

Riinnnnnggg.

Cole jerked in her embrace, his lips stilling against hers as the harsh ring pierced through the sound of fast breath and wet kisses.

Megan tensed. A cop to his core, Cole never let anything get between him and his sworn duty. Even on his day off. She closed her eyes and started to count to one hundred, trying to cool her body and bring herself back from the edge as she prepared for yet another night on the razor's edge of sexual frustration.

To her shock, the cell phone kept ringing. Cole curled his fingers more tightly in her hair and resumed kissing her with that almost primitive intensity. Wow. *Cole must really want me if he's ignoring it.* A thrill rippled through her at the thought.

A second after the ringing stopped, it started again.

"Fuck!" Cole roared.

Exactly what I had in mind, she thought. "I guess you better get that," she sighed.

Cole nodded and let out a string of curses as he pushed himself off of her and grabbed his cell from the end table. "Jorgensen, why the hell are you calling me on my afternoon off?"

It was his partner, Nick Jorgensen. Megan sighed and tried to swallow back her disappointment. If she really wanted a relationship with Cole, she would have to get used to the demands of the career he loved.

Party's over. Megan sat up and pulled her dress back over her breasts and tugged her skirt down to cover her legs. Cole was silent for several seconds, his dark brows pulling into a tight frown over eyes that were losing their sensual haze.

She could make out a little bit of what Jorgensen was saying on the other line, but not enough to figure out exactly what was going on. Something bad, she guessed from the grim look on Cole's face.

"I'm off today," Cole said. "Why don't you handle it—"

Jorgensen answered loud and clear. She heard every word. "This is a slam dunk, asshole. Get over here now."

Cole's broad shoulders slumped, and he clawed his fingers through his hair. "Fine, I'll be there as soon as I can." *I'm sorry,* he mouthed to her.

Megan gave him a feeble imitation of an understanding smile, her sexual glow dimming by several watts.

"What's the address?"

Megan's stomach seized as she heard Jorgensen give Cole the number and street.

She had to have misheard.

Cole disconnected the call, zipped up his pants, and reached for his shirt. "I'm sorry, Megan, but I have to go—"

"Did he just say the address is Forty-five Appleton Street?"

He didn't confirm. His face was cold and wiped clean of all expression.

"Cole, that's my brother's address. What's going on?" Panic roared through her veins, stealing her breath, replacing the heat of arousal with the cold bite of fear. Cole was a homicide detective. There was only one reason he would be called to Sean's house. She sprang from the couch and grabbed his arm. "Is my brother dead? Did something happen? You have to tell me!"

Cole grabbed her in a brief, fierce hug. "I don't know the details. I'll call you as soon as I can." He pulled away, and when she looked up, she saw that he'd gone into full-on Robocop mode. He reached for his phone and his jacket. "Just stay here and wait for my call."

The door hadn't even closed behind him before she grabbed her phone and dialed her brother's house. Straight to voice mail. "Sean, pick up!" she yelled, even though she knew he couldn't hear her. She yanked on a fleece pullover and stuffed her feet into flip-flops, dialing Sean's cell phone as she rushed out the door.

Her call went straight to voice mail and she left another message.

She slipped on the damp wooden stairs that led out, barely catching herself before she tumbled down the last two to the paved driveway below. She took a deep breath and gathered her trembling legs under her before continuing.

Please God, let everything be all right. Please let Sean

be okay. Sean had done ten years in the military, including his last tour in Afghanistan. He couldn't have survived that only to return home and...

She wouldn't let herself think it. Her fingers shook so hard she could barely get the keys into the ignition. She made the drive in five minutes flat.

Her heart seized in her chest as she pulled over. Flashing lights from an ambulance and two Seattle PD squad cars created a swirling eddy of blue and red in the twilight. Cole's Jeep was parked behind a black-and-white, but he was nowhere in sight.

Neither was Sean. Megan sprinted across the street, hearing the harsh catch of her breath and the pounding of her heart in her head. The ambulance blocked the driveway. She skirted around and saw two EMTs standing by the back door.

"What's happening?" she said. "Is someone dead? Is my brother dead?"

"Hey, you can't be here," one of them said.

"Somebody tell me what the hell is going on."

Neither responded, but the two men shared a look.

She didn't realize she'd started screaming Sean's name until a uniformed cop got right up in her face.

"Hey, this is a crime scene." The cop, with his blond hair sticking out from under his cap and ruddy cheeks, looked barely old enough to shave.

"This is my brother's house," she yelled, and tried to shove past him. "You have to tell me if he's okay."

The cop grabbed her by the shoulders and gently but firmly made her move. "Back it up."

"Get your hands off of me!"

"Is there a problem, Officer Dicks?"

Megan whipped her head in the direction of the familiar voice just in time to see Cole's partner, Nick Jorgensen, rounding the ambulance.

"Megan?" He motioned for the cop to let her go but caught her as she attempted to sprint up to the ambulance. "You need to get out of here."

"Is my brother in there, Nick? Is he dead? You have to tell me."

His closed, careful expression didn't provide any reassurance. "Megan, go home. Wait for someone to call you—"

"Not until I know—" She stopped when she saw Sean appear in the doorway. The constant strobe of emergency lights made him fade in and out. He looked out of it, like he didn't know exactly where he was.

"Sean," she yelled, a half sob, half laugh, so relieved to see him alive she almost fell to her knees. Sean's head turned at the sound of her voice. He took a step toward her, his leg nearly buckling under him as he stumbled on the first step.

Someone jerked him hard from behind, halting his fall. Then Sean staggered forward a few more steps as though someone was pushing him, his hands cuffed behind his back.

Other details became clear in that split second, her brain registering them in a series of high-definition freeze-frames. *Snap.* She saw that her military-neat brother was wearing a torn khaki undershirt stained with reddish brown streaks. *Snap.* Her brain registered those same streaks on his pants. *Snap.* A spattering of it across the part of his arm she could see with his hands handcuffed behind him.

Oh my God. Blood.

Snap. The man walking behind her brother, shoving him down the sidewalk, was none other than her would-be lover, Detective Cole Williams.

Megan leaped from her frozen stupor. She tried to shake off Nick, but he held her arm in an iron grip. "Sean, are you all right?"

Cole's dark eyes locked on her for a fraction of a second. He didn't make a move in her direction, but instead steered Sean to a squad car. Sean's mouth moved, but the words were obliterated by the din of radios squawking and shouted orders. Neighbors came out to their front stoops to gawk.

Megan's stomach lurched as she watched Cole with her brother. She had been at the scene of enough arrests to recognize someone being Mirandized.

"Let go of me!" She shoved at Nick and yanked until her shoulder threatened to pop from its socket, but he wasn't about to let her go anywhere. "Cole, tell me what's happening."

He shoved her brother into the back of a black-and-white and slammed the door behind him.

"Cole, answer me!"

His wide shoulders were vibrating with tension as he stalked up the lawn toward her, giving a nearly imperceptible nod at Nick. The grip on her arm eased.

She ran, not toward Cole, but to the squad car where Sean waited. She could see his face in the window, panic in his eyes. "Sean, Sean, it's going to be okay." Strong arms wrapped around her waist before she could reach the car. "No, let me go! I need to talk to him!" she screamed. In another second the squad car pulled away from the curb.

Megan wheeled on her captor, shoving at Cole's chest. "How could you? How could you arrest my brother?"

"I told you to stay home—" he started, his low, too-calm voice kicking her fury higher.

"Fuck you! You can't expect me to stay home and wait by the phone. You should have told me what was happening—"

"Megan, I can't give you details—"

"I told you this was my brother's house!"

"I have a job to do. I can't break the rules. Even for you."

His eyes were flat, black chips of ice. Megan stepped back, unable to believe this was the same man who had spent the day laughing and flirting with her. The same man who less than half an hour ago had his hand up her skirt and his mouth on hers, holding on to his control by a thread as he slid her panties down her legs.

Right now he stared at her as though she was just another freak who'd showed up at a crime scene.

Rage dissolved into fear, leaving her desperate. "You have to help me, Cole. Help me get him out of this."

Cole's look thawed a degree, but his mouth stayed in a straight, bitter line. "I don't know what to tell you. Sean's in big trouble."

"No! There has to be something you can do."

He shook his head. "You really want my advice? Get a damn good lawyer."

She went numb.

Cole looked over her head and spoke to someone behind her. "Get her out of here."

"Come on, miss, let's get you home." Male hands gripped her arms, pulling her toward the street as the man she loved turned his back and walked away.

Chapter 2

Seattle Tribune, January 20, 2008

DECORATED WAR VETERAN SENTENCED TO DEATH
A King County jury has formally sentenced thirty-year-old Sean Flynn to the death penalty after being convicted of raping and killing a young woman.

Flynn was convicted last month of the aggravated rape and first-degree murder of Evangeline Gordon, twenty-one, who Flynn met at Seattle nightclub Club One. Gordon was seen leaving with Flynn on the night of June 4. Her body was found the next day in Flynn's house.

Flynn's was the first case in which King County prosecutors sought a death sentence in nearly a decade.

Flynn's attorneys say they plan to appeal the verdict.

—⚬⚬⚬—

Outside Walla Walla, Washington, Two Years Later

An all-too-familiar tight feeling settled in Megan's stomach as she took a right turn off Highway 12 in Walla Walla and the towers of the Washington State Penitentiary, aka the Walls, came into view.

The sight of the squat brick buildings never failed to send a wave of dread through her, as it had every single Saturday for the past two years, ever since Sean had been sentenced.

It still struck her as surreal, impossible that Sean could ever be convicted of murder, much less sentenced to the death penalty.

She'd been devastated when she'd learned that the prosecutor planned to ask for death in Sean's case. Prosecuting attorney Mark Benson had been up for reelection and had been reeling under the upsurge in violent crime. He seized on Sean's case as the perfect opportunity to take bold action and set an example. To show that no one, not even a decorated war hero with an otherwise spotless record, could escape due punishment for his crimes.

Despite Sean's continued assertions of innocence and the support of the best attorneys they could afford, it had taken a jury less than two hours to return with a guilty verdict.

Even Megan, in her weaker moments, was forced to admit it looked bad. If she hadn't known her brother to his very soul, she might have questioned his innocence too. The victim, Evangeline Gordon, had been killed by multiple stab wounds, and there was little question the weapon was the Randall knife Sean and the other members of his Army Ranger regiment had had specially made. Evidence of sexual assault put the final nail in Sean's coffin, as had the testimony from the victim's friend that he had been stalking Evangeline before she died. . . .

Seemingly irrefutable evidence that gave the judge and jury ample reason to levy the ultimate penalty.

Megan refused to believe in her brother's guilt. She

knew, with every fiber of her being, that Sean was innocent. The man she knew wasn't capable of what they'd
accused him of. Sean was fiercely protective and would
never deliberately hurt a weaker person. He would never
hurt a woman, much less rape or kill one.

Too bad no one else gave any weight to her assertions
that Sean, who had been drugged along with the victim,
had been framed by the real killer.

She'd taken her story to anyone who would listen, until
almost everyone outside of Sean's attorneys had written
her off as delusional, unwilling to face the truth.

But she knew the truth, she thought as she took the
turn toward the prison. The truth was that Sean wasn't
guilty, and Megan didn't care if people dismissed her as a
whack job. She wasn't going to stop until Sean was free.

A dream that still felt impossibly out of reach.

Gloom had settled like a wet wool blanket on her
shoulders on the drive here. Now she struggled to shrug
it off and put a goddamn smile on her face. Though she'd
had hours to prepare herself, she was still practicing her
cheerful pep talk as she checked in at the entrance and
pulled into visitor parking. She checked her reflection in
the rearview mirror and made a feeble attempt to conjure
a smile that didn't look like a grimace.

Suck it up, Flynn, she scolded herself. *Sean's already
got it bad enough. He doesn't need you coming in looking
like death warmed over.*

A half laugh, half sob scraped her throat at her mental
phrasing.

There's still time, she reminded herself.

She pulled her purse into her lap and took out her
makeup kit. Just as she had every Saturday for the last

year and a half, Megan worked a little last-minute magic. Concealer to disguise the dark circles under her eyes from sleepless nights. Highlighter along the top of her cheekbones to make the hollows underneath look less pronounced. Blush to coax to life what was left of the peach in her peaches-and-cream complexion. Last, tinted gloss so Sean wouldn't see that her lips were as drained of color as the rest of her.

The results were far from perfect, but maybe it would keep Sean from noticing the toll insomnia and stress had taken on his little sister's face.

Yeah right. Sean had the kind of eagle eye that had qualified him for sniper training in the Army Rangers. He wasn't going to miss the red eyes and road map of fatigue lines, no matter how much powder and sparkle she applied.

Megan got out of the car and felt her shoulders start to slump and her mouth turn down. She stopped herself short and paused for her weekly mental asskicking. *Get your act together, Megan! Sean needs you to be strong. Sean needs to see you're okay. Now put on a fucking happy face like you do every Saturday.*

But it wasn't just any Saturday, and the thought made the soles of Megan's black Converse All Stars move at a snail's pace toward the visitor check-in center. She was already tired. It was a four-hour drive from Seattle to the Walls. When Sean was first convicted and sent to the penitentiary in Walla Walla, Megan had considered moving to be closer to him. But Sean had told her to drop the subject or he would refuse all future visits. *No way am I going to let you move out here to the ass end of nowhere just so you can see me for two hours a week.*

Megan had been secretly relieved. She hated it out here. If she were objective about it, she'd probably find the rolling hills, increasingly populated by vineyards, and acres of lush farmland beautiful. But to Megan the wide-open space and sparse population represented exile. The weekly drives took their toll on her long-suffering Honda, but they helped her cope. She used the drive here to prepare for her visit, to think up topics of conversation, stories about the kids and families she was working with. Brace herself for Sean's grim silence, his monosyllabic answers, the forced smile that didn't do anything to erase the despair in his green eyes.

When she left, she guiltily relished her ability to leave the prison behind and drive west, literally into the sunset. She would roll down the windows and let the wind scrub off the sickening smell of Lysol and despair that seemed to cling to her, welcoming the transition from bright sun to Seattle's cool, cloudy sky. A rush of shamed relief would bring her back to her own world, her own life.

She checked her watch and forced herself to step up her pace. Visiting hours for the Intensive Management Unit, or IMU for short, were set in stone, and if she didn't make it through processing by 1:00 p.m., she was screwed. And today of all days, she knew Sean would be counting on her to provide some sort of friendly contact from the outside world.

Megan went through the check-in process automatically, showing her photo ID and walking through the metal detector. After her first visit, which seemed like centuries ago, she'd learned to lock her purse in the trunk of her car and not carry anything but her driver's license.

She kept her eyes forward and her face impassive,

never making eye contact with anyone in the waiting room. She'd chosen her clothing as much for modesty as for warmth. The heavy turtleneck sweater and baggy jeans gave no hint of skin or curves. Still, she could feel the eyes of the other male visitors, even the male prison guards, making her skin crawl under her dowdy clothes.

Finally she was escorted to a booth to wait for Sean. The slight relief at no longer being on display gave way to the heavy sadness that never failed to surge as soon as the guard locked the door behind her.

While she waited, she tried to swallow back the lump that had taken residence in her throat the day Sean was arrested and expanded to near choking size each week when her butt hit the hard orange plastic of the waiting room chair.

But this week the lump was bigger—like a softball lodged at the base of her throat. And now tears were pricking at the backs of her eyes. She angrily swiped them away, hoping she didn't rub off the concealer in the process. No way was she going to let Sean find her crying. He already thought she was too emotional to deal with his problems. Today she needed to be strong. For him. For herself.

Earlier in the week, the Supreme Court of Washington denied Sean's second appeal. Adam Brockner, Sean's attorney, tried to console her, telling her it was just a setback. When Sean's death sentence had been held up in the state's mandatory review process, that, too, had been a mere setback.

Adam Brockner was full of it.

Her brother was still stuck in this hellhole for something he didn't do. She'd call that more than a setback.

She'd said as much to Brockner when he'd called her on Wednesday after the three judges on the panel had issued their ruling.

Nothing she could do about that. She'd written a lot of freelance pieces about criminal cases, and her volunteer work as a child advocate gave her some knowledge of the legal system, but she was no defense attorney. All she could do was what she'd been doing since the night Sean was arrested. Put on a brave face for her brother.

That, and explore every shred of evidence that might lead to Evangeline Gordon's real killer. The appeals process could keep Sean alive for years, but finding the real murderer was Sean's only true shot at freedom.

After a few minutes, Megan was summoned by a guard and instructed to sit in a booth in the prison's no-contact visiting area. A few moments later, she watched through the Plexiglas divider as Sean was led in. Cuffed and shackled, he shuffled into the room, his shoulders hunched slightly because of the cuffs. Even so, her brother's tall body radiated power and strength.

He and Megan shared their mother's high cheekbones and dark hair and their father's deep green eyes, but the resemblance ended there. Megan's wide eyes, small nose, and full mouth gave her face a soft, frustratingly childlike quality—at twenty-nine, she still got carded when she bought drinks. Sean's features were stronger, sculpted. The rigors of prison had honed his sharp cheekbones and squared-off chin until his features looked chiseled from granite.

And his eyes, thickly lashed but deep-set under strong brows, gave him a tough, almost menacing look that Megan knew others found intimidating. Now, with his skin pulled tight over muscles and bones, he didn't look like anyone you wanted to mess with.

But he was not a monster. He was not a murderer. She would never believe that her brother—who at fifteen years old had held her thirteen-year-old hand at their parents' funeral and promised her he would always take care of her—could be capable of raping and killing a woman.

Still, she could see why the guard moved away quickly once he unlocked Sean's cuffs and slammed the cell door behind him. Not that Sean had caused any trouble during his incarceration.

Sean settled his long form in a molded plastic chair and reached for the handset as she did the same. As Megan put it to her ear, she braced herself to meet her brother's eyes.

She never got used to it, the way his eyes, which used to glint with humor and crinkle at the corners with his easy smile, were now flat, dark pools staring out of his skull. No light. No joy. Only the desperation of a man trying to make it through one more day. It hit her like a sucker punch to the gut every time.

She pulled her mouth into a smile. "Hey, Sean."

"Hey, Bugs," he replied.

Megan's smile morphed from pasted on to the genuine article at her brother's use of the old nickname he'd given her when she was seven, before a mouthful of braces had taken care of her striking resemblance to a certain animated rabbit. She'd hated the nickname at the time, but now it gave her a little burst of hope that maybe the Sean she grew up with wasn't lost after all.

When she met his eyes through the glass, something like relief swept through her at the expression in them. For the first time since his conviction, there was something there that looked less like hopelessness and more like resolution. Like he had a purpose and finally knew what he was fighting for.

Her brother on a mission was a force to be reckoned with. They were going to get through this, no matter how long it took, no matter how many rocks she had to turn over to find the truth.

"You look tired."

She scoffed in mock offense. "Thanks a pantload. I drive four hours to see you and you tell me I look like crap?" There was no venom in her tone, and she relished the opportunity to bust his chops a little. "You better tell me how gorgeous I am or I won't come see you next weekend."

Something flickered in his gaze. "You shouldn't come so much. You have better things to do with your time."

She rolled her eyes. "Why do we always have to have this conversation? I don't have a life. If I didn't come visit you, I'd spend my Saturdays sitting on my couch eating Ben and Jerry's from the carton and watching movies on Lifetime. I might even get a cat," she said with a shudder. "You're saving me from a couch full of hairballs and an ass the size of Jupiter."

Sean didn't smile. He never did. "The only reason you don't have a life is because of me."

"That's not true." At least, not the way she saw it. Sure, most of her friends had gotten tired of what they saw as her delusional devotion to her brother and belief in his innocence. And she'd gone through all of her savings and racked up a mountain of debt to pay private investigators to look into Sean's case and help her come up with alternate suspects in Evangeline Gordon's murder. But Sean was family, the only family she had left. "And even if it were true, it wouldn't matter. I would do anything for you—you know that." Sean had given up a big chunk of his own childhood to help raise her after their parents were killed in a car accident. Even if Megan didn't love Sean more than anyone on the planet, she would have owed him for that.

His mouth softened into something approaching a smile. "Yeah, I know. But you need to live. You should be out, having fun, dating guys I'd want to beat up."

"I'm only up here on Saturdays. Who says I don't go out?"

He cocked a dark eyebrow at her, his knowing expression so familiar it made her chest hurt.

She shrugged. "Dating is overrated. Besides, I'm busy. I just got an article accepted in *Seattle* magazine and have a new corporate copywriting client. And I just started working with this new girl—oh my God, her family is such a mess." Sean let her ramble on about fourteen-year-old Devany and her alcoholic, absentee dad and meth-addicted mother. Last month, Megan became her court-appointed advocate, and after a few rocky interactions, they were starting to hit it off. "Before she moved in with her aunt, she went between her mom and foster care ten times in six years. She's run away twice and lived on the streets. Her mom gets out of court-ordered rehab in a couple weeks, and Devany's afraid she's going to have to move again. I'm doing what I can to make sure she has some stability for a while."

Megan had started as a court-appointed advocate shortly before Sean got out of the army, and she had loved it so much she'd considered going back to school to get a master's in social work. Sean's arrest, the trial, the lawyers, sucked up any energy—not to mention funds—she might have had for graduate school. So she'd kept up her freelance writing to keep the creditors from blowing down her doors and thrown herself into her volunteer work.

"She's lucky to have you on her side. All the kids you help are."

Megan felt tears prick at the backs of her eyes. "Thanks. Not everyone has a big brother protector like you, but I do my best." It gave her some comfort to be able to give victimized kids a voice, to have some impact on their situation when she couldn't help Sean.

Sean was silent, staring at her with a funny expression on his face. Oddly affectionate, like he was trying to memorize her face. Totally different from the grim, stony visage she'd encountered on nearly every visit for the past three years.

"What is up with you?" she finally asked. "You're acting all weird."

"What do you mean?"

"You seem, like, not happy, but, uh, content? After what happened..." She licked her lips, paused. Might as well acknowledge the giant elephant in the room. "The ruling on your appeal, I mean. I expected you to be in a much worse mood."

"Yeah, well, it wasn't like it was unexpected," he said with a shrug. "We need to talk about what happens next."

"I talked to Adam and he's already working on a collateral appeal."

"I know," Sean said. "I told him to withdraw it."

Megan cocked her head to the side. "You're going to fire Adam and appeal on the grounds of faulty counsel?"

From what Megan had read, that was one of the more common ways to get a new trial granted.

Sean shook his head, his eyes grave. The warmth in Sean's unexpectedly pleasant mood faltered. "There aren't going to be any more appeals," he said.

Megan's head jerked to the side, like she hadn't heard him correctly. "What do you mean?"

"I've decided to waive my right to any further appeals. I'm tired of trying to work the system just to draw out the inevitable."

"But that means...they'll set an execution date."

His head moved in an almost imperceptible nod. "Yeah."

Her stomach flipped over and her turtleneck sweater started to itch around her neck. "No. No. I know you feel discouraged right now, but once you've had time to think about it—"

"I've had three years to think about it. Trust me, when you spend most of your time alone, there's a lot of time to contemplate your life. I just want this over with."

"I can't let you quit." But she could see the resolve on his face. Her heart thudded with panic and her fingertips went numb. He meant it. He was going to give up.

"You can't leave me, Sean. You can't do this to me." Angry tears burned the backs of her eyes, and it felt like a giant fist was squeezing her chest.

For the first time today, Sean looked angry. "I'm doing this for you, Megan. I won't let you waste your life—"

"No! Don't you put this on me."

"Fine," he snarled. "I'm a selfish fuck. I'm doing this for myself. But I can't take it anymore, Megan."

His voice cracked and her heart ripped in half. His

eyes were once again dark and desolate, bright with unshed tears. "The first appeals took two years. The next one will take at least that long. Years I'll spend in a nine-by-nine cell. And once in a while they let me out to walk around the yard like a fucking dog."

"You're alive," she said, unable to choke back her sobs.

"I'm in hell."

She shook her head, though she couldn't deny the truth. She and her brother had grown up camping and exploring the wilderness in the Cascade Mountains. Sean was never happier than when he was out in the open air, nothing around but the vastness of nature to explore. For him to be confined to a cage was nothing short of torture.

But she couldn't let him go so easily.

"Sean, I won't let you die for something you didn't do. We just need more time, and when we find out who the real killer is—"

She stopped at Sean's derisive snort. "Come on, Megan. It's been three years. Three fucking years and I still can't remember a goddamned thing about that night. If there were any leads, any trace of evidence against someone else, someone would have found it by now."

"Don't say that. Convicts who've been on death row for decades have had their convictions overturned because of new evidence."

"Yeah, DNA evidence. And the only DNA found on or around Evangeline Gordon was mine." He shook his head. "Hell, maybe we're both wrong. Maybe I did do it."

Megan swallowed back a surge of nausea. "Don't say that. We both know you're not capable—"

"You don't know. You don't know what I saw when

I was deployed. Shit like that changes a person, Megan. You see things, and you kill in the name of your country—"

"Shut up," she hissed. "Do not spew that shit at me." She'd heard enough of it during his trial, the experts spouting off about operational stress exposure, post-traumatic stress disorder, and traumatic brain injuries that could alter a soldier's behavior. "You think I'm going to change my mind about you? It won't work."

Sean shook his head, suddenly looking a hundred years old. Beaten down. Utterly defeated. "All I know is that we're both stuck. I don't want this life for either of us."

Megan could only shake her head as she struggled to swallow back her sobs, tried to conjure the words that would convince him to turn from this drastic course. "Please," was all she could come up with. "Please don't leave me alone."

His firm mouth trembled a little as he spoke. "It'll be better this way. You have to trust me on that."

"How can it possibly be better for you to die for something you didn't do? This isn't right. This isn't fair. You have to give me time to fix it."

He shook his head and pressed the palm of his hand up to the Plexiglas divider. Megan placed her own palm against his. "Some things can't be fixed. You know that. Sometimes you get dealt a shitty hand, and you just do what you can to pick up the pieces and move on. That's what I want you to do."

"No. I don't know what kind of suicidal bullshit you're trying to pull, but I don't accept this. I'm going to talk to your attorneys, and when I come back next week—"

"Don't come back."

Megan stopped short, pulling her hand away from the glass. "What?"

Sean swallowed hard and shifted in his seat, straightening up like he was bracing for something. "This is it, Meg," he said, his voice barely audible through the handset. If she hadn't seen his lips move, she might have believed he hadn't spoken at all. "I don't want you to visit anymore."

"Shut up, Sean. Of course I'm coming back."

He shook his head. "I won't see you."

She fell back in her chair. He would do it too. He'd refuse to accept her visits, and the prison wouldn't force him. "How can you do this to me, Sean?"

He closed his eyes and shook his head slowly. When he opened his eyes, they held the same peaceful resolve she'd found so reassuring just moments ago. "I'm tired of you seeing me like this. I know it kills you a little every time you come here, and I won't keep doing this to you."

"It's my choice, Sean! Believe me, I can handle this as long as I know there's still a chance you'll get out of here alive."

"There is no chance. And it's time you accepted that."

She had no words to convince him otherwise.

"I love you, Megan. You know that, right?"

"I love you too! But how can you say you love me and make a decision like this?"

"It's all going to work out for the best," he said. "Someday you'll see." He kissed his fingers and pressed them up to the glass. "Bye, Megan."

Before she could react, he placed his handset back in its cradle.

"Sean! Wait!" she screamed, even though he couldn't

hear her through the soundproof glass. Sean rose from his chair and went to the door to summon the guard.

Megan pounded her fist on the Plexiglas, but Sean didn't so much as look back.

——m——

Sean silently followed the guard out the door. With the thick layer of plate glass muting her, he could pretend Megan wasn't there. He didn't turn to watch her go. He had to push it away, couldn't let himself get taken in by her pain. Megan was strong. She would recover.

He shoved all thoughts of her aside. The emotion that had overwhelmed him at seeing her drained out as quickly as it had filled him, leaving him edgy and overstimulated like he always was after her visits.

The guard wrapped a hand around his arm and steered him through the visitor's complex and back to the IMU cell block. Sean struggled to slow his breath, quiet his mind as every cell resisted the idea of going back to his hole.

He counted every clank of his shackles as they walked down the concrete blue corridor with its yellow cell doors. One, two, three, four ... By the time he got to ten, he knew he wasn't going to try to throw his cuffed wrists around the guard's neck.

Eleven, twelve, he heard his guard speak. "What?" Sean said as he lifted his head. Then he realized the guard wasn't speaking to him, but to another guard escorting a prisoner out of his cell for his exercise hour. It was the guy two cells down from Sean's, the guy whose screaming jarred Sean from sleep most nights. He didn't know what the guy was in for, didn't care.

It was the first time in two years Sean had seen the man's face. Their eyes met for a split second, and Sean registered a doughy face and a green tattoo creeping up the guy's neck before he broke contact. He could feel the guy's stare as the guards continued their conversation. Sean kept his eyes locked on the floor like a wary dog.

He had no interest in making any connection, no matter how small.

The slide of his metal cell door drowned out the squeak of footsteps, and Sean stepped inside. He clenched his teeth as the door clanged shut and put his hands through the slot without being told. Rattle, snick, the cuffs came loose and Sean pulled his hands back inside.

He sat down on his bunk. Stood up. Went to the sink, bent his head to drink from the faucet. Paced the length of his cell, forward and back, tracing the groove that had worn into the concrete floor from the feet of dozens of poor bastards like him.

Lying down on his bunk, he closed his eyes and tried to conjure up the blue sky and snow-dusted mountains surrounding his father's fishing cabin. But all he could see was Megan's face, pale and tight and wet with tears.

And another face, beautiful, delicate, with wide-set dark eyes that he'd sworn were pleading for help. His stomach twisted, and for the millionth time he wished he'd never agreed to go to Club One, where his "friend" Jimmy Caparulo had been working as a bouncer. Wished he hadn't given in to his friend's pleas to make amends after what Jimmy had done to Megan.

But he'd gone to meet Jimmy, and that night he'd met her. Evangeline Gordon. Beautiful, mysterious, and in Sean's eyes, vulnerable, though he'd never figured out exactly why. But she had that lost-little-girl-in-need-of-saving vibe he'd always been a sucker for, and once he'd picked up on it, he couldn't let it go. Not that she'd given him a whole lot of encouragement. He'd barely convinced her to go on a couple of coffee dates in the two weeks he'd known her, and she never gave up anything about herself other than what he already knew. Still, he couldn't stop himself from trailing after her to the club, even though Jimmy was off that night and he had no other excuse to be hanging around. She was upset to see him, but she wouldn't say why. After that, the details went fuzzy. He had a vague memory of her agreeing to leave with him, a blurry recollection of her looking up at him with big, scared eyes and asking if he would protect her.

The memories after that were brutally clear. Her naked body, her cut throat. And blood. On the walls, staining the sheets.

Staining his hands.

He couldn't protect her. He couldn't protect himself.

He sat back up, his chest tight, his body coursing with nervous energy. He sprang to standing, bouncing on the balls of his feet. Jumping jacks. Ten. Twenty. A hundred. A thousand. Now jumps—bend, spring, land, until his legs shook and his breath labored. Push-ups, sit-ups, more jumping jacks.

For hours he bounced around the cell, until a tray of food passing through the slot in his door startled him from his frenzy. Ignoring the food, he collapsed on his bunk, his face salty with sweat and tears. He turned his face to the wall.

—w—

Megan's hysteria rapidly gave way to numb purpose. No way was she letting Sean do this, she thought as she stalked away from the main building out to her car. She had Sean's attorney on the phone before she even backed out of her parking space.

"We can't let him do this, Adam," she said as she turned onto Highway 12. "We have to stop him."

Adam Brockner let out a long-suffering sigh. "I'm not sure there's much we can do."

"Bullshit. There are always options. We can file a writ of habeas corpus, have Sean declared mentally incompetent—"

"Sean's depressed but he's not mentally deficient, and no judge will declare him so. We can try to delay, but Sean has made his wishes very clear, Megan. Don't you think you need to respect that?"

Fury rose in her chest and she clung to it, its fiery sting so much better than the crippling grief at the thought of giving up on her brother. "He's either suicidal or on some fucked-up martyr kick, trying to save me from myself, and you think I should respect that?" Thick raindrops spattered against her windshield. She forced herself to slow down as red brake lights flared in front of her.

"Sean has his own reasons for wanting to take this course," Adam said in his low, measured voice that usually soothed her but now raised her hackles. How dare he be so calm? "I spoke with him at length, and I believe he's decided to accept the inevitable."

She wished Brockner was in the car with her so she

could hit him in the face. "An innocent man is going to be executed, and all you can say is it's inevitable?"

Thick silence hovered over the line.

"You think he did it," Megan said, disbelief sharpening her tone even as she wondered how she could be so stupid. She'd just assumed...had never bothered to ask him flat out if he believed Sean did it.

"You can't deny the evidence is damning," Adam said.

Yeah, tell me something I don't know.

"But you defended him."

"I can believe a client is guilty and still believe the state has no right to kill him. The two aren't mutually exclusive. You should know that by now, Megan. And he'll never admit it out loud, but I think Sean has finally come to terms with his guilt. And even though I don't agree with how the state wants to deal with it, I respect Sean's decision."

"Sean is *not* guilty," she said through clenched teeth. "And if he really believed it, if he remembered something after all this time, he would tell me."

"Would he? Your brother is very protective of you. Maybe you don't know him as well as you think."

"I know Sean better than anyone," she snapped, and disconnected the call.

But as her car flew down the highway, an ugly thought emerged from a dark corner of her mind.

Was it possible she could have been wrong all this time? Was it possible she was as self-delusional as the press, the police, hell, most of her friends had painted her?

No. She mentally yanked that sprout out by the roots and poured cyanide on it to boot. Yes, the evidence was damning, as Brockner had said. But from the beginning, she'd always thought it too damning. Too neat, too tied up in a convenient bow for the police.

Her brother was smart, ex–Special Forces, trained in covert operations. She believed that if Sean wanted to murder someone, he wouldn't have been nearly so stupid about it.

Too bad no one wanted to listen to her theories. Not even the few people she should have been able to count on to at least hear her out.

A vision of hot, dark eyes turning cold, lips full and red from passionate kisses going tight and mean. She tightened her grip on the steering wheel, shoving Cole's image out of her head. Even thinking of him made it hurt to breathe.

No time for wallowing. No time to spare even one conscious second of thought on that asshole.

Unconscious...that was another story. Megan had long ago ceded control of her dreams, in which Cole Williams popped up more frequently than she'd like, in scenarios that left her alternately sobbing with heartbreak or burning with unfulfilled desire—in pain and unsatisfied either way she sliced it.

In real life, Cole didn't want to listen to her theories—no one did. So be it. Megan knew in her soul that Evangeline Gordon's real killer was still out there. Lurking like a dark stain, a creeping shadow no one could nail down.

She just needed a break. A tiny shred of something to point her in the right direction. As her Honda ate up the miles between Walla Walla and her apartment in Seattle, Megan whispered up endless prayers, for something, anything, a single clue. Before Sean got what he wanted and it was too late for them all.

Chapter 3

He moved the TV a few inches to the left and studied the screen. Still not quite right.

He reached up to the bookshelf where he'd positioned the camera in the trailer's cramped bedroom and tilted it slightly down. He checked the TV again.

Perfect.

Blood rushed to his groin and a smile stretched across his face. At this angle, the camera displayed the bed from headboard to footboard, close enough to capture every detail but with enough vertical and horizontal clearance to make sure no heads or other body parts would be cut off from view.

He would be able to see everything.

He squatted in front of his laptop, which was connected to the camera and placed one shelf below. A few keystrokes and they were rolling, the computer recording everything about to be displayed on the screen.

Time to retrieve the talent.

She was huddled against the wall, long, black hair spilling over her face as her head lolled forward. He reached out a gloved hand and tilted her chin up. Her eyes were dark, lazy slits that showed no recognition of where she was or what was about to happen.

He hefted her onto the bed and positioned her against the pillows. He did a quick check to make sure the camera had a clear view of her face. He adjusted the latex cap on his head, grimacing as it pulled at his close-cropped hair.

It was hot and made his head itch, but it ensured no stray strands of hair would escape. He diligently shaved his body whenever he was called into action, but he'd be damned if he'd walk around looking like a cue ball.

"C'mon, sweetheart, time for your close-up."

She shook her head and moaned, but otherwise didn't stir.

He reached in his pocket, pulled out an envelope of smelling salts, and ripped it under her nose. Her head snapped back and whacked against the trailer's wood-paneled wall. Her dark eyes went wide, instantly alert, though unfocused as they looked wildly around the unfamiliar room.

Then her gaze landed on his face.

And she knew.

His already burgeoning cock went rock hard, tenting out his sweatpants. God, he loved that moment of shocked realization, the split second when they realized exactly what was about to happen.

He was the bogeyman, the grim reaper. The one who came after you if you pushed too far. He left his message in slash marks and pools of blood, and yet some girls never learned. He was still summoned to practice his craft.

He'd started the cleanup work years ago, allowing him to channel his appetites in a way that helped the organization. He knew his appetite for the wet work made them uneasy. He knew they saw him as a loose cannon, a barely caged beast.

He liked letting them think that.

And he loved the opportunity to indulge in his specialty. Fear. Pain. His weapons against chaos.

Later he would watch this moment, stroking himself to climax again and again as he savored her look of fear. Of recognition. The moment when she realized this man who she'd known, who'd even been a protector of sorts, was the monster of her worst nightmares.

Even now it was hard to control himself. But he wanted to savor it, for this would end soon. His plan was well into motion now, his dreams of the future so close to becoming reality he could nearly taste it. There would be no need for this at the next stage.

Like an alcoholic about to enter rehab, he wanted to take his time, enjoy this last bender, appreciate the sights, the sounds, the *sensations* this night would offer.

He reached for the pack of cigarettes he'd placed next to the bed. He lit one and took several long drags, trying to slow his heartbeat, trying to cool the lust sizzling in his veins, urging him on.

Such a delicate balance. Every time he had to work harder to keep control, to force himself to savor every second of the pain, every molecule of their fear.

This one's fear was like a palpable force in the room, her mewls behind the gag high and hoarse. Acrid sweat bloomed on the surface of her smooth, flawless skin, displayed so beautifully by the scrap of silk she wore. So smooth, so perfect, so beautiful.

He yanked a thin strap down her shoulder, exposing her breast, exposing more flesh the texture and color of warm cream. He took another deep drag of his cigarette, then pressed the tip against the underside of her breast.

Her scream was muffled by the gag and the roaring in his ears. He breathed deep through his nose and mouth, sucking in the scent of burning flesh, the flavor of her terror. He yanked the dress down her chest, rending it in half when he was stopped by her bound hands. She kicked and thrashed, but she was no match for his far greater strength. His laugh turned into a groan as he ground his erection against her, her bucking and gyrating threatening his control.

He put the cigarette against her stomach, her chest, her nipple, left a trail of burns down the tender skin of her inner thigh. Soon her muffled screams had faded to hoarse moans behind the gag. Her thrashing weakened and her eyes closed, as though she could block out any of what was about to happen to her.

Not a fucking chance.

He stubbed out the cigarette and quickly stripped out of his clothes.

He stroked himself, looking at the bed as he did so. She'd opened her eyes and was staring at his cock, tears streaming from her eyes.

That's right, baby. The thought made his dick throb, and he knew he better cover up. Rip, snap, and a condom was in place to catch any stray bits of precome that might leak out and contaminate the scene.

He flipped her onto her stomach so her head was at the foot of the bed. He knelt behind her and yanked her up on her knees so her perfect ass pointed in the air, her cleanly shaved cunt exposed to his view. He reached over beside the bed, his gloved hand curling around the handle of his blade. A warrior's blade. Custom made, honed to an edge so keen he could shave his beard with it.

He slashed the knife across her back in the same instant he drove into her. He closed his eyes and clenched his teeth as he struggled for restraint. Her body squeezed his dick like a vise as she convulsed from the pain seizing her from inside and out. He looked at the TV screen, watching himself as he pounded her from behind.

Her head was down, hanging in defeat, his body jarring hers like a rag doll.

That wouldn't do.

He smiled at himself as he reached out and grabbed her hair, forcing her head up until her face was visible on-screen. His other hand reached out. The blade rested against her neck, its glare casting a glow around her face like a twisted halo.

"Open your eyes," he ordered. They snapped open at the first bite of the blade. She tried in vain to shrink away. "You watch," he said, over and over as he pumped into her. With each stroke, the blade sliced at her neck until bloody rivulets ran down her chest and neck.

He watched his face tighten with ecstasy, saw his lips peel back to bare his teeth, saw his muscles cord in sharp relief under his skin as his climax came thundering down.

Watched himself deliver the killing blow.

—⚇—

"So do you think you'll still live here after your mom gets out?"

Devany Sinclair looked up from picking at a chip of blue polish on her right thumbnail. Sixteen-year-old Amber, who lived three trailers down and whose mother worked the same whacked schedule as Devany's aunt Kathy, was buried shoulder-deep in their ancient Frigidaire like she was digging for treasure. Kathy's hyperactive terrier mix, Skeeter, danced a hopeful circle around Amber's feet.

"I don't know." Devany shrugged. "It all depends on what my mom wants to do."

"Sorry, dog, no treats for you," Amber said, brushing Skeeter aside with her foot. She emerged with a couple of silver aluminum cans and presented one to Devany.

"We can't," Devany protested. "My aunt will totally notice."

"Don't worry," Amber said, rolling her eyes as she popped the top on the beer. "I have more stashed. Jesse hooked me up earlier." Jesse was Amber's too-old-for-her boyfriend. He had a beater car and a fake ID, which made him the closest thing to Prince Charming that Redwood Acres Mobile Home Park had to offer.

"Then why didn't you bring it?"

"Well, duh, it's warm," Amber said, rolling her dark eyes again as she took a swig from her can.

Devany popped the top and slurped at the foam, grimacing at the bitter taste. "Next time tell Jesse to get a bottle of Popov, okay? I can barely drink this shit." She took three quick chugs and shuddered. "You got the exact same brand, right? Last time I almost got busted. And we need to get it in the fridge in time to get cold."

"Stop worrying," Amber said, flipping her thick black hair down her back as she plopped on the faded rust-colored couch.

"You're not the one who will land her ass back in a group home if we're busted."

Amber shrugged. "So do you want to stay here, or what?"

Devany flopped down next to her. Skeeter followed, curling next to Devany, his chin resting on her denim-clad knee.

"This is the longest I've lived anywhere, and my aunt's not so bad." Really, she didn't want to think about what would happen when her mom was released from her latest stint in court-mandated rehab.

She drained her beer and started on another. A mellow glow spread through her limbs and loosened her tongue. "Doesn't matter. I know my mom will try to get me back, which wouldn't be so bad if she could just stay clean." The first time her mom had gone to jail for meth possession, Devany had been eight. At the time, she'd believed her mom's vows that she loved her and would get clean for her sake. Devany would be in foster care for only a little while, Janna Sinclair promised. *Once I get out, we'll be a family again.*

That had been six years, four arrests, and ten moves ago.

"I'll probably have to go live with her, until she fucks up again." Which was a given. For all the turmoil in Devany's life, her mother's talent for fucking up was pretty much the only thing she could count on.

"But if your aunt decides to fight it..." Amber let the rest trail off.

Devany shrugged. Truthfully, she didn't expect Aunt Kathy to put up much of a fight. She suspected her aunt's generosity had more to do with the county's subsidy check than anything. She didn't expect Kathy Davis to go to the trouble of taking the matter to family court, that was for sure. "Maybe they'll remember that last time I went to live with Mom, she moved us in with a registered sex offender." Devany had been twelve and had taken off after the guy had cornered her in the bathroom and tried to shove his hands down her pants. She'd hit him with a faceful of Aqua Net and a knee to the balls, but she knew not to press her luck and had headed for the streets. She'd managed a month before she got picked up for shoplifting and sent to another group home.

Maybe Megan will help me, she thought. *Ha! Like there's really anything she can do.* Megan was a volunteer advocate, not a miracle worker. Not even a judge or a social worker. Still, Devany felt a tiny pinch of guilt as she took another swig of her beer.

Just stay straight and keep yourself out of trouble. That's the best thing you can do to make sure you get to stay with your aunt.

Right. Like a drafty double-wide in a crappy part of town was such paradise. And no matter how good she was, she knew her aunt would off-load her the first chance she got.

Still, she declined when Amber offered her a couple Oxys she'd taken from her mom's medicine cabinet. "Why are we talking about all this shit anyway? It's stupid. Whatever. I don't want to talk about my stupid mom anymore."

She grabbed the remote off the coffee table and cranked up the TV. She and Amber spent the next two hours working their way through a six-pack.

Devany wandered back to the kitchenette for a snack and swore as she caught the display on the microwave. "Shit, Amber, it's ten-fifteen already. Aunt Kathy will be home by eleven." She didn't need to spell out what would happen.

Amber scrambled up from the couch. "I'll be right back—I just have to go out to my car." She yanked on her fleece-lined boots and flung open the trailer's screen door.

"Watch out for—" Devany called, but it was too late. Skeeter had seen an opportunity and seized it, his little body nothing but a brown and white streak as he hurled himself through the crack in the door.

"He'll come back, won't he?" Amber asked. "He always does."

"Yeah, but last time he got into Dreesen's rabbit hutch and almost killed one of them. He said if he catches Skeeter again, he's going to snap his neck."

Neither girl questioned that their half-crazed Vietnam vet neighbor was serious.

"Shit. I'll get the beer—you get the dog. Meet you back here."

Devany nodded, pulling on her sneakers and following Amber outside. Amber went right, down two trailers to her car, and Devany cut left and over two rows. She called Skeeter's name in a soft voice, punctuating her calls with an occasional whistle. Cold, damp air haloed the weak outdoor lights spaced regularly on poles throughout the park. Devany could see the silvery clouds of her breath, but her fleece hoodie and fast jog staved off the chill of late fall.

She slowed to a walk in front of Dreesen's double-wide. "Skeeter," she said in a high whisper, "come on, boy." Nothing. She called his name again, a little louder this time, casting a wary look around to make sure she hadn't attracted anyone's attention. Devany had lived in worse neighborhoods, but Redwood Acres had more than its share of scumbags and lowlifes. It was not a place Devany wanted to be wandering alone after dark.

She heard a sharp bark in the distance and cocked her head, closing her eyes to make sure her beer-addled brain wasn't playing tricks. Another high-pitched yip, followed by a series of barks that said Skeeter had found something interesting and wasn't shutting up soon. And dammit, it sounded like it was coming from the woods all the way on the other side of the park.

Devany took off at a sprint, wincing as every dog in the neighborhood joined Skeeter in a chorus of yelps and howls. Woozy from three beers, she could still hone in on Skeeter's bark. By the time she got to him, she was panting hard, nausea churning in her stomach.

One of the streetlights in this row of mostly vacant trailers had been smashed, and the remaining light did little to illuminate the trailers or the neighboring woods. She made out the white patches in Skeeter's coat as he poised on his haunches in front of the last trailer, barking his head off. There was probably a raccoon on the roof or something, she thought as she walked slowly toward Skeeter.

"Skeeter, come here," she said in her softest, most beseeching tone. She crouched low to the ground and made kissing noises.

Skeeter paused his barking for a second and whipped his head around to look at her. Then he charged up the stairs of the trailer. Devany yelled, "No," and sprinted after him, but she wasn't nearly fast enough to keep him from slipping through the front screen door, which hung partially ajar.

She looked around to make sure no one was watching—not that anyone around here was likely to get their panties in a wad over her trespassing—and followed the dog through the door. "Skeeter," she whispered as she came through the dark kitchenette. The trailer smelled like mold and dust, and underneath that was a heavy, metallic scent Devany couldn't place.

She heard a scuffling sound from the back bedroom and picked her way through the dark living room and down the short hallway. Light spilled through the open bedroom door.

Devany's stomach clenched with nerves. "Is someone here? Hello?"

She tried again when no one answered. "Sorry to bother you. I'm just here for my dog." Skeeter let out a funny, warbling whimper.

She crept down the hall and pushed open the door. Her view of the bed was blocked by the door, but she could see the dog standing on the floor in front of the TV. "Skeeter, get over here," she whispered through clenched teeth.

She snapped her fingers and called again, and her gaze skidded across the image on the TV screen and froze.

A woman, naked and facedown, her head turned to the side so Devany could see her sightless eyes staring out from the screen. For a split second she thought it was a horror film, one with really realistic-looking effects. But why would someone break into an abandoned trailer to watch a movie?

Then she stepped into the room. And she saw the blood.

Striping the naked back of the woman on the TV screen. Pooling under the gash in her throat.

Flowing like a river down the bedspread and staining the carpet two inches from Skeeter's front paws.

Her scream caught in her throat as her horrified gaze took in every detail of the bloodbath in the room and on the screen. Instinct took over and she ran over, snatched Skeeter in her arms, and ran like hell into the dark night.

———

Megan jerked awake, discombobulated and surprised to find herself facedown on a couch cushion. She sat up, eyes sticky from having fallen asleep with her contact lenses in. The TV was still on, and her half-eaten turkey sandwich was drying out on the coffee table.

After three nights in a row spent staring into the darkness—her acid-soaked stomach clenched in a knot as she thought about Sean and the execution that had been scheduled to take place only a week and a half from today—her exhaustion had caught up with her.

A guitar lick blared through the room, and Megan's fogged brain registered that it must have been her cell that woke her. She staggered off the couch, squinting to see through her gummed-up contact lenses, and snatched the phone off her kitchen table.

Even as she thumbed the button to look at the call log, the phone started ringing again. *Dev,* the display read. Megan's stomach sank a little as she wondered what reason the girl would have for calling her at—she squinted at her watch—ten twenty-two on a Tuesday night.

"Hey, Dev, what's up—" she started to say around a jaw-cracking yawn, but she couldn't get a word out before Dev's voice cut her off.

"Oh, thank God you answered. I don't know what to do. You have to get over here."

The pure terror in Dev's voice sent a shot of adrenaline through Megan's veins and banished the last cobwebs from her brain. "Whoa, Dev, calm down and tell me what's going on." Megan took a deep breath, trying to calm herself as her mind raced with infinite ways a fourteen-year-old girl could get herself into deep trouble.

She'd barely managed the thought before Dev's next words froze her in the act of walking to the bathroom. "I think she's dead, Megan. And there was so much blood."

"Where are you, Devany? Who's dead?" Panic rippled through her limbs as she struggled to make out Dev's explanation through her sobbing. She quickly removed her contacts and put on her glasses. "Dev, I can't understand you. You need to talk more slowly." She put the girl on speakerphone to yank on warmer clothes and finally deciphered that Dev was home, that her aunt's dog had gotten out and made a gruesome discovery in an abandoned trailer.

"Did you call the police?"

"No," Dev said. "I didn't know what to do—there's no one here, and I'm so scared."

"You must call the police," Megan said firmly.

"But I don't—"

"You won't get in trouble, Dev." She knew why Dev was hesitating. In her short life, the cops at her house meant only bad news—her mom getting busted, Dev being taken away and moved to yet another new home. Megan couldn't blame Dev for being reluctant. "I want you to hang up and call nine-one-one, and tell them exactly what you saw. Stay in your house with the door locked, and don't open the door for anyone except me or the police."

Megan yanked on rubber rain boots, slid a waterproof shell over her shirt, and raced out to her car. She made it to Redwood Acres in a record seven minutes, figuring that if a cop tried to stop her, she'd just lead him straight to the murder scene.

Because she wasn't under any illusions that Devany had stumbled across anything else.

She skidded to a stop in front of Dev's trailer. There was no sign of the police, and both trailers on either side of Dev's were completely dark. Megan jogged down the path to Dev's trailer and banged on the door. "Dev, it's Megan. Did you call the police?"

She saw one of Dev's brown eyes peek around the edge of the curtain that covered the door's square window. With Megan's identity verified, she opened the door for her to enter. Dev was trembling, mascara smeared under her eyes. The dusting of freckles across her nose stood out in stark relief against her ashen face, and she scrubbed her pierced nose with the sleeve of her flannel shirt. Gone was the tough-talking fourteen-year-old Megan knew. Dev's usual attitude had disappeared, leaving behind a wide-eyed, gangly girl who was scared out of her mind. Dev cradled Skeeter in her arms as if he were a baby. Megan pulled Dev in for a quick hug, then quickly released her. "You called the police, right?"

Dev nodded, her eyes wet and haunted-looking. "I thought they'd be here by now," she sniffed. "What if they think I was joking?" She tried to tuck her dark bangs behind her ear, only to have them fall back across her eyes.

Devany was almost as tall as Megan, but Megan guided the girl to the shabby couch as if she were a small child and sat down next to her. She covered Devany's hand with her own and tried to calm the girl's shaking. Megan wanted to pull her close, but the courts had strict physical contact guidelines for advocates like herself. Megan understood that such rules were necessary to avoid lawsuits and misunderstandings, but constantly having to rein in her natural tendency toward physical affection got old. Especially at times like this, when Devany could really use a big hug. "They'll be here," she assured. "Sometimes it takes them a while." Especially in a part of town like this, where all the patrols were likely tied up with the steady level of criminal activity that plagued this part of Seattle. As she gave Devany a quick squeeze around her shoulders, she caught a whiff of Dev's shampoo, which smelled faintly of bubblegum, and something else that made her mouth tighten in disappointment.

"You were drinking, weren't you?"

Dev stiffened and jerked away. "No."

"Don't BS me. You smell like you crawled out of a keg."

"I was bored, okay? Aunt Kathy grounded me for sneaking out last week. Don't tell her, please? She'll kick me out."

"Trust me, Dev, if you saw what you think you saw, we have bigger things to worry about." Dev's choked sob made Megan's throat go tight. Poor kid, as if stumbling onto the scene of a grisly murder wasn't enough, she lived in constant fear of being kicked out and sent to yet another foster home.

"But my aunt ... she'll kill me ..."

Megan's heart pinched at the genuine dread in the girl's voice. She and Sean had been comparatively lucky after their parents had died. They had each other and they'd gone straight to their grandmother and stayed out of the foster system. But she remembered how it felt to live with a relative who wasn't overly enthusiastic about caring for teenagers, someone who made you feel that with one wrong move, you could end up at the mercy of the system. "I promise I'll take care of everything," Megan said.

Dev snapped her mouth shut as a car pulled up outside the trailer. Through the filmy curtains, blue and red lights circled the walls of the trailer. Within seconds, a hard fist was pounding at the door.

"Just tell them what you told me," Megan said as she moved to answer the door, "and everything will be fine."

Megan quickly explained who she was and why Dev had called her before she'd called the police. Devany gave one officer directions to the abandoned trailer while the other uniform, who'd introduced himself as Officer Roberts, stayed behind to take Dev's statement. Dev hugged Skeeter to her and took a deep, bracing breath, then spilled her story to Roberts, whose hulking bulk took up the majority of space in the living room.

"So you were here by yourself when the dog got out?" he asked.

Megan saw Dev's eyes flick to the side before she answered. "Uh, yeah."

Uh-oh. Someone had been here. Megan hadn't even thought about it, so overwhelmed by Dev's shocking discovery.

Roberts locked eyes with Dev. It was the kind of cop stare Megan was sure they taught the first day at the academy. "Do I smell alcohol on your person?"

Dev swallowed hard and gave a guilty nod. "Just a couple of beers," she said, and Megan winced as a little of Dev's attitude sprang to the surface.

Roberts cocked an eyebrow. "You're sure there was no one else here?" Dev nodded.

The radio hooked on Robert's belt squawked. "Go ahead, Mendez," Roberts said, and listened intently.

"I'm here at the trailer. We're definitely looking at a one-eight-seven."

"Ten-four, I'll call it in," Roberts said. He excused himself and went out to the squad car to call in the homicide.

"Who was here?" Megan hissed as soon as the door had closed behind the officer.

"No one," Dev hissed back.

"Dev—"

"She didn't see anything, okay? And if she gets caught drinking, she'll be in worse trouble than I am, so please don't say anything."

Megan shook her head. "I can't go along with that—"

"You said I could trust you!" Dev cut her off with a harsh whisper. "You promised I could come to you with anything." The latch on the door clicked, warning of the cop's return. Dev hit Megan with a warning glare.

Megan was torn. Dev was so used to being screwed over by the adults in her life; she would see Megan's exposure as ratting out her and her friend. On the other hand, buzzed teenagers weren't known for having the best judgment. Withholding information from the police—no matter how harmless—wasn't a good idea for a lot of reasons.

Still, Megan remained silent, listening as Dev told Officer Roberts in excruciating detail about the few seconds she'd been in that trailer.

"I couldn't see that well," Dev said. "There was no light except for the TV. At first I thought it was a movie or something, like someone had paused it." Dev closed her eyes and took a shuddering breath. "Only a sicko would pause on a scene like that, right? On a close-up of . . . Then

I saw the blood and realized that what was on the TV was in the room."

Something nudged the back of Megan's brain, like a polite fingertip trying to get her attention, but she didn't have a chance to hone in on it. At that moment, Dev's pale cheeks took on a greenish cast and she swallowed hard. Acting on pure instinct, Megan wrapped her arm around Dev's shoulders, hauled her off the couch, and herded her into the kitchen. They made it to the sink just in time to prevent the beer and Cheetos Dev had consumed from splattering all over the floor.

Megan got Dev a glass of water and rubbed her back as the girl rinsed and spit. She stood at the sink, her back to the door, and held Dev's hair as she heaved into the sink again. *Poor kid.* She heard a car pull up outside, followed by heavy footfalls on the trailer's front steps. A knock, a murmur of masculine voices was all shunted to the background as Megan focused on preventing Dev from completely falling apart.

"If you don't mind, Roberts, I'll take it from here."

Everything inside Megan froze at the sound of that voice. Common sense told her to stop being ridiculous, that it couldn't be him. Even if it was, there was no reason in hell for her body to react this way.

Her body had different ideas, and warmth radiated out from her center as every nerve ending sparked with heightened awareness. Her traitorous body, which didn't give a damn that he'd turned his back on her in the name of duty when she'd needed him most, didn't care that he'd broken her heart so bad she knew it would never be the same.

Her senses knew what her mind refused to accept.

She turned slowly, bracing herself as Detective Cole Williams stepped inside the trailer.

Chapter 4

Megan rubbed Dev's back as she gagged over the sink, wondering when this would all be over.

Cole started to introduce himself as she turned to face him. "I'm—" He stopped short, his dark eyes widening, his body visibly jolting with shock. "Megan?" His hand twitched as though about to reach for her, but he regained his composure almost immediately. All emotion fled and his eyes got that flat, dead, cop look that never failed to unnerve her.

Waves of hot and cold shuddered through Megan as she attempted to follow Cole's lead. "Hello, Detective Williams." Her voice trembled a little at the end, and even as she mentally kicked herself, she reminded herself she could hardly be expected to be calm in a situation like this. It wasn't every night she was called to the scene of a gruesome murder.

Confronted with the man who, after all this time, after everything he'd put her through, still had the power to make her knees shake when she looked at him. It seemed impossible that he should still have this effect on her. He'd put her brother in jail for Christ's sake, hadn't lifted a finger when she'd asked—no, begged—for his help. Then when their relationship had been exposed in the press, Cole had told reporters his feelings for Megan weren't serious, certainly not serious enough to interfere with his job. Which took priority over everything.

Yet she took one look at that hard, chiseled face; that rangy, broad-shouldered body; those big, long-fingered hands, and her stomach did a completely irrational, adolescent flip-flop.

"You know him?" Dev whispered.

"Yeah, we go way back," Megan replied, proud of the way her tone sharpened, happy to feel the fresh burst of anger in her chest chase away the rest.

Something flashed on his face—regret? Then it was gone as his gaze shifted from her to Dev. "I understand you called Miss Flynn after you found the victim?"

Dev's gaze flicked anxiously to Megan, who gave her an encouraging nod. "Yeah," Dev said softly. "She told me to call the police."

Cole's full mouth pulled into a half smile. "Smart woman." He started to say something, then paused as the trailer door opened behind him.

"This is my partner, Detective Olivia Petersen," Cole said. "Petersen, this is Megan Flynn and Devany Sinclair."

With her tall, athletic body, short blond hair, and cleanly sculpted features, Detective Petersen looked like some kind of Nordic goddess of war. Her eyes did the cop sweep around the room, taking in every detail.

"You found the victim, correct?" she asked Dev.

Dev nodded.

"And who are you again?" she asked Megan, who tried not to bristle at the woman's sharp, businesslike tone.

"I'm Dev's court-appointed advocate."

Detective Petersen's perfectly arched brows knitted into a frown. "Why is your name so familiar?"

Megan fought not to squirm as the woman's blue stare pierced her. "Most likely because my brother Sean is on death row and recently waived his right to appeal," she said, her voice flat and emotionless. "His name is in the press lately because in less than two weeks he'll be the first person executed by Washington State in over a decade." She felt her mouth stretch into a sneer. "And whenever they talk about Sean, my name comes up. The crazy, delusional sister who won't believe her brother is guilty." Her eyes narrowed and she couldn't resist a look at Cole.

He watched her silently, his eyes dark and full of sympathy that bordered on pity. Goddamn him. She didn't need his pity. "Stop looking at me like you feel sorry for me, Cole. We both know how you feel about Sean."

Cole opened his mouth to protest, but Megan cut him off as she turned back to Detective Petersen. "None of that matters tonight. Dev has already been through a lot. Maybe we should pick this back up in the morning—"

"We'll try to get through this as quickly as possible," Cole said, his low voice somehow soothing, now that he was once again all business.

"It's okay," Dev said. "We can talk now."

He motioned for Dev to sit on the couch and took a seat on the edge of the coffee table while Petersen remained standing, arms across her chest. Megan sat on the couch next to Dev, pressing herself as far back into the cushions as she could. Still she couldn't escape the claustrophobic sensation, like Cole had sucked up all the space and air in the room.

Dev wasn't having nearly the same reaction, and

Megan couldn't blame her. Had she not known better, Megan would have fallen under Cole's spell too. There was something about the way he leaned in to listen, watched with those dark eyes, asked pointed, probing questions in that deep voice that made you want to give up all your secrets.

She'd been such a sucker for it, believing he cared, believing the intense focus, the way he hung on every word, meant he was falling as hard for her as she had for him.

Now, wiser, she realized it was just another layer to his cop facade, one he used with great success on civilians and suspects alike. As she listened to Cole question Dev, she understood how Sean, fighting off the effects of drugs after his arrest, had given up way too much incriminating information before Megan had been able to get a lawyer in there.

She shook off the memories of that night and forced herself to listen as Dev described what she'd seen. "Like I told the other cop—uh, police officer—at first all I saw was the TV showing a close-up of a dead girl. I thought it was like, a horror movie. It was only when I looked over where Skeeter was that I saw blood all over the floor." Dev swallowed hard, fighting back the urge to vomit the little bit of water she'd just swallowed. "That was when I realized it wasn't a movie."

Megan didn't miss the way Olivia's head cocked to the side, nor the seconds-long look she and Cole exchanged. "What is it?" she asked.

Another look. Jealousy twisted in Megan's gut at the fluent, silent communication and intimacy that flowed between the partners. Megan tried to shove the emotion aside. She had no business wondering or caring about how intimate Detectives Williams and Petersen were.

Nevertheless, there was a bitter ache in Megan's throat as she asked, "Why are you looking at each other like that? What aren't you telling us?"

Cole countered with another question. "Devany, when you were chasing Skeeter, you didn't see anyone else, inside or outside the vacant trailer?"

Devany shook her head. "No one. There was no one else there."

"You're sure?" Detective Petersen said. "Think really hard, Devany. Maybe you saw something, heard something?"

"I didn't see or hear anything," Devany said.

"You think the killer was still there when Dev found the body?" The thought sent ice crystals through Megan's veins.

Petersen shared another look with Cole before she responded. "When Devany found the body, the TV was on. Based on what Devany told us, the killer had a camera hooked up to capture what has happening on the bed," Detective Petersen said. "Our first responders reported that when they arrived on the scene, the television was on but it was just showing a blue screen. No camera was found."

Dev turned impossibly paler. "Oh my God. What if he thinks I saw him? What if he comes after me?" She turned to Megan, her eyes wide with panic. "You can't believe what he did to her, Megan. I mean, her back, everything, it was awful."

"It's okay," Megan reassured her. "Everything is going to be okay. You're going to be protected no matter what."

She shot Cole a meaningful look over Dev's head. He nodded.

What Devany described sounded eerily similar to what had happened to four other victims in the past year.

About nine months ago, a woman had been found murdered in an apartment in downtown Seattle. Since then, three more had been found in different locations in the Seattle area.

Though many details about the murders had been closely guarded, enough information had been released to the press that Megan couldn't shake the suspicion that the girl Devany had discovered was the killer's latest victim. But she held off on voicing her suspicions to Cole. Megan didn't want to bring up her concerns in front of Dev. The poor kid was terrified enough.

Not to mention, Cole was so careful about doing everything by the book, he'd never confirm her suspicions before he'd done a thorough investigation himself. And maybe not even then, depending on what the police department wanted the public to know.

A feeling of uneasy anticipation prickled down her spine, but she shoved it away. *Maybe this time I'll find a link.* She smacked the thought down before it could even fully form. She'd looked as deeply as she could into the previous four victims' cases in an effort to find similarities to Evangeline Gordon's murder.

Every time she'd hit a brick wall. Even Megan was aware she was something of a joke—considered the crazy chick who had chased down every scrap of information about every woman who'd been killed by a knife in the past two and a half years in a desperate attempt to get her brother off death row.

Nothing had ever come of it. No reason to think this time would be any different.

And yet . . . she couldn't shake that weird electric buzz, like something was about to happen; she just didn't know what.

Cole flipped his notepad closed and rose from the coffee table. "I think you've answered everything for tonight, but—"

He was cut off by a commotion outside. Screeching tires, followed by a car door slamming, a woman's high, shrill voice yelling at the patrolmen outside. Skeeter raced to the door, dancing in circles, his sharp yaps threatening to pierce Megan's eardrums.

Dev's frown deepened. "Aunt Kathy," she said over the din.

Megan stepped forward to intercept Kathy as she slammed into the trailer. Megan knew firsthand how volatile and unreasonable the woman could be, and she hoped to spare Dev any more trauma tonight.

Kathy was a wiry woman of fifty. She'd changed from her waitressing uniform into worn jeans that hung off her hip bones and a thick sweater that practically swallowed up her thin form. Her hair was a uniform shade of dark red that didn't occur in nature and was twisted in a knot at her nape.

She dumped her purse on the counter with a thud, her gaze bouncing from Megan to Cole to Olivia, finally narrowing on Devany. Wisps of smoke swirled around her head as she lifted a lit cigarette to her mouth and took a deep drag.

"Devany? What the hell didja do now?"

"I didn't—" Dev began.

"Dev didn't do anything, Kathy," Megan said at the same time.

Cole held up his hand, palm out, silencing them both. In the other hand he flashed Kathy his badge. Detective Petersen did the same. They quickly introduced themselves and explained the reason for their presence.

Kathy's ruddy complexion went pale. "Jesus, when Carol from three trailers down said there were cops at my house...I had no idea." She looked at Dev, and Megan was relieved to see genuine concern on the woman's face. "Devany, honey, are you all right?"

Kathy crossed to Devany and gave her a comforting, if slightly awkward, hug. Dev threw her arms around Kathy's waist and buried her head in her thin shoulder. Kathy tightened her hold and rocked Dev back and forth half a dozen times before releasing her.

"It was so scary," Dev said, and the tears that had been going on and off since Megan got there started up again. Not that Megan blamed her. "And they even think he was still there—the killer, I mean—when Skeeter and me were in the trailer. He could come after me."

Kathy's eyes widened with alarm. "Is that true? You think he's gonna come after her?"

Detective Petersen shook her head. "We have no reason to believe that."

Megan was glad—a little shocked but glad—that Kathy seemed to have dropped her usual gruff attitude for a more maternal one toward Devany. At the same time, she suddenly felt a little lost. She wasn't needed here anymore.

She looked up, blinking, and found Cole staring at her. She hardened her expression, not wanting to give him any more reason to feel sorry for her. "I should go," she said, telling herself she was happy to get as far away from Cole as possible. The man was a master at messing with her already-fragile equilibrium.

She reached for her coat, then froze as long fingers closed around her upper arm. Even through the thick cotton of her sleeve, she could feel the heat of that touch. Racing through her veins, sparking reactions in every nerve cell, generating sensations she had no business feeling on a night like this.

With a man like him.

"Unless there's something else you need from me, Detective," she said, tilting her chin up to glare at him.

Big mistake. Because the frown tightening his mouth and the sincere concern in his dark, heavy-lidded eyes nearly sent her to her knees. The way he said, "I'm sorry to hear about your brother, Megan," in that low, raspy voice that made her want to fling herself into his arms and cry on his big, brawny shoulder. Then drag him back to her apartment, beg him to strip her naked, pin her to the bed, and make her forget for a week, a month, a year, the black hole of despair her life had become.

Instead she seized on that despair, used it to fuel her anger at Cole. That he had the balls to apologize, to actually try to comfort her in all of this, was unbelievable. "Yeah, I'll just bet you are." She jerked her arm from his hold, then grabbed her shell and shrugged it on.

Tears clogged her throat and she knew that in about thirty seconds she was going to break down and cry. The last thing she wanted was for Cole to see her so weak.

Again.

She managed a good-bye and a promise to call Dev in the morning and hurled herself out the door.

Cole followed her to her car. With her blurry eyes and shaking hands, she couldn't get the door open before he reached her.

His hand closed over her shoulder and he spun her to face him. "Megan, dammit, I am sorry."

"Spare me. You put Sean in jail yourself. You believe he's guilty. You are not sorry that he's going to die."

He closed his eyes. "I'm sorry for what you've had to go through. I never wanted to see you hurt."

She let out a watery laugh. "And yet you didn't do anything to keep it from happening." She took off her glasses and scrubbed her eyes with the heels of her hands. "You didn't even bother to return my calls, because you were afraid it would make you look bad to be in contact with me—" She snapped her lips closed. Now was so not the time to let on how badly his abandonment of her after Sean's arrest had crushed her. She spoke again, her tone calmer. "I don't need you to feel sorry for me. I don't need you to believe Sean." She put her glasses back on. "But I do want to know something about what happened here tonight."

He stuffed his hands in his pockets and rocked slightly back on his heels. In the faint glow of the streetlight, she saw one thick brow arch. "I'll tell you what I can."

"Do you think this is the same guy who killed the woman outside of Renton last month?"

"We won't know anything until we get the medical examiner's report. And even then you know I can't give out those kinds of details yet."

"Right. Always by the book. No matter what." She shook her head and turned to unlock her car, wondering why she'd bothered to ask.

Cole watched Megan's taillights disappear, still reeling from the gut punch that had hit him the moment he'd recognized her. He felt poleaxed, same as the first time he'd laid eyes on her nearly three years ago when she'd crashed—literally—into his life by backing her little Honda into his unmarked squad car in a parking lot near the courthouse.

"Oh my God, I'm so sorry. I'm running late for family court. I'm an advocate and one of my kids is about to be sent back to his aunt's house, which is a totally bad idea since I know for a fact that her boyfriend is running a meth lab in a trailer on the property. I totally didn't see you backing out."

Normally he wouldn't have responded with anything but irritation at her breathless excuses. But something about her dark, wind-whipped, wavy hair; glossy, pink mouth; and sparking green eyes washed his irritation away in a matter of seconds. Add a set of tight, trim curves and world-class legs, showcased by her knee-length skirt, and he was ready to let her take out his other taillight if it meant he got to look at her a little longer.

But he wasn't about to let her off scot-free. *"You might have seen me if you weren't peeling around the corner like Jeff Gordon,"* he said.

Her eyes narrowed. *"Since you were backing out, technically I had the right of way, Cochise."*

Just like that, he'd been toast. So when she gave him her phone number, supposedly to exchange insurance information, he knew he was going to use it to ask her to dinner. And even when he was trying to convince himself that she was too young, too wide-eyed and idealistic for a cynical bastard like himself, every male instinct was firing on all cylinders, demanding he grab hold and never let go.

Instincts that roared to life again, things he had no business feeling given their history and the grisly circumstances that had brought her crashing back into his life tonight.

He and Petersen had briefly stopped at the crime scene to take a look before going to the witness's trailer. They both wanted to get the girl's statement while everything was still fresh and raw in her mind. The longer she had to think about it, the more the memories would fuzz as her brain started to fill in missing pieces until she forgot things that were there and started believing things that weren't.

The patrolmen had been short on details—like the witness's name—when they called it in. It had never occurred to him that the "woman identifying herself as the girl's advocate" would be Megan.

He closed his eyes, tilted his head back, and deeply inhaled the cold night air, trying to calm the blood rushing through his veins. Adrenaline made him jumpy. Always did when he was called to a scene. Seeing Megan had kicked it into overdrive, along with a whole host of other things he was unprepared to deal with right now. They had a dead woman, tortured, raped, and killed. This was no time to deal with the need that twisted him in knots every time he so much as thought of Megan.

Forget actually getting close enough to touch her soft skin, smell her flowery musk scent. One look at her—pink lips pressed tight, stubborn chin pointed in the air as she'd mouthed off to Detective Petersen—and he was practically shaking with the need to pull her into his arms. Because under all that bravado, he knew there was an ocean of pain, threatening to consume her. She'd fought its pull for the last three years.

And now it had gotten even worse.

"Good news, Cole. Flynn's going to get it."

His former partner had called Cole. Under normal circumstances, Cole might have shared his sense of triumph, that rare satisfaction he got when he really nailed the bad guys. No plea bargains, no deals cut, no endless taxpayer dollars spent keeping a worthless turd alive on death row while he filed appeal after appeal.

But he couldn't shake thoughts of Megan and what this must be doing to her. He'd brushed it aside, told himself her grief was collateral damage, nothing he could help or prevent.

Seeing her tonight had brought it back into razor-sharp focus.

Gravel crunched behind him. "Is her involvement going to be a problem for you?" As usual, his partner cut straight to the quick. Cole turned to face Petersen. The streetlights bounced off her sculpted features and light blond hair.

"Of course not," Cole replied. He could feel her studying him, and he shoved all thoughts of Megan aside and schooled his face to reveal nothing. Petersen had worked vice for years before moving to homicide, and she could read almost anyone like a book. Her skill was invaluable, but he didn't want her using it on him.

He breathed a silent sigh of relief when Petersen's phone rang.

"Crap, it's Karen. I need to take this."

Saved by the lesbian. Petersen had married her partner, Karen, a little over a year ago, and now they were expecting their first child. Like any cop's wife, Karen got nervous every time Petersen walked out the door. As they walked back to the abandoned trailer, Cole listened to Petersen's side of the conversation, the way she tried to keep the frustration out of her voice as she assured her wife she'd be home as soon as humanly possible.

Cole didn't envy his partner. The few relationships he'd sustained over the course of his career had been full of similar complaints about how much he worked and angry phone calls demanding he come home.

Unlike Petersen, who believed she could have some kind of work/life balance in this job, Cole had acknowledged early on that he was more committed to his job than he ever could be to a woman, and that being the case, it was probably best to keep himself unattached. It sure as hell made long nights like this easier to endure. It was no big deal to work till 4:00 a.m. when you had nothing but an empty house to go home to.

The crime scene buzzed with activity. In the time he'd been questioning Devany, the coroner's truck had arrived, joining the ambulance and paramedics who'd been dispatched before it was clear their presence was unnecessary. Cole donned latex gloves and slipped disposable booties over his shoes and entered the trailer. A flash of light came from down the hall. The crime scene technician was in there taking pictures.

He and Petersen entered the bedroom and were greeted by the coroner, Dr. Mark Pineta. "Based on the core temperature and the tackiness of the blood, I'd say she was killed sometime after ten p.m.," Pineta said, not wasting any time on small talk.

"Devany didn't miss it by much," he murmured.

Pineta nodded curtly. He was a short man in his early fifties, his Filipino heritage evident in his complexion and dark, almond-shaped eyes. Pineta had been the King County coroner for over fifteen years. As such, he'd seen just about every type of dead body imaginable, and now he delivered the preliminary facts of the woman's death with the same level of emotion he would have given to reading a laundry list.

"The victim died of exsanguination, caused by the cutting of her jugular and carotid."

Another flash popped, illuminating the savage slice the killer had made along the right side of the girl's spine. "That wound was made antemortem, as were the cigarette burns on her breasts and stomach. The ones on the buttocks, however," he said, "were delivered postmortem. I'm confident the autopsy will reveal other pertinent details," he said meaningfully.

Cole nodded. He felt only a mild sense of revulsion. His first dead body had made him puke and haunted him for days. The years had toughened him, and now he was able to take the facts, the sights, even the smells of death, and file them away. Rather than dwelling on the horror, he'd learned to use them as tools to help solve the case. To an outsider, he knew he looked callous, jaded. *Robocop,* Megan had once teased him. But he knew the hardening was part of becoming a better cop.

Still, it was never easy to see a vic close up. Particularly one who had been so savagely brutalized.

"And this wasn't the first time someone cut her," Pineta

continued, indicating a set of marks across the woman's right shoulder blade. There was a pattern of raised, pale scars—several years old by his guess—and on closer look, Cole could see that it was a crescent moon surrounded by four tiny stars.

"Intentional scarification," Cole said, making a note. While tattoos were now as common as pierced ears, the average tattoo parlor didn't offer the more extreme alternative. If they could pin down the artist who did this, maybe that would lead to something.

Cole did a quick sketch of the mark in his notebook and continued his examination of the victim. She hadn't been moved from the bed. She was on her knees, her legs spread at an awkward angle. Her chest rested on the mattress, her bound hands trapped beneath her. Her face was turned to the side. A gag was tied around the lower half of her face, and Cole could see the tufts of material sticking out of her mouth. The killer had stuffed another bandana in her mouth to muffle her screams.

Blood pooled under her head and had streamed onto the floor below, where it was drying in a sticky black puddle.

Cole leaned in closer to look at her face. Above the gag, her features were delicate, her nose small, her cheekbones high. Her eyes were dark and deep set, lending her features an exotic cast.

"She was beautiful," Petersen said.

"And young," Cole added.

"I'd guess her around twenty, twenty-one." Pineta nodded.

Barely more than a kid.

Cole straightened and caught Petersen's eye. She quirked a brow and sighed. "So do we call the feds?"

"Let's wait until the autopsy is complete," Cole said, though he knew in his gut he was only delaying the inevitable.

But she was just like the others. Four in less than a year. With nothing in common other than that they were beautiful and in their early twenties. Two were still unidentified.

No one seemed to know anything about them—who they were, where they'd come from. Like they didn't exist until Fate dropped them into the hands of the sick fuck who tortured them, raped them, and finally cut their throats so they bled out facedown on the bed.

Tension pulled at his shoulders and Cole sighed. They had their work cut out for them. After the third victim, the feds had gotten involved, as it was determined they had a serial killer on their hands. This was the first victim to turn up in his jurisdiction, but Cole had followed their investigation closely and knew full well there had been little progress made.

He took another look at the beautiful, nameless girl lying dead and shook his head, unable to deny the truth. The Seattle Slasher had found another victim.

—∽—

Megan Flynn.

All these years he'd forced himself to keep his distance, unsure of his ability to control himself if he got too close.

Tonight she'd been so close, like a gift dropped from the sky.

His hands shifted on the steering wheel of the car he'd

boosted from a strip mall parking lot located two streets down from the trailer park. Blood raced through his veins, euphoria from the kill sending him higher than any drug. But tonight he was even more exhilarated.

Because of her.

He almost hadn't lingered at the scene, knowing it was risky, thanks to the girl who had stumbled into the trailer. He still had been naked and in the process of packing up, about to crack the fucking dog's neck when the girl with dark, purple-streaked hair had burst in.

He'd slipped into the closet and watched, waited. A smile stretched across his face and he had to stifle a laugh as he remembered her scream of terror, the way she scrambled out with the stupid dog in her arms.

He was relieved when she ran screaming, eliminating the complication of having to kill her too. And avoiding complications had helped him maintain a perfect record after all this time. He'd taken on a dozen cleanup jobs over the years, and still the cops had no fucking clue about him. Even with his particular methods and practices.

But goddamn, he wished he'd had the camera turned on the girl when she realized the image on the television was real. The expression on her face, the abject terror when she realized she was in the room with a blood-soaked body ...

He'd known the smartest move was to leave, but he couldn't resist the urge to slip into the dense woods surrounding the trailer park and take out his high-powered binoculars and wait for the cops to arrive.

He loved this part, the Keystone Kops routine that inevitably followed when one of his victims was discovered. Rushing around like morons looking for clues they'd never find. Nine months and they still had no idea who they were looking for. The press had even given him a name—"the Seattle Slasher." Stupid of them, since his kills extended far beyond the city limits.

And with many more than the five victims he'd left for them to find. Fucking idiots, thinking they could pigeon-hole him, profile him. They had no clue what he was capable of. They had no clue how hugely they were being played. No one did.

He watched the scene play out, knowing exactly what would happen. Clueless cops would do a ham-handed assessment of the crime scene before calling in the equally clueless feds.

So predictable. And yet he never tired of loitering around, waiting for the victim to be found, watching the chaos that ensued.

But tonight, to his shock, before the first squad car had arrived on the scene, Megan had appeared in his field of view. Big green eyes, dark tumble of curls down her back. The subtle curves just hinted at by her loose clothes. So beautiful she made his heart stop. So close, he'd reached out a hand as though he might touch her.

It was a sign. It had to be. He always knew she was meant to be his, from the first moment he'd laid eyes on her. And recently with the news of Sean Flynn's pending execution, he knew the time for them was getting close. Now it seemed Fate had stepped in to bring them together even sooner.

They'd tried to keep him away from her, tried to convince him that he couldn't control his baser urges, that if he got too close to her, he'd lose control and hurt her. Perhaps even kill her. He would put them all at risk, and it would be impossible to protect him.

He'd played along, let them send him away, pretend he agreed with them even though they were blind to the truth—that he and Megan belonged together. That she and she alone had the power to change him, to save him.

She would be his. And if anyone tried to stop him... it would be fun to send their world crashing down around them.

He wanted nothing more than to go to Megan, right then, experience her purity, her light, have it wash away the darkness and filth that threatened to overtake him. But the squad cars began to arrive, his cue to go. The police would start canvassing the area soon, and there was no way for him to plausibly explain his presence anywhere near the trailer park.

He had summoned every ounce of the iron-clad control that had allowed him to get this far without being caught and had torn himself away from the mesmerizing vision of Megan Flynn.

He held her face in his mind as he drove. Elation poured through him, pure and clean, washing away the fervor of the kill.

Patience. He just needed to be patient for a little while longer, and then they could be together forever. Like they were meant to be.

But tonight, he still had business to attend to.

He waited until he was more than six miles from the trailer park before he turned on his phone. Even though he'd had special security features installed, it didn't hurt to be careful. He hit the first number of his speed dial and listened as it rang twice, as always.

"Gino's Pizza. Takeout or delivery?" a voice on the other end answered.

He rolled his eyes at the hokey but necessary ruse.

"Takeout."

"Please hold."

He waited several seconds before the line clicked over.

"You're calling to confirm?"

"Yes. The order has been filled."

"Good. You'll get your usual tip. After you finish cleaning up, get over here. We need to go over the logistics for this week's deliveries."

He hung up and smiled. He'd gotten off. He'd gotten paid.

And best of all, he'd gotten a live, close-up look at Megan.

Not bad for a night's work.

Chapter 5

Blood was everywhere. Covering the walls, the bed, the floor of the dumpy, abandoned trailer. As Megan approached the bed, she could feel the blood under the soles of her shoes, tacky and sticky. The salty, metallic smell of it saturated the air. She reached out a trembling hand to the woman lying facedown on the bed.

She was naked and bound, like the others. But there was something about her, something strange and eerily familiar that Megan couldn't put her finger on.

"Megan!" The whisper came from the darkness behind her. She whirled around, heart in her throat.

"Sean?" Her brother stood in the corner, his face in shadow, but she knew it was him. She took a step away from the bed, toward him.

"Megan, you have to run. You have to get out of here."

"But I have to help her." She turned back to the woman on the bed. The room had changed. It was no longer the trailer. It was her own bedroom, her own bed.

"Megan!" Sean yelled again, but she ignored him, reaching toward the girl, placing her hand on the blood-smeared cheek and turning the girl's face so she could see her in the blue glow that illuminated the room.

Megan leaned closer to see.

And realized she was staring into her own sightless eyes.

She staggered back, screaming. But nothing came out except a high-pitched wheeze. She turned to run, but the blood on the floor had turned thick as tar, pulling at her feet until she was trapped.

"Megan, run!" Sean's voice again.

I'm trying. But she couldn't get the words out.

From behind, a gloved hand covered her mouth. Cold metal kissed her throat.

Megan sat up with a gasp, her hand clutched around her neck. Her breath sawed in and out of her chest as her heart pounded so hard she could actually see her T-shirt tremble with every thud.

He's here.

Her eyes darted frantically around the room, searching for the figure in the shadows. Searching for Sean. Her throat still tingled from the feel of the knife. The sensation was so vivid she had her phone in her hand and dialed 9 and 1 before her brain finally kicked into gear.

Just a dream.

The realization didn't dampen her panic right away, adrenaline pumping through her as the too-vivid images slowly faded.

She sat up straighter and rubbed her eyes with the heels of her hands as if she could wipe her mind clean of the dream. Bits and pieces clung to her consciousness, and her stomach flipped over at the memory of looking at her own dead face.

Oh, Sean . . . A wave of sadness swelled up to mingle with the shakiness. Sean, trying to protect her even in her dreams. She shook her head and sniffed back tears.

She reached over to the bedside table and slipped her glasses on. Maybe if she brought the real world back into focus, the creepy dream hangover would loosen its hold. Most of the time she didn't mind living alone, but nights like this she wished she had someone lying next to her. A muscular back to curl up against, someone warm and solid who would slip a strong arm around her and stroke her back until she calmed back down.

An image of Cole's solid chest, long corded arms, and big hands flashed in her brain. She shoved it away and swung her legs over the edge of the bed. She reached for the bedside lamp, then froze as she realized what was weird about the room.

She'd fallen asleep with the TV in her room on. Which in and of itself wasn't unusual, but somehow the input selection had gotten messed up, so instead of late-night infomercials, her TV displayed a blank blue screen. She must have rolled over the remote in her sleep. The room was suffused by an eerie glow, casting her shabby chic furniture in ominous shadows.

The TV.

That was what had been bugging her all night, the little finger tapping at the back of her brain when Devany was telling first the patrol officer, then Cole, exactly what she'd seen in that trailer.

The TV had been on.

Just like when Sean found Evangeline Gordon next to him in that bed. He'd described the scene in grueling detail over and over, to the police, to his lawyer, and to Megan. She'd been over Sean's case files so many times she could recite every statement from every witness word for word.

I woke up and found her next to me in the bed. There was blood everywhere. On the sheets, on me, all over the rest of the house. I have no memory of how we got there. I left the room to find the phone and noticed that the television was on.

Both Sean and the first responders reported the TV had been on, remarkable only because there was no display, only the blue screen. It had seemed strange to Megan, since Sean had just moved in and hadn't had his cable installed yet. He'd bought a new TV, but he'd given Megan his old DVD and stereo and hadn't replaced them.

So why would Sean turn the TV on if there was nothing to watch?

No one took the question seriously, and on some level even Megan had felt she was grasping at straws.

But now the question sprang to life again. What if the man who killed Evangeline Gordon had a camera hooked up to Sean's TV?

Just like the man who killed the woman in the trailer. The serial killer the press had dubbed the Seattle Slasher.

Something like optimism leaped in her chest.

Do not get ahead of yourself.

But her brain raced, wondering if this, of all the known facts and odd coincidences, could be the one shred of information she'd been looking for?

Even she had to admit it was a long shot.

But right now it could be the only shot Sean had.

—⁓—

Megan tucked a stray curl behind her ear before she entered the building that housed the SPD south precinct.

Her nerves were shot from adrenaline and caffeine. Her dream had woken her at a little past three-thirty in the morning, and she hadn't gone back to bed. Instead, she'd pored over her copy of Sean's case file for five hours and consumed a full pot of coffee in the meantime.

She thought she managed to keep the quaver out of her voice as she told the desk sergeant her name and asked to see Cole. But she couldn't stop the toe of her boot from *tap tap tapping* at the linoleum floor, even when the desk sergeant flashed her an irritated look.

She turned her back on him. The coffee churned in her stomach as she tried to figure out exactly what to say to Cole. The cardboard of the accordion file that held Sean's case files grew soft and mealy in spots from her damp, clutching fingers, and she willed herself to calm down, stay focused.

"Megan?"

Her heart spasmed when Cole called her name. Purely from the caffeine overload, she told herself.

He was dressed almost exactly as he'd been last night, in dark slacks and a white cotton shirt that stretched across his broad shoulders. The only difference was the tie. He'd swapped out yesterday's navy for a maroon one. He stared at her, his brows knit.

"I have something I need to talk to you about. About the woman Devany found last night."

"You know, you could have called. You didn't have to come all the way down here. Not that I'm not happy to see you," he said. He cleared his throat but regained his cool almost immediately.

"It's kind of complicated," Megan replied. "I wanted to go over it in person."

He nodded and led her back to a small conference room that held a small round table and three padded chairs. "Do you want some coffee?"

Her stomach lurched at the thought. "God, no."

He motioned for her to sit down. "Let me just get Detective Petersen—"

She held up a staying hand. "I'd rather go over this with just you, if you don't mind."

Cole frowned at her but took a seat in the chair across from her.

Megan plunked the accordion folder down on the table.

"What's all this?" Cole said as he reached for the folder.

"Sean's case files. I think whoever killed that girl last night might have killed Evangeline Gordon too." Oh crap, she hadn't meant to blurt that out so quickly. She hadn't exactly worked out what she was going to say, but she'd had some vague plan of leading with a question about the television and camera in the trailer, bringing up the similarity to the crime scene at Sean's house. Hell, maybe even getting the lightbulb to go off in Cole's head all by itself.

Instead she could see him shutting down in front of her. His eyes glazing over, his mouth tightening, the subtle shake of his head as he looked at her with a combination of exasperation and pity.

"No, just listen," she said, feeling the muscles in her neck tighten like rubber bands. "There are similarities—the TV thing." She opened the accordion file and pulled out the crime scene report. "The TV was left on at Sean's house, just like in the trailer."

"Megan, you have got to let this go."

"But look." She pointed to a paragraph in the report. "The evidence showed that Evangeline was killed in the living room, in front of the television, then moved to the bed."

"And you think that's evidence that the Slasher killed Evangeline Gordon and framed your brother for it?"

She fought not to shrink under his barrage. Cole thought she was batshit, and Megan wasn't even sure she could blame him. Hearing herself say it out loud...her theory sounded crazy to her too. She shook off the doubt. Crazy, maybe. Far-fetched, definitely. But this was the one shred of hope she had, and she wasn't letting go so easily.

"Look, all I want is for you to look into it. What about the other victims? Was there this camera/TV thing going on with them? What about the wounds? Have you ever compared the autopsy reports side by side to see if there were any similarities?"

Irritation sparked in his dark gaze. "Tell me something. Would I let Sean rot on death row if I thought there was a possibility he wasn't guilty?"

"But if you'd just—"

Cole's broad palm slammed down on the table with enough force to make his empty coffee mug jump. "I don't want Sean to be guilty any more than you do, Megan. That's why when the first vic was found, I looked at the reports. I compared the autopsy and crime scene information to Evangeline Gordon's. And I can tell you that the only similarities are that they were both sexually assaulted and killed with a knife."

She was mute for a moment, struck dumb with shock by what he'd just revealed. "Why didn't you ever tell me?"

"Well we weren't exactly on speaking terms. And I didn't want to get your hopes up," he snapped.

He pushed back from the table, and she knew her time was running out. "Please, just let me see for myself," she said, wincing at the pleading tone in her voice.

"You know I can't give you that information with the investigation still ongoing."

"Please, Cole. No one has to know." Her hands balled into tight fists, fingernails biting into her palms. She hated him. Hated—being in a position where she had to grovel and beg him for help.

But she sensed a crack in his hard surface. He wasn't completely immune to her—she'd seen that last night. He still had some feelings for her, still cared a little, even though he'd dropped her like she was on fire after Sean's arrest.

"I would know," he said simply.

She swallowed hard, feeling like she'd had a hole blown through her chest. "And you can never bend the rules, even if it might lead to a break in your investigation." She restacked the papers she'd pulled from the folder, careful to put them back in precise order.

"Actually, technically it's not my investigation," he said.

She froze in the act of paper clipping the stack together. "Not because of me?"

He gave her a puzzled look that quickly morphed into understanding. "The feds opened a file after the third victim, and a team flew in from D.C. this morning. My role now is to support their ongoing investigation," he said with a humorless smile.

Great. A dead weight settled in her stomach along with the knowledge that the feds would be even less willing to investigate her theory. She packed the files back in the folder and stood. Cole rose too. "Is the agent in charge available?" she asked briskly.

"Don't do this, Megan. You're just going to drive yourself crazy, and you're not going to find what you're looking for."

"How can I not, Cole? How can you stand there and tell me I shouldn't do everything I possibly can to help my brother?" She tilted her head to the side, eyes narrowing. "Then again, I guess that's the difference between you and me. You have no problem turning your back on the people who need you."

—⁓—

Cole watched as Megan exited the conference room and brushed past Petersen with a nod. The front of her hair was pulled back in a clip, leaving the rest to tumble down her back, bouncing and shifting as she moved through the office at a sharp clip.

Every male eye was glued to the bounce of her round ass. While Cole couldn't blame them, that didn't stop him from wanting to punch every single one in the face.

"What was that about?" Petersen asked. Cole noticed she, too, was admiring the last glimpse of Megan before she disappeared from view. Though she and her partner had recently celebrated their anniversary, Cole supposed Petersen couldn't be faulted for looking. She turned to face Cole.

"She thought she had some information that might be relevant. Turned out to be nothing."

Petersen stared at him like she knew he was hiding

something. "What was all that about giving up on people you care about?"

He shook his head. "Just bullshit. Nothing important." He wasn't about to let Petersen see how hard Megan's parting words had hit their mark. He and Petersen were friendly and worked well together, but they didn't go around sharing painful experiences from their pasts.

So unless she'd done some digging on her own, Petersen wouldn't know that Megan had scored a direct hit with her reference to another woman he'd failed—his high school girlfriend, his first love who had been murdered while Cole was out of town on a college scouting trip. Kelly had wanted to join him, but Cole had wanted to hang out with the basketball coach who was recruiting him and the other team members without having to make sure she was having a good time. So he'd left her behind in their hometown of Billings, Montana.

He'd revealed all of this one night over dinner with Megan, when she'd asked him why he'd become a cop. He'd never told anyone the truth before—that the unsolved murder of his girlfriend ate at him, drove him, until he abandoned his original plan to study civil engineering and studied criminal justice instead. Obtaining justice for other victims had helped him make peace with the fact that Kelly's murder was still unsolved.

That peace had allowed him to move on, even though Kelly's death had left permanent scars. At the time, Megan had taken his hand in hers as her eyes gleamed with sympathetic tears.

"Whatever," Petersen said, jolting him back to the present. "I just wanted to tell you Agent Whitmore called. He had a couple questions about your report."

Cole nodded and went back to his desk to return the call from the FBI. As he filled in the gaps and clarified a few points, Cole couldn't ignore the gnawing sensation in his chest where Megan's comment hit its mark. He tried to brush it off, knowing she was lashing out. It was nothing he should take so seriously.

But her dig picked away at the scar tissue, exposed the festering guilt over the fact that it had been nearly twenty years, and the guy who did it was still out there.

Guilt ate at him now, and not just over his inability to find Kelly's killer.

He'd let Megan down too. No matter how he justified it in his head, no matter how certain he was that he'd done the right thing arresting Sean, the way he'd treated Megan in the aftermath still didn't sit right. Convincing himself it was best not to talk to her, refusing to return her calls because it could only get uglier between them. And when she'd leaked details of their relationship to the press, he'd told the world there was no way his feelings for Megan were strong enough to influence his treatment of the suspect.

The way they'd quoted him made it sound like he hadn't cared for her at all, which couldn't have been further from the truth. But he'd told himself it was better to let her think that, better to let her hate him if that's what she needed to do.

Now he couldn't chase away the regret, and seeing her again made him wish he'd acted differently. It didn't matter if he thought he was doing the right thing at the time. When it came down to it, he'd watched her world blow apart and left her to dangle. He still couldn't keep from failing the people he cared about.

Fuck it. This was no time to get maudlin. Megan wanted his help, and it was long past time he gave it—even if his instincts told him it wouldn't bring her anything but more grief.

Cole knew she wouldn't get anywhere, that she was chasing ghosts. He knew that better than anyone. She was only going to drive herself crazy or get herself into trouble. And none of it would keep her brother alive.

He hoped by stopping her in her tracks he could shut her down, keep her from getting her hopes raised only to get them crushed. He should have known better. Megan had never lost faith in her brother's innocence, in her belief that Evangeline Gordon's real killer was still out there.

Why should Cole expect that to change?

He grabbed his phone and dialed before he could think better of it. He was taking a huge risk, and if anyone found out he'd leaked the reports, he would be in deep shit.

But right now he couldn't see any other way to help Megan put this behind her once and for all. The only way was to give her exactly what she claimed she wanted: the truth.

—⁓—

Floating. Helpless.

Megan was right back where she started. The flash of insight, the rush of hope smacked down with one blow of Cole's big, broad palm.

Now, after talking to the FBI agent in charge of the investigation, Agent Tasso, she was even more deflated. As Megan was the first person Devany called after finding the body, he was interested in talking to her. But as predicted, he'd brushed off the idea that the Slasher murders could be related.

"I can imagine how hard it is to accept that your brother was capable of such a thing," Tasso said, his tone so condescending Megan fully expected him to reach across his desk and pat her on the head. "But the evidence left little room for doubt. If you knew the details of the other victims' murders, you'd understand why there's nothing to support your amateur detective work."

She'd left his office with a bitter taste in her mouth and no idea where to go next. Without Cole or another inside source, she had no hope of getting her hands on the sealed reports. And without a side-by-side comparison, there was no way she could prove that her hunch had any truth to it.

Maybe not even then.

But she couldn't bear to sit around and do nothing. After calling to check in on Devany, she'd decided to come here. Back to the source.

It had all started here, where her brother had met Evangeline Gordon.

It had always struck Megan as a strange location for one of the city's most exclusive nightclubs. Club One took up half a city block in Seattle's seediest neighborhood. It was only four-thirty in the afternoon, but from where she was parked across the street, Megan had already seen two drug deals, and she was pretty sure the woman in the orange micromini and thigh-high white boots leaning into the window of a car in front of her was not giving the male driver directions.

Yet every night, a line of Seattle's most hip and beautiful snaked out of Club One's door and around the block, the patrons even more attracted to the club because of the dangerous location.

Now, though, the sidewalk that fronted the nondescript warehouse that housed the club was empty. The crowd wouldn't start showing up for several more hours. Plenty of time for Megan to get some answers, even though as she crossed the street to the club she still wasn't sure what questions she should ask.

All she could think of was to go back to the beginning. To the place Sean had been seen with Evangeline Gordon before her murder. To talk to the woman who swore under oath that according to Evangeline, Sean had been practically stalking her in the week before her murder.

She ignored a panhandler and an offer to buy crystal meth and pushed open the door of the club.

"Can I help you?" a deep, male voice boomed as she stepped over the threshold. It took a moment for her eyes to adjust to the dim interior, but she spotted a huge, dark-haired man standing at the club's lower-level bar. His black T-shirt stretched across about an acre of chest, and his black pants hinted at thick, muscular legs. He stood with his legs slightly apart, arms loose at his sides. Not aggressive, at the moment. Just watchful.

He reminded her oddly of Sean. Full of coiled energy and ready to pounce if she made any sudden moves.

Megan walked slowly toward him. As she got closer, she saw that he was good-looking, in a square-jawed kind of way. His blue eyes would have contrasted nicely with his dark hair if he could have eased up on that disconcerting stare that made her fight not to squirm. "I was hoping to talk to Talia Vega, the beverage manager? Her sister told me I could find her here."

Talia had moved up in the world since Megan had last seen her. When Talia had taken the stand at Sean's trial, she'd been living in a small apartment in a rough part of downtown, working as a cocktail waitress to get by. Now she shared a house with her teenage sister in Seattle's Queen Anne neighborhood. No longer a cocktail waitress, Talia was now the beverage manager at Club One. A job that obviously paid enough to support Talia and her sister in comfort.

"Can I tell her your name?" the man asked.

"Megan Flynn."

He nodded curtly and disappeared through a door at the back of the club. Megan surveyed the club, with its black marble bar lined with plush red velvet bar stools. Booths lined the lower floor, and heavy velvet curtains were drawn back to reveal velvet-upholstered banquettes and black-lacquered tables. Besides the main bar, there were two fully stocked bars on opposite corners of the lower level. Upstairs was another floor, accessible from a wide staircase that curved dramatically into the middle of the lower-level dance floor. Up there was a VIP room with private tables and red velvet love seats.

The whole place reeked of hedonism. She tried to imagine her rugged, outdoorsy, beer-drinking brother in a place like this but couldn't. But being at Club One was the last thing Sean remembered from that night.

Megan turned at the swift tap of heels against the lacquered floor. Talia was as stunningly beautiful as ever, though more polished in the years since Megan had seen her last. Her glossy, straight black hair was pulled back tightly from her face, emphasizing her high cheekbones and huge eyes. Her dramatically arched eyebrows, red mouth, and hourglass figure reminded Megan of a comic book bombshell.

Talia's expression was guarded as she cocked her sleek head to the side. "Is there something I can help you with, Megan?"

Megan wasn't surprised by the wary undercurrent in Talia's voice, or by the way she shot a "stay close" look at the man who had greeted Megan. Talia had testified against Sean at his murder trial. For all she knew, Megan could have been driven completely over the edge by recent events, out to get revenge on everyone who'd helped convict Sean.

Megan tried to conjure a convincingly sane, friendly smile, though there was no denying the resentment she harbored toward the woman staring back at her. "I'm assuming you know about the murder at Redwood Acres last night," Megan said.

Talia's perfectly arched brow quirked higher. "Of course. It's terrifying." Talia sounded more annoyed than terrified as she folded her arms across her chest.

"I know this is going to sound crazy—"

"Do you mind?" Talia snapped before Megan could finish. But Talia's irritation was aimed at the man who had greeted Megan and fetched Talia for her. He had gone behind the bar and taken down a highball glass from the bar and was filling it with water. She marched over to the bar and snatched the glass out of his hand. "I have that all set up for tonight. You can get your drink in the back."

He snatched the glass back, put it to his lips, and drained it in three deep swallows. Whatever had those two bristling at each other went way beyond a conflict over what glassware to use.

Talia glared at the man for nearly a full minute before turning back to Megan. "Our new head of security seems to think he can do whatever he wants around here."

The man ignored Talia and refilled his glass.

"Sorry. You were saying?"

"This is going to sound crazy," Megan started again, "but I have a...hunch—for lack of a better word—that last night's murder and Evangeline Gordon's death could be related."

Megan wouldn't have thought it possible, but Talia's expression closed even further. "I don't see how that's possible, since Evangeline's murderer was convicted. There was no disputing the evidence," she said pointedly, though not unkindly.

Megan forced herself to unclench, to not fly off the handle at Talia. No love lost between them, but if there was any information to be gained from Talia's memories of that night, she'd get a lot further if she minded her manners. "I know that's what everyone thinks. But there are similarities, and I don't know where to start except at the beginning. The night you claimed you saw Sean follow Evangeline out of the club."

"I didn't claim anything," Talia replied, her voice dripping icicles. "I *saw* your brother. I *heard* Evangeline tell me that he'd been hounding her for a week before she died."

"Maybe there's something you missed, something you don't even realize you saw or heard. Something that was ignored because it didn't help the prosecution's case," Megan said, hating how her voice pitched higher with every syllable.

Something in Talia's cool expression flickered, a crack

in her porcelain facade, but it was gone so quickly Megan wondered if she'd imagined it. "I told the police and the prosecution everything I knew before and during the trial. Many times over. Now, if you'll excuse me, I have a lot of work to do. Brooks," she snapped.

"Yes?" The big man was leaning on the bar, watching their exchange like an anthropologist studying a foreign tribe.

"Do your job. Escort Ms. Flynn out." Without another word, she spun on her stiletto and *tap tap tapped* her way back to the club's shadowy depths.

Feeling like her lifeboat had been punctured by a harpoon, Megan didn't even protest as the man gestured her toward the door. She started to hurry out, but he stayed her, curving one massive hand around her biceps. "You shouldn't walk around here alone, even at this time of day."

She let him accompany her silently across the street, all the while her mind racing, grasping, trying to figure out the next step. All she could see in front of her were brick walls.

As the man reached out for her keys to unlock her car, the sleeve of his T-shirt slid up, revealing the bottom edge of a tattoo on his left biceps. Without thinking, she grabbed his arm and leaned in for a closer look. It was a black-scaled snake coiled around a beret-wearing skull with a sword stabbing up through its mouth. Sean had a similar one in the same location, but his skull was minus the beret.

"You're Special Forces," she said.

"Green Beret," he confirmed.

"My brother was too. Captain Sean Flynn, seventy-fifth Ranger Regiment."

"Major Jack Brooks," he said. "I heard about your brother. Hate to see a fellow soldier end up like that."

Megan jerked her hand from his arm and waited for him to elaborate. He didn't, just stared down at her, a steady, inscrutable look in his dark blue eyes. As she met his gaze, Megan got an uneasy feeling in her gut, as though he'd known everything about her even before she'd walked through the door of the club.

Flustered, she yanked at the handle of her car door. "I guess I should get going," she said, and slid into the driver's seat.

"Yeah, you should."

Something in his tone made her look up as she clipped her seat belt.

The measured look he gave her was like an icy finger down her spine. "Don't come back here," he said. "This isn't a safe place for you."

They both knew he wasn't talking about the neighborhood.

Chapter 6

Megan tucked her headphones into her ears, cranked up the volume on her iPod, and forced herself to concentrate on the screen. She usually had no problem drowning out the din of the crowd at her favorite café, but after the events of the past few days, she hadn't been able to focus enough to make herself a peanut butter sandwich, much less write the article she was supposed to have turned in to *Seattle* magazine two days ago.

Located just two blocks from her flat, Café Norte was a favorite of students at the university and freelancers like herself. As usual, the place was crowded with patrons, echoing with low-pitched conversations and the *tap tapping* of fingers on keyboards. Usually she found the vibe conducive to writing, the energy of others working and studying adding fuel to her own creative fire.

"Come on," she muttered to herself. "Just fucking write it already." Small wonder she couldn't focus on an article about how Seattle's diverse immigrant population shaped the city. But if she didn't turn in this article ASAP and get a check cut, she was going to have a hell of a time making rent this month.

She blew out a frustrated breath, jaw clenching as she

willed the crowd of Café Norte to shut the hell up or disappear entirely. She'd come early for her coffee date, hoping the change of scenery would encourage productivity, having given up on working at home. Her high-speed Internet connection there proved too tempting and distracting—instead of making phone calls to a district high school to discuss how schools were being impacted by larger immigrant populations, she'd spent the past two days obsessively Googling every article she could find about the Seattle Slasher and his victims, looking for a sliver of information that might support her theory that they might be connected to the murder of Evangeline Gordon. She'd found nothing she hadn't read before, except for an article about the latest victim found in the Redwood Acres trailer park.

Other than a brief statement by Special Agent Tasso of the Seattle FBI office, the article was short on information. Mostly it was a recap of the history of the Slasher and his past victims, the details of which were frustratingly sparse as investigators did their best to keep the details out of the press.

In the end, all she'd had was a short list of investigators on the local precincts where the other victims had been killed whom she planned on contacting as soon as she got this damn thing written.

So far she had two whole paragraphs. Awesome.

Her eyes did another pass at the door. She checked the time. Her coffee date was two minutes late by her watch. Maybe he wouldn't show up. She almost wished he wouldn't. She really needed to get the article done. And Sean... It seemed wrong somehow to be catching up over coffee with one of his old army buddies when Sean... God, the clock was ticking. Two more days gone since

her dead-end meeting with Cole and her useless visit to
Club One.

*Maybe I should just bail before he gets here. I'm not fit
company for anyone.*

Don't be like that, she scolded herself. In all this chaos,
she needed a friend. Especially a friend like Nate, someone who knew her, who knew her brother and everything
that had happened over the past three years. For that reason she'd agreed to meet Nate for coffee when he called
her out of the blue yesterday. Amazing who came crawl-
ing out of the woodwork now that Sean's name was back
in the press.

She'd avoided most of them—especially Jimmy Caparulo, who had called every day since the news hit, and she
couldn't bring herself to call him back. She just didn't feel
up to dealing with the mixed emotions she had about the
man who had once been as close as a brother to Sean. So
close they'd gone to the army recruitment office together
and been in the same class at Ranger school. She could
have forgiven him for what he'd done to her. But she would
never forget that it was Jimmy who had brought Sean and
Evangeline Gordon together, Jimmy who had testified as a
witness for the prosecution that he knew Sean had devel-
oped immediate and strong feelings for Evangeline the
first time he met her at Club One.

Logically, Megan knew Jimmy hadn't had any choice
but to testify, and to his credit, he'd done his best to stand
up for Sean and not let the prosecutors twist his words.
He'd even emphasized his issues with drugs and alcohol
to make himself seem less credible on the stand. But she
couldn't get over the fact that if it hadn't been for Jimmy,
Sean never would have met Evangeline.

She knew Jimmy was genuinely sorry, for everything, but no matter how much she missed her surrogate brother from childhood, right now Megan couldn't stand to talk to him, even to hear his apology.

But when Nate had called her earlier this week, she'd surprised herself by accepting his invitation to meet for coffee. Maybe because Nate was the only one of Sean's friends to actually back off when she pushed everyone away, one of the few who didn't keep trying to push their way back into her life, all the while looking at her with pity in their eyes—pity for her inability to accept the truth of what her brother had become. Her refusal to see the monster lurking within.

And unlike guys like Jimmy, Nate had emerged from his stint in the military unscathed from his combat tours. That alone made the prospect of seeing him again appealing. Megan could only handle one emotional breakdown at a time, thank you very much. Namely her own.

Five minutes past ten and Nate still wasn't here. Maybe he was going to stand her up.

She felt equal parts disappointment and relief at the prospect as she sucked down the last of her coffee. She asked a girl with a nose ring and improbable red dreadlocks at the next table to keep an eye on her stuff while she went for a refill. She already had four cups churning in her gut, but after more sleepless nights, caffeine was the only thing keeping her on her feet.

She gave the cashier a quarter for her refill and dosed it heavily with cream and sugar. As she turned to walk back to her table, she got a prickly sensation at the nape of her neck, quickly followed by a nauseating twist in her stomach. The mug trembled in her hand, and coffee sloshed over her wrist. Megan didn't flinch, oblivious as her heart pounded in her chest and cold sweat bloomed on her skin.

She took several deep breaths, trying to calm down before she succumbed to a full-fledged panic attack. The third one in two days.

She'd had her first attack three years ago, the week after Sean was arrested. At the time, she'd been convinced she was dying. She'd had them on and off throughout the year of his trial and had finally overcome them after a brief stint in therapy and a couple months on prescription antianxiety meds.

She hadn't had one in years; then—bam—the other day after she'd left Club One, it had hit her like a freight train. At least this time she knew what was happening. She knew she wasn't dying and had the presence of mind to pull over before she plowed into a parked car. Though she'd shaken off the attack, a looming sense that her world was about to come to an end stayed with her.

Because it would. Unless she could figure out a way to keep the needle out of Sean's arm.

She abandoned her coffee on the counter and lurched back to her table on legs that threatened to buckle with every step. Her heart rate had nearly slowed to a gallop, but a large masculine hand clamping around her forearm sent it back to warp speed.

She gasped and jumped about a foot. Her elbow flew into a rib cage and the crash of a trayful of dishes echoed through the small café, permeating the deep thrum of her own heartbeat.

"What the hell is your problem?" a sharp, feminine voice snapped behind her.

"Megan, are you okay?"

Megan looked up at her would-be assailant and felt like an idiot. Nate Brewster stared down at her, his clear blue eyes dark with concern. He slackened his grip and moved his hand up her forearm in a light caress. "Sorry if I scared you. I thought you were about to fall."

Megan tried to slow her breath so she wasn't panting like a greyhound and shook her head, willing away the irrational fear that clawed its way through her insides. "No...I'm just really jumpy." She looked down and saw ceramic fragments at her feet. Heat rushed to her cheeks when she saw a waitress with full-sleeve tattoos kneeling on the floor, wiping up a puddle of coffee.

"Oh God, I'm sorry," Megan sputtered, and started to sink to the floor to help.

"Don't worry, I got it," the waitress said.

Nate took out his wallet and, ignoring Megan's clumsy protests, handed the waitress a ten. "For you."

The waitress gave him a surprised smile and stuffed the bill into her apron.

Humiliated, Megan let Nate guide her to her chair, grateful for a steady hand as she lowered herself on still-shaky legs. "I'm really sorry," she began.

"No worries." Nate flashed her a smile worthy of a toothpaste commercial. His vivid blue eyes still held traces of concern. "Talk to me."

Megan shrugged and pushed back a lock of hair with shaky fingers. "I've been having panic attacks. I thought I was over them but..."

"Not surprising with everything that's happening." He heaved a sigh. "I know how hard you must be taking all of this."

Megan's spine stiffened and she looked for signs of pity or condescension on his face, but saw only concern.

"I just don't understand why he gave up."

Nate shrugged. "I have no idea what Sean must be going through in there, but I imagine being locked up like that, especially for a guy like Sean, would mess you up pretty bad."

Megan swallowed around the lump lodged in her throat and nodded.

Nate reached over and gave her hand a quick squeeze. "Let me get you something to drink." He took her drink order—decaf this time—and walked up to the bar. Megan watched him move through the crowd, standing out like a preppy beacon among a sea of hipster black, grunge flannel, tattoos, and piercings.

No one could deny that Nate Brewster was easy on the eyes. Though he was big—almost as big as her brother—he moved with the easy grace of an athlete. With his blond hair, blue eyes, and finely chiseled features, Nate had always reminded her of some kind of Nordic aristocrat. His was the kind of handsome that could have almost been called pretty if the rest of him hadn't been so masculine.

Totally the opposite of Cole.

No! You are not about to ruin a perfectly good coffee date brooding over you-know-who.

She couldn't get Cole's face out of her mind, with his dark, almost black hair and eyes. Rough-hewn features just this side of craggy. Nothing pretty about that face. And yet...

Just thinking about him made her stupid. Especially considering the role he'd played in making her life a living hell.

The role he was still playing.

Nate returned with two full mugs and a plate holding two biscotti. "Here," he said. "If you're this shaky, you should have something to eat to absorb the acid."

A warm feeling washed through her. Unfamiliar, but... nice. Funny that such a small gesture could mean so much, but it had been so long since anyone had looked after her that she'd forgotten what it felt like.

Nothing dramatic. But it was nice. And right now nice was about all she could deal with.

"I owe you an apology," Nate said, looking at her a little sheepishly over the rim of his coffee mug.

"What for?"

"For being out of touch for so long. For not making more of an effort to keep in contact with you." He was silent a beat. "And Sean."

Megan curled her hands around her coffee cup and gave him a feeble smile. "It's all right. As for Sean—" She broke off, her eyes suddenly stinging with tears and the knot in her throat threatening to close off her breath. "He won't see anyone. Not even me." Not even one last time before he died. She refused to blink, afraid it would break the seal on her tears and then she'd really lose it.

"Look, I had to go away for work, but I could have done more," Nate said. "So when I heard about Sean's decision, I thought maybe you could use a friend."

Megan nodded. "You were right."

There was an awkward moment of silence; then Nate spoke again. "I know the circumstances are totally screwed up, but it is great to see you again. You look—"

"Like shit," she said with a wry smile.

"I've seen you look better," he conceded. "But you're beautiful, Megan. You always have been."

His smile had faded, and she squirmed a little under his suddenly intense look. "I have a mirror. Don't try to flatter me." She lowered her gaze to the table and took a long drink of her coffee.

"I can't imagine how hard this must be on you."

She nodded, grateful he dropped the subject of her looks and supposed beauty. Though Nate was pleasant company, she'd seen the undeniable spark of attraction in his eyes and wasn't prepared to go there.

"Yeah," she said with a mirthless smile. "The last few years have been pretty much all about work." She gestured at her mostly blank laptop screen. "I'm supposed to be writing an article. You can see how far I've gotten. And when I'm not working, I'm…" She hesitated. She hadn't known Nate all that well before Sean's arrest.

All he has to do is read a newspaper to know that's what the rest of the world thinks. May as well lay it all out there early.

He raised a curious eyebrow and gave her an encouraging nod.

"The rest of the time I've spent searching. For evidence, a lead, anything that could help me prove that they were wrong about Sean. There's no way he could have murdered that girl."

Megan's stare was a challenge.

Nate nodded. There was no surprise, no doubt, and *thank you God,* no fucking *pity.* Like her conclusion was perfectly logical.

"I hired a private investigator, but we never got any

leads," she said, upping the ante. "But I know in my heart Sean is innocent."

Nate merely nodded again as he finished off his biscotti. "Who did you use?"

"Use?"

"What investigative service? Someone local?"

"Parker and Fishman," Megan said.

Nate dusted the crumbs from his hands with a mild look of disgust. "They're a bunch of hacks. Good for a basic background check and not much else."

Megan chuckled weakly. "Wish you'd been around to tell me that before I spent six thousand dollars with them."

"I've worked with Dennison Investigations," Nate continued. "I like to know the details of who I'm doing business with before I do a deal. Dennison always delivers. They get booked up solid, but I'll make sure they'll see you."

Not that it would do any good. Megan had contacted Dennison right after Sean was arrested, only to find out they were way out of her price range. Nate's computer-consulting business must be doing pretty well if he could afford to use them regularly. "Thanks for the offer, but I kind of blew my budget on the other guys. Anything I find now will have to be on my own."

Nate's dark blond brows knit above his blade-straight nose. "Wish I'd known that."

Megan waved him off. "I didn't tell you. Like I said, I closed off anyone and everyone who wasn't willing to jump on the 'Sean is innocent' bandwagon. You had your own life to deal with."

"But Sean was my friend, and I turned my back on

him. And you. I'm sorry for that." He reached across the table and covered her hand. His fingers were warm as they lightly caressed the back of her hand. "Go ahead and call Dennison. If you're worried about money, let me contribute."

Megan's hand jerked in surprise. Nate's fingers tightened to keep it in place. "That's...that's really generous of you," she sputtered, "but I don't think—"

"Megan, compared to the amount we already spend with them, your case would be nothing."

Megan shook her head, momentarily speechless. She wanted desperately to take him up on the offer. The idea that she could have one of the top private investigation firms in the country at her back was an overwhelming temptation. But it would also put her in Nate's debt, to the tune of tens of thousands of dollars. "That's too much—"

"It's not just for you. It's for Sean too."

Oh, he really knew how to stab at her heart. Still, she and Sean had always fended for themselves, never accepted a handout from anyone. She didn't like the idea of being so deeply obligated to Nate.

As she opened her mouth to respond, she froze at the sight of a tall, masculine figure weaving its way through the crowded restaurant.

Everything about Cole shouted cop. The way he moved through the room, unconsciously in charge, the way his dark gaze took in every detail of every person in the crowded café. Megan wasn't the only one who noticed it. The mostly student crowd darted furtive glances his way, careful not to make eye contact, shifting uneasily on their chairs as though afraid he was going to sniff out the dime bags and stray Vicodins stashed in their beat-up backpacks.

But Cole had only one target today.

Megan swallowed hard as his dark gaze locked on her, focused, intent. His already grim expression darkened as he assessed her companion. His eyes narrowed to icy black slits when he saw Nate's hand covering hers.

Her core temperature went up about ten degrees, and her stomach did that stupid flippy thing it always did when he was around. She jerked her hand from Nate's, then cursed herself for caring that Cole caught her holding hands with another man.

"I need to talk to you," Cole snapped without preamble, not even bothering to acknowledge Nate.

Nate, ever the gentleman, gave a guarded smile and said, "You know this guy, Megan?"

"Nate Brewster, meet Detective Cole Williams."

Nate stood and offered his hand. The two men briefly shook, all the while eyeing each other like two fighters circling the ring.

If it came down to it, they would be evenly matched. Cole had Nate on height by a couple inches, but Nate matched him in sheer muscular bulk.

"How did you know I was here?"

"I stopped by your place. Mrs. Makowski said she'd seen you take off with your laptop case. I figured you might be here working."

Megan swallowed hard and told herself it was of no significance that Cole remembered her favorite work-away-from-home spot. None whatsoever. She pasted a smile on her face and gestured toward Nate.

"Nate's an old friend of Sean's," Megan said. "And, Nate, you might remember Cole as the man who arrested Sean."

"Sorry to interrupt whatever it is you have going on here," Cole said, not even trying to sound sincere, "but Megan, I need to talk to you. It's important."

Megan settled back against the firm wooden frame of her chair and folded her arms. "So talk."

"Alone," Cole added, not so much as offering an apologetic glance at Nate.

Megan fought the impulse to do exactly as he asked on the tiny scrap of hope that he might actually be willing to help her this time. She damn well knew better, after all this time. Still, she couldn't completely squelch the burst of anticipation. "Is it official police business, Detective?"

His full lips flattened into an irritated line. "Not exactly."

She sat back in her chair and crossed her arms over her chest. If he wouldn't give, neither would she. "Well I'm busy with my friend, and I think you said everything you needed to say in your office the other day."

Cole blew out an impatient breath and hooked a thumb in his waistband, a gesture that flipped his leather coat back just enough to provide a glimpse of his Glock tucked securely in a shoulder holster and the badge clipped to his waistband. Megan wasn't sure if the gesture was deliberate, but it and the hard look at Nate had the desired effect.

Nate pushed his chair back. "It's not a problem," he said, his affable smile not quite reaching his eyes. "I really need to get back to work anyway."

"Nate, you don't have to go," Megan said, reaching out to stop him as he stood.

Don't leave me alone with him, she wanted to plead. Instead she stood, too, and let Nate pull her into a hug tight enough to push the bounds of friendly. Though the hard press of Nate's chest against hers didn't exactly set off bells and whistles, she let the hug linger a few seconds longer than she might have otherwise.

And felt the tight curl of satisfaction in her gut at the flash of heat in Cole's eyes. It was gone in a nanosecond, shoved behind the wall of his impassive cop's gaze, but she knew what she saw.

"Think about what we discussed," Nate said. He dropped his arms but trailed one hand down her forearm to loosely grasp her hand.

"I will," Megan said.

"Seriously," Nate said, giving her hand a shake for emphasis. "And if there's anything I can do, day or night, you call me. I'm here for you, Megan."

He left with a wave. Megan watched his tall form weave through the crowd, bracing herself as she turned to face Cole.

Any feelings of warmth or reassurance she might have enjoyed from Nate's words fled when she looked at Cole. His face was perfectly neutral, but she didn't miss the way his eyes tracked Nate across the crowded café. Quietly watchful, like a predator stalking his prey.

Unease prickled her skin as he turned that dark, assessing stare on her. "So what's so important?" she snapped, and started to sit.

He stopped her with a sharp shake of his head. "Not here. Somewhere private."

She rolled her eyes. "Fine. Let's go back to my place." She shut down her laptop and shoved it into her computer case. Cole waited and gestured for her to walk in front of him. The crowd had peaked with the lunchtime rush, and she had a hard time weaving her way through. She stiffened when Cole's hand rested lightly on the small of her back, fighting the urge to jump even as a tiny—okay, not so tiny—part of her relished the way he used his body like a human shield, using his size and authority to magically open a path through the throng.

He'd always been able to do that, make her feel safe and protected just by being in the same room with her.

Right. Safe and protected until he brought your whole world to a crashing halt.

She put as much distance between them as she could and rushed to the door. A light drizzle was falling, and the cold, moist air felt good on her overheated skin. "Do you mind telling me what all this is about?"

"You want information. I have it."

She cocked her head to the side, unsure she'd heard him correctly. "You mean the information about the other victims?" Even if he hadn't been so adamant, she knew Cole. No way would he break the rules. Not for her. Not for anybody.

No wonder, then, that his reply made her feel like she'd been hit with a Taser. He leaned in close and spoke so softly she strained to hear. "I pulled the autopsy and crime scene reports for you. Now, do you want to keep standing out here in the rain, or do you want to get this over with?"

Chapter 7

Megan popped open her umbrella, then handed it wordlessly to Cole to hold. He held it up, and she scooted under for the short walk back to her place where his car was parked. She stood as far away as she could and still remain under the meager shelter of the umbrella.

That left a good two inches between them. Close enough that Cole could catch the scent of her shampoo emanating from her rain-damp hair. Close enough to see the baby-fine curls springing from her tight braid, tempting him to coil one around his finger to see if it was still as silky soft as he remembered. Close enough to swear he could feel the warmth radiating from her skin, even through the layers of his jacket and her shell.

He tightened his grip around the umbrella handle, trying to summon up some self-control. Inside he was a seething mass of messy emotions, ranging from lust to guilt and a lot of other stuff he didn't even want to put a label on. Feelings for Megan he thought he'd buried. He shoved it all down, so far down he'd thought they had all but disappeared, except for a few wistful what-ifs every once in a while.

And, of course, his subconscious loved to torture him

on a regular basis with dreams ranging from the wickedly hot sex they had never had to visions of a future he'd been stupid enough to hope for, before the whole world came crashing down around them.

He told himself the dreams didn't count. His brain, his heart, everything that mattered knew it was beyond over with Megan, that it had been the second he locked the cuffs around Sean's wrists.

Had he been disappointed? Yes, bitterly so. But he was over it. At least that's what he'd thought until his chance encounter with Megan three days ago.

One look was all it had taken for everything to come bursting back to the surface. Where it stayed. Simmering, seething, threatening his common sense and control.

And now, today, seeing her with that Ken-doll clone, he'd managed to add a healthy dose of jealousy to the emotional mix. An emotion so unfamiliar, he didn't at first recognize it as the force that made him want to grab the hand covering Megan's and snap it like a twig. Fortunately his common sense prevailed, but even with Mr. All-American out of the picture, Cole found himself struggling to keep from doing something stupid.

Pulling up confidential autopsy and crime scene reports didn't qualify?

He was doing it to be altruistic, he told himself. For the sole purpose of putting Megan's wild theories to bed once and for all so she could finally move on.

Sure, Ace. Keep telling yourself that it's not just an excuse to get close to her again.

"So what's with what's-his-name—Nate?" He strove for casual and failed miserably, the question just this side of accusatory.

Megan slanted him a look from under her lashes. "Like I said, he was a friend of Sean's. They met in basic and realized they'd grown up practically next door to each other."

"You never mentioned him."

"He was Sean's friend, not mine. I met him only a couple times. But he saw all the recent news coverage and said he wanted to get back in touch."

Wanted to get in your pants is more like it. "Nice of him."

"It is. And he even offered to help me get an investigator from Dennison Investigations to help with Sean's case. There's no way I could afford them, but Nate offered to help cover the cost."

Hoping you'd pay him back how, exactly? Cole kept that to himself but couldn't suppress his skeptical grunt as they turned down Megan's street.

"What?" she snapped as he clicked his key fob to unlock his unmarked Crown Vic, which was parked across the street from her place.

Don't get into it, he warned himself. "You realize he wants to fuck you, don't you?" He could have kicked his own ass for saying it out loud. He was jealous. Bleeding black with it. Nothing he could do about that. But laying it out there for her to see? Now, that was just plain stupid.

Megan looked up at him, her dark eyebrows arched over her wide, challenging stare. "If he can help me prove Sean's innocence, maybe I'll let him."

The muscles in Cole's shoulders tensed as he reached in the passenger seat of his car for a large accordion folder. "If that's the case, you have no idea how much I wish there was something in these files that could do just that."

When he turned back, Megan was staring at the asphalt, but her cheeks were so pink they practically glowed. Her tongue flicked out to moisten her soft, pink lips. The gesture sent a spark of lust straight to his groin.

She risked a furtive glance, and in that split second, he saw an awareness so intense the air between them crackled with heat despite the cold, damp weather.

Before he could breathe, she'd lowered her thick lashes and was walking briskly across the street, her slender back so straight it looked like she had a metal rod running up her spine.

Cole paused, momentarily dumbstruck. It was the first time since Sean's arrest that Megan had indicated she felt anything other than hatred for him. He'd been convinced anything good she might have felt for him had been lost in the tidal wave of anger and resentment.

That hot green gaze flashed in his mind again. *Apparently not.*

What a fucking disaster.

It was bad enough that he'd pined after her like some pathetic fifteen-year-old the last three years. Knowing that anything she might have felt for him was dead kept him from dwelling on it too much. He could carry a torch for her to rival the Statue of Liberty's, but it was never going to get him anywhere.

But now he knew different. Emotions that strong didn't just disappear. Not for him anyway.

And evidently not for Megan either.

And it didn't do him a goddamn bit of good. All it did was make his chest ache that much more, make the regret that much keener over what they'd lost. What they should have had.

It was as hopeless as it had ever been, yet he couldn't silence the voice in his head urging him to use what he'd discovered to get her to open up to him, just a little bit. Tempting him to see if he could get that flash of lust to come blazing back up to the forefront.

You can't have everything. But maybe you don't have to settle for nothing.

His cock thickened behind the zipper of his trousers. He was pretty sure he'd identified the source of that voice.

Never one to let his little head do his thinking, he shoved the thought aside and followed her across the street, up the flight of rickety wooden stairs that led to the apartment she rented on the second floor of the house, doing his damnedest to keep his libido in check.

That was easier said than done when he stepped into the warm darkness of her apartment. He immediately steeled himself against the memories as the familiar vibe of Megan's place assailed him.

It was small and cozy, full of overstuffed furniture and colorful pillows that invited a person to flop down and relax with a warm cup of coffee or a couple fingers' worth of good whiskey. It was the opposite of his town house, which was little more than a place to sleep and store his stuff.

And that smell...He'd always loved the way Megan's apartment smelled. A combination of the spicy black tea she drank, the green smell of her many plants, the fresh scent of clean laundry. And under it all, the sweet, spicy smell of the woman herself.

It was all Cole could do not to close his eyes and inhale a deep, lusty breath.

"You can hang your jacket in the closet. I'll make some coffee." Cole shrugged off his coat as Megan moved past him into the front room and flipped on a table lamp, flooding the room with golden light.

As she rattled around in the postage-stamp-sized kitchen, Cole did a quick survey of the place, confirming his initial impression that nothing had changed. Same pillows. Same oversize armchair parked in front of the television.

Same couch.

His core temperature spiked as he was suddenly hit with the memories of the last time he'd been in Megan's apartment. The last time he'd been on Megan's couch.

Smooth, hot skin under his hands. His lips sucking the bullet-hard tip of her breast. The feel of her hands stroking the skin of his back and arms, her mouth sucking at his like she couldn't get enough. Never get enough. The hot, sweet squeeze of her sex around his fingers. Tight, slippery wet, aching for him to slide inside...

The sharp trill of the phone jerked him out of his flashback.

Megan picked up the phone, checked the caller ID and grimaced, but she didn't answer. Avoiding the couch, Cole settled himself at Megan's small kitchen table and set the folder down on it with a thud.

The answering machine clicked on as she spooned coffee into the filter.

Cole smiled when he heard Megan's cheerful outgoing greeting. That hadn't changed either. "Here in the twenty-first century," he said, unable to resist a dig, "we have something called voice mail."

She rolled her eyes at him and hit the coffeemaker's power button.

Any trace of humor fled her face as a man's voice filled the apartment. "Hey, Megan, it's me, Jimmy. I really wish you'd call me back. I just want to talk to you. You know how to reach me."

Cole settled back in his chair and tried to ignore the twist in his gut. But it was obvious from Megan's pale, strained face that this Jimmy was important to her, whoever he was. "Boyfriend?"

Megan's sharp, "Hah!" cracked across the kitchen. She filled two mugs with coffee, put cream and sugar in one and left one black for him. "That," she said, inclining her head toward the answering machine, "was Jimmy Caparulo."

Cole had a flash of recognition. "That was the bouncer from Club One, right? The guy who testified at Sean's trial."

Megan nodded, her mouth pulling tight. "It was more than that. He was Sean's best friend growing up. They joined the army together after they graduated from high school. They were even in the same class in Ranger school. That's where they met Nate." Megan gave him a sad little smile and set a mug in front of him, and then settled into the empty kitchen chair. "They were as close as brothers until . . ."

"Let me guess—until Sean got arrested."

"Nope. They were on the outs weeks before Sean got arrested, but Jimmy finally convinced Sean to come by Club One so they could talk. Don't you remember? That's how Sean met Evangeline in the first place."

Cole didn't have Sean's file memorized like Megan did, but now the little details were falling into place.

"What was their falling-out over? I don't remember it ever coming out in his testimony."

Megan flashed him a bitter smile. "It was because of me. Remember how Sean had a barbecue a couple weeks after he got back? I invited you but you couldn't come because you were too deep into the Pachevsky case?"

Cole nodded. In the end, he'd had to miss it to fly to Portland, where a money-laundering investigation had revealed a link to the murder of Sergei Pachevsky, a restaurant owner with ties to the Russian mob. Cole's investigation had consumed the better part of the month. The first time he met Sean Flynn in person, he was cuffing and stuffing him into the back of a squad car.

"Anyway, Sean had told me Jimmy was having trouble adjusting to civilian life. He was discharged a few months before Sean after an IED almost took him out. Even though he mostly recovered, he never really got over it, you know? I saw him some before Sean came home, and I knew he was drinking too much, and I'm pretty sure he was going pretty heavy on the painkillers. He was barely holding on to his job at Club One—he was a mess. Anyway, that night at Sean's, things got kind of out of hand."

The muscles in Cole's back tightened. "What do you mean, out of hand?"

"When I went inside to get the stuff to throw on the grill, Jimmy cornered me in the kitchen. Told me some BS about how he'd always had a thing for me, and he was so glad to be home where there were nice girls. He went in to kiss me, and when I pushed him away, he got a little rough."

Cole's hands fisted against the tabletop. "How rough?"

Megan shook her head and put up a hand as though to stay him. "Nothing major—he shoved me against the refrigerator and knocked my arm against the door."

"You told me you got that bruise when you hit it against a door frame."

She shrugged. "And that was the truth. I really don't think Jimmy wanted to hurt me—"

"No, he just assaulted you."

"He didn't assault me! I honestly think he was so messed up he didn't realize what he was doing."

"Why the hell didn't you tell me?"

"Because you had better things to do, and Jimmy was having enough problems without me siccing my cop boyfriend on him! Sean came in right then, saw what was happening, and yanked him off of me and told him to stay the hell away from me or he'd kill him."

"Has he been bugging you this whole time?"

She shook her head. "No. He called a couple times after the trial to apologize." Her breath caught and she sniffed hard. "Like that would help. I mean, I know he had to testify, but..." She squeezed her eyes shut and wrapped her arms around her waist. Cole's own arms twitched to pull her close and give her the comfort she needed. "He called me last week when he heard about Sean."

"Promise me you won't go see him alone."

"I don't think that's going to be an issue since I'm not even taking his calls. Even so, I don't think he wants to hurt me or anything—"

"He shoved you up against a wall!" The thought made Cole want to plant his fist in the other man's face.

"He was drunk. From what I've heard, he's been in rehab and is keeping it together. I think he's just sorry for how everything went down."

"We all are," Cole said. He made a mental note to run a check on Jimmy Caparulo when he got back to the station. Megan amazed him with her ability to see the best in people. It was a kind of faith he'd always admired, when it didn't drive him crazy. But regardless of what she thought about Jimmy, Cole would find out everything there was to know about him and make sure he kept the hell away from Megan.

—⁕—

"Can we get started already?" Megan asked, indicating the thick accordion file taking up nearly the entire surface of her minuscule table. Not only was she eager to dive into the reports, she needed to distract herself from her nearly overwhelming awareness of Cole, from the memories of what had happened the last time they were alone in her apartment.

Stupid, irrational, and inappropriate, she scolded herself. There was something wrong with her, some sick twist in her DNA. That was the only explanation for how, after everything that had happened, she still felt that same electric buzz along every nerve when she got close to him. How his scent—man plus a hint of cedarwood—could make her want to bury her face in the crook of his neck and breathe him in as if he were oxygen. How her fingers could ache to comb through his thick, dark hair.

It was a chemical quirk. Totally meaningless. She had more important matters to deal with than her libido, which for some unknown reason roused only around big, dark, roughly handsome police detectives who didn't let anything as silly as feelings get in the way of doing their jobs.

With that in mind, Megan pulled her focus back to the

folder. Despite Cole's certainty that there would be nothing in the reports to help Sean's case, Megan was buzzing with anticipation to see what was inside.

Cole was wrong. He had to be. There had to be something, something everyone had missed because they didn't know what they were looking for. But Megan knew, and if there was any information, no matter how small, linking the murders of five prostitutes to the death of Evangeline Gordon, she would find it.

"Some of this is going to be pretty rough," Cole said. "The photos are very grisly—"

"I'm a big girl, Cole. I've been over Sean's case file literally thousands of times. Not a lot bothers me." That wasn't entirely true, and she hoped he wouldn't call her bluff. Sure, the pictures of Evangeline, naked, her throat slashed open like an obscene smile, her torso nearly black with a curtain of blood, had stopped making her gag after the first dozen viewings. But Megan would never be immune to them, nor to the cold, clinical descriptions of how she had been raped and sodomized, how deep slashes had been cut into her breasts, buttocks, and thighs before her throat had been cut.

She braced herself as Cole slipped the elastic from around the folder and extracted the manila folders for each case.

Megan picked up the first one, marked *Jane Doe*. The Slasher's first victim. "So thin." They all were.

Cole ran a hand through his short, dark hair and let out a frustrated sigh. "It's everything we have. Crime scene report and printouts of digital photos, the ME's report, the autopsy, and toxicology reports. Blood-spatter analysis. But, yeah, it's not much. We know nothing about her, how she ended up in that house. And nothing about the sick fuck who did that to her." He flipped open the folder and indicated a photo with a blunt finger.

Megan suppressed a shudder and swallowed hard at the gruesome image before her. A woman lay naked on a bed, on her stomach, her knees still bent as though she'd been on all fours and fallen forward. Her arms were trapped beneath her chest. Her long, blond hair obscured her face, the ends matted with the blood that had pooled under her, saturating the sheets.

Her pale skin was marred with angry red slashes. Megan flipped through the rest of the photos. A shot of the blood spray that had arced from the foot of the bed onto the floor in front of it. A close-up of three slashes the killer had cut into the smooth skin of the woman's back.

As Megan turned to the next picture, her vision started to tunnel and she heard a loud buzzing in her head. This one was from the ME's report, after they had moved the body in preparation for the autopsy. The victim lay on a gurney, positioned on her back. With her fine features, closed eyes, and blue lips, she looked like a wax doll.

Like Evangeline, she had a gaping wound across her throat. Circular marks covered her breasts and stomach. "Cigarette burns?" she asked, fighting back the wave of dizziness.

Cole nodded and reached out to flip through some of the pictures. "He also burned her inner thighs."

A cold sweat bloomed on Megan's skin as she looked at the mutilated swath of pale skin. "And of course the other knife wounds." In addition to the cuts on her back and legs that Megan had already seen, the killer had sliced at her breasts.

The last photo was a close-up of one of those wounds, cut into the underside of the woman's left breast. There was a latex-gloved hand in the picture, lifting the breast up to show the severity of the wound.

Megan couldn't stifle her gasp of horror. The killer had slashed the woman so deeply, he'd nearly cut off her breast. "And he did all of that before he killed her, right?" She picked up the autopsy report, as much to distract herself as to verify the information. The typed words and diagrams swam in front of her.

"Yeah," Cole said. "Though he got a little more conservative with subsequent victims."

"Conservative?" Megan whispered, nausea burning at the back of her throat.

"The cuts on this first victim are much deeper than with his later victims. Like he was still getting the feel for it. You'll see with his later victims, the wounds are much shallower, the cuts much more controlled, only cutting through to the fat layer, not into the muscle. Like he's toying with them, not wanting them to bleed out until the very end."

That was it. One second Megan was trying to focus on the ME's written description of the wounds, struggling to process the image of the victim bound, helpless, awash in blood. The next, she was sliding out of her chair, the hardwood floor of her kitchen rushing up to greet her.

"Shit!" Cole's curse was muffled, like Megan was surfacing from the ocean. She blinked slowly and tried to sit up.

"Did I pass out?" Humiliation surged through her, providing the energy to sit up.

"This was a mistake." Cole was kneeling beside her,

his arm wrapped around her shoulders as he helped steady her. Megan scrambled to her knees but wobbled when she tried to stand.

Cole swore again. "Hold on. Let me help you."

He tightened his arm around her shoulder and helped her to stand.

She told herself she leaned into him only because she was still dizzy.

"Let's get you to the couch," he said, and started to steer her in that direction.

"No!" she said, a little too forcefully. She was having enough trouble keeping her mind from wandering to what had happened—nearly happened—on that couch. "Here's fine." She heaved herself back into the kitchen chair, took a deep breath, and grabbed the folder on the slasher's second victim. She flipped open to the first photo. Any memories of how it felt to be under Cole on that couch retreated on a wave of dread.

Cole tried to slide the open folder away. "This was a bad idea. You're obviously not up to it—"

"I'm fine," she snapped. "Just low blood sugar."

Cole's look said he didn't believe her for a minute. "So eat something."

She swallowed back bile at the mere thought of food, but no way was she going to cave, not when she finally had the information she needed. She rose from the table and carefully made her way to the cabinet on only slightly shaky legs. She peered around for something her stomach might be able to handle and settled on a few Ritz crackers. She sat back down at the table and stuffed a cracker into her mouth, staring pointedly at Cole all the while. Then she ruined the effect by coughing as the cracker immediately turned to sawdust in her mouth. She washed it down with a mouthful of water as Cole stared at her, one thick eyebrow cocked.

"Just don't throw up, okay?" he said when she finally composed herself. "I don't do well with vomit."

"Really? You can look at bloody crime scenes all day, but you can't handle vomit?"

He shrugged. "We all have our weak spots."

Megan picked up a picture of the second victim and looked down at it. "At least she had a name," Megan said. Molly Dennis.

"Lot of good that's done us. According to our files, the real Molly Dennis died in 1985, a year after she was born. As far as we know, she was handed Molly's identity six months before she was murdered, and we know nothing about her up until that point. No one seems to know who she was, who she knew. Like all of them. They might as well all be Jane Does, even the ones who do have names."

As he spoke, Cole's expression grew grimmer, the grooves on either side of his mouth deepening, his features hardening. She had to fight the urge to go to him, to comfort him somehow.

He always seemed so strong, so in control. But she, more than most, knew the deep currents that ran beneath the surface, the emotions Cole had to keep in check just to get through the day. But every once in a while, even he cracked. It was impossible to keep the mask firmly in place in the face of such brutality.

Megan didn't say anything. Instead she tried to take a pointer from Cole and look at the files analytically, detach herself from victims and look at them instead like pieces to a puzzle.

One she desperately needed to solve.

"And she was a prostitute?" she asked, reading a scribbled note in the file.

Cole nodded. "Hard to tell when none of them were in the system for previous arrests and no one came forward to give us any information. But that's the theory Tasso's going with."

Megan pulled a face. Condescending bastard. "He wouldn't like you telling me any of this."

Cole huffed out a humorless laugh. "He'd probably try to have my badge over it."

Megan's eyes met his across the table. He wasn't kidding. The scale of the risk he was taking sank in. Sure, the chances he'd get caught were slim as long as she kept her mouth shut. But there was little reason for him to count on that, based on her past behavior. For Cole, being a cop wasn't just his job. It was his life. It was who he was.

That he would risk all of that to help her was... humbling. And a whole lot of other things that were too complicated for her to dwell on right now. "Thanks for showing me these, Cole. It means a lot."

He looked up from Sean's file, his faint smile etched with regret. "You might not feel that way once you realize you won't find what you're looking for."

Don't be so sure.

But after two straight hours poring over the files, comparing them side by side with Sean's, Megan acknowledged with a sick feeling that Cole might be right. He'd managed to shoot down every plausible link. "The Jane Doe in the house in Renton—the first officer on the scene reported the television was left on. All of the victims were killed in front of one."

Cole shook his head. "And now we know from the latest victim that the killer likes to watch and probably record his own kills. That doesn't tie it back to Sean."

Megan gritted her teeth against the headache forming behind her eyes. She slipped the elastic from the end of her braid and unraveled her hair, trying to relieve the tension. "There has to be something here, something we're not seeing."

Cole lifted his hands in exasperation. "There's nothing. As much as I wish there was something in these reports that would point to Evangeline Gordon's murder being the early work of the Slasher, I can't." He picked up Sean's file, flipping through the pages in quick, jerky motions. "To start, the victim doesn't fit the profile. Evangeline Gordon was no saint, but she was far from a prostitute. Second, the wounds." He paused, his eyes narrowing as he focused on something in the ME's report.

"What?" Megan demanded, a shot of adrenaline spiking her blood pressure.

Cole didn't answer as he grabbed the latest victim's file, flipping through the pages until he found what he was looking for.

"What do you see?" She grabbed for Sean's file as Cole grabbed the third victim's folder for a side-by-side comparison. His lips moved but she couldn't make out the words.

She launched out of her chair to his side of the table and peered over his shoulder. He was studying the section of the ME's report that described the knife wounds on the victims' throats. In addition to the killing blow that cut the victims' carotid and jugular, there were short, shallow slices inflicted before death. This information hadn't been released to the public. Reading it now, Megan realized it was a calling card, part of the killer's ritual, his sick need to play with his victims.

He doesn't want them to bleed too much till the end.

She didn't need to reread Sean's file. She knew the damn thing by heart, knew that similar wounds were found on Evangeline Gordon's neck. At the time, the investigators had attributed it to hesitation, a few false starts as her brother supposedly worked up the courage to kill.

"It's the same," she breathed. "The same wound pattern around the throat." She unconsciously lifted her hand to her own neck.

Cole shook his head. "It's just a coincidence."

"You need to reopen the investigation—"

"I can't do that, not based on this."

"Are you so fucking afraid to admit you were wrong that you're willing to let my brother die?"

Cole whirled around. "I took a big risk to help you—"

"Help me? How is refusing to use information that could help reopen Sean's case helping me?"

His shoulders were rock hard, almost vibrating with frustration. "Megan, you're overlooking a key piece of information in all of this." He pulled out the ME's report for the Slasher's latest victim. "The Slasher is right-handed." He emphasized his point with a thump of his finger on the report.

Sean was left-handed. She shook her head, refusing to give up so easily. "Some people are ambidextrous," she said. "Maybe the killer knew Sean is left-handed and wanted to frame him."

Cole stared at her, his face a mask of disbelief. "Really? *Really?* You think they're going to let me drop everything and reopen Sean's case based on that?"

"It's worth a shot," Megan snapped, feeling helpless as the trickle of hope was washed away by harsh reality.

"Stop it. Stop torturing yourself."

"If I want to torture myself, that's my business."

"You've thrown your whole fucking life away over this, and I can't stand it."

"No. You can't live with the guilt knowing you made it happen."

He shot her a look so full of rage she took a step back, but it was gone in a flash and replaced by a cool, calculating gaze as he reached out and locked his hand around her arm. He pulled her in front of him, her back to his front. His grip wasn't painful, but it was tight.

"What are you doing?" Her heart pounded against her rib cage as he propelled her into the front room. She swallowed back her alarm, knowing in her heart he would never hurt her. And yet . . .

"I'm going to show you why you're wrong," he said, his voice calm. "So you can understand what really happened once and for all." He guided her to the floor, positioning her so she knelt in front of him.

The pressure on her back pushed her forward until she caught herself with her hands, on all fours in front of him. "The Slasher kills his victims like this," he said. His hand took hold of the hair at the nape of her neck and exerted enough pressure to make her lift her head. His other hand came in front of her neck. He pretended to hold a knife and mimicked a sawing motion. "He makes half a dozen or so smaller cuts before"—he jerked his hand violently to the right—"he slices their throats." Abruptly he released her.

Megan fell forward, barely catching herself before her face hit the hardwood floor.

"With his right hand."

Before she could process that, he flipped her onto her back, positioning himself with one knee on either side of her torso. "In contrast, when Evangeline died, your brother—"

Megan tried to howl a protest but it came out more like a sob.

"Stabbed her in the chest." His hand arced down in a stabbing motion. "Hard enough to pierce through her breastbone."

Megan tried to buck him off, but he was too strong, too heavy. She knew all of this, had even watched a digitally animated re-creation during the trial. But she couldn't fight the surge of panic exploding in her chest. "Don't," she whimpered, hating how defeated she already sounded.

"Then he put the knife to her throat. By now, blood was gushing out of her chest, getting all over her, all over him," he continued, still so calm, so matter-of-fact, oblivious that she was breaking down in front of him.

"Stop it!" she yelled, louder now. She swung her fists and tried to sit up, but he caught her wrists, easily subduing her with one hand and pinning her wrists above her head.

"Not until you understand what happened that night in Sean's house," he said, his dark eyes full of determination. "It's like he saw all the blood and realized what he'd done. He hesitates, cutting her but not deep enough to kill, like he's not sure he can go through with it. But he knows she's too far gone—he has to finish her off. So he takes the knife and slices her throat. With his *left* hand."

Megan closed her eyes against Cole's words but found no relief. Instead her mind was flooded with images of knives dripping with blood, slashed skin. Her blood went cold, her heart racing as she got a minuscule taste of what those poor girls must have felt in the seconds before they were killed. The terror. The helplessness. The knowledge of their impending deaths and that no one was coming to save them.

The idea that Sean could inflict such horror . . .

Megan burst into tears.

Chapter 8

Aw, shit. Megan's sobs hit Cole like a bucket of ice water, dousing his cold determination and replacing it with the bitter bite of shame.

What the fuck was he thinking? He swung his knee over so she was no longer pinned, but she didn't get up. She just rolled to her side, sobbing so hard her entire body shook. Guilt burned like acid in his gut as he lifted her off the floor and wrapped his arms around her.

Instead of shoving him away and punching him in the face like he deserved, she let him pull her up onto the couch, her legs across his. He tucked her head against his neck and buried his face in her hair. "I'm sorry, baby. I shouldn't have done that."

She responded with another shudder and a sob, and Cole blundered forward, compelled to explain himself even though there was no excuse for what he'd done. "I just need you to understand, to accept what happened," he said. But that was bullshit. His motivation hadn't been at all altruistic or even that calculated. He'd let his frustration get the best of him, and he'd gone after her in the coldest, bluntest way he could think of in an effort to force her to see the truth.

And if she does that, maybe you can let yourself off the hook for ruining her life the day you arrested Sean.

Cole shoved the thought aside. He was a cop. He'd done his job. If anyone had ruined Megan's life, it was Sean.

Still...Cole tightened his hold around her, wishing there was some way he could take away her pain. Wishing the truth really would set her free. But even that was bullshit. If she accepted Sean was a killer, where was the relief in that?

"I hate this. I hate how this is hurting you," he murmured. Her misery ate at him like an open, festering wound in his chest.

Megan lifted her head. Her green eyes were swollen and red, her nose was red, her pale skin blotchy. She was so beautiful it felt like his heart was being squeezed by a giant fist every time he looked at her. "So help me," she whispered. "Help me find out the truth."

"Goddamn it," he whispered through clenched teeth. "I showed you the truth. It sucks, and it's awful, but there's nothing else to do." He brushed her hair back from her face and cradled her cheek in his palm. Unable to resist touching her. Torturing himself with the silky grain of her skin under his fingers.

Megan's full lips trembled. "I can't accept that, Cole. I won't. Sean's all I have. I'll never believe he killed Evangeline Gordon. And if I let him die without doing everything I can to prove you wrong, I'll never forgive myself."

So brave. So delusional. He wondered what it felt like to be loved like that. To inspire faith like that.

How would it feel to be loved like that by *her*? He'd almost had it once. Had been so close he could taste it.

He became aware of her weight on his lap, the firm

curve of her ass against the muscles of his thighs. The softness of her breast where she rested against his rib cage. His breath hitched and warmth spread in his groin.

Her mouth was mere inches from him, plump, succulent. Megan's cheeks flooded with heat, and when he looked in her eyes, he saw it again, that flash of awareness that told him he wasn't the only one here with unresolved feelings.

Get up, get out of here, and stop torturing yourself with this. It's a dead end. The only reason she even let you near her is because you pushed her into an emotional meltdown.

But he couldn't resist. He bent his head the last few inches, tasted her soft gasp as his mouth covered hers.

Ah, sweet, so goddamn sweet. Even that slight pressure sent heat surging through him. One taste, one brush of her lips and he was as hard as a spike.

His hips rolled under her, pure reflex as he sought to get closer. He wove his fingers into her hair, angling her face to kiss her deeper, harder.

He knew he was taking advantage of her, knew she was in a fragile state that he'd created. Knew this was going nowhere, that in seconds she'd probably come to her senses and slap him silly.

He didn't care. He parted her lips with his tongue, sucked on hers, drinking in her taste. Greedy, selfish, unable to resist taking everything he could get.

But Megan surprised him with her own hunger. Her hands came up to cradle his face as she kissed him with a ferocity that rivaled his own. Hot, wet, deep. She tasted so good, felt so good. He wanted to bury himself inside her, lose himself until the rest of the world fell away.

His hand skimmed down her back, his fingers dipping into the waistband of her jeans. Warm, smooth flesh gave under his fingers. He slid his hand back up, burrowing under the hem of her sweater to stroke baby-soft skin.

She gave a little shiver as his hand coursed over the curve of her waist and the bumps of her rib cage. Silk and lace, her flimsy bra was no barrier against the heat of his hand.

The sound of pure delight she made as his hand closed over her breast sent his cock straining against his zipper. He brushed his thumb across her nipple, deepening his kiss to swallow her moan of pleasure.

God, she felt so good in his hands. Soft and round and big enough to fill his broad palms. Making him ache to see them, taste them with his lips and tongue. Tearing his mouth from hers, he pulled her sweater up and over her head and pressed her back into the couch.

He went for her pants next, unbuttoning and unzipping with shaking fingers before he pulled them down her legs.

He wanted her with a force that bordered on insanity. An asteroid could hit the earth and it wouldn't distract him from the driving need to have her, all of her, to find out once and for all how it felt to sink his cock into her wet heat.

To finally feel the sweet grip of her body as she came with him buried deep inside her. Maybe if he finally had that, she would stop haunting his dreams.

He paused for a moment, transfixed by the sight of her laid out on the couch in front of him, wearing nothing but a couple of scraps of cream-colored silk. She stared up at him with hot green eyes, a delicate flush spreading across the curves swelling over the top of her bra. Slender curves and pale silky skin. More beautiful than his fevered memories, sexier than any fantasy he ever could have conjured.

He came down over her and captured one nipple through the flimsy silk of her bra. It nudged eagerly against his tongue. He shoved the bra out of the way and sucked her in, groaning at the taste of her, salty sweet. Megan moaned and dug her fingers into his hair, urging him on.

He sucked her hard as his other hand slid down to cup between her legs. Hot, damp, pulsing against his hand. Something that sounded like, "Oh please" escaped her throat.

She wanted this, wanted *him* as much as he wanted her.

The thought almost made him come, right then and there.

He reared up off of her and fumbled with his belt. He wanted to spend hours, days, exploring every secret spot, licking and sucking every inch of skin from the top of her head to the soles of her feet until he knew her body as well as he knew his own.

But he was so primed he knew he'd be lucky if he lasted more than a few thrusts.

Just this once. This is all I'm going to get and I promise I'll never ask for more.

He was dragging his zipper down when his phone rang in his pocket, the vibration against his aching dick almost knocking him off the couch.

Déjà fucking vu.

He considered ignoring it, but even if he did, it was too late.

The cell phone's sharp ring had snapped Megan out of her haze. She scrambled up to sitting and looked down at herself in horrified disbelief, as though shocked to find herself nearly naked and about to have sex with him.

Again.

Cole zipped his pants and yanked the phone from his pocket. He didn't try to stop her when she scrambled off the couch, grabbed her clothes, and made for the bathroom, slamming the door so hard the walls shook.

He looked at the caller ID. "What's happening, Petersen?" he asked, hoping nothing in his voice would tip Olivia to the fact that he was nursing a massive case of blue balls.

"Why are you breathing hard?"

Shit. "I was walking fast."

"Where are you anyway?"

My own personal hell. He considered lying, then quickly dismissed it. Petersen was too sharp for that. And he didn't want to lie any more than he had to. "I'm at Megan Flynn's place," he said. A cover story always worked better when it included some truth.

Dead silence echoed across the phone line.

"I wanted to ask the girl, Devany, more about the night of the murder. But I wanted to check with Megan on her emotional state first." That sounded reasonable.

"You couldn't do that over the phone?"

"Petersen, do you have something to tell me or not?"

Megan emerged from the bathroom then, carefully averting her gaze, once again covered from neck to toe by her heavy wool sweater and tight-fitting jeans. Her wavy brown hair was again pulled back in a tight braid. Prim, proper, and buttoned up like nothing had happened.

But one look at her flushed cheeks and red, kiss-swollen mouth and it was all he could do not to throw his phone against the wall, toss her back down on the couch, and pick up right where they'd left off.

"Is she what's making you pant like that?"

You have no idea.

"Wait, don't answer that. Just get back to the station. We just got an ID on the latest victim."

Anticipation pricked the hairs at the back of his neck as he buckled his belt. *Don't get your hopes up.* "Two of the other victims were ID'd, too, and that led nowhere."

Megan, who was sitting back at the kitchen table, pretending he didn't exist as she put the case files back in order, snapped to attention.

"It's different this time," Olivia said, excitement evident in her voice.

"This must be good. I haven't heard you this excited since you heard Heidi Klum was going to be on the cover of *Playboy*."

"Come on, with Karen's pregnancy hormones kicking in, I have to get my thrills where I can. Anyway, one of the FBI's computer jockey's ran the vic's picture through the facial-recognition system and linked her up with a cold case in San Diego. We need to verify, but it looks like our victim was really Bianca Delagrossa, who disappeared at age sixteen on her way home from a party."

"We have a real name. A real person this time." It was flimsy, but it was something. Every victim had a story. Maybe this one would finally be able to tell them something. "I'll be there in fifteen."

"A real name? What does that mean?" Megan snapped as soon as he hung up.

He paused, weighing how much to tell her. On the one hand, the information wasn't public yet. On the other, it was likely Tasso would release the victim's name and alias to the press in a call for any information on the victim. "We have an ID on the latest victim."

"Who is she?" The pale, pinched look was back on Megan's face. That tight look of despair that had disappeared for a few minutes in the heat of passion.

He reached out to her but she jumped back. "Don't. Don't touch me." It was then he saw something else in her eyes. Shame. Guilt. Like she'd done something dirty by letting Cole touch her.

Or worse yet, betrayed someone she loved.

Fuck it. He couldn't wipe away the grief or the guilt. But he could throw her a bone. Knowing the victim's name before it was released to the press wouldn't help her, but it wouldn't hurt the investigation either. "Until Tasso makes a statement to the press, what I'm about to tell you is strictly confidential."

—◊◊◊—

Megan looked at Cole as he walked out the door. Her body hummed with a combination of unfulfilled sexual need and nauseating guilt.

She sank into a kitchen chair and buried her face in her hands. What was wrong with her? Not only did she let him touch her, kiss her, she'd kissed him right back, given as good as she'd gotten. She could make up all the excuses she wanted about her fragile emotional state, but bottom line, she knew if Cole hadn't gotten that phone call, she would be under him on her couch right now with him buried deep inside.

The thought was enough to send a jolt of desire straight to her core, so keen it nearly hurt. Her skin felt too tight for her body, so sensitive that the silk of her bra felt like sandpaper across her nipples. She shoved away from the table and retrieved her laptop from her bag, determined to take her mind off Cole and what had almost happened.

She pulled up a search engine and typed in the name of the Slasher's latest victim, Bianca Delagrossa. Cole had surprised her by telling her the victim's name, but she figured he was trying to make up for refusing to pursue the connection to Sean's case.

And maybe for some of the other stuff that had happened.

Not that there was much information to be found, she realized as she quickly scanned through the results of her search. The articles were all old, dated over six years ago when Bianca had first disappeared. An apparent runaway, then sixteen-year-old Bianca had gone missing from her home in San Diego sometime in the middle of the night and hadn't been seen since.

Megan clicked over to a Web site that kept a database of missing children and pulled up a photo and description. She swallowed hard, trying to reconcile the beautiful, smiling girl in the picture with the images of her mutilated body from the crime scene. Megan had known too many girls like Bianca, girls who ran away from a bad situation only to find that what waited for them on the streets was a thousand times worse.

She got more depressed as she scanned through what

little was written about her disappearance. Because she was a runaway from a working-class family that didn't have the resources to launch a massive media campaign, Bianca's disappearance had received minimal attention beyond the first week. And it didn't help that Bianca's family and close friends depicted her as a troublemaker who'd already been in trouble with the police after she was caught trying to sell Percocet she'd stolen from her parents' medicine cabinet. The most recent article had been published a little over two years ago, when Bianca had turned eighteen, when a reporter revisited cold cases from his neighborhood. By that time, even her parents had given up. "If she wanted to come home," her mother said, "she would have done it by now."

Megan's stomach hurt reading it. They had no idea how lost a girl could get, how even if no one was forcing her, it would seem impossible to go home.

Her cell phone blared and she recognized Devany's ringtone. Megan snatched it up, grateful for the distraction. "How are you doing?" she asked when she answered. Devany was still pretty shaken up from the other night. "Did you manage to sleep?"

"Yeah," Dev replied. "I kinda need to talk to you about that. I've been having these dreams."

She could relate. "The nightmares are normal, Dev, and they'll pass. But you should definitely bring them up in your counseling session tomorrow."

"It's not that.... It's—" She broke off. "Do you think the killer saw me?"

Megan bit her lip. She didn't want to lie, but she didn't want to ratchet up Dev's anxiety. "The important thing is you didn't see him," Megan replied.

"That's the thing. I've been having these dreams, and I think I did see something after all."

Megan sat up straighter. "You think you saw the killer? You have to call the police—"

"Not the killer—the dead girl. I think I know her."

"From where?"

The other line was silent for several seconds. "A couple years ago, before my mom got busted the last time, I took off for a while."

Megan knew all of this from Dev's file. She'd run away from the house her mom shared with the boyfriend who turned out to be a registered sex offender and had spent nearly two months on the streets. The thought of twelve-year-old Dev out there on her own still made her queasy, but somehow the girl had made it through without being sexually assaulted or seriously injured. "You met her then?" Megan's skin broke out in goose bumps. If she could find information about where Bianca had worked, who her pimp was . . . "You're sure?"

"I didn't recognize her at first when I saw her. . . ." Dev's voice trailed off, and Megan heard her swallow. "But I keep dreaming of that night, of finding her, and this morning it finally stuck. She has a mark on her shoulder, kind of like a tattoo, but it's not a tattoo. It's a scar, in the shape of a moon and some stars."

A crescent moon surrounded by three smaller stars, to be exact. Megan had seen it in the autopsy photos Cole had shown her. But Megan couldn't let Devany know that without outing Cole for feeding her information.

"Do you remember her name?"

"She said her name was Bibi, and I met her a couple times when I was crashing at the mission down on Thirty-ninth."

Megan knew Mission St. Jude—and its director, Sister Mary Theresa Goczeski—well. "So Bibi was homeless too?"

"No . . . at least, I don't think so. She never said, but she was too clean and dressed too nice, and when I saw her, she was mostly helping out with meals and stuff. But I remembered the scar because she would wear these tank tops and the nun who ran the mission was always telling her to cover up."

"If she wasn't homeless, do you know where she lived, where she worked?"

"No," Dev said. "She didn't talk much about herself. She just always told me I should go home before I got into real trouble."

"We need to tell the police."

"No!"

Megan could hear real fear in her voice. "If you're worried about getting in trouble for not telling them sooner, don't worry. This kind of thing happens all the time. I'll go with you if you want—"

"You don't get it. If I tell them, they're going to start snooping around, asking questions, and if it gets out that I'm the one who sent the cops around, I could end up worse than Bibi."

Megan sighed, knowing Dev's fear wasn't completely unjustified. "Fine, I'll tell them and I'll be sure to keep your name out of it. Deal?"

"Deal."

—⚯—

Thirty minutes later, Cole ducked into the conference room and slid into a seat next to Petersen.

The rest of the task force was already in attendance, and Special Agent Tasso stood at the front of the room. Behind him was a whiteboard with pictures of the victims, as well as a map of the West Coast. "Now that Detective Williams is here, we can get started. As you all know, we've identified the Slasher's latest victim as Bianca Delagrossa, who was reported missing on August twelfth, 2004." Tasso indicated a photo that stood out from the rest because it wasn't taken at a morgue. In it, a pretty teenage girl gave a flirty smile to the camera through thick, dark lashes. Glossy black hair spilled over her shoulders.

"The San Diego police treated it as a runaway case based on information given to them by her mother. They could find no trace of her, until now." He pointed to another photo. There was no smile in this photo. Bianca lay silent and still, her dark hair dull, her pretty features looking as if they were carved in gray marble.

"As of now, we don't know anything about her other than her name. Not how she got up here, where she lived, who her pimp was. But if we can find that out, maybe we can figure out what links her to the other victims."

Tasso started to toss out orders. "Blake, I want you to run the other victims through the facial-recognition program again, see if we get another hit on a cold case. And be sure to cross-reference internationally. No reason to think some of these girls weren't trafficked in."

Agent Blake, who sported a goatee and heavy-framed glasses, nodded.

"I plan to release a statement in the next forty-eight hours, but for now, the victim's identity is strictly confidential. We haven't even notified her parents yet."

Cole's collar went a little tight around his neck, and he

told himself to relax, reminding himself that Megan had promised to keep it quiet.

But she's leaked stuff to the press before. When it comes to her brother, do you really think you can trust her?

He shoved aside the doubts. Leaking the victim's identity wouldn't serve any purpose, and Megan wouldn't do it out of pure malice.

"Detective Williams, Detective Petersen, I want you to find out everything you can about our victim, where she lived, who her friends were."

"Yes, sir." Cole stood, followed by Petersen. "We thought we'd start by running down people in the city who do these scar tattoos," Petersen said, indicating the close-up of Bianca's moon and stars. "We're hoping that will get us an address, maybe a neighborhood she was working."

Cole nodded. "It's a place to start." Not that Cole thought it would get them anywhere. Even if they could nail down where she lived, it had been clear from the first victim, and was more so now, that if the victims were prostitutes, they weren't part of the ordinary downtown crew. These girls were high-end, well maintained, free of disease or any indication of drug abuse.

And well protected from the police. Any prostitute who worked the same territory ended up in the system eventually, whether through a roundup by vice, a drug bust, or an assault that landed her in the hospital.

Whoever worked these girls had resources to keep them off the streets, out of the system; they had the ability to erase their lives and give them entirely new identities.

And whoever was killing them worked on the inside.

Now tell us something we didn't know, Sherlock.

"Who knows, maybe there's something about Bianca

that will pull this whole mess together," Cole said as he and Petersen exited the conference room.

"Detective Williams," Tasso called after him. "A word, please?"

"I'll catch up with you," he told Olivia. "Yes, sir?"

Though Cole topped him by about three inches and thirty pounds, Tasso still cut an imposing figure. With his military bearing and piercing stare, he wore his authority like an invisible cloak. "I noticed you requested copies of the victims' files."

Shit. Should have known Tasso would keep close tabs on everyone. "I wanted to go over them on my own. See if anything new jumped out at me."

Tasso cocked a thick eyebrow. "And? Anything of interest?"

Nothing to do with this case. He didn't know Tasso well, but he knew his work and respected him. Having always prided himself on being up front and honest, Cole didn't like having to go behind his back. "Nothing we weren't already aware of."

"Keep me updated on any new information you discover."

He didn't even consider bringing up the perceived similarities with Sean's case. Megan had already gone to Tasso herself and had been dismissed out of hand as a delusional woman who was desperate to grasp at anything that might exonerate her brother.

Tasso's assessment was pretty dead-on.

Still, some of Megan's delusion must have rubbed off on him, because as he headed back to the bull pen, he couldn't shake that nagging feeling that maybe they were missing something. First the TV left on, then the cuts...

An ambidextrous killer and a calculated frame job. It was like something out of a movie, nothing that could happen in real life.

As much as he wanted to help Megan, it would be career suicide to push to reopen Sean's case on such flimsy evidence.

Yet he couldn't get Megan's haunted face out of his head.

"Ready to go?" Olivia said as he passed her desk.

Whatever follow-up he was going to do on Sean's case would have to wait for later. "Let's hit it."

Chapter 9

Mission St. Jude was located just within walking distance of the famous Pike Place Market. During the day, the downtown area was spit shined for the tourists. Few visitors ever realized that only a few blocks away was the dark world of Seattle's homelessness, drug trade, and prostitution.

Megan had a twinge of conscience as she approached the entrance. She'd promised Dev she'd tell the police, and she would, she promised herself. After she'd had a chance to ask a few questions on her own.

She wasn't interfering with the FBI's investigation, she rationalized. She was going to tell Cole what Devany had revealed. But not before she found out everything Sister Mary Theresa—or Sister MT as she was known in the neighborhood—remembered about Bianca Delagrossa.

Megan had first met Sister Mary Theresa four years ago when she'd gotten involved as a court advocate. Within a week, thirteen-year-old Courtney had run away and Megan eventually tracked her to the mission, just two streets over from the girl's apartment. Sister MT had spotted Courtney lurking in a doorway, huddled against the cold and damp. When Megan arrived, Courtney was wrapped in a sweater two sizes too big, sipping cocoa and playing a board game with a group of kids. Within five minutes, it became clear Sister MT kept tabs on everyone.

Homeless, drug addicts, prostitutes, and runaways, Sister MT greeted them all with open arms, and she never forgot a face.

Megan showed Sister MT the photo she'd downloaded from the missing-and-exploited-children's Web site. "A friend of mine said Bianca used to come in here," Megan said.

"Oh yeah, Bibi." Sister MT's eyes flashed in recognition. "She was an interesting one. Showed up here the first time about four years ago, looking for a bed and a hot meal. Beautiful girl, but so beaten down. She worked the neighborhood for a while and I'd see her every so often."

"Do you know who her pimp was?"

Sister MT frowned. "Ruby," she called over to a young woman who sat hovered over a cup of coffee. "You remember this girl? You know who her pimp was?"

Ruby pushed herself up and made her way slowly, carefully across the room. As she drew closer, Megan could see why she was moving like an eighty-year-old. One eye was swollen nearly shut, and a purple bruise blossomed across her left cheekbone. Her skintight jeans and hoodie hid other painful injuries, if the way she carefully sank into her chair was anything to go by.

Megan felt a tug of sympathy and darted a look at Sister MT, who quickly verified her suspicions.

"Ruby got knocked around by a trick the other night, so she's hiding out with us for a few days," Sister MT said, with her typical matter-of-fact delivery and complete lack of censure. She held out her hand, and Megan handed over Bianca's picture.

Ruby shook her head. "I don't think I seen her working around here."

Megan looked at Sister MT. "But you're sure she was hooking around here."

The nun nodded. "That was a while ago. I didn't see her at all for a couple of years; then she showed up with an envelope of cash and said she wanted to volunteer."

"Was she still hooking?"

Sister MT shrugged. "She never talked about it, but she showed up here a couple times with a big donation and no explanation how she got it."

"When was the last time you saw her?"

"Last Monday. It was the strangest thing. She hadn't been down here in months, and then she just showed up with a big pile of stuff. Clothes, shoes, books, like a whole house worth. Said she was moving away and didn't need it anymore."

Last Monday. By Tuesday night she was dead. Did she know who she was running from?

"She didn't say anything about where she was going?"

"No. She was jumpy, though, and in a really big hurry to get everything unloaded. I went to get a donor receipt for her, you know, for taxes, and by the time I came back, she was gone."

"Do you still have everything?" There was a chance she'd left something behind that might provide a clue.

Sister MT shook her head, strands of her graying hair catching the light behind her. "Most of what she had was already sorted and given out, but I think there were a few things we kept aside to sell in the church thrift shop."

Megan's heart sank as she followed Sister MT out of the mission's common room, down a narrow hallway to a large utility closet. By now, Bianca's stuff had been distributed to dozens of different people. No way was she going to be able to track it all down.

Sister MT switched on the single-bulb light. Boxes lined the walls, neatly labeled by type of clothing or item the box contained. "That's all the free stuff over there," Sister MT said, gesturing to the left side of the closet. "Over there's the stuff that's nice enough to resell," she said, indicating a few boxes to the right. She walked over and retrieved a small cardboard box. "I think this is mostly Bianca's stuff. You're welcome to look through it."

Megan jumped at the sound of a loud crash coming from down the hall. "I'll fuckin' cut you, motherfucker!"

"Oh Lord, that sounds like Snoopy. I better go see what's going on." Sister MT rushed from the closet, and Megan could hear her yelling down the hall. "I told you, Snoopy, you keep causing trouble and you're gonna find yourself sleeping on the sidewalk!"

Megan marveled at the steely toughness of the tiny woman, matched only by her boundless heart. She could make out the tone more than the words, but it sounded like Sister MT was scolding Snoopy as if he were a fifth grader in Catholic school. He must have known you don't mess with Sister MT, because the ruckus quieted almost immediately.

Megan settled on the floor and flipped open the lid of the box. Of the boxes of stuff Bianca had dropped off, only two pairs of shoes, a pair of designer jeans, a gray cashmere sweater, and an assortment of gold and silver jewelry remained. Megan picked up the jeans and searched the pockets for a business card, a scrap of paper, even a receipt. Nothing.

She lifted out the shoes for closer examination. Black patent leather with a peep toe. When she flipped them over, she recognized the trademark red sole of a well-known designer. These shoes ran several hundred dollars a pair. Not your ordinary hooker fuck-me shoes by a long shot. The simple cashmere pullover was also made by a high-end designer.

If Bianca had been still hooking, she'd moved up to the high end, with very generous clients. No twenty bucks for a quick blow job for her.

As Megan went to tuck the sweater back into the box, she realized something had been hidden underneath it. A small beaded handbag was tucked into the corner. She reached for it, her fingers shaking with anticipation. *Please, please let there be something.* She flipped the silk-covered catch on the clutch and peered inside.

It was empty except for a receipt from the Mekong Noodle House, dated three days before she was killed.

Megan sat back on her heels, her heart sinking to her stomach. *What did you expect? A note detailing the last week of her life, including who killed her?*

At least you know she fills up on pho before a big night out. That's helpful.

Megan shook her head, wondering for the thousandth time if she really was just crazy. Even if she found out more about Bianca—hell, even if they found the killer—there was no guarantee they'd find anything to link him to Sean's case.

As usual, Megan was acting on nothing but a hunch and blind desperation. But she couldn't give up now, no matter how high the odds were stacked against her.

Against Sean.

A wave of grief settled over her like a wet wool blanket as she thought of him. Alone in his cell, refusing to see anyone. Waiting to die.

She tucked the purse back in the box and heaved herself to her feet. There had to be someone, somewhere who knew something about where Bianca lived and her recent activities. No one existed in a bubble.

And she had an address for the restaurant, which was only a few blocks south. A neighborhood joint, and she'd be willing to bet anything Bianca lived nearby.

She stopped in the kitchen to say a quick good-bye to Sister MT before heading out. She turned her collar up against the chill on the five-minute walk to the restaurant. It was a dingy hole-in-the-wall, with chipped Formica tables and cracked linoleum. But the décor couldn't detract from the mouthwatering aroma of savory broth and exotic spices. Even well before the dinner rush, the place was packed with customers slurping down mouthfuls of noodles.

Finally Megan worked her way to the front of the line and got the attention of the woman working the cash register. "What number?" the woman asked.

Megan held up a hand. "I'm not here to eat," she said, and extracted Bianca's photo from her pocket. "I wanted to know if you recognize this woman, if she lives around here."

The woman put a laminated menu in front of Megan and tapped it with her fingertip. "You pick number. Make order."

"I don't want to eat—"

Megan was cut off as the woman let loose with a string of Vietnamese and gestured at someone behind Megan.

"Can I help you?" Megan turned to see a Vietnamese boy of about sixteen. His hair was cut so short it stood up like a brush, and his slim body was swallowed up by a green-and-black flannel shirt and baggy jeans. "My grandma doesn't speak good English."

Megan showed him Bianca's photo. "I'm trying to find this woman," she lied. "I think she might live around here."

"Oh yeah, I know her house."

Megan's head jerked in surprise. "You do?" Really, was it going to be this easy?

"Yeah, I deliver to her house sometimes. Her and her roommate, they like the number four with tofu and chicken. Nice. Pay cash. Good tipper."

A roommate. "What's her address? And do you know her roommate's name?"

The kid's eyes narrowed warily. "Are you cop or something? You going to get them in trouble?"

Megan shook her head. "I swear I'm not a cop. I just want to check on my friend."

The kid rubbed his chin, his dark eyes shrewd. "I don't know. Maybe I'm wrong. Maybe I'm thinking of different girl, different house."

Megan rolled her eyes and dug a twenty from her wallet. "Maybe this will help with the early onset Alzheimer's."

The kid's eyes did a quick sweep of the restaurant as he palmed the twenty. Megan keyed the address into her phone as he recited it.

"And she lives with another girl—Stephanie, I think her name is."

Bianca, or Bibi as she was known around here, lived in a tiny two-bedroom house on Seneca Street, about a

ten-minute walk from the Mekong Noodle House. Megan
was vaguely familiar with the neighborhood. If Bianca
really was a high-end escort, she wasn't spending any of
her money on rent.

She pulled her coat tighter around her, steeling herself for the walk. The farther she got from the Market
Place and the tourist traps, the seedier the neighborhood
became. Even in the early evening, it wasn't a great place
for a lone young woman. But the cabs didn't troll this
area of town for fares, and Megan didn't have any time
to waste. At some point, Cole would show up at Bianca's
house, if he hadn't already.

She walked swiftly, with purpose, ignoring catcalls
and kissing sounds, careful not to make eye contact with
anyone. Finally she reached Bianca's street, where she
found a long row of small houses in varying states of dis-
repair. The street was eerily quiet, with no evidence of
human activity. Somehow that was even scarier than the
gauntlet of pimps, dealers, and junkies.

She stopped in front of a small, one-story house, its
blue paint chipped and fading. She double-checked the
address the kid at the noodle house had given her against
the fading numbers on the mailbox. Cold gray mist swirled
above a patch that was more dirt than grass.

"What are you doing here?"

Megan's heart galloped in her chest as a strong hand
wrapped around her arm, nearly lifting her off her feet as
she was spun around to face her assailant.

Her panic faded only marginally when she recognized
the new head of security at Club One.

"I asked you what you're doing here." Though his
voice was low, his blue eyes were icy with something that

looked like malice. A black knit cap covered his hair, and a black wool overcoat hung from his huge shoulders. She hadn't heard so much as a whisper of his approach. How in God's name did such a big man move so quietly?

Megan swallowed hard, trying to shove back the bite of fear and failing miserably. She couldn't put her finger on it, but something about Jack Brooks, with his too-watchful eyes and shadowlike stealth scared the ever living crap out of her. "I'm v-visiting a friend," she managed, wincing at the stutter. She tried to pull her arm free of his grip. The leather-glove-covered fingers tightened.

He looked at the house and back to her. "You expect me to believe you have a friend who lives here?"

"What business is it of yours?" She yanked at her arm again, and this time he let her go. "What are *you* doing here anyway?"

"I live close by. It's convenient to work."

Megan had gotten a little turned around, but she remembered the club was about a half mile away. Maybe Jack knew Bianca.

But an internal alarm bell went off, stifling the question before it passed her lips. Something in her gut told her not to reveal any secrets to this man. "You better go before you're late, then."

"And you better get the hell out of here."

Scared or not, Megan's hackles rose at being bossed around. "I missed the part where you became the boss of me."

Jack yanked her close and got right in her face. "You need to be careful. I know you think you're helping your brother, but you might want to think twice about nosing around where you don't belong."

"Maybe you should tell me what's going on." Uneasiness ate like acid in her stomach and her mouth went bone-dry.

His laugh was dry and mirthless. "Trust me, little sister, it's nothing you want to get mixed up in. Now why don't you take yourself home?"

Anxious to get away, Megan took off down the street as soon as he released her, in the opposite direction of Club One. It was easier to pretend to run, tail between her legs, and then double back once he was gone than to try to reason with him.

Megan rounded the corner and ducked into an alleyway between two houses. She waited five minutes, and when she was satisfied Brooks hadn't followed her, she doubled back to Bianca's house.

This time she kept one eye over her shoulder as she went up the walkway to knock on the door. No answer. She knocked again, this time calling for the roommate. "Stephanie? Are you there?"

She tried the knob. Locked.

A black SUV drove by, the bass pumping so hard Megan's insides quivered. But other than that, the street was quiet. Deserted.

She did a quick sweep of the street to reassure herself no one was around then darted around the side of the little house. She felt a little stab of satisfaction when she saw the sliding window midway up the side of the house. It wasn't even closed all the way—probably a bathroom window left cracked to let out the moisture.

In any case, to Megan, who had locked herself out of the house enough times as a kid to become an expert on breaking and entering, it was as easy an access point as a wide-open front door.

She pulled a pair of thin leather gloves from her pocket and slipped them on and did another scan to make sure she was clear. She reached up and carefully pried the screen from the frame and slid the window the rest of the way open, then grabbed the sill and jumped up. It was a tight fit, but she was able to twist her shoulders and hips through the small window. She lowered herself carefully to the floor, making as little noise as possible.

The bathroom had a narrow stall shower with the usual array of feminine toiletries. Towels hung on a rack above the toilet, but they had hung there, unused, long enough to dry.

Megan was no forensic scientist, but she knew that in Seattle's moist climate, that took at least a couple days.

She crouched on the bathroom floor for a beat. Hearing nothing, she went to the door and looked out into the short, dark hallway. She flicked on the light in the bathroom, its dull yellow glow enough to illuminate the hall. She turned to the left and walked into the small living area that flowed from the kitchen. It was empty but for a couch and a shoddy faux wood coffee table. Fashion magazines were piled high on the table. Megan looked through all of them, but there were no subscription labels. No additional information on the mysterious "Stephanie" who supposedly lived with Bianca.

The kitchen was sparsely furnished, the few dishes tucked neatly away in the cabinets. It was weird. The refrigerator contained a six-pack of Diet Coke, a half-empty bottle of wine, and a gallon of milk well past its expiration date. The freezer was empty. The rest of the cabinets revealed a box of saltines and a box of Cheerios. Other than the pile of magazines and scant food, the place showed very little sign of being lived in.

The bedrooms revealed little else. One room, which she assumed had been Bianca's, looked like the scene of a robbery. Closet doors hung open; dresser drawers lay empty on the carpeted floor. The entire room had been stripped bare. Sister MT hadn't been exaggerating when she said it seemed as though Bianca had donated everything she owned.

A search of the other room showed a few more clothes, but nothing else. No papers, no odds and ends, no bills with the inhabitants' names. All of the wastebaskets in the house had been emptied, but underneath the kitchen sink, far back in the corner, was a crumpled piece of paper. Megan fished it out and smoothed it. It was faded and food-stained, but she easily recognized Bianca in the black-and-white photo of the woman reclining on a bed wearing a black lace bra and matching panties. She saw the address in the upper right corner and realized it was the printout of a Web page.

Megan felt a buzz of excitement as she pulled out her phone and entered the URL to check later. She wouldn't know until she checked, but she bet this was how Bianca was reaching out to clients. Maybe it was how the killer found his other victims too. It was unlikely it would provide the link to Evangeline she was looking for, but it was something. She crumpled the paper back up and tucked it into the corner for the police to find when they eventually searched the house.

Megan went back to Stephanie's room and pulled open the closet, determined to do one last search for information.

It was in the back pocket of a pair of black leather pants that she found it. A cocktail napkin with a crimson smear of lipstick against the snowy-white backdrop.

Megan's stomach clutched at the logo embossed in the corner.

Club One.

You have no idea what you're sticking your nose into.

The bedroom door flew open, slamming into the wall with a crash. Her heart leaped to her throat as she whirled around; then her stomach bottomed out when she saw the uniformed officer in the doorway, her standard-issue Glock trained on Megan. "Drop to your knees. Hands in the air."

Megan obeyed, wincing as the officer wrenched her arms behind her and snapped the cuffs around her wrists, the sharp metallic click echoing through the silent room.

———

Cole slipped his cell phone out of his pocket, grimacing when he saw Tasso's number on the caller ID. The SAC was calling for an update.

"You got anything yet?"

"We narrowed down the neighborhood where Bianca has been seen around, and we're still trying to find anyone who knows where she might have lived."

At Cole's voice, Petersen looked up from where she was talking, or rather trying to talk, to a working girl who was shaking her head and trying to pull the *no hablo inglés* on her.

Cole rolled his eyes and mouthed "Tasso" at her.

The truth was, they'd been canvassing downtown, questioning the usual crew for hours now and had fuck all to show for it. If Bianca had ever set foot in this part of town, no one was willing to open up to the cops about it. The gangs who ran in this part of town hadn't been shy about letting people know what happened when you snitched. Recently a local store owner had been found stabbed to death with his tongue cut out. It made a population already disinclined to trust the cops even more tight-lipped.

Trying to reassure folks that the guy they were after had nothing to do with the gangs didn't help. A cop was a cop and a rat was a rat as far as they were concerned.

"So you haven't found any new information about her?"

Cole didn't like the edge creeping into Tasso's tone. "Nothing substantive," Cole said, his grip tightening around the phone. "Is there anything else you needed, sir?" If Tasso was going to chew his ass out over something, Cole wanted to get it over with. If not, Cole needed to get back to work.

"No, but I thought you might be interested to know Megan Flynn was arrested for breaking and entering."

Cole shook his head, sure he hadn't heard right. "She what?"

"And that's not the best part. She claims she was there because some kid from a noodle house told her that's where Bianca and her roommate lived."

Cole felt the bottom drop out of his stomach. *Fuck.* He'd passed on the information to Megan, convinced there was nothing she could do with it. When was he going to learn to stop underestimating her and the power of pure desperation?

—⁂—

"What is it with this chick?" Petersen said as they pulled into the parking lot. "You're a good cop, Cole. You follow procedure and you don't fuck up. And you sure as hell don't leak confidential information to civilians not involved in the case."

Cole shook his head. "Drop it, Olivia." The truth was he didn't have an answer for why Megan Flynn made him so fucking stupid and reckless.

"For you of all people to think with your dick—"

"It wasn't like that. I wanted to help her."

"Yeah, well, you helped yourself into getting thrown off an investigation that could make you a sergeant. Hell, Lieutenant Chin could fire you for this."

The truth was like a fist knotting in his gut. Petersen was right. And Chin didn't even know about him showing Megan the information on the other victims. He was trying to be a good guy, help Megan get some closure. Instead he was at serious risk of losing the career that had defined his entire adult life.

Talk about a warning sign to stay the hell away from her.

Yet the first thing Cole did when he got to the station was ask the desk sergeant where he could find Megan Flynn.

"Are you kidding?" Petersen gaped. "Tasso and Lieutenant Chin are waiting for you."

He knew what she was thinking—that the Detective Cole Williams she knew would never consider leaving his superiors waiting. Hell, that Detective Williams would never do something so stupid, so reckless, as to deserve the kind of ass reaming he had coming.

But he'd dug himself in this far, and he needed to talk to Megan face-to-face, find out what the fuck she thought she was going to accomplish that the police couldn't.

No surprise, rather than being booked and tossed in a cell with the other petty thieves, Megan had been taken upstairs for questioning by Tasso and Chin. They would want to know why she was at Bianca's house, what she was looking for.

What else she knew.

Fuck. Cole was a master of interrogation, and he knew all the tricks and tactics they would use. Even if she was inclined to protect him, Megan would be helpless if they really turned the screws.

But deep down, did he really want her to lie for him? He'd dug his own grave, fucked himself over. He couldn't really blame her.

He found her, mercifully alone, in an interrogation room. Under other circumstances, he might have admired her ability to nose out Bianca's address before he had. Right now, all he felt was angry, not just at the prospect of losing his career, but also at her for going by herself to a sketchy neighborhood. He knew Megan thought of herself as tough and street smart, but just the idea of her walking around there alone was enough to make him want to keep her locked up for her own safety.

Cole turned off the monitors and cameras and ducked inside the room.

Some of his anger dissipated when he saw her, small and fragile, sitting at that table. Her shoulders were hunched, her dark hair spilling forward to hide her face. They'd removed the cuffs, but she was rubbing her wrists like they still hurt.

The urge to hug her was as strong as the urge to shake her.

He closed the door quietly behind him.

Megan's head snapped up, her face melting into a mask of guilt the second she recognized him. "I'm so sorry, Cole—"

He held his hand up. "Save it. This whole thing is my own fucking fault for being so stupid. I should know by now that being around you only causes me trouble."

She winced at that, but Cole was so pissed, mostly at himself, he couldn't muster any sympathy. "What I want to know is what the hell you think you were doing, going by yourself to that part of town, breaking into someone's house."

Megan licked her lips and stared at the table. "Two years ago, Devany ran away and ended up at Mission St. Jude. Bianca was a volunteer there. Devany didn't realize it was her right away, but she remembered the mark on her shoulder."

"And instead of calling me immediately, you decided to interfere with the investigation and go nosing around yourself."

"I was going to tell you, I swear! I just wanted to take a look myself, because I might see something you guys won't."

"You used confidential information to go off half-cocked and then neglected to relay information that could help us learn more about the victim."

"I didn't conceal it," Megan said. "I just didn't tell you right away. I knew you wouldn't tell me if you discovered anything in her house, so I wanted to get there before you—"

"Don't rub it in. Even if I do keep my badge, no one's ever going to let me live that down. I leak information to a fucking court advocate, for Christ's sake, and she tracks down the victim's address before I can."

"I was going to tell you about Devany and anything else I found out."

"You should have left it up to the police—"

"Right, because you're so willing to entertain the idea that these cases are connected to Sean's? After today, why would I trust you to do that?"

Just like that, Cole was back in her apartment, Megan stripped almost bare beneath him. His hands running over her silky skin, the salty-sweet taste of her in his mouth. He felt himself thicken as blood rushed south. "After what happened today, wouldn't you think I'd be more inclined to help you out?"

Hot color flooded her cheeks, and her green eyes skittered away from his. "I was talking about what you *said*. About the knife wounds. I wasn't talking about what you *did*."

"*We* were both on that couch, Megan." He took a step closer and heard her breath catch. He leaned over the table, so close he could smell her hair. "I did what you asked and showed you the files. You saw for yourself there was nothing in there to prove your theory." He shook his head in exasperation. "Or you should have. But instead you had to break into the victim's house. I'll be lucky to get off with just a suspension."

Her mouth pulled down at the corners, shame mingling with guilt. "I'm sorry, Cole. I had no idea anything like this would happen." She ran her eyes around the interrogation room. "Obviously."

"It's my own goddamn fault. I know better." He rubbed his eyes. "Do you have an attorney you can call?"

She nodded. "I called a friend, and a lawyer should be here soon. And I really was going to tell you if I found out anything. Like you should know—"

Before Megan could get the words out, the conference door opened again. Lieutenant Chin's face tightened with anger. "What the hell are you doing in here, Williams? I told you to come to my office as soon as you got back."

Cole had always had a solid relationship with his lieutenant, but now he fought the urge to pop him in the face as payback for chastising him like a child. "I was just on my way."

Another man followed, and it didn't take years as a detective to recognize that the navy pinstriped suit and expensively trimmed graying hair spelled *lawyer*. "Ms. Flynn, I'm Michael Levin. Mr. Brewster called me on your behalf."

Megan nodded and murmured her thanks.

Brewster? The tool from the coffee place?

"I'll see you in my office, Detective," Chin snapped, and closed the interrogation room door in his face.

Sure enough, as Cole crossed the bull pen on the way to Lieutenant Chin's office, he spotted Nate Brewster in his Ken-doll, all-American glory, cooling his heels in the waiting area. The knife twisted in Cole's gut. He shouldn't care—should be relieved, even—that Megan's moneyed, wannabe boyfriend had come to her rescue.

Yet the very idea of Megan counting on any man but Cole for help stuck in his throat like a giant uncoated aspirin.

Unfortunately, Nate spotted him too. "Detective," Nate called, standing and waving a big hand to get his attention. "Nate Brewster, we met the other day."

As though Cole could forget the man he'd caught drooling over Megan. Once again the man was dressed like he was fresh from the country club, a heavy platinum watch gleaming on his thick wrist.

"I remember," Cole said, accepting the handshake. He imagined a lot of people found Nate's smile charming. Cole was hard-pressed not to shove his fist into it. "Nice watch," Cole said, gesturing to the piece that probably cost enough to feed a third world nation for a month.

"Thanks." Nate's smile was a flash of blinding white. "I got it as a present for myself last year when my business grew three hundred percent."

"Really? What business is that?"

"Computers—nerd stuff," Nate said in a way that told Cole he didn't expect a meathead cop to be able to grasp it. "Have you seen Megan? How is she?" The smile was gone, replaced by a look of deep concern.

"She's okay. The lawyer's in there with her now."

"We got here as soon as we could. I couldn't believe it when she called me for help. Breaking and entering? What was she thinking?"

"She wasn't," Cole said flatly. "There's a lot of that going around today. Now, if you'll excuse me."

Nate nodded and said good-bye with a quick wave, and then sat back, his too-handsome face pulled into a mask of concern. Wealthy Prince Charming ready to use his money to dig his damsel in distress out of her hole.

Cole went to Chin's office, sank into a leather armchair, and waited to find out if he still had a badge.

Chapter 10

By the time Nate led her from the station and tucked her into the passenger seat of his BMW, it was after ten. It had taken several hours to work everything out, but Lieutenant Chin finally conceded that it was better not to press charges than tell the public that their detective had leaked key information in a high-profile investigation.

In exchange, Megan told them everything she'd discovered about Bianca—her work as a prostitute, the restaurant she'd frequented, her donation to the mission, and the probability that she had a roommate named Stephanie who'd left very little evidence of her existence at the shared house.

The only pieces of information she held back were the napkin she found from Club One and the picture from the Web site. It wasn't a big deal, she told herself, since the police were likely to find it themselves when they searched the house. Megan wanted to look at the Web site, and more importantly, she wanted to get to Club One before the cops. She was afraid the staff and patrons would likely clam up once the police started nosing around.

She flipped on her cell phone and saw Devany's number come up in the missed calls list. She'd called three times in the last fifteen minutes.

Dev answered on the first ring. "Where have you been?" Dev's harsh whisper was all teenage indignation.

Megan forced back a snappy retort. "I had my phone off. Do you need me for something?"

"I need a ride," Dev said, again in a whisper.

"It's almost eleven on a school night."

Megan could hear muffled music and voices in the background.

"Don't give me a hard time, okay? You always said you'd come get me if I needed you to, and tonight I really need you to."

"Where are you?"

Megan winced when Devany gave her the address, not too far from Mission St. Jude. Not a place for a fourteen-year-old girl alone at night. "Hang on." She covered the mouthpiece and turned to Nate. "I hate to ask you this, but I need another huge favor."

Ten minutes later, they pulled up in front of a low-rise apartment building. A small crowd milled out front, drinking beer and smoking cigarettes. Megan spotted about half a dozen girls around Dev's age, along with a bunch of guys who looked several years older. She dialed Dev's number, squirming in her seat as a few of the guys approached Nate's car. She wondered if, on top of everything, they were going to get carjacked. The guys stayed back but kept a wary eye on their car. "We're here."

Dev appeared at the front of the complex in seconds. Megan waved her over. Nate clicked the lock and Dev dove into the backseat in a cloud of Everclear punch and pot smoke.

"Can we go, please? I want to get out of here before Davos realizes I left."

"And you're welcome for the ride," Megan snapped. "Dev, this is Nate. The man nice enough to come to this lovely part of town to pick you up. Maybe you could at least say hi."

"Hi, and thank you for the ride," Dev said, her kohl-rimmed eyes rolling, red mouth sullen. She slumped back in the seat.

After several blocks, it became clear she wasn't about to offer any explanation.

"So, you want to tell me what the hell you were doing there?"

"My friend's boyfriend knew about this party, so I decided to go."

"I thought you were still grounded."

"Aunt Kathy had to go back to work tonight, and I started freaking out by myself, okay?"

"You should have called someone—"

"I did call someone. I called you, and you weren't around."

Because she was too busy breaking and entering, Megan thought with a stab of guilt. "I'm sorry about that. I got hung up."

"I can see why." In a flash, Dev went from brat to flirt. "He's cute. Cuter than that cop."

Megan rolled her eyes but didn't contradict her. "So what happened at the party?"

"It just got a little weird, and my friend didn't want to leave."

"Who's Davos?" Nate asked.

"A guy at the party, not that it's your business."

"I'm your ride. I think that makes it my business."

Megan could hear the thread of irritation in Nate's voice.

"Sorry," Dev mumbled. "He's this guy I've seen around. Usually he's okay, but tonight he was on Molly—a bunch of people were."

Megan's stomach clenched. "Please tell me you didn't take any." Molly was Ecstasy cut with coke, or occasionally heroin.

"I'm not an idiot. But Davos was getting all amped up and grabby—everyone was—and I kind of freaked out and hid in the closet."

"I'm glad you called," Megan said, meaning it. "I'm sorry I wasn't around earlier."

"Me too."

They were silent as Nate pulled the car into the trailer park entrance. Megan directed him to Dev's dark trailer. Nate parked, got out, and opened Megan's and Dev's doors. "It doesn't look like your aunt is home. Do you want us to stay with you?"

Exhausted as she was, Megan was touched by Nate's consideration.

Dev shook her head. "Kathy will be home soon. I'm just going to crash."

They followed Dev up the short steps and waited as she turned on all the lights in the trailer. Megan told her good night, but Dev stopped her as she turned to go. "I almost forgot to tell you—my mom called today. She's getting out early." Dev tried to say it casually, but Megan knew she had to be freaking out. That news, as much of being scared, had sent Dev out into the city to blow off some steam.

"I'll set up a meeting with Rhonda tomorrow, okay?" Megan knew Dev's case worker would recommend Dev stay with Kathy. Megan hoped that was enough to convince the judge this time.

"Thanks," Dev said, and flashed them both a shy smile, "for everything."

—◊◊◊—

"Here we are."

Megan lifted her head from where it rested against the cool glass of the window as Nate walked around to open her door. "How are you holding up?" he asked.

Megan nodded. After brushing off her effusive thanks and dishing out a couple of "what were you thinkings," Nate was mercifully silent, seeming to appreciate that after nearly three hours of nonstop questioning, Megan wasn't exactly in the mood to talk.

Especially not about what was really bothering her. Yeah, the arrest was traumatic, and the thought that a record would prevent her from continuing her volunteer work was devastating, but it was nothing compared to what she'd done to Cole.

She closed her eyes, but she couldn't erase the memory of him as he confronted her in the interrogation room. Anger, betrayal, self-recrimination at his own stupidity in trusting her. She had very likely ruined his career.

She tried to tell herself that any collateral damage was justified if it helped Sean, but that didn't stop her from feeling like something scraped off someone's shoe.

Somehow she'd make it up to him, but hell if she knew how. At the very least she'd let him in on her Club One lead. Who knew, maybe if he was able to unearth new information relevant to the investigation, they'd let him back on the task force.

That assumes he hasn't been suspended, or worse, fired. Another twist of guilt.

She walked up the creaky wooden stairs to her apartment and tried to tell herself that she was only disappointed because if he was thrown off the case, she would lose her source of information.

Deep down, she knew that wasn't true. If one thing had become clear in the past couple of days, it was that no matter how hard she tried to convince herself that everything she'd ever felt for Cole had mutated into hatred, on some level she still cared about him.

Deeply.

Like a genetic defect that had been injected into her DNA, Cole was part of her now, and damned if she knew how to get him out.

She pulled out her key as she reached the top step, fumbling a little in the dark. She made a mental note to replace the bulb in the motion-sensitive light above her door, which had burned out over a month ago. It hadn't really bothered her up until now, but with everything that had happened in the last few days, the dark had taken on an added hint of danger.

She shivered a little, glad to have Nate's large bulk behind her. Her gratitude gave way to a gasp of fear as a tall figure emerged from the shadows. Nate shoved her behind him just as the man called out Megan's name.

"Megan, it's cool! It's just me, Jimmy!"

"Jimmy?" Megan unlocked the door and flipped on the outside light from the inside. Sure enough, there was Jimmy Caparulo, his dark hair clipped close to his skull. Though his face had the same intensity as the last time she'd seen him, at first glance he looked sober. His dark

eyes were focused, and there was no scent of booze cling-
ing to him. His face had filled out a little, too, his bold
Italian features still sharp but not gaunt like the last time
she'd seen him. "You scared the hell out of me."

"I know you don't want to talk to me, but it's
important."

"This isn't a good time," Megan said, and started to
step around him.

Jimmy reached for her, and Megan shrank away, flashing
back to that night at Sean's, remembering how awful it had
felt to be pinned against the wall, terrified someone she'd
always trusted was about to hurt her. But tonight Jimmy
took the hint and backed off. As Megan's shock faded, she
realized Jimmy's presence was a stroke of luck. She loaded
Bianca's image on her phone screen. "I'm actually glad
you're here." She held the phone out to Jimmy. "Do you recognize this girl? Do you ever remember seeing her at Club
One?" It was a long shot, she knew. Jimmy had quit his job
at the club after Evangeline's murder, and it wasn't likely
Bianca was hanging out at the club three years ago.

A muscled arm hooked Jimmy around the neck.

"Get the fuck away from her," Nate said in a tone so
menacing it sent shivers up Megan's spine.

Jimmy grunted and landed an elbow in Nate's gut,
hard enough that Nate loosened his hold. Jimmy spun
around and tried to tackle him, but Nate shoved him off
and swung a right hook to Jimmy's face. Jimmy blocked
the blow and countered with a left to Nate's jaw. Megan
could barely understand Jimmy over her own shouts for
them to stop, but she caught the words "Leave her alone"
and "Sean would kill you for touching her."

They were well matched, both trained in hand-to-hand

combat. Jimmy had gotten himself back into shape, and though he wasn't as thickly muscled as Nate, he moved with a speed and fluidity that had Nate dodging and blocking to keep from getting his face pounded to a pulp.

Oblivious to her screams to stop, Jimmy swept Nate's feet out from under him and knocked him to the ground. As he launched himself on top of Nate, Megan dove onto Jimmy's back. "Stop it!" she shouted in his ear. "Jimmy, stop right now."

Her voice in his ear seemed to bring him out of his rage and Jimmy froze. Nate shoved him to the side, then helped Megan to her feet.

"I'm sorry," Jimmy said grimly. "But you shouldn't be around him." He took a step forward, then froze as Megan shrank back against Nate. Jimmy held up his hands. "You need to listen to me. You can't be around him—"

"No, I want you to go," she said, a slight tremor in her voice. "I don't want you here right now. Either you leave, or I'm calling the police."

Jimmy shot a look at Nate over her head. "I'm watching you," he said before he turned to go.

Megan felt a pinch of sadness through her unease and wondered how out of control Jimmy had gotten that he was seeing enemies at every turn. Even in the face of a man who had once been a close friend.

"I'm sorry about that," Megan said when she turned to face Nate. "He's been trying to get in touch with me, and I just don't want to deal with him."

"It's okay," Nate said, carefully probing his jaw as he worked it open and shut.

"I didn't realize you two had a falling-out as well," Megan said.

Nate flashed her a wry smile. "I didn't either. I haven't seen him in almost three years. Not since..." His eyelashes cast dark shadows on his cheekbones as he averted his gaze.

Right, she didn't need him to say the milestone out loud. As she started to walk through her door, she spotted something on the ground and picked it up. "Jimmy must have dropped his phone."

Nate held out his hand. "I'll make sure he gets it. Probably better for you to keep your distance."

Megan agreed. "Let me get you some ice." She ushered him into the apartment, went to the kitchen, and filled a baggie full of ice cubes.

She flopped next to Nate on the couch and dug her fingers into her scalp. She could feel the fatigue manifesting in a headache that shot tendrils of pain from the back of her neck up into her eyeballs.

"It's like the perfect shitstorm. First I'm arrested, then Devany acts out, and then Jimmy shows up and goes berserk."

Nate shook his head. "Devany seems like a real handful."

"She's had a tough couple of weeks. She's the one who found the latest Slasher victim."

"That's terrible."

Megan nodded. "She's been completely messed up about that, not sleeping, nightmares, everything. And now they're afraid her mother's going to somehow use that as leverage to get custody. Claim Kathy's trailer doesn't provide a safe environment or something."

"Maybe I can help," Nate said, lowering the ice pack as he slung his arm along the back of the couch and turned to more fully face her. "I've done business with a lot of people all over the city. I could pull a couple of strings."

Megan shook her head. "That's so nice of you, and you've been so great helping me with everything, but I think I've taken enough advantage of you for the time being." The acknowledgment made her uneasy.

Nate waved her off with a smile. "You're not taking advantage. I'm happy to help you however I can."

Her lips curved into a feeble smile. "Thanks."

He was perfectly still for a moment, and she felt as much as saw his gaze shift to her mouth. His hand slid closer to her shoulder along the back of the sofa, and she knew he was going to kiss her before he dipped his head.

She tilted her head up to meet him, her lips soft and slightly parted in invitation. His kiss was perfect. Not too dry, not too moist. His full lips applied the perfect level of pressure to make her lean in for more. His hand curled around the nape of her neck, big and warm and solid.

Megan laid a tentative hand against his neck and leaned closer. She closed her eyes tighter, focusing on the firm pressure of his mouth, the clean soapy scent of his skin.

Tried desperately to feel something more than a mild, pleasant warmth.

Frustrated, she parted her lips, inviting his tongue to venture inside. He did so, slowly, skillfully. No lip smashing or shoving his tongue down her throat—it was possibly the most technically proficient kiss she'd ever experienced.

And yet.

And yet.

There is seriously something wrong with you when you

can't even get a mild heart flutter for a man who's practically perfect, but Cole can throw you around the living room, lay you on the couch, and kiss you so senseless you're stripped down to your panties before you even realize it.

She pulled away with a sigh and let her hand fall from Nate's cheek. "I hate to do this but it's been a really long day."

"Right. I'm sorry. I shouldn't have pushed you after everything you've been through."

And after he'd saved her ass, a kiss was the least she could do for him, but try as she might, she couldn't muster up reciprocal attraction. If things were different, if she hadn't that very day been starkly reminded of the combustible chemistry she still shared with Cole, she might have pushed it, convinced herself that if she told herself she was attracted to Nate, eventually she would be.

But Nate deserved better than to be with a woman who couldn't stop remembering, couldn't stop feeling, couldn't stop aching for the touch of another man.

"It's okay," she said, grasping for the words to let him down easy. "You're great, but right now things are really complicated...with Sean." Her grief, never far from the surface, pushed to the forefront.

"Of course," Nate said, all warmth and understanding. "It's a very emotional time, and I don't expect you to jump into something."

She shook her head and sniffed back tears. "What are you, like, an *Oprah* addict? How do you know exactly what to say?"

"I don't know about that. All I'm saying is I can be patient. I'll be here when you need me, as a friend for now, until you're ready for it to be something more."

As he hugged her good-bye, Megan struggled not to dwell on how hurt he'd be when he finally figured out that "something more" was never going to happen.

It was only after she closed the door behind him that she realized that in the midst of all the drama, Jimmy had never answered her question about Bianca Delagrossa.

She retrieved her laptop and clicked on her e-mail. Any worries about Nate fled as she typed an address into the "to" field. She really didn't want to open up communication with Jimmy, especially after what happened tonight. But any fallout would be worth it if it gained her any more information that connected Bianca's murder to Evangeline. She attached the picture of Bianca, typed a quick note asking Jimmy to take a second, closer look to see if he recognized her, and hit SEND before she had a chance to think too hard about it.

She clicked open a browser window and typed in the Web address that had been above Bianca's picture.

Megan wasn't sure what she thought she was going to find, but that didn't stop anticipation from flooding her as the page loaded. It was just a Web site, she reminded herself. But maybe this clue to Bianca's life would provide the link Megan had been searching for.

The page was blank except for a message across the top: *Welcome. Please enter your username and individual access code.*

She was no computer expert, but depending on the site's security, there might be a way to get in. Megan frowned and typed gibberish into both fields and pressed ENTER.

For a split second, another page came into view, and Megan barely registered the images of several young women before her screen went blue and filled with rows of white text.

Crap.

Stomach sinking, she restarted the computer, praying the site hadn't permanently hosed the machine. To her surprise and relief, everything restarted okay. But when she pulled up her browser and tried to reload the site, she received a *page not found* message. Even more odd, her browser had been wiped clean of history, bookmarks, everything. As though the Web site had entirely reset the program.

Her search for the URL came up empty. Somehow the Internet had been wiped clean of all evidence of the mysterious Web site, as though it had never existed.

Chapter 11

*H*urry, Sarah, you have to hide!"
He could hear the car coming down the drive, the rumble of the muffler vibrating in his belly, twisting his guts until he nearly doubled over with pain.

Eleven-year-old Sarah ignored him, her dark head bent over the log cabin she was carefully constructing from sticks she'd gathered from the scrubby trees surrounding their dusty yard. "I'm busy."

"But he's coming. You have to get out of here." Despite the searing heat of the summer afternoon, goose bumps prickled his arms and legs. The rumbling was getting closer, and he could see the dust kicked up by the truck tires, a faded yellow cloud rising up to the almost painfully blue summer sky. Sweat beaded at his hairline and trickled down his neck, yet he shivered in the late-afternoon heat.

Sarah flipped a glossy brown braid down her back and shot him an exasperated look over her shoulder. "He's here to see Mom. He never pays attention to us."

But Sarah was wrong—mostly anyway. Yeah, Scott was here to see Mom, but the bitch had forgotten to eat breakfast that morning, and now, half a box of wine in, *she was already passed out on the couch. He knew what that meant. Without Mom to fuck and knock around, Scott would be looking for something else to entertain him.*

It was easier during the school year. He'd been able to sign himself and Sarah up for all kinds of extracurricular activities or send Sarah home with another kid to play. By the time they got home, Mom would be passed out for the evening and Scott would have left for his job working the night shift, packing and loading produce from all the local farms.

Now it was summer and it was tougher to get away. Without school, they had little refuge. Their few friends were gone, visiting relatives or at camps his mother couldn't afford. He tried so hard to keep Sarah out of the house when Scott came around, but he could only keep her at the community pool for so long before she started complaining. And today she'd flat out refused. She was sick of the pool and wanted to stay home and play with her own stuff.

He'd nervously checked the front window, listened for the truck. Scott usually showed up sometime after lunch, after he'd slept for a few hours after getting off work. He and Mom would watch TV, her with her box of white zin-fandel, him with his twelve-pack of beer. Inevitably she'd piss him off, say something stupid or spill his beer, and he'd catch her with a backhand or a punch upside the head. Then the crying would start, the I'm-sorry-I-didn't-mean-its....

The bedroom door would slam and he'd hear his mother's pleas, hear Scott's demands for her to show him exactly how sorry she was.

Scott wasn't the first bad seed Mom had brought into the house, allowing him to use her body in exchange for a few dollars toward rent and food in the fridge. Allowing him to yell at her kids and occasionally knock them around because she needed someone to keep her company; she was so very lonely.

But Scott was different, and he'd realized it way too late. If he'd known, he never would have let Scott catch him outside the bedroom door, never would have glared at him, all disgust in his thirteen-year-old heart plain on his face.

Call him a coward. But if he'd known, he would have run.

But Scott had seen him. Scott had emerged from his mother's room, his shirt unbuttoned, his pants half unzipped, a look of satisfaction on his sweaty, piggy face. "What are you looking at, you little shit?"

He'd just stared for a minute, his lip curling in disgust, like he smelled a pile of rotting trash. "Nothing."

For a chubby guy who was usually more than halfway to drunk, Scott moved like a striking snake. He didn't see the blow coming; all he knew was pain exploding in his nasal cavity, up through his eye sockets. The second blow caught him on the cheekbone, hard enough to stun him to his knees.

"Who do you think you are, you little shit, turning your nose up at me? You little fuckin' punk. I knew punks like you when I was in the joint. You want to know how I handle punks like you? How I show them who's in charge?"

Scott pushed him into the bedroom he and Sarah shared. Thank God Sarah was at a friend's house working on a school project. He fell to the floor, Scott's heavy weight pressed against his back, shoving his face into the floor. He focused on the rough nap of the worn carpet against his face. The sound of a neighbor's dog barking in the distance. Anything but on what was happening. His pants and underwear ripped away. Rough hands grabbed his hips.

Unimaginable pain and humiliation.

"Teach you to fuck with me," Scott muttered, smug satisfaction ringing in his voice as he pushed off him and left him there, crumpled on the floor. He didn't move for a long time. By the time he limped out, Sarah was home, eating a bowl of Cheerios at their kitchen table. His mom had roused herself from bed and sat, nursing another goblet of pink wine in front of the television.

"What happened to your face?" Sarah asked, spoon halfway to her mouth.

He caught his reflection in the oven door. His nose was swollen to twice its size—most likely broken. There was a lump over one cheekbone, and one eye was swollen nearly shut. He looked kind of like Sloth from The Goonies.

He became aware of a throbbing in his face, a pulsing ache that made nausea twist in his gut. He focused on that, ignoring pain in other parts of his body, the burning ache in his ass, the feeling that he had been torn apart from the inside out.

"I tripped and hit my face on the table," he said, looking not at Sarah but at their mother.

She tore her gaze from the TV and spared him a glance, her eyes widening when she saw the condition of his face. He saw the flash of guilt in her eyes as she took another gulp of wine.

She knew.

She knew exactly what Scott had done to him.

But all she said was, "You better get some ice on that."

After that, he'd done everything he could to get himself and Sarah out of the house when Scott was likely to be around. But sometimes they ran out of places to go. He came to dread the sound of Scott's muffler buzzing up the driveway.

Became physically ill at the smug, knowing leer on Scott's face if he showed up and their mother was already passed out.

And the fucking bitch knew exactly what would happen if Scott came around and she was too drunk to fuck him.

And she didn't fucking care, as long as Scott threw her a little extra cash and saved her from her self-imposed loneliness.

The rage in him built every day. Every time he was beaten, used like an animal. But he kept it in check, because he had to protect Sarah. He didn't tell anyone, knowing if he did they'd be separated, and he couldn't bear to be away from her, the only good person in his life. The sister who took care of him after Scott got his hands on him.

At least, he let Sarah tend to the black eyes and busted lips. But he'd never let her know the rest. He couldn't bear the humiliation if Sarah knew he let himself be used, even if it was for her protection.

But then a few weeks ago, he'd caught Scott looking at Sarah in her tank top and cutoffs. Running his piggy eyes over her long skinny legs, licking his greasy lips at the sight of her small breasts, just barely making an impression against her shirt.

He'd done his best to get them away from the house, and when they were stuck, he would antagonize Scott to keep his attention focused on him, away from Sarah.

He knew it was only a matter of time. He knew he couldn't protect Sarah forever. Sooner or later, Scott would get his hands on her.

As he watched the cloud of dust get closer and closer, watched as Sarah continued cluelessly with her construction project, he had a gut-twisting hunch that today might be the day.

"Sarah, you have to get out of here!" he said again.

Their bikes leaned against the side of the house, but it was too late. Even if he could get Sarah on her bike in this heat, they'd have to ride by Scott to get out to the road.

Scott's view of the yard was obscured by the scrubby bushes that lined the driveway. There was still time. "Go to the neighbor's okay? Just for an hour or two," he pleaded.

Sarah stood up and threw down the stick in her hand. "No! I'm tired of this! This is our house, not his. Why should we have to leave whenever he comes over? Why do you put up with the way he beats on you? When he gets here, I'm gonna tell him to get out of here or we're gonna call the police."

Fear choked him as he envisioned what would happen if Sarah made good on her threat. Sarah, bloody and beaten on the floor, sobbing from the pain of having her soul stripped away. He couldn't let that happen. But he couldn't tell her that; he didn't want her to live in fear like him. "If you call the police, we'll be taken away. We'll be separated," he said, frantic now as Scott's truck drew closer.

She tossed her chin. "No, they won't. We'll just tell them he's the one beating on us. They'll take him away."

Sarah was too little to remember the one time he did tell someone one of Mom's boyfriends had slapped him. The terrifying week when he and three-year-old Sarah had to go stay in the group home where the older kids pulled her hair and stole her food.

Now he was starting to wonder if maybe being in foster care would be better if it meant Sarah was safe from Scott.

Even so, Scott could do a lot of damage before the police came.

He had only seconds. He grabbed Sarah by the arm and yanked her over to the driveway. Ignoring her protests, he pushed the button on the trunk of his mom's ancient Buick and shoved Sarah inside.

"Stop it!" she yelled. "You can't lock me in here—"

He finally lost it. "If he finds you, Scott is going to hurt you! You think he just beats on me, but that's not even close to the worst of it! I've seen him looking at you, Sarah, and if he gets his hands on you, he's going to hurt you, way worse than he's hurt me."

Something in either the words or the tone finally registered. Green eyes wide with fear, Sarah ducked into the darkness of the trunk. "Don't leave me in here for too long," she said in a thready whisper.

"I won't close it all the way. As soon as we get inside, you get out and run next door and call the cops." He would distract Scott, get him to take out his violence on him and give Sarah plenty of time to make a run for it.

Hands shaking, he carefully placed the trunk door so it rested against the bottom but didn't latch.

He stepped away just seconds before Scott screeched to a stop in front of their house.

Scott got out of the car, adjusting his belt under the beer gut that spilled over the waistband of his Wranglers.

"Mom's inside," he said, arms folded across his skinny chest, chin tilted with as much defiance as he could muster.

A stained Seahawks cap shadowed his features, but he could see Scott's squinty eyes darting around the yard. "That ain't who I'm looking for. Where is she?"

He backed away, toward the house. Scott followed, stalking him up the driveway. "She's gone. At a friend's house."

"Little fuckin' liar. Her bike's here. I know she's here."

He swallowed hard as Scott got closer to the Buick. "She walked."

"Don't you fuckin' lie to me!" Spit flew from Scott's mouth, and his heart froze in his chest as Scott's fist slammed down on the trunk of the car, hard enough to make a dent.

Shit. Sarah was locked in. Stay quiet, Sarah, please stay quiet.

"You think you can keep me away from her? Her skinny little ass is mine, same as yours!"

Rage swelled up in him, a blinding red wave. Before he knew what he was doing, he launched himself at Scott, kicking, screaming, punching, scratching, biting. He got in only a few blows before Scott threw him down, steel-toed boots hitting his ribs. He lay there, stunned, helpless to defend himself against blow after blow.

He was vaguely aware of being dragged inside, thrown to the floor of the kitchen. Another kick and something cracked. Everything went black.

He woke up, the pain hitting him like a Mack Truck.

He'd been out for a while, judging from the way the sun slanted across the kitchen floor.

He rolled to his side, tried to push himself up, only to collapse under the weight of the excruciating pain. This was by far the worst Scott had ever gotten him. Every nerve roared with pain, inside and out.

But at least he'd taken it, and not Sarah.

Sarah!

She was still in the trunk. Holy fuck, she was still in the trunk.

Pure adrenaline launched him off the floor, past Scott snoring on the couch, out the front door as his brain frantically tried to calculate how long he'd been out.

How long had Sarah been trapped in the trunk of the car, the sun beating down in the triple-digit heat?

Long shadows crawled across the front steps and patchy lawn. The temperature had cooled a couple degrees, but the yard and the driveway were still glowing under direct sunlight.

Please, please, please.

She looked so peaceful, curled up in the trunk. Her dark wavy hair half hid her face; her thick, dark lashes cast shadows on her cheek. One hand pillowed her face, palm up, like she'd settled in for a nap.

But he knew with an instinctive, crippling dread, Sarah wasn't just asleep. Her limp hand, her skin, already cooling despite the heat. Her total lack of response as he dragged her out of the trunk, screaming her name at the top of his lungs.

He laid her out on the lawn and put his mouth over hers, trying to breathe for her and pumping her heart like he'd seen on TV.

He sat back on his heels, the pain in his body fading as he sobbed. Sarah. His baby sister. Dead. She must have been so scared when she couldn't get out. Trapped in the trunk, cooking like a chicken in an oven.

They'd done this. They'd killed her.

Rage propelled him inside, where the worthless sack of shit lay sprawled on the couch. He went to the kitchen and grabbed a carving knife from the block on the counter. He was going to gut him like a fucking fish, but first things first.

He went to the medicine cabinet, got two packs of the smelling salts his mother kept around in case there was an emergency and she needed to be roused from her alcoholic stupor.

He went into her bedroom. She was laid out like a beached whale. Her blotchy skin was shiny with sweat and grease, a trickle of drool pooling under her on the mattress. Her tank top rode up her back, leaving a six-inch swath of skin bare. He wondered how she'd feel if he peeled her skin off as if she were a banana.

He cracked the smelling salts and waved them under her nose. He wanted her awake. Fully aware of what was being done and who was doing it to her.

She roused with a snort and rolled onto her back. Her gaze was fuzzy at first, but he knew the split second she realized what was happening.

The terrified knowledge in her eyes, the choking sound as she tried to scream, sent a rush through him, pleasure and power so extreme, it almost filled the hollow ache left by the thought of Sarah's lifeless body sprawled on the lawn.

He raised his right hand, the knife clenched in a death grip.

Wait.

Scott was left-handed.

He quickly switched hands.

He was almost as good with his left hand as his right, a fact he'd discovered when he was six and had broken his wrist.

Before she could scream, before her drunken body could catch up with her brain's warning to fight, he brought the knife down as hard as he could. The blade cut through the skin like butter, obliterated the resistance of bone as it penetrated the soft tissue underneath. She let out a feeble choke as blood bubbled out of her mouth and spread like a lake across the front of her shirt.

He yanked the knife out, adrenaline coursing through him as he stared at her horrified eyes.

"You fucking cunt," he yelled. "It's all your fault. You let him do it. You knew all along, and you let him do it. You're a fucking whore who whored out your own kid."

Her mouth moved. No sound, but he could read her lips.

"I'm sorry."

Red mist fogged his vision. His blood felt like it was boiling out of his skin.

Sorry.

Sorry.

She could take her sorries to the Devil when she met him in hell.

One last slice across her neck and the bitch was gone, gaping like a trout as her bloodshot eyes filmed over.

He made sure Scott's prints were on the knife, too, before he roused him. Scott put up more of a fight, even managed to turn the knife on him and slice him across the arm.

Then Scott was gone, too, the knife buried to the hilt in his chest.

He staggered outside, fell to his knees next to Sarah. Sobbing her name over and over, begging for forgiveness for not keeping her safe, not killing them sooner.

In the dream she changed, her features morphing, changing. She was no longer a child. She still had the same green eyes and dark hair, but the face and body were those of a woman.

His body jerked as he realized he wasn't holding Sarah.

He was holding Megan.

Her dead eyes opened and she reached up to caress his face. "You were supposed to save me. We were supposed to be together."

He jerked awake, his heart galloping in his chest, cold sweat filming his body. He squeezed his eyes shut, trying to hold on to the last shreds of the dream. He wanted to hold on to it, hold on to Megan, reassure her everything was going to be fine. They would be together. He wouldn't let anything happen to her.

He flung his forearm over his head, swallowing back a wave of guilt. He thought of Sarah all the time, lived with the guilt every day, but he hadn't thought about what led up to her death for a long, long time. Had shoved it so far back he could almost pretend it had never happened, that it was all a bad dream.

When he did let himself remember, he remembered only the good parts. The euphoric power that surged through him when he cut his mother's throat. The rush of feeling the blade pop through Scott's breastbone.

He felt his cock harden under the sheet at the memory. Like a first kiss or a first fuck, there was nothing like the first kill. It was the one and only time he'd killed on pure, savage impulse. Now his kills were deliberate, purposeful, and carefully managed and directed.

He'd learned so much that day. Like how good it felt to have someone at his mercy, begging for their miserable, worthless lives.

Not to mention how easy it was to fuck with the cops. They'd gulped down his self-defense story like a fish sucking down a juicy worm. They'd even called him a hero, fending off a maniac who had already broken his wrist, cracked his ribs, not to mention the other damage.

As for Sarah, he told them she'd locked herself in the trunk. He hated to do that, make her look foolish, but there was no other way.

Sarah...Her face floated in his mind again, smiling. His sweet sister, the only one who'd ever really loved him. The only one he'd ever really loved.

But she must have forgiven him, because how else was he getting this second chance?

Megan was his second chance at a normal life, a normal love. No more living under the thumb of those who considered themselves his masters, who thought that without their influence, he would be nothing but a mindless, soulless killing machine.

He'd show them. He'd once had a soul. He remembered what it was like to be normal. Before Sarah died. Megan could give that back to him. Her love would vanquish the darkness, wash away his sins.

He felt a form rustling beside him and reached out, his hand meeting smooth, feminine flesh.

He ran his hand down her arm, over her stomach. He squeezed his eyes shut. If he did that, he could almost pretend it was Megan. But the hip under his fingers was too skinny, the bones protruding into his palms. And she smelled like heavy perfume and dirty sex. Nothing like Megan's fresh flowers and clean laundry scent.

His fingers tightened around her hip, and he heard her gasp as the bone ground beneath his grip. It was nothing like what he needed, but the sound sent a faint tickle to his balls. He gave up the fantasy and opened his eyes. He couldn't have Megan yet, but at least he could use this bitch for what she was good for. And deliver a warning in the meantime.

"Sorry," he said, pasting a sheepish grin on his face. "Sometimes I don't know my own strength."

She gave him a feeble smile from where she sat huddled against the headboard, her short blond hair standing up in spikes. "It's okay. I know how excited you get." The sheet clutched to her chest hid most of the marks he'd put on her earlier, but he could see a faint purple bruise darkening on her shoulder.

She was so easily duped, believing his roughness was a combination of overenthusiasm and lack of skill. They all were, accepting him as the nice, fumbling guy they would throw a free bang to as part of the deal. They had no idea of the monster that lurked beneath, no idea how every wince and cry of pain got him rock hard.

The marks would put her out of commission for a couple days, but it didn't matter. There were plenty of other girls, willing and eager to service Stephanie's regulars. Not that they would want her lately, even without his marks. Her face was drawn, her eyes bloodshot and ringed with dark circles.

"You need to take better care of yourself, Steph," he said.

She started to flinch as he reached out his hand, then relaxed and flashed him a tentative smile when he traced his fingers gently down her shoulder.

"I haven't been sleeping much lately, after what happened to Bianca," she whispered.

"Did you know what she was planning?"

"No." She ruined the lie by casting her gaze to the sheets, then looked back up to meet his pointed look. "Well, we lived together and I knew she was up to something. I told her not to do anything stupid, that whatever she was planning she couldn't get away with it." Her breath caught on a sob. "And she didn't."

He slid his arm around her shoulder, pulling her close, the comforting friend. "It's terrible what happened to her."

She nodded, buried her head in his neck. He grimaced as she slimed him with snot and tears. "I can't stop thinking about her. How scared she must have been, how much pain she was in..."

You have no idea. His cock grew painfully hard at the memory of Bianca screaming behind the gag. The tight clench of her sex as her body convulsed in pain. "I'd hate to see something like that happen to you." Oh, he could see it now. Stephanie up on her knees, her long, skinny legs splayed open for his invasion as she whimpered against the cold kiss of his blade.

It would be so easy, and so good, so much more satisfying than what he had to get by on between kills.

But he wasn't authorized, he thought bitterly. They'd told him to deliver a warning. To make sure she understood what would happen if she did something stupid like go to the cops to talk about her former roommate and colleague.

Like a dog on a too-short leash, he strained to be free. But he couldn't break free, not yet. There were a few more details, a few more pieces to put in order before he could free himself from their imagined hold.

In the meantime . . . "The police will be looking for you. You know that." He slid his fingers in her short, choppy hair, tightening his grip until she raised wide, frightened eyes to his face. "Now that they know who Bianca really is, they'll be looking for anyone connected to her." Which pissed him off to no end. He left no loose ends, and he couldn't be blamed for this one. It wasn't his fault they hadn't done a good enough job covering up Bianca's past. And now the police knew who she was, where she'd lived, and so did Megan.

Megan, who was going to find herself in serious deep shit if she didn't stop sniffing around places she didn't need to be. She'd found the Web site, as he'd discovered last night from the access report. Not that he was worried. He knew there was no way she could access it without a code or find out who was running it. Still, the bits and pieces of information she was picking up were bound to lead somewhere if they weren't careful. He couldn't let them be discovered. Not until he was ready.

Stephanie's bottom lip quivered.

"You won't talk to them, will you?" She shook her head, and the fear in her eyes, the knowledge of what would happen if she talked, made his cock throb in time with his heartbeat. "That's good," he said. "I'd hate to see anything happen to you."

His breath sped up as he flipped her onto her stomach

and yanked her to her knees. He shoved into her tight, unwilling body, reveling in her gasp of pain. Good whore that she was, she quickly muffled it with a feigned moan of pleasure. But he could see the way her hands fisted in the sheets, white-knuckled desperate. The way her skin flinched when he put his hands on her.

She took it, like they all did. They knew what to expect when they were called in to see him. Did they suspect that he was the monster of their nightmares?

Whore. She made herself available to anyone who would pay for it. She may have catered to an exclusive clientele, but that didn't change what she was. She deserved every ounce of pain he inflicted. She wasn't worthy of pleasure.

He'd save all of it, the gentle touches, the passionate kisses, for Megan. He'd worship her body when he got the chance, drown her in pleasure until she forgot everything but his touch.

Soon, he thought as he collapsed on top of the blonde. *Soon.*

Chapter 12

If Cole had learned anything over the past few days, it was that he should stay the hell away from Megan Flynn. After a fifteen-year career in which he'd followed all the rules, dotted every I, crossed every T, he was now holding on to his detective shield by the skin of his teeth. All because Megan Flynn had a way of drawing him in, getting under his skin, and getting him to make stupid choices in some misguided attempt to protect her.

He should be home, relaxing with a beer in front of the TV. Or better yet, he should take advantage of the break in the weather and take his boat out to the San Juans, use his enforced vacation to get his head together. Focus on what was important and not let himself get dragged down by a desperate woman chasing a lost cause.

Yeah, he should be doing a lot of things besides sitting here in the dark, parked across the street from her house like some creep, waiting for her lights to go out so he could go home and get some sleep. But damn her, she'd thrown herself into her misguided mission to save her brother with no regard for her own safety, had put herself in dangerous situations. It was only a matter of time before she ended up hurt. Or worse.

And the need to protect her overrode everything, including any last shred of common sense.

He was hopeful that her run-in with the Seattle PD and Special Agent Tasso had reined her in a bit. Cole had spent the day tailing Megan. Her first stop had been to pick up Devany to take her to breakfast at a diner near the trailer park where the girl lived. Cole couldn't hear their conversation, but Devany was pissed about something. She slumped in her chair, picking at her food as Megan talked to her. After only a few minutes, Devany pointed an accusing finger at Megan and stormed out.

After breakfast, Megan had dropped Devany back home. To Cole's surprise, Megan didn't go back to Redwood Acres. He wouldn't have put it past her to take the opportunity to go poke around the Slasher's latest crime scene.

Instead she headed back toward her place, to the café where she liked to work. She spent several hours on her computer and made a few phone calls. Nothing out of the ordinary.

And no visit from the knight in shining armor who had so gallantly rescued Megan from the clutches of the evil police, Cole thought with a grimace. Not that Cole had wanted to see Megan charged with breaking and entering, no matter how big a part she played in getting him suspended—that was all on his stupid ass, and he was kidding himself if he tried to convince himself different.

But it stuck in his craw that Captain America had been able to come in with his money and big-shot lawyer and make Megan's mistake disappear, all while Cole was sitting in Lieutenant Chin's office getting his ass handed to him.

A background check on the guy had revealed nothing—the guy was as perfect on paper as he was in the flesh. College, a stint in the army Rangers with honorable discharge. Now he owned his own computer-consulting company, which clearly provided enough money and connections to help him bail Megan out of any scrape she found herself in.

That wasn't the only background check Cole had run in the past couple days. Sean's pending execution was bringing people out of the woodwork and into Megan's life, not all of them with records as spotless as Nate Brewster's. Guys like Jimmy Caparulo. Cole grimaced as he remembered the story Megan had told him about Jimmy.

Based on what Cole had discovered, since he'd left the army a little over three years ago, trouble was pretty much a constant in Jimmy Caparulo's life. His record was spotted with multiple DUIs and two arrests for assault. After his gig at Club One, he'd been hired by a private security firm, basically working as muscle for hire, his employers willing to overlook his past brushes with the law. Megan wasn't totally off in her assessment, though—turned out Jimmy still lived with his aunt and contributed a significant portion of his paycheck to pay off her medical bills.

Ailing aunt or not, Jimmy was trouble, no doubt about it, and the way Megan attracted trouble like bees to honey . . .

Right, chump. If that's how you want to justify following her all over the place and sitting out here in the dark with your thumb up your ass, that's your business. Admit it. You can't stay away from her. You can't stop thinking about how it felt to kiss her, touch her, but you're too much of a coward to go up those stairs to her and go after what you really want.

Cole slammed his head back against the seat. What was he doing, lurking after her, telling himself he just wanted to keep her safe, when all he wanted to do was go up there, strip her naked, take her to bed, make the world disappear for both of them for a while.

He was so fucking pathetic, sitting down here in the dark, hard as a spike at the thought of her, knowing he wasn't going to do a goddamn thing about it. He wasn't being arrogant when he acknowledged that if he showed up on her doorstep, if he put on the full-court press, he was confident he could get Megan into bed.

The chemistry was still there, blazingly hot on both sides, as evidenced by their scorching, near-naked tussle on her couch the other day. And Megan, for all that she tried to hold herself together with her iron will, had so many cracks in her veneer that she would shatter into a million pieces with a mere poke of his finger.

But she'd hate herself afterward. Cole could live with her hating him, but he didn't want to put self-loathing on the menu with all the other stuff she had to deal with. As for himself…she had him so twisted in knots without even trying. He'd done nothing but fuck up since he'd seen her again, and no good could come from getting more deeply involved.

Which was why he needed to get his ass home, and first thing tomorrow he was going to pack up his boat and head out to Lopez Island. He'd rent a cabin, fish, run, spend the next two weeks getting his shit together.

Sean's execution was only six days away. By the time Cole got back, it would be all over, and Megan would be forced to move on, one way or another.

He swallowed at the morbid thought. But he could do nothing to save Sean, and despite his misguided efforts, he couldn't save Megan from her pain.

The light in Megan's living room went off. She was calling it a night, and now Cole could too.

He was reaching to turn the key in the ignition when something caught his eye. *No fucking way.* Megan appeared on the landing, her slim form hidden by a heavy overcoat. She picked her way carefully down the stairs, and as Cole squinted to see her in the murky streetlight, he saw that she was wearing lethally high heels.

She minced her way to the car, and as her face came into full view, Cole jerked back in surprise. Since he'd known her, Megan had always gone light on the makeup unless it was a really special occasion.

Cole wondered what the hell she was up to tonight. Even from across the street, he could see the slick red lips and heavily lined eyes. Her usually wavy hair was pin straight, spilling down her back almost to her waist. She slipped her coat off to toss it in the backseat, and Cole nearly choked on the sip of water he'd just taken.

In defiance of the frigid, wet weather, Megan wore a sleeveless dress with a plunging neckline and a skirt so short Cole wondered if maybe technically it should be called a belt. He couldn't make out the exact color in the dim light. All he could tell for sure was that it was dark and looked as though it had been shrink-wrapped to her body.

He wondered where the hell she was going at ten-thirty at night, dressed like a slut.

A date? With Captain America?

Jealousy churned in his gut as she pulled her car away

from the curb. He waited a few seconds, then followed. If she was going to meet someone, so be it. Cole would just have to restrain himself from putting his fist through the guy's face.

And no matter what happened, he had a sinking feeling that his fishing trip was going to be postponed.

———⁓———

The sound hit Megan like a wall as she stepped inside Club One. Even on a weeknight it was packed with people. She tugged at her skirt and gave her neckline a quick check to make sure her boobs hadn't popped out. She'd put the dress on and taken it off half a dozen times before she'd mustered the courage to wear it out of the house, worried it was too much. Or, to put a finer point on it, way too little.

But as she looked around, she realized she didn't need to worry. Most of the women here wore clothes that were equally, if not more, revealing. Megan tottered on her heels as a woman brushed past her wearing a sheer blue top and no bra, having no qualms about showing her small, dark nipples to the world.

Megan, in her fuck-me shoes and barely there dress, blended in perfectly. She gave a little sigh of relief. She didn't want to attract any more attention than necessary as she did her little recon mission. She did a quick scan of the crowd and looked over by the main bar.

No Talia, at least not that Megan could see. Megan knew the other woman wouldn't be happy to see her, especially if she realized Megan wasn't just there to throw back a few drinks and hit the dance floor.

Megan worked her way across the main floor, surveying the crowd, her heart sinking a little as she took in the scale of her self-imposed mission.

It had seemed so clear-cut back at her place, as she'd been tarting herself up like a little girl playing dress-up. After the Web site yielded nothing, she decided she needed to do some on-site research. *Go to Club One. Blend in with the crowd. See if anyone recognizes Bianca and can help you track down her roommate.*

Right. Now she looked out at the sea of hundreds, trying to figure out where the hell to start.

There was a trio of guys sitting at a table near the bar, leaning back in their chairs, eyes raking every woman who walked by. They would notice a beautiful girl like Bianca. Might as well start with them.

They spotted her a few steps from their table, all three raising their eyebrows in interest as they scanned her from head to toe and back again. They were decent-looking, with their carefully tousled hair, tight button-down shirts, and even features. Still, the way they eyed her and leaned in to whisper to each other made her skin crawl. Megan pasted a smile on her face and forced herself not to cross her arms in front of her chest.

She was so glad this wasn't her regular scene. And she wondered, not for the first time, what had drawn Sean here in the first place.

Megan felt a stab of grief explode in her chest, and she faltered on her four-inch spike heel. She willed herself not to fall, to keep it together, and forced the thought of Sean out of her head. Lately, if she wanted to function, she couldn't even think about him, couldn't let him come to the forefront of her consciousness without completely falling apart.

She threw her shoulders back and sauntered to the table under the trio's appreciative gazes. She could succumb to mingled despair and anxiety later. Right now she was on a mission.

"Hey, guys," she said, leaning in and pitching her voice to be heard over the loud thump of music and the din of the crowd.

Three pairs of eyes glued themselves to her cleavage. Megan grimaced and resisted the urge to look down and check just how much of a show she was giving. Hell, the club was dark, and if they produced useful information, so what if they caught a glimpse of nipple?

"Sit down and have a drink." The hipster in a striped shirt hooked the back of a chair and dragged it over, while his friend motioned to a cocktail waitress. The third slid his gaze slowly from her chest to her face with a grin she supposed was meant to be flirtatious but made Megan feel like she'd been painted with a coat of slime.

She refused the drink but gratefully took a seat. She'd been on her feet for a measly five minutes and already her feet were killing her.

"I'm looking for information on a friend." She pulled the picture of Bianca up on her iPhone and passed it across the table.

All three guys squinted at the picture. "Hey, I think I do know her. Why do I recognize her?"

Probably because Bianca's picture was all over the news, after the police had officially released the information about the Slasher's latest victim. Their leering smiles dropped when she shared that bit of info. "What I really need is information on her roommate—Stephanie, I think her name is? Have any of you guys ever seen

Bianca here at the club? Do you know who she hangs out with?"

They all shook their heads. "I've never seen her here," said Striped Shirt, "and I don't know any girls named Stephanie."

Like you really thought it would be that easy? Megan sighed and winced as she rose to her feet. She had a bad feeling it was going to be a long, unproductive night in very uncomfortable shoes.

The guy protested. "C'mon, sweet cheeks, one drink. You've got all night to look for this Stephanie chick."

Megan flashed a smile that was more a baring of teeth and rapped on the table. "Thanks, guys, but I really need to find her. Besides, I make it a policy not to accept drinks from guys who call me sweet cheeks." She turned her back and sauntered back into the crowd.

A hand on her arm stopped her short, and she jumped as a masculine voice yelled in her ear. "Megan, what are you doing here?"

She turned, shocked to find Nate behind her. But it was easy to see how she'd missed him in this crowd. While he'd stood out at the boho Café Norte, here he was just another button-down shirt in a sea of financiers and wannabe software moguls.

She felt herself flush as his gaze took in her skimpy dress and lethal heels. His mouth pulled tight like he was irritated.

She moved closer but still had to yell to be heard. "I could ask you the same thing. I didn't realize you hung out here."

He shook his head. "I don't. I'm here with clients." He gestured over his shoulder with his thumb to a table in the far corner. She could make out the shadowy figures of two men in dark suits. He gave them a quick wave and pulled Megan to a slightly quieter area of the first floor. "When they found out I set up all the networking and communications for the club, they asked me if I could get them in. It's just business," he said, as though trying to reassure her. She didn't have the heart to tell him the thought of him picking up a honey from the club didn't bother her in the least. His blue eyes narrowed on her cleavage. "What about you? Are you meeting someone here?"

She didn't miss the underlying jealousy. She was going to have to set him straight soon. "Not exactly. I'm trying to find out information about someone." She pulled Bianca's picture out of her bag and showed it to Nate.

"Is that the woman they found in the trailer?"

Megan nodded. "Her name's Bianca Delagrossa. She used to come here. And I'm trying to find out if there's anything that links her to my brother's case."

"I know the manager," Nate said, reaching for her arm. "I can get you in to talk to her—"

Megan held up a hand and backpedaled as fast as her heels would allow. "No thanks. She and I aren't on good terms. She testified against Sean."

Nate closed his eyes briefly. "Oh, Jesus, I'm an ass. It never registered—"

"No reason it should have. Her name wasn't in the press much. But do me a favor. If you see her tonight, don't tell her I'm here. So, do you recognize Bianca?"

Nate shook his head. "I've never seen her. To be honest, I'm usually here in the daytime, before this whole scene unfolds." He gestured at the dance floor full of gyrating bodies.

"You better get back to your clients, then."

"I guess," he said. "You really think you'll find anything?"

She couldn't blame him for his skepticism. When she'd come up with the plan, it had seemed so simple. But now the sheer mass of people and thundering noise was overwhelming.

"I have to try."

"You'll let me know if I can help."

She nodded and tilted her face up to accept a quick kiss on the cheek before he melted back into the crowd.

An hour later, the sass was decidedly missing from her step as her predictions about tonight's recon mission proved true. No one she talked to seemed to know anything about Bianca or a roommate who may or may not be named Stephanie.

She asked the bartenders and cocktail waitresses, who she hoped might be more likely to remember Bianca's face, especially if she and her roommate were regulars. No dice. She studied the curving staircase that led to the second floor and the VIP area.

Stood to reason if Bianca and her roommate came here often enough, they might be hanging with the high rollers. *Not that you have any indication Bianca was a regular based on who you've talked to so far.* Still, she'd be stupid not to check it out.

As she carefully placed one precarious shoe on the first step, she felt a warning tickle in between her shoulder blades and her heart picked up speed. She whipped her head around and scanned the crowd, suddenly overwhelmed by the certainly that she was being watched. She'd experienced it several times in the last few days, that creepy feeling that someone was following her, tracking her every move.

She laughed silently and shook her head. *You're out in a club wearing hooker shoes and a dress made with less fabric than a handkerchief. Of course you're being looked at.*

Still, she did another scan, but she didn't see anyone staring particularly hard at her. The table where Nate and his clients had sat was now occupied by a new group. No Talia Vega glaring daggers at her from behind the bar. No Jack Brooks watching her with his cold, impassive gaze.

Then again, something told her if Jack were watching her, he'd never let himself be seen. Her skin prickled with goose bumps despite the heat generated from hundreds of bodies moving through the club. She tossed her hair down her back and continued up the stairs, telling herself she didn't give a crap whether Club One's menacing head of security was watching her or not. If he saw what she was up to, so far he hadn't interfered.

Still, the thought of him watching her from the shadows made part of her want to turn tail and head for home.

The VIP area was located at the back of the second floor, hidden behind a wall of frosted glass. As she approached, she watched as dozens of people approached the doorway to the inner sanctum. The men were dressed expensively and were of varying levels of attractiveness, but there wasn't a woman who went through the door who wasn't model-perfect.

Megan ducked into the bathroom and checked her reflection. More glam than average? Definitely. Model-perfect? Absolutely not.

As she was applying another coat of lipstick, a woman

emerged from a bathroom stall. She was small with short, spiky blond hair. Megan had a flash of recognition. The Web site. The blonde's picture had flashed up there for a split second; Megan was almost certain of it.

The woman's thin frame was showcased by a skintight, white satin top and equally tight leggings that looked like they were made of vinyl. She was beautiful in a delicate, elfin sort of way. Megan knew she would have no problem getting into the VIP room.

Megan waited until the woman washed her hands before she shoved her phone with Bianca's picture in her face. "Sorry to bother you, but I wondered if you know anything about this woman." She watched the woman's reaction carefully.

The girl drew back in surprise, and her lips moved for a moment without sound. "Uh...uh...isn't that the girl who—" She broke off, swallowing convulsively, her skin paling.

"She was the latest Slasher victim," Megan said matter-of-factly. "I'm trying to track down her roommate."

"Why? Are you a cop?" the girl asked warily.

Megan shook her head with a little laugh. "Hell no."

"You're a friend of hers?" The woman cocked a hip and surveyed Megan up and down.

"Not exactly," Megan conceded. "I have a..." How should she put it? "A personal stake in her case, I guess you could say. I have a theory that the Slasher murders might be connected to another murder three years ago."

"It's really scary what happened," the woman said as she took another look at the photo on the screen. She bit her lip and gave a little shudder, then lifted her eyes to meet Megan's again. "Sorry, but I didn't know her."

Megan sighed and put her phone back in her purse. "Doesn't seem like anyone else did either." She turned to go, but as she put her hand on the door handle, the girl called out, "I saw in the papers they're doing everything they can to find the guy. Brought in the FBI and everything."

Megan nodded.

"A lot of effort for a handful of dead hookers."

Megan's head snapped back. The police had released Bianca's identity to the press, but they hadn't mentioned their suspicions that the victims were prostitutes. "How did you know they were hookers?" Even though Megan hadn't seen more than a flash of an image, her gut was telling her this was one of the girls.

The woman shook her head, eyes wide. "I just assumed. Isn't that how it always is on TV?" she said with a forced laugh. "Creepy killer stalking and killing hookers because no one cares enough to look after them?" She rummaged through her clutch purse, avoiding Megan's eyes as she pulled out a tube of lipstick.

Megan moved behind her until she could see her reflection over the woman's shoulder in the mirror. "Everyone has someone who cares about them. But unless someone cares enough to tell the truth about what's going on, he's just going to keep getting away with it."

The woman's gaze flicked to Megan's reflection in the mirror as she smoothed her lips with slick pink color. "I'm sorry for those girls and all, but I've got plenty of my own shit to worry about, you know?"

Yeah, I know all about having other shit to worry about. Like my brother dying of a lethal injection in a week if I don't find enough of a connection to raise reasonable doubt. "Fine. But in case you suddenly remember something about Bianca or anyone else who might know her, here's my number." She pulled a business card from her purse and slapped it on the counter. She went to the bathroom door and gave the blonde one last look.

She still hadn't picked up the card.

Megan knew she should have pressed her harder, but she'd learned from experience with her kids in the system that if someone didn't want to tell her something, there was no way to force it out of them.

To hell with it. Maybe she should just call the cops and have them deal with it. She could imagine how that conversation would go: "Right, Agent Tasso. Remember how I broke into Bianca's house and snooped around? Well, I found a Web site for what I'm pretty sure was an escort service which may or may not have featured Bianca, but I managed to crash it before I told you about it. I also found a cocktail napkin with Club One's logo, you know, the same club where Evangeline Gordon was working when my brother supposedly killed her? And I thought, what a coincidence..." and so on until they hung up or arrested her again for interfering in their investigation.

Nope, she was out on her own, and she didn't want the woman, whoever she was, to get spooked. And, Megan told herself, chances were if she'd found one person tonight who'd known Bianca—even if she didn't want to admit it—she was bound to find another.

She stepped out of the bathroom, eyeing the VIP door from across the upper level's bar area. She stopped at several tables, interrupting couples and groups as she flashed Bianca's picture. All she got were a lot of head shakes and annoyed looks that she'd interrupted their fun with questions about a dead girl.

At one point she saw the woman from the bathroom slip by her and dart into the VIP room. Megan sighed. Time for her to stick out her tits, lay on the charm, and follow suit.

———∾∾———

Cole hung back in the shadows, nursing his beer as he watched Megan move through the crowd with all the finesse of a bull in a china shop. He had to give her points for determination. She was, if nothing else, a woman dedicated to her mission as she shoved that iPhone in the faces of anyone who would pay attention. Taking every head shake, every annoyed brush-off on the chin as she moved on to her next target.

Now she was headed for the VIP area. This should be interesting. Even with her heavy makeup and wardrobe from Sluts R Us, Megan didn't fit in with the crowd here at Club One. She was too sober, too purposeful to fit in with the kind of crowd that had the time and the means to knock back twenty-dollar designer drinks until the wee hours on a Thursday night.

Not that he didn't appreciate her efforts to blend in. The heavy red lipstick he could do without, but that dress...It was absolutely criminal what that tight, short, low-cut dress did for her legs.

And her breasts.

And her ass.

And Cole was far from the only one who noticed. He'd spent the past hour watching guys' eyes glaze over, losing focus on the questions Megan peppered at them as their gazes locked on the soft inside curves of her breasts displayed by the plunging V of her neckline. His right hand felt like it was permanently clenched in a fist as he fought not to slam it into yet another club patron's leering gaze. And when Captain America had appeared out of the crowd and put his hands all over her, Cole had nearly lost it.

He held himself back, relaxing when Nate returned to the two guys he was with. He tailed Megan through the crowd, making sure she didn't get herself into too much trouble, keeping close tabs to see if it looked like anyone was actually giving up any relevant information.

While he was pretty damn certain this mission of hers—whatever had sparked it—was a bust, there was always a chance she'd come up with something. After all, she had come up with Bianca's address before he had, he reminded himself with a fresh spurt of irritation.

This time he intended to be there if she managed to uncover any leads.

Watching Megan from behind as she approached the entrance to the VIP area, Cole smiled as she stuck her ass out and tilted her head back, one hand on her cocked hip as she talked to whoever was manning the door.

Next thing he knew, she had disappeared inside.

Huh. Well, this was Seattle, after all. Not like it's L.A. or even Vegas, chock-full of celebrities and high rollers.

Yet when Cole tried to get in, he was told no dice, no way, no how. He knew he wouldn't get in without causing a scene, and he didn't want to ruin Megan's night—not yet. If this is what she needed to do to get through the night, to give her a sense of purpose while she dealt with the shit sandwich her brother had served up, who was he to interfere?

And now you have an excuse to question her later. His mouth curved into a grim smile as he let himself fantasize for a moment about some creative interrogation techniques.

Cole found a table near the VIP room where he could sit with his back to the wall and keep an eye on the door. He ordered another overpriced microbrew from a passing server and settled in to wait.

—∿∿—

Megan scanned the VIP area, her stomach churning with discomfort. The vibe in here was decidedly different. *Welcome to the land of the beautiful people.*

Check that. Welcome to the land of the beautiful people about to have sex.

Everything about the room was sexually charged. Older men held court at tables crowded with beautiful young women willing to exchange a couple gropes or something more for endless free drinks. She watched a server who could have been a model drop off a bottle of liquor, flashing a smile when the fat cat she served gave her a pat on the ass.

Megan wasn't sure, but she thought she recognized a local athlete at a table with several friends. He whispered something in his waitress's ear, and within seconds she had recruited two young women dressed like twins to go sit at their table.

Was this how it all started?

Couples, threesomes, even foursomes lounged indolently on plush velvet couches. Even those who weren't actively kissing or groping leaned in close to one another, speaking in intimate whispers over the heavy music thumping from below.

Smoky haze filled the dim room, and Megan smelled tobacco, pot, and other things she didn't recognize and didn't want to think about. Apparently there was an anything-goes policy here in Club One's VIP room, and yet again she wondered what her straight-arrow, military-bred brother had found appealing about this kind of indulgence.

It wasn't the club; it was the girl, she reminded herself. Then she wondered what it said about Sean that he would go after a woman who ran with a crowd like this.

Maybe you didn't know him so well after all, that evil, nagging little voice that liked to chime in when she was nearing rock bottom hissed at the edges of her consciousness.

No. I know Sean. And just because he hung out here doesn't make him a sleaze, and it sure as hell doesn't make him a murderer.

And he'd never mentioned being up here in the VIP room, which was a world away from the dance club and bar scene going on below. This was an orgy waiting to happen, she realized as she watched a man snake his hand up a woman's skirt while their female companion leaned in to give her an openmouthed kiss.

Megan tottered through the room, her whole body blushing, feeling dirtier and dirtier by the second. She was at a loss as to how to jump in and start asking questions. Not to mention, the people in here were so sexed up and drugged out, it was unlikely they'd register their own names, much less Bianca's.

The handful of staff that catered unobtrusively to the

crowd watched her curiously. When Megan showed them Bianca's picture, she was told politely but firmly that here in the VIP room they were known for their discretion.

Frustrated, Megan was just about to give up and slink home on her aching feet when she spotted the woman from the bathroom ducked in a booth near the back of the room. She was with a man, and before Megan could approach, the couple stood and disappeared behind a heavy black velvet curtain hanging along the back wall.

Megan darted a quick look over her shoulder to see if anyone was watching and followed suit.

Behind the curtain was a dimly lit corridor, and as Megan stepped through the curtain, she saw the blonde and the man disappear through a door. Her heels echoed as she hurried to follow, but when she tried the handle, she realized the door was locked. She looked closer and saw that the door was protected by some kind of keycard security system.

She jiggled the handle and smacked the door with her bare hand. "Hello? Is anybody back there—"

Brutal hands gripped her bare shoulders and whipped her around. Before she could so much as breathe in the air to scream, a huge hand covered her mouth, crushing her lips against her teeth as she was shoved up against the door.

Though she couldn't make out his face in the dim light, she recognized that clipped voice immediately. "What part of 'authorized personnel only' don't you understand?"

Chapter 13

Megan relaxed only marginally as Jack lifted his hand off her mouth and eased his hold enough that she wasn't crushed against the wall. "Do you know that girl out there? The blonde?" Megan said, figuring it couldn't hurt.

He rolled his eyes and didn't answer. Without a word, he pulled her back into the VIP room, his hand wrapped around her upper arm in a viselike grip as he propelled her across the floor.

"What's back there? Where did she go?"

"None of your business." He looked tough and scary in his black T-shirt and pants, the shadow of his beard dusting his jaw. In the low light of the VIP room, the snake on his tattoo seemed to pulse and writhe as his fist clenched and unclenched in frustration.

"I wasn't doing anything—"

"I've been watching you for the last hour. It's time for you to go."

She tried to yank her arm from his grip, noticing the way the people in the VIP room looked up to watch as Jack marched her to the door. With every step, her heels threatened to buckle. "You don't have to manhandle me," she spat as he shoved her toward the door.

"Yeah, I do, because apparently you can't take a hint. You're not welcome around here. And the next time you show up and harass customers with your questions about dead girls, I'm not going to be so nice."

"You call this nice?" she said as he dragged her out to the main part of the floor.

"I didn't break anything, did I?"

"Get your hands off her, asshole."

Megan jumped at the masculine roar behind her. Her stomach did a little flip when she recognized Cole.

Jack released her arm, and the two men squared off like heavyweight fighters circling the ring. "She with you?"

"Yeah," Cole said, and slid a proprietary arm around Megan's waist. Heat surged through her, arousal mixing with adrenaline, making her legs tremble so hard she had to lean against Cole for support.

"You should keep a better eye on her. She has a bad habit of turning up in places she shouldn't." ·

Cole's eyes narrowed and his lips stretched into a smile that looked more like a snarl. "I'll keep that in mind."

Jack stepped back and she saw him nod to someone behind her. Megan turned and caught a glimpse of Talia Vega before she melted into the dark periphery of the club.

"Get her out of here," Jack said to Cole, though his cold, hard stare was locked on Megan. "And if you want to keep her safe, don't let her come back."

Megan shrank against Cole under the blast of that icy blue glare and didn't protest as he tightened his arm around her waist and steered her to the staircase.

She braced herself for him to lay into her, blast her for dressing like a slut and risking pissing people off by showing up where she wasn't welcome and shoving Bianca's picture in everyone's faces. But Cole was grimly silent as he guided her down the stairs, other than a harsh "Careful" when she staggered on her heel and would have taken a header down the metal stairs had he not grabbed hold of her elbow.

As they reached the teeming mass on the first floor, she couldn't stand it anymore. She whirled on him, figuring the best defense was a good offense. "Why are you following me?"

His dark eyes narrowed. "Because like the guy said, you seem to have a knack for getting yourself into trouble lately."

"It's not your job to keep me out of trouble, Cole."

He flashed a smile that didn't quite reach his eyes. "Since I've been suspended for leaking Bianca's identity before Tasso released it, I have a lot of free time."

Megan felt a stab of guilt. He must have been going crazy, not being able to work the case and, worse, knowing his career hung in the balance because of her recklessness. "I know it doesn't help, but I'm really sorry. You know I didn't mean to mess anything up for you this time."

"Yeah, we're all sorry about a lot of things," he said as he steered her to an empty table near the end of the bar. Megan hung her purse on the back of the chair he pulled out and took a seat. "Now, how about you tell me what the hell you thought you'd accomplish by coming here."

Megan darted a nervous glance around the club. "Shouldn't we go? Jack was pretty adamant...."

Cole shrugged his broad shoulders, unconcerned. "I'm not worried about him."

That makes one of us.

He flagged down a waitress and ordered a round of drinks, a single malt for himself and an extra-dirty vodka martini for her, extra olives.

Megan tried to tell herself there was no significance in the fact he remembered her favorite cocktail.

"How do you know that guy?" Cole said, an edge creeping into his voice.

"I met him here last week, right after Bianca was murdered. I came here to find out if they knew anything. If there was any way…" She trailed off, shaking her head.

"If you didn't find out anything then, why come back tonight?"

Megan shifted in her chair, grateful when the waitress appeared with the drinks. It took two bracing gulps of icy vodka before she could bring herself to meet Cole's dark cop stare. She leaned across the small lacquered table even though no one was likely to hear her over the music. "I found something in Bianca's house."

Cole's hand smashed down on the table hard enough to make the ice in his glass jump. "Please tell me you told Tasso and Lieutenant Chin."

"It really wasn't much of anything, just a cocktail napkin—"

"For fuck's sake, Megan! Breaking and entering? Removing items from a victim's residence—"

Megan put a hand up in defense. "I didn't remove anything, I swear! I was looking through some clothes in one of the closets and found a Club One cocktail napkin." She held up the one that came with her drink for emphasis. "But I left it there, for you guys to find. And I left the picture of Bianca from the Web site too," she said, as though it had just occurred to her.

"What Web site?" Cole asked, his voice grim.

"I think it might have been advertising an escort service," Megan said, "but I couldn't access it." She ignored the pinch of guilt for not providing all of the details about the site and her suspicions about the blonde.

"And you didn't mention this when you were questioned because..."

Megan shrugged. "People tend to clam up once the police get involved, and even if they did talk, the cops aren't looking for the answers I need." She tilted her chin up, refusing to feel like a scolded teenager under his censure. "If Agent Tasso and the task force decide those are leads worth following, I haven't done anything to stop them. Besides," she said, heaviness settling over her shoulders as she took another drink, "no one here seems to know much of anything." Or if they do, she thought as the blonde's face flashed in her mind, they're not inclined to talk about it. "But maybe Tasso and Chin will have more luck than I did."

"No matter what, Megan, you've got to promise me you'll stop doing this. If you're not careful, you're looking at an obstruction-of-justice charge."

She looked at him across the table, his expression both frustrated and concerned. For her. When he looked at her like that, she wanted to promise him anything he asked.

"I need to go," she said, jumping abruptly from her chair. Another sip of vodka and this night was going to end very, very badly.

His big hand clamped down on her arm. "Wait. Promise me you'll stop."

She shook her head. "I'm out of options, Cole. If I think there's any way I can help Sean, I'm going to do it."

"Then let me help you. I'm a detective. This is what I do."

She smiled thinly. "Really? You'll help me prove the innocence of a man you believe with every fiber of your being is guilty?"

His dark gaze didn't waver. "I'll help you find the truth, whatever it is."

She wanted to believe him. She so badly wanted to have someone to help her through this.

Not just anyone, she admitted to herself. She wanted Cole. She wanted to be back in that place with him where she could trust, where she felt safe, protected, and though he'd never said it out loud, loved.

But there was no going back, and as much as she wished she could take him at his word, Cole was a cop, first, last, and always, suspension or not. He would help her only as much as it helped him protect his job.

"Promise me," he prodded. "Promise you'll call me before you go off chasing another crazy lead."

"I'll think about it." She paused. "And if I do, will you promise to stop tailing me all over the place?"

His lips curved into a half smile as he rose from his chair. "I'll think about it."

He walked her to the front of the club, retrieved their coats from the coat check, and walked Megan to her car. She rummaged through her purse for her key, flustered at the way he stood so close, blocking her in, keeping her safe, his gaze constantly scanning for danger that might come from any corner.

He snatched the key from her hand, unlocked the door, and reached for the door handle. This brought his face level with hers, so close she could smell the sandalwood scent of his aftershave, the smoky aroma of scotch on the breath that wafted across her cheek. He paused there for several seconds, and she could feel the coiled tension emanating from his body.

A quarter turn and her lips would be on his...

The door latch clicked, and the door swung open. Megan slid into the driver's seat. "Drive safe," Cole said, and closed the door.

Megan wasn't surprised to see Cole's headlights tailing her home or to see his Jeep pull up behind her. She shook her head as she got out of the car. Even if she'd been suspicious of him following her, she would have been looking for an unmarked Crown Vic. At least now she knew what to look for.

"You don't have to come up with me," she protested as Cole opened his door.

He gave her a hard look and held out his hand for her keys.

Megan handed them over, too tired to argue, and led him up the stairs. He unlocked her door, opened it, and ducked his head in for a quick look around before he moved out of the way.

Her chest went tight at the small gesture of chivalry. It had surprised her at first, that under his hard, almost gruff exterior lived a gentleman who opened doors for her, held her arm when they crossed a street, and never let her walk alone into a dark apartment. She hadn't realized until that second how much she'd missed the feeling of having someone look after her.

"Well, good night," she said hastily before her case of the warm fuzzies made her do something stupid.

"Hey," he said, catching her by the shoulder before she could go inside. His hand rested there, in the curve where her neck and shoulder met. His thumb stroked along her collarbone as he looked at her with an expression of lust...but there was something else there too. Something she knew would send her right into his arms if she thought too hard about it. "You don't have to do this on your own. But I can't help you if you keep things from me."

He bent his head, and she braced herself to push him away even as her lips tingled in anticipation of tasting his. But his lips landed on her forehead instead, warm and comforting and somehow even harder to resist than if he'd gone for all-out seduction.

"You stay safe," he whispered, and jogged down the stairs before she could reply. She told herself she was glad he left, because she wasn't sure she would have had it in her to push him out if he was determined to stay.

And yet, she couldn't suppress a wistful sigh as she snapped on the light and waved to him from the front window. She felt the tug of regret as she watched his tail-lights disappear into the night and hopelessly wished that she could manipulate the time-space continuum and somehow go back to before any of this had ever happened. Push the reset button and get her life back on the path it was supposed to travel.

Love. Marriage. Kids.

With Cole.

Well, she'd been on that path, she thought. Bitterness chased away the wistfulness as she remembered how she'd been so sure she and Cole were meant for each other that she hadn't even noticed that Cole wasn't exactly on the same page.

She shook her head and scrubbed her eyes against the sting of tears. What was it her grandfather said? *Wish in one hand and shit in the other and see which one fills up first.*

Right. That about summed it up.

She sank to the couch, yanked off her toe-crunching heels, and grabbed her evening bag to retrieve her driver's license and credit card to put back in her wallet before she forgot.

She grabbed the plastic, her phone, and the little stack of business cards she'd brought with her. She put the pile on the table, her heart rate picking up when she saw that one had something written on the back.

Please meet me tomorrow, 1pm, at the Hillside Motel, room 104. Please come alone.

Megan read the polite meeting request twice. It was from the blonde; it had to be. She must have slipped it into Megan's purse.

Promise you'll call me before you go off chasing another crazy lead.

She sat back, flicking the card with her thumbnail. Guilt stabbed her conscience, but she resisted the urge to call him. She'd made Cole no promises. And while he was full of reassurance, he hadn't made any promises not to go straight to Tasso or Chin with any information she brought him.

Besides, she'd tell him everything she found out, providing there was anything worth telling.

—⁂—

Stephanie stared at the door and used the butt of her current cigarette to light the next one. She'd been in the room only half an hour and was almost halfway through the pack. The smoke seared her throat and stung her eyes, but she sucked it down, desperate for the nicotine's calming effects.

It had been so long since she'd smoked; she was almost feeling high. That was one of the many rules. Clients could do whatever they wanted, but the girls couldn't smoke. They weren't allowed to be noticeably intoxicated or use drugs—unless the client insisted.

Some guys couldn't get off unless they knew you were sharing the high.

They also had to keep themselves immaculately groomed from head to toe, and especially in between, and maintain their appearance in accordance to specifications, which varied from girl to girl.

She ran a shaky hand through her hair. First thing she was going to do after she left today was to dye her hair dark, maybe get a weave until she could grow this shit out. Or shit, shave it off altogether. Anything but the platinum-blond, spiky pixie cut that had come to symbolize her role, her part, her character. The edgy, slightly exotic elfin girl who would do anything you wanted with a smile on her face, the one whose delicate, adolescent body let you indulge in fantasies of fucking your teenage daughter's girlfriends. Or hell, your teenage daughter herself.

It wasn't her job to judge. It was her job to follow the rules.

And she was about to break the number one, most important rule of all.

Don't talk. About herself. About them. About what she did and who she did it with.

Because everyone knew what happened to the few who tried to get out before their time was up, the handful who threatened to tell, thinking that would be a ticket out.

It was a ticket out, all right, if you considered being stuffed in a body bag with a cut throat a good means of escape.

Her stomach twisted and she rose from the bed, telling herself she should get out of here before Megan showed up. Hadn't Stephanie just received a friendly warning to keep her mouth shut just two nights ago?

He just said not to talk to the police. He didn't say anything about not talking to anyone else.

Right. Try to argue that with your throat sliced.

She was taking an enormous risk, and for what? A bunch of dumb girls with stars in their eyes who knew what they were getting into from the beginning and should have damn well known whether or not they could handle it.

But Bianca...She had been her friend. She'd looked out for Stephanie from the start, taken her under her wing, taught her how to survive with some piece of her soul intact. Bianca was already three years into the business, while Stephanie was only six months into her contract, such as it was. Bianca had seen a lot more shit go down, had girls she knew disappear on her, victims of a fate they all suspected but no one wanted to say out loud.

She couldn't blame Bianca for wanting to get out, for wishing she could reconnect with her family and start life over. Stephanie rubbed away the sting of tears. Bianca had known the risks, but she didn't deserve what had happened to her. None of those girls did.

Risky or not, Stephanie couldn't sit quietly by and let her friend's killer get away with it. Besides, even if they were watching her, there was no way anyone could have seen her slip that card in Megan's purse.

There was a knock at the door, and Stephanie stubbed her cigarette out and checked her watch. Megan wasn't supposed to be here for another ten minutes. She went to the door, rising up on tiptoes to look through the peephole, but she couldn't see anything. Fingers trembling, she flipped the security latch and cracked the door.

Her stomach flipped when she saw who it was. *Shit.* She was such an idiot, scheduling the meeting at the motel where she'd been crashing.

"Let me in, Stephanie."

She swallowed hard. "I don't have time to see you right now, but if you want to come back later—"

He shook his head. "You know that's not what this is about. Now come on. Let me in. We need to talk before you do something stupid."

"I didn't do anything," she protested. "Please don't rat me out, please!"

"I'm not going to rat you out," he said, with what looked like genuine concern on his face. "I don't want to see you get hurt. Only a couple people know you've made contact, but I can help you fix this. Just let me in so we can talk about it, okay?"

Stephanie weighed her options. If they didn't know what she was up to, there was still a chance she'd be okay. On the other hand, what would he want in return? He'd always treated her and the other girls pretty decently but...

Screw it. She'd fuck him for free for the rest of the century if it meant saving her from ending up facedown in a pool of her own blood. She flipped the safety latch and opened the door.

"I don't know what I was thinking," she said as she turned away. "I'm just so freaked out and sad about Bianca. I felt like I should do something to try to stop it."

"There's nothing you can do," he said. His voice was like an icy hand down her spine. "There's nothing anyone can do."

His huge arm wrapped around her neck, choking off her air supply. She struggled, clawing at the sleeves of his shirt. His gloved hand pressed into her right cheek with bruising force, while the fingers of the other dug into her skull.

"I wish I had time to do this right, to take my time. Feel you clench around my cock when I make the first slice."

Oh God. His breath was coming hot and fast on the crown of her head. Tears stung her eyes, and she let out a choked whimper when she felt his erection bumping against her back.

Adrenaline coursed through her as she struggled with every fiber against his hold.

"Unfortunately, time is tight, and I have a message to send."

A jerk of his hands. A sickening crack of bones and cartilage.

I'm sorry, Bianca.

Megan looked over both shoulders as she got off the bus. She'd managed to ditch Cole back at the coffee place, but she knew he'd get suspicious when she didn't come out of the bathroom after a reasonable time. She hoped that taking the bus instead of her car would help throw him off too.

She looked around, saw no sign of him. So far, so good. She half walked, half jogged the two blocks to the motel where she'd been instructed to go, presumably by the blond woman from Club One.

At least, she hoped the message was from the blonde. Anxiety-induced adrenaline coursed through her veins. It wasn't lost on her that she could be walking into a trap set by someone who didn't want her sniffing around Bianca's murder and whatever connection she had to Club One. She'd quadruple-guessed her decision to ditch Cole, but she was sure if she told him about the card, he would insist on doing the meeting himself. Megan knew she was taking a huge risk going to the meeting by herself, but she was desperate. Sean's execution was only five days away, and she couldn't risk scaring off the only person willing to talk to her.

If she's even the one who set up the meeting.

Megan forced the thought aside. She couldn't afford to panic now, not with so much at stake.

The Hillside Motel was a squat cinderblock building with rooms that opened to the parking lot. Not exactly a rent-by-the hour establishment, but a few rungs below even a Holiday Inn. Megan approached room 104 cautiously. She slipped her hand inside her pocket and felt the reassuring weight of her phone which had 911 dialed in. If anything went amiss, she told herself, she'd press the SEND button and call the police.

She tapped softly on the door. No answer. "Hello? Is anyone here? It's me, Megan. From the club." Still no answer, but the knob turned and the door swung open. She stepped inside and felt a tingling foreboding as her eyes struggled to adjust to the dim interior of the hotel room.

She barely took two steps into the room before her instincts started to scream, *Run*! There was something not right here; she could feel it in her blood....

Then she saw the body. Time seemed to stop, her vision tunneling in on the sight of the woman crumpled on the floor. Her dark eyes were wide, staring, her head at an impossible angle. There was a lump at the base, a bone stretching the delicate skin.

Blood roared in her head, and she wheeled around to the door as her hand fumbled for her phone.

Too late.

A hand caught her by the neck and jerked her back against a hard, muscular chest. Megan's phone went flying as hard fingers dug into her throat, squeezing either side of her windpipe.

She tried to scream but all that came out was a sick, choking sound as she clawed at the arm digging into her chest. The sound of rending fabric pierced the air as the fingers dug harder into her throat.

Her heartbeat echoed in her head, the loud whooshing sound of her blood almost drowning out the sound of his voice. "I don't want to hurt you, Megan," the voice said. "I never want to hurt you. You need to leave this alone before it's too late."

Megan struggled to absorb his words, but her vision was dimming by the second, her struggles weakening as she tried to escape his hold.

The door opened, crashing into the wall.

Megan fell to her knees, gasping as her attacker abruptly released his hold.

"I'm going to kill you, motherfucker!"

Cole!

The building seemed to shudder as Cole slammed her attacker against the wall and buried his fist in the man's stomach. He doubled over, and Cole grabbed at the ski mask pulled over her attacker's face.

She caught a metallic glint just as Cole jumped back with a grunt and grabbed at his side. Her assailant fled from the room, the soles of his sneakers slapping against the asphalt as he sprinted away.

She hurried to Cole's side, the throbbing in her throat forgotten when she saw the crimson stain on Cole's hand. A dark stain had already bloomed along his right side. "Oh my God," she cried as she tugged his shirt from his waistband.

"It's not that bad," Cole said, brushing her hands away. "Forget about me. I need to call this in."

Megan went to the bathroom and grabbed a stack of well-worn but clean-looking towels as she listened to Cole rattle off a series of codes and a description of the victim. She carefully avoided looking at the body on the floor as she returned to his side. Still, she couldn't get the image of that grotesquely torqued neck, the staring eyes, the voice screaming this was Megan's fault out of her head.

"Tell me about the woman." Cole peeled up his shirt, and Megan's blood drained to her feet at the sight of the bloody slice.

She swallowed hard and forced herself forward on wobbly legs, willing herself not to faint like she had when she'd seen the crime scene photos.

"Who was she?" Cole said.

Megan shook her head and tried not to think about the

blood—Cole's blood—staining the towel a dark crimson. Her words came out in a rush. "I talked to her last night at the club. I didn't say anything before, but when I first went to the Web site where Bianca's picture was posted, there was a flash of pictures on the screen. I'm pretty sure she was one of them. When I talked to her, she said she didn't know anything about Bianca, but she slipped a card into my purse telling me to meet her here. She didn't tell me her name, but if I had to guess, I'd bet she's Bianca's roommate, Stephanie."

"Stephanie—no last name, no past, no future." Cole sighed. "What the hell were you thinking, coming here by yourself? Did it occur to you for one second that you could have been walking into a trap?"

Her hands started to shake so hard she could barely hold the towel to the wound at Cole's side. "Of course it did," she said, blinking back tears. "I'm not an idiot. But she said come alone, and I didn't want to risk spooking her."

Cole winced at the pressure of her hand, and she whispered an apology. Blood stained the white cloth, and she closed her eyes against the stain as guilt welled inside her.

"I'm sorry," she said again. "I didn't want to drag you into this."

"I told you I would help you," Cole snapped. "You should have called me. We would have figured out a way for you to have the meeting without putting yourself in danger."

"Oh, right. I'm sure you would have gone along with me and not called Tasso at the first opportunity."

Her glare faded under the force of Cole's dark, steady stare. "I told you I would help you, and I meant it."

Megan felt a series of hairline fractures snake through the barrier she was so desperately maintaining between them. She was terrified to open herself up to him again, only to have him turn his back on her once more.

And yet, he'd already risked his career for her. And today he'd risked his life. Her stomach rolled as she felt the damp warmth of his blood soaking the towel. "There's so much blood," she whispered.

He put his hand over hers, hissing as he pressed it tighter against his side. "Trust me, I've had worse than this. Clean slice, no penetration."

"I'm sorry you got hurt," she said. Cole shook his head and pulled her to him. It seemed like the most natural thing in the world to rest her cheek in the crook of his neck.

"I'm just really fucking glad I got here when I did," he said in a shaky whisper.

Megan swallowed hard, wincing at the pain in her throat. "Me too."

Sirens sounded in the distance. Megan lifted her head from Cole's shoulder. Her gaze involuntarily went to the crumpled form on the floor, and it all hit her again with the force of truck.

It came back in a rush, details snapping into sharp focus. "He knows me," Megan said, panic inching her voice up another octave. "He knows me. He said my name when he was choking me. He said my name."

Chapter 14

He knows my name.

"Are you sure? It's possible she told him before she was killed."

Cole led her out of the room to wait in the parking lot as the sirens grew louder. She tried to shut out the noise, the buzzing aftermath in her own head, and focus on the man's voice in her ear.

Another spike of fear hit her, and Cole's matter-of-fact tone did nothing to calm her down. "He told me he didn't want to hurt me," she said, her voice rising in concert with her racing heartbeat. "Who says that while he's choking you? What kind of sick—"

Cole put a firm hand on her shoulder. "Calm down. Focus, and try to remember every detail of what happened, no matter how small."

She shut her eyes, but all she could see was a ski mask, a big, powerfully muscled body, the glint of a knife.

Focus.

"I ripped his shirt," she said, wiggling her fingers as she remembered. "Maybe there will be fibers."

"Be sure to tell the officers that when they arrive, along with everything else you know." He put his hand on her shoulder and gave her a meaningful look. *"Everything."*

The next two hours passed in a blur as Megan and Cole were loaded into an ambulance and taken to the ER for treatment. Megan was relieved that Cole's wound was considered minor, even if it was six inches long and needed twenty-five stitches.

They each gave their statements to the police, and this time Megan followed his advice, even to the point of sharing her theory that Stephanie's and Bianca's murders could somehow be connected to her brother's case. She ignored the look the cop shot at the nurse checking her oxygen levels, the one that said "crackpot."

Her brother was set to die in five days. Today she'd nearly died herself. It wasn't like she had much to lose.

After he gave his statement, Cole planted himself on her gurney. Relief washed through her at the sight of him and she inched closer.

"How's your neck?" he said, brushing her hair aside to get a better look at the bruising.

She didn't have a chance to reply before Agent Tasso burst through the exam room doors, trailed by a grim-faced Detective Petersen.

"I should have kept you locked up after your little stunt the other night," Tasso snapped. Megan felt herself shrink under his glare and reflexively shifted closer to Cole. "As it is, I can nail you for interfering in an investigation."

"Hey," Cole snapped, "why don't you lay off her?"

Tasso turned his glare on Cole. "I suggest you shut up, Williams. You're on thin ice as it is."

Megan spoke before Cole could open his mouth and

get himself into more trouble. "I didn't interfere with anything! I just wanted to ask some questions."

"I told you to stay away from my investigation. It was part of the deal your boyfriend and that shark of his cooked up to drop the charges."

"He's not my boyfriend," Megan said quickly, cursing herself for caring what Cole thought. Stupid, especially under the circumstances, but it was suddenly vitally important to her that Cole know that Nate was not her boyfriend. "I'm just trying to find out information about my brother's case."

"Which seems to have somehow led you directly into my case."

Maybe it was the trauma of the day or the aftermath of the terror-induced adrenaline rush, but she couldn't keep her mouth shut. "Not my fault I seem to be able to find information before you guys."

"She's got a point," Cole said.

A vein bulged in Tasso's forehead, and he pressed his lips into a tight line. "Petersen, follow up with Ms. Flynn. Williams, come with me."

She felt Cole stiffen beside her, his resentment at being ordered around coming off him in waves.

"I'll be fine," she said softly.

He got up from the gurney. "Don't even think about leaving without me."

The warmth curling in her belly at Cole's protective attitude fled as she turned to meet Petersen's frosty glare.

"Why do you have to mess with him?" she said as she flipped open her notebook.

"I'm not," Megan said, not even trying to pretend she didn't understand.

"You dragged him into this, and if it goes any further, he's going to lose his badge."

Megan held up her hands in defense. "I didn't want to cause any trouble for him."

"Bullshit. You were in his office the day after the murder. Next thing I know he's pulling case files for the other Slasher victims, and you're breaking into the latest victim's house before her name's gone public."

Guilt twisted in her stomach. "I'm just trying to help my brother," she said.

"And ruining another man who cares about you in the process. He could have been killed today. Do you even care?"

The knife in her gut twisted deeper. "Of course I care! I didn't know Cole was going to follow me, and I never wanted to see him get hurt—"

"Well he did, and now he's getting his ass reamed because of it. He'll be lucky to have a badge at the end of this. Or maybe that's your angle. You're pissed at Cole because he arrested your brother, and now you get to have your revenge by ruining his career?"

"No!" Did Cole think that? The idea twisted her stomach into a knot, her guilt compounded by the fact that it wasn't like the thought hadn't occurred to her.

After she'd leaked information about their relationship to the press and Cole had been forced to recuse himself from Sean's case, Cole had told reporters who questioned his objectivity, "My job is the most important thing to me. I would never let a casual romantic relationship interfere with my work as a detective."

When she'd read that quote, Megan felt like her chest had been cut open. She'd be lying if she said she hadn't entertained fantasies of ruining the career that meant so much more to him than she did. But she wasn't vindictive enough to carry them out.

Now she might really cost him his job without even trying. "I never meant for Cole to get in trouble. I didn't think he'd get so...involved."

In fact, he'd surprised her at every turn. She'd never really expected him to pull the case files when she asked, not when he'd so easily turned his back on her before. But he had. And now he was tailing her. Not to mess with her investigation, but to keep her safe.

For three years she'd lived with the hurt, convinced herself Cole had abandoned her when she needed him. Now she had to consider the idea that maybe there was more going on with him than she'd known. And if nothing else, he was getting a damn good start on making it up to her.

Detective Petersen's derisive sniff pulled Megan out of her musings over her feelings for Cole, which were getting more complicated by the hour. "It says here you didn't get any information from this woman, who you presume is Bianca's roommate, Stephanie?"

Megan gave Petersen a brief recap of their meeting in the bathroom of Club One. "She said she didn't know Bianca, but I got the sense she was lying. I also saw her a few minutes later in the VIP room. It was weird—she led some guy through the back of the VIP room, down a hall to another area that's protected by a security system."

Petersen's blue eyes flickered with interest as she wrote something down. "But you didn't see her or anyone else slip the card into your purse?"

"No."

"What can you tell me about your attacker? You said he knows you?"

Cold sweat bloomed on Megan's skin, and her heart started thudding at the memory of rough hands grabbing her, hard fingers squeezing her throat. "He called me by name. But I didn't see his face. He was wearing a ski mask."

"Try to remember everything you can. How tall he was, the sound of his voice."

Megan shook her head, her brain muddled as it tried to put all the pieces together, but it was like her mind wanted to block it all out. She closed her eyes, forced herself to put herself back in that room, feel him jerking her back against his body. "He was big. Muscular and tall." She made herself block out the terror to focus on how tall he was compared to her. "His chin was on top of my head. He was wearing a long-sleeve shirt, like a dress shirt. Black. I tore one of the sleeves." Her fingers shook as she remembered struggling, clawing at his arm to pull it away, the harsh rending sound of the cloth.

"That's when Cole came in," Megan continued. "They struggled and I saw the knife." Her voice hitched at the memory of seeing the gleaming steel arc toward Cole's body. "I thought he was going to kill Cole, but Cole jumped out of the way." Still, she'd never forget that split second as the killer's knife plunged for Cole, his gloved hand clenched around the hilt, the muscles of his forearm tense as he went in for the kill....

His arm.

"He had a tattoo," Megan blurted out. "I saw part of it, on his right biceps. Dark ink. I couldn't see the design."

She jerked back as the truth thudded home, so obvious even her thick brain could comprehend it. "It was Jack Brooks," she said, feeling like an idiot that it had taken her this long to connect the dots. "The security guy at Club One," she clarified at Petersen's quizzical look.

Megan gave Petersen a rundown of her brief acquaintance with the shadowy former Special Forces guy, emphasizing his repeated warnings for her to steer clear of the club. "He could easily be the Slasher. He works at the club—he had access to the victims. Find out where he was the night Evangeline Gordon died. You never know—"

Petersen cut her off. "How about you let us handle the investigation for a change? I'm sure we'll make a lot more progress without you stumbling around getting potential witnesses killed."

Guilt slammed her as she thought of Stephanie's body splayed like a broken doll on the floor. If Megan hadn't been snooping around . . . She looked up as the door to the exam room was pushed open. Cole stood in the doorway, his face pulled into grim lines. "You about done in here?"

Petersen nodded and flipped her notebook closed. "We'll follow up with Brooks," she assured Megan. "And we'll let you know if we need any more information. I'll call a squad car to take you home."

"I've got her," Cole said, his tone brooking no argument.

That didn't stop Petersen from trying. "You sure you want to do that, Cole?" she said, straightening to her full height and squaring off against him. "She's caused you nothing but trouble," Petersen said as though Megan wasn't sitting two feet away. "If you give a shit about your job, you need to stay the hell away—"

"Whoever did this knows her," Cole bit out. "And unless you can guarantee her twenty-four hour protection until he's caught, she'll be with me."

Megan felt herself shrink under Cole's stare, feeling vulnerable and all but naked in the flimsy hospital gown. "You don't have to give me a ride home, Cole. I've caused you enough problems. If you just give me a minute to get dressed, I can go home with another officer."

"I'll give you five minutes," Cole said, and walked out.

——————

Megan slid reluctantly into the passenger seat of his Jeep, which one of the patrol officers had been nice enough to drive to the hospital.

She could feel the tension emanating from him. Cole was closed up in that silent, self-contained way he had that didn't invite conversation. But she had to try. "What happened with Tasso?"

"I don't really feel like talking about it."

Though his tone wasn't harsh, Megan felt the sting of his brush-off. Leaving him to his brooding, she curled up against the passenger door. She tried to tell herself that she was only doing what was necessary. She wanted to save Sean; she didn't have any time for guilt. But today she'd seen up close the kind of collateral damage she was causing. And for the first time in three years, she wasn't in this alone. Now Cole was getting hurt too.

A month ago she might have been spiteful and told herself losing his badge was nothing less than what Cole deserved. But after the last week . . . nothing was so black-

and-white any more. "I'm sorry I dragged you into all of this."

Cole held up a silencing hand. "You didn't drag me into anything. I made my bed when I decided to give you confidential information."

"And I want you to know how much I appreciate that," Megan said. "I know I haven't exactly been generous with my gratitude—"

"Can we just drop it for now?" Cole said wearily. "I don't really feel like dwelling on the fact that I'm pissing away a fifteen-year career."

Megan slumped in her seat as they turned down her block. He parked in front of her driveway and led the way up the stairs to her flat. When she went to unlock the door, he took the key from her hand. He opened the door slowly, and Megan jumped back when a gun seemed to appear out of thin air into his hand.

"What are you doing?" she whispered.

He raised a finger to his lips and hit her with a glare. "He knows you. He most likely knows where you live. I'm not taking any chances." He motioned for her to wait while he did a sweep of the apartment, then beckoned her inside.

"Um, okay, I guess that means you can go now." Megan wrapped her arms around herself and forced back a shudder. Despite the tension between them, she didn't exactly relish spending a night alone.

"Are you kidding me?" Cole looked at her like she'd just lost about forty IQ points. "You're not staying here." He moved down the hall to her room. Without asking, he rummaged through her closet until he found a small duffel bag. He tossed it on the bed. "Pack enough to hold you for at least a few days. You're coming home with me."

—⁓—

They drove to his house in silence so thick it was like a physical presence between them in the car. She'd tried to convince him to take her to a hotel, reminding him how it would look to Lieutenant Chin and the rest of the review board if they knew she spent the night at his house, but he completely bulldozed over her protests. Short of making a break for it and trying to elude him, Megan didn't see that she had much choice.

And really, after what had happened, she knew she wouldn't feel safe alone, even in a hotel with the dead bolt thrown. Knowing Cole stood between her and the psycho who had tried to kill her made her feel secure in a way that she hadn't in a very long time. She warned herself to be careful with Cole—she'd made the mistake of reading too much into his actions before and got burned for it.

But tonight, she wanted to lean into him and let him chase all her demons away.

Cole turned down his street in his development and drove past a row of nearly identical houses. He pulled into his garage, grabbed her bag, and walked into the house without a word. She followed and watched as he tossed her bag onto the couch. His place hadn't changed at all in the nearly three years since she'd seen it. The same plain coffee table and leather sofa. He'd upsized his flat-screen TV, but there was still no art on the plain, off-white walls.

The place was devoid of personality, without so much as a book or stray DVD to hint at the interests of the man who lived here. On the handful of occasions she'd been over here while they were dating, she'd entertained stupid fantasies of how she might enliven the décor when she moved in with him.

She shoved away the tug of sadness that she'd never had the opportunity. That his house had remained as boring and sterile as it had been the last time she saw it. Like his life had gotten just as stuck as hers.

And there's obviously not any woman coming around to put her feminine touch on things.

Not that she cared, she told herself firmly as she walked into Cole's living room. Still, it was hard to forget what had happened the last time they were alone together.

After the last adrenaline-fueled hours, she was suddenly so drained she could barely keep on her feet. She sank into the leather armchair and felt like she could close her eyes and sleep for the next forty-eight hours.

Cole's voice roused her. "I've set up the spare room as an office, so I don't have a real guest room." He rubbed his hand wearily against the back of his neck. "You take my bed and I'll take the couch."

Her? Sleep in his bed? His stuff, his sheets, his scent all around her. "Absolutely not. You're almost a foot taller than me—you won't even fit on the couch."

"I'm not going to debate it, Megan."

She pushed herself up from the chair. "I don't want to put you out. I can stay at a hotel for a few days—"

"Right, and you'll be out on your own trying to find the guy who attacked us today. You really think I'm going to let you out of my sight?"

She swallowed, wincing at the ache in her throat. "What else do you expect me to do? Sit around and twiddle my thumbs and wait for Sean's execution date? I'm out of options, Cole."

He shook his head. "If you decide to go off half-cocked over another barely there lead, I'm gonna be with you. And you're staying here. No negotiation. And while you're staying here, take the fucking bedroom." He turned his back on her and went into the kitchen, where she could hear him rooting around the refrigerator like a bear in a garbage can.

She followed him, protesting. "You don't have to do this. I'll be fine on my own." After what happened today, she wasn't sure about that at all, but she could feel herself starting to lean on Cole and it was feeling a little too good.

He whirled around on her, so fast she took a startled step back, stopping only when the ridge of the countertop dug into the small of her back.

Streaks of angry color stained his high cheekbones, and his eyes were molten with fury. "Goddamn it! After what happened today, could you just stop fucking arguing with every goddamn thing I say? You almost died today, Megan! And for what? A fucking note on a scrap of paper!"

She swallowed, wincing at the ache in her throat. He was pulled tight, every sinew coiled with tension, like he didn't know whether to kiss her or shake her. She broke her stare, unable to look at him, knowing he was right. Knowing she had put her life and his career at risk for a barely solid lead.

The memory of her attacker's fingers digging into her windpipe sent a shiver of fear down her spine. "I had to take that chance. Don't you understand? Unless Sean changes his mind, he'll be dead in five days. I have to do something, no matter how crazy or far-fetched it seems."

He moved closer, so close she could feel the heat of his thigh muscles against her hips, and planted his palms on the counter on either side of her hips. "You could have died."

Her pulse throbbed in her throat at the feel of his hot breath on her cheek. She dropped her gaze from his face and struggled to get her traitorous body back under control. "I think that would make your life easier, wouldn't it? Get me out of your hair once and for all." Her weak attempt at lightening the mood backfired. Now he was even angrier, his dark eyes practically spitting fire.

"Don't even fucking joke about that!"

Before she had time to react, his mouth was on hers, hungry, desperate as his lips crushed hers. God he felt good, strong and powerful. Heat exploded in her veins, and just like that, she melted into a puddle at the first touch. Helplessly, she parted her lips to drink him in, suck his tongue into her mouth, tangle it with hers.

His kiss immediately gentled, and he pulled away, cradling her face in his hands as he whispered again, "Don't even fucking joke about that." Soft, nipping kisses rained on her mouth and cheeks. "Do you have any idea how it felt to walk in that room and see you . . ." His voice broke, and a shudder rippled through him. "I'm going to have nightmares for the rest of my life, thinking about what would have happened if I hadn't shown up in time."

He kissed her again. "I can't stand the thought of anything happening to you. It kills me that he touched you, that you were hurt. So don't ask me to leave you alone, not when I'd cut my own arm off if it kept you from getting hurt."

Before she could absorb what that implied, Cole leaned

closer, pressing her into the counter. Unable to stop herself, she wrapped her arms around his waist, then jerked away when he let out a hiss of pain.

Megan jerked back to reality. She wasn't the only one who had gotten hurt today. This was so crazy; they were both riding high, their resistance pummeled by adrenaline and fear. She couldn't give in. "This is a really bad idea."

In the past, he would have played the good guy and backed off at the first sign of resistance. Hell, more often than not, he'd been the one to stop them in their tracks. How many times had he pulled away, telling her that he didn't want to move too fast, that he didn't want to push her into anything she wasn't ready for?

Until she was so ready she could barely see straight, only to have reality come crashing down all around her.

But Cole didn't budge. "Actually, I think this is the best idea I've had in a really long time." His big hands cupped her face, holding her still as he took her mouth.

She'd had a taste of this Cole a few days ago. The one who didn't try to fight the lust no matter how they might kick themselves later. Relentless. Determined.

He pulled her hair to the side and sucked her earlobe into his mouth, a touch that sent a jolt of heat to her core. She made a last grasp for sanity. "This is so stupid, after everything." She bit her lip on a moan as his big palm squeezed her breast through her shirt. "You know this can't go anywhere."

"I'm so fucking tired," he muttered as his tongue traced her bruised throat, "of thinking about what happened before and what's going to happen after." He pulled his head up and stared at her as his hands undid the top button of her blouse. Then another.

Daring her to stop him.

God, why does he make me so weak?

"All I know is that I want you, Megan. I've wanted you every day for nearly three years. I buried it, and I could keep you out of my mind most days. But ever since I saw you again, it's like this ache, eating away at me until I can't think of anything but kissing you, touching you." He gave her breast a squeeze that sent sparks singing through every nerve ending. "And being inside you," he said, closing his eyes, his voice so deep and reverent it made her ache with need. "You have no idea how bad I want to be inside you."

Her pulse throbbed between her legs. Oh yeah, she had a pretty good idea. And it was getting more difficult to resist by the second as he whispered hot, dirty things he wanted to do to her, all the ways he'd imagined having her.

So different from how he'd been before. Back when they'd dated, he'd been reserved. Careful not to reveal too much. Cautious of moving too fast. And when everything had gone to hell, he'd been quick to deny that what he'd felt for her was serious.

Now all the barriers were coming down as he told her in no uncertain terms what he wanted and how. "You almost died today." His whisper was almost accusing. "You could have died, and I would never have been able to touch you again." His fingers traced her cheeks; his lips nipped at hers like he couldn't get enough, couldn't stop touching her, tasting her. "Just one night," he pleaded. "Just one night where I don't have to think about anything but how much I want you, how good I'm going to make you feel."

He slid his hand between her legs, cupping her sex through her jeans. "You do want that, don't you, Megan?" As though he couldn't feel the heat and dampness of her sex through the fabric. One finger ran against the seam of her pants, pressing against her clit until it was all she could do to keep her legs from buckling under her.

God, yes. But all she could do was moan into his mouth as his finger circled her, teasing her through the suddenly constrictive fabric of her jeans.

This is so wrong. She tried desperately to remind herself of all the reasons why nothing good could come of giving in.

Her protests evaporated like mist as he popped the button on her jeans and buzzed her zipper down. His hand slid into the waistband of her panties. Thick, callused fingers pressed against her, the firm pressure of his fingertips against her clit almost enough to make her come right then and there.

His breath hitched in his chest as he delved farther, until his fingertip teased her opening. "God, you're so wet. Jesus, you do want me."

If his tone had been at all smug, she would have shoved him away. Kneed him in the balls and locked herself in his bedroom all night. He sounded... wondrous... like he was the luckiest man in the world to have her want him.

His euphoria was infectious. *Just one night,* a reckless, needful voice urged her. After everything she'd been through, everything she'd sacrificed, didn't she deserve this? One night of pleasure with the man who had haunted her dreams for the past three years? One night to finally know, after years of wondering, wanting, needing, how it would feel to be taken by this man who wanted her so much.

And who you want right back. She rocked her hips against his hand and shoved his shirt up his waist. He released her mouth as she yanked his shirt over his head, and she moaned a protest when he pulled his hand from her panties. Their fingers tangled as they both rushed to remove their own and each other's clothing. The kitchen echoed with the sounds of panting breath, wet kisses, and pleasured moans.

Within seconds they were naked, the hot press of Cole's skin against hers driving her crazy. The rough dusting of hair on his chest teased her nipples to painful hardness. Every nerve ending was on high alert, buzzing with arousal so acute it bordered on pain. Her hands and mouth were everywhere, reveling in every patch of hot, smooth skin, the salty taste of him on her tongue, his woods-and-musk scent wrapping around her.

His cock pressed against her belly, thick as a club and just as hard. She wrapped her hand around it, her mouth going a little dry as she measured his substantial length. Smiling against his mouth, she swallowed his shuddering groan.

She stroked him harder, loving the way he felt in her hand. Hot, velvety soft skin over marble hardness. Thick and pulsing with life. As she watched, mesmerized, a thick bead of precome welled to the surface. An answering rush of moisture pulsed between her legs.

"I want you so much. I don't think I can go slow," Cole said, and she could feel the tremor in his hands as he lifted her onto the countertop and stepped between her legs. He was shaking like a racehorse, his every muscle standing out in sharp relief as his body went taut with rapidly dwindling restraint.

Megan leaned back, bracing herself with one hand, the other still stroking his cock. "It's okay," she panted, so turned on she could barely see straight. "I don't need slow. I need you."

He groaned, hooked her leg over his hip and wrapped his hand around hers. She licked her lips in anticipation as he rubbed the thick head against her, parting her lips, circling her clit as he bathed himself in her juice. It was the most erotic thing she'd ever seen, both their hands circled around his cock, guiding him up, down, around her slippery flesh until they were both shaking with need.

But it was nothing compared to how he felt, squeezing inside, the broad head of his cock stretching her until she danced on the edge of pleasure and pain. His hips rocked forward, sinking him halfway, and he paused at her sharp gasp.

"I'm sorry, baby. You're just so tight, and you feel so good." He squeezed his eyes shut, his face a mask of agonized pleasure. But he held himself there, perfectly still as he waited for her to adjust around him.

"It's okay," she whispered.

He bent his head and closed his mouth over her nipple, the hot suction making her jerk against him, taking him a little deeper. He didn't move his hips as his lips, tongue, and teeth teased her agonizingly sensitive nipples, sucking, licking, biting, until she couldn't stand it anymore.

She rocked her hips, moaning his name as every thrust took him a little deeper.

"That's it, Megan," he breathed. "Show me how you want it. Show me what you need."

Her inner muscles tightened around him, greedy for him as she rocked harder. Finally, finally, he was buried to the hilt, filling her up, deeper than anyone had ever been before.

He pulled almost all the way out and squeezed slowly back in, one heart-stopping inch at a time. He pulled his mouth from her breasts and pressed his forehead against hers, his eyes cast down, his face tight with concentration as he watched his cock sink into her. Over and over, so slow and so deep, until she felt like she was going to burst out of her skin.

She needed *more*. She threaded the fingers of one hand through his hair and tugged his mouth back up to hers. She sucked his tongue into her mouth and slid her other hand down to grip the hard muscle of his butt, urging him harder, faster.

She leaned back on the counter, bracing herself against his thrusts as she wrapped her legs tighter around him. The lust coiled inside her like a spring, tighter and tighter until she was moaning and shaking with the need for release. "Oh God, Cole," she moaned, needing something, needing *him*. His thick cock sank into her, his hands roughly gripping her hips as he held her still to take him and take him and take him.

He stared down at her, his face tight with need as he slid his hand between them and pressed his thumb against her clit. Tight circles, firm brushes up and down in time with the heavy thrust and drag of his cock.

Sharp sounds she didn't even recognize as hers erupted from her throat as he drove her higher. Then she was shaking, shuddering, coming around him, so hard she could feel her inner muscles squeezing and releasing him. The ripples of her orgasm radiated out from her core in waves, sizzling through her limbs and making even the soles of her feet tingle.

Cole wasn't far behind. A bead of sweat trickled down his cheek as he threw his head back. An agonized groan tore from his chest, and then he was holding himself deep, jerking and spurting inside her.

—⁂—

Cole's heart hadn't stopped thundering against his ribs, his breath barely slowed, before he felt her stiffen against him. The last ripples of her orgasm had barely faded and already the gears of her brain were churning so hard he could practically hear them as regret tried to worm its way in and ruin the afterglow.

Not if he could help it. He looked down at her troubled green eyes staring at him, her cheeks flushed, her mouth swollen and red from his kisses, her hair a wild tangle spilling over her shoulders. She looked exactly like what she was, a blazingly hot woman who had just been fucked within an inch of her life. No way was he going to let her slide into a spiral of self-recrimination. Not until he really gave her something to feel guilty about.

"Cole," she warned as he leaned down to kiss her. She tried to turn her face aside at the last second, but his hand on her jaw held her in place.

She was still at first, her lips closed as he probed at them with his tongue. "Don't," he whispered, his tongue tracing the seam of her lips. "Don't pull away from me. Stay here with me." He kissed her again, and this time she softened, her lips parting to let him in. He swept his tongue inside, savoring her heat, her taste. "Be with me tonight."

She surrendered with a sigh and gave herself over to his kiss. His cock surged inside her as he felt her melt against him, her arms wrapping around his back, her legs looping around his hips. She gave a little squeal when he cupped his hands over her ass and lifted her off the counter. "What are you doing?" she gasped.

"Taking you to my bed," he replied, unable to keep the satisfaction from his voice. *His bed.* If life had worked out in his favor, he would have taken her there three goddamn years ago and she never would have left. The thought squeezed his heart like a fist, and he shoved it away. No use whining over the way life should have turned out. He had her tonight, and he was going to make the goddamn most of it.

He took a few steps and her breath hitched as she squirmed against him.

"Oh my God," she breathed, her legs and arms tightening around him. "You're still..." She squirmed again.

"Hard," he said, unable to suppress a grin as he rocked his hips against her for emphasis. "I've waited a long time, thinking about how good it would be to fuck you."

She let out a little moan and clenched around him so tight his knees nearly buckled. He barely made it to the bedroom, his cock hardening with every step, and Megan's answering moans and squirms tempting him to sink to the floor and take her again right there.

Fuck, he was thirty-six years old, well past the time that he could stay hard and go two rounds back-to-back. But by the time he'd made it the fifteen steps to the bedroom and laid her down on the bed, he was primed and ready and afraid he was going to come in about ten seconds if he wasn't careful.

He came down over her and ordered himself to take it slow. *Easier said than done.* Especially when she felt so unbelievably good. Soft and slick from her orgasm and his come, but still so tight around him it was like being squeezed in a wet fist. He wanted to explore, touch and taste and take in every detail of her, but he couldn't make himself leave the hot clasp of her body.

He'd spent hours, days, years fantasizing about being with Megan, how it would feel to have her naked, under him, her body stretching around him as he went as deep as he could possibly go. No fantasy could do this justice, he thought as he buried his mouth against her neck and sucked a dewy patch of skin. Even the smell of her drove him crazy, flowery shampoo mixed with the tang of sweat and the sultry musk of sex.

She moaned and shifted underneath him, wrapping her arms and legs around him to hold him close. He propped himself up on his elbows and lifted his head to look at her. He held himself still, buried in her body, wrapped in her embrace.

He cupped her face in his hands, stroking the curve of her cheekbone with his thumb, feeling like his heart had lodged somewhere up around his throat.

This was all they could ever have, all they could ever be. The thought made something primitive inside of him take hold, an unfamiliar, territorial need to mark her, brand her so that no matter what happened, she would never forget what it was to be with him.

He bent and took her mouth like a starving man, drinking in her taste, reveling in the way her lips sucked greedily at his tongue. He rocked deeper, twisting his hips so she could feel him from every possible angle. He hooked her knee over his elbow and shifted his angle, knowing he had it right when she gave a little gasp and her muscles rippled around him. He stayed that way, buried to the hilt inside her, twisting his hips to rub her in all the right places inside and out.

Soon she was chanting his name and rolling her hips, her hands sliding up and down the sweat-slicked skin of his back. She was close, so close, whispering "please" with every stroke.

He could feel his own orgasm building, his balls pulling tight against his body, his thigh muscles clenching as the tingling started at the base of his spine.

One last roll and grind, and she came hard, stiffening in his arms as every muscle in her body clenched and released around him. He rode her through it, fighting for control as every pulse, every ripple of her tight heat around his cock threatened to hurl him over the edge.

He clenched his jaw to hold back his release until the last wave had receded. Only then did he give in, letting loose with a harsh groan as he shot inside her. Weak, spent, he collapsed, rolling to his side at the last minute to avoid crushing her with his weight.

He gathered her to him and struggled to catch his breath. He closed his eyes and savored the feel of her next to him.

Jesus, who knew sex could make you feel like your whole world had been blown off its axis? He'd never put too much emotional weight into sex, viewing it as a fun way to pass the time with a consenting partner. But work kept him too busy to ever get serious with anyone, and after too many failures, he'd learned to keep it light.

Then Megan came along, and he'd immediately realized he needed to be careful. That whether he liked it or not, sex with Megan would have serious emotional consequences. Idiot that he was, he'd convinced himself they'd all be on her part. He was the badass who would be able to fuck her and walk away, and by not sleeping with her, he was protecting her from his own inability to maintain a functional relationship.

Now, lying beside her, feeling her heartbeat slow against his, he realized how foolish he'd been, thinking she was the only one who would get the raw end of the deal.

Emotionally overwhelmed, Megan had given in to temptation tonight, but no matter what happened, she'd never allow herself to be with him. A hot ache settled in his chest, creeping its way up his throat until it threatened to choke him.

He tried to shove it away. He was a grown-up, and he'd accepted a long time ago that what he had with Megan was over. One night of hot sex was no excuse to get all bent out of shape. But as he stared into the darkness, he couldn't shake the feeling that it was going to wreck him when he had to let her go.

Chapter 15

The rain sounded like bullets on his windshield as he waited in the parking lot.

He clenched and released his jaw, trying to evaporate some of the tension knotting the muscles of his shoulders. The neurons were still firing over what had happened in the hotel room, but now he had to focus or he would make a mistake. The remaining moves were so critical, so delicate, he needed every bit of concentration.

He blew out a breath, counted the too-loud raindrops spattering on the windshield. *One, two, three.*

He clenched and unclenched his hands, cursing his stepcousin Carl for running late.

He had better fucking places to be.

Megan. His soul cried out to be with her. He wouldn't talk to her, not tonight, but he wanted—needed—to see her, to make sure she was okay after what happened.

A fist gripped at his chest as he remembered Megan's throat under his fingers, the sound of her choking on her own fear. He'd hated to hurt her, but he'd also been elated.

He'd passed the test. He'd meant to only give her a warning, but part of him had feared that he wouldn't be able to stop himself. That once he held her life in his hands, felt her fear, the demon would tear free and take the decision from his hands.

He'd felt none of the usual urges, even after killing the whore in such an unsatisfying way.

He finally had his proof that she was different and that he could be different. He'd been wrong to avoid her all this time, to believe what they said about him.

He finally knew, to the depths of his soul, that with Megan it wouldn't be a matter of passing for normal.

With Megan, he could be normal. She alone could put the demon to rest once and for all, give him a second chance at the life he would have had if Sarah hadn't died.

He pulled himself from his daydream as headlights flashed in the distance. Carl's black Mercedes pulled into the parking lot and slid between two semi cabs. He got out of his car and turned his collar up against the rain, forcing his face into a pleasant expression as he jogged across the parking lot to meet his stepcousin.

He heard the car door slam and saw Carl's broad shoulders silhouetted against the hazy yellow parking lot lights. Though he couldn't see Carl's face, he knew his stepcousin would be wearing a faint sneer, his lip curled ever so slightly as the scar that bisected his cheek pulled at the corner of his mouth. But he knew the scar wasn't the only reason Carl looked at him like he'd caught a whiff of shit. It was no secret that Carl didn't like him; if his stepcousin had had his way, his uncle would have written him off years ago, left him to his own devices and the mercy of the justice system when his overwhelming needs finally got the best of him.

Which was why he loved greeting Carl with a bland

smile, like he was clueless to the other man's feelings, too socially fucked up to notice the animosity radiating from the other man in waves.

"The shipment is running late," he said to Carl with a smile, "but they should be here soon. It will be interesting to see what Roman sent us."

"If it's anything other than grade A, we're sending it back," Carl said.

A dark sedan pulled up behind Carl's sedan and parked. Two men got out. Though he couldn't make out their faces, their size and the outlines of their AK-47s held loosely at their sides marked them as heavies from his uncle's security detail.

Another man emerged from the car, and a tremor of surprise shook him when he recognized his uncle's thick head of salt-and-pepper hair as he came to stand next to Carl. At fifty-three, David Maxwell was still as strong as a bull, his muscular build similar to that of his nephew. Though his face was lined, it still had the same brutish handsomeness that had helped him charm his way into Margaret Grayson's bed and secure his position in one of Seattle's wealthiest and most influential families.

"David." It was always just David, as he was careful to never publicly acknowledge their relationship. As far as he knew, other than David himself, only David's wife, Margaret, and Margaret's son Carl were the only ones who knew about their relationship. Seeing to his nephew's care after the violent death of his sister was one of the few noble things David Maxwell had done in his life. "I'm surprised to see you here."

Tonight it looked like David was regretting that long-ago act of familial charity. Even if his grim expression didn't broadcast his mood, the fact that David was here at all couldn't mean anything good. David liked to keep himself as far away from the deliveries as possible, as though his lack of presence somehow kept his hands clean.

"You fucked up today, big-time," David said bluntly, his footfalls crunching on the ground as he approached. One of the heavies walked discreetly beside him, holding an umbrella to keep the rain off David's two-thousand-dollar overcoat. "You were not sanctioned to kill the girl."

He willed his fingers to relax. "She was going to talk. It was necessary."

"Then you wait for the call and you do it discreetly. All this showboating, all this going off half-cocked on your own—it's creating attention we don't need."

Exactly. And very soon they'd realize that despite what they thought, they'd never been in control of him.

"You injured Megan Flynn and stabbed a fucking cop, for Christ's sake. And not just any cop—the cop who arrested Flynn!"

His mouth tightened at the reminder. He hadn't expected Cole to come bursting in like Megan's personal guard dog, and kicked himself for not seeing it coming. But he hadn't foreseen Detective Williams jeopardizing his career to sniff around Megan like a dog in heat. That Williams still wanted to fuck her was obvious, but risk his badge over it? Didn't match what he'd said after Sean's arrest about not letting his "casual" relationship with Megan interfere with his police work.

Even if it meant arresting Megan's brother and wringing a confession out of him.

Williams had unintentionally helped him that night.

For that reason, he hadn't driven his knife into his belly in the hotel room.

"After today, you're done," David continued. Disappointment deepened the lines bracketing his mouth. "We're shutting down the operation at Club One, and you're leaving for Amsterdam tomorrow. No more going out on your own, no more Slasher. You had your fun. Now it's back to basics."

He faked a meek nod. He'd listened to them once. Tucked his tail between his legs and fled, let them pack him up and ship him away, away from *her*. They'd tried to convince him he was a monster, not fit for human relationships, a barely tame beast who should be thankful they let him fulfill his darkest needs.

At the time he'd believed it. And though he'd known he'd had nothing to fear from the police—he'd done such a masterful job of giving them Sean Flynn on a platter that the police had never bothered to so much as look at another suspect—he'd let them convince him that he couldn't have Sarah.

No, not Sarah. Megan.

Sarah was dead, but he could still have Megan.

Did his uncle really think he could stop him? He clamped down the urge to let the beast free. To show his uncle, show them all, he wasn't some meek lapdog who took orders and licked their boots out of gratitude for the "protection" they provided.

Other than a little help he'd needed cleaning up after Evangeline Gordon, he'd never needed their help. He worked clean. He'd never be caught unless he wanted it that way. They didn't know it, but he was calling the shots.

They wanted him out of town? They'd get it. He had new identities set up for him and Megan, passports to go along with them, and over ten million in a numbered Swiss account. Enough to keep Megan like a queen. Just a few more days until Sean Flynn was executed, and then he and Megan would disappear forever.

Headlights approached from the opposite end of the parking lot, and the low rumble of the diesel engine cut through the steady patter of freezing rain. A shipment from down south, courtesy of the Russian gangsters David had recently partnered with. David's idea, to bring girls from out of the area into the operation.

He didn't like anything about it. Not working with the Russians, not importing from who-knew-where, not using girls who were lured by promises of well-paying jobs or outright kidnapped. All it took, he told his uncle, was for one underage illegal to get busted by the cops for the whole house of cards to come crashing down.

Now, the girls they used, girls like Evangeline, girls like Bianca, they were smart enough to fly under the radar. Unlike the poor souls so desperate for a better life they were willing to leave their homes on a promise of a job as a chambermaid, the girls who worked the clubs knew the score. They knew exactly what they were getting into and what they wanted out of it.

David hadn't listened, insisting that the practice of using the current stable of girls to get new recruits was too limiting, not to mention dangerous. These girls got the mistaken idea that because they'd gone in to it willingly, they could leave the business whenever they chose, and it was becoming a problem. Look how many they'd had to kill in the past six months.

The truck parked, and the driver and his partner went to the back of the vehicle.

"You're going to have to take them back," Carl said. "We're shutting down the operation."

The driver ignored him and opened the rear cargo area.

There was a shuffling sound, and his stomach tightened as he heard the muffled whimpers.

"No, we don't want the girls. You need to take them back."

He tried not to look at the girls, but he couldn't help it. He bit back a swear. Even if David wasn't demanding that he shut down the Club One operation, these girls would never do. There were five in total, and the oldest couldn't have been more than seventeen. Disheveled, dirty, and scared to death, they shivered as the cold winter rain soaked the flimsy dresses that were supposed to be sexy. Instead the thin fabric showed off one's flat chest, another's too-plump thighs, and another's shoulder blades that were so sharp they threatened to rend the material.

The driver and his companion looked at them expectantly, and the driver held out his hand, indicating they should pay him the money he was expected to collect.

David shook his head. "No, I'm not paying you. Take the girls back."

The driver and his companion looked dumbly at David, then at each other.

"Tell them," David said to him.

He'd picked up some Russian in the military. "Take them back," he said, making a shooing motion with his hands. "We don't want them anymore."

The driver shook his hand and started arguing vehemently. "I bring girls—you give money."

The girls stood in a frozen, huddled knot, shaking and crying. "Get back in the truck," he told them. A spasm of guilt squeezed his chest. He wasn't doing them any favors sending them back with the driver. They would end up somewhere, with another buyer who would work them for weeks, months straight until their bodies gave out.

But at least he wouldn't have to look at them. He wouldn't have to look at those accusing eyes as they were subjected to a fate none of them deserved.

The driver and his friend began yelling in Russian, and one reached inside his jacket. Shots rang out as David's security detail took them out in two shots.

The girls' screams died as the security goons swung the guns in their direction.

"What the fuck was Roman thinking?" David circled the girls, scanning them up and down like he was searching for redeeming features. He shook his head. "They're not even worth trying to move ourselves."

"But the loss—" Carl broke in.

"We'll eat it," David said. "And then we'll let Roman know what happens when he misrepresents his merchandise." He paused then. "You."

Tension snapped down his spine as his uncle pinned him with a cold stare.

"Take care of them."

He shook his head. His hands started to shake.

"What's the problem?" Carl sneered. "This should take the edge off for at least a couple of weeks."

He swallowed hard, tried to control the tremors coursing through him as he struggled to keep the beast caged as it foamed at the mouth, urging him to wrap his hands around Carl's throat and squeeze until his eyes popped from their sockets. They didn't understand how it worked. Girls like Evangeline, Bianca, Stephanie had chosen their fates, chosen to let men use their bodies because they were too lazy or too stupid to do something worthwhile.

All whores, just like his mother. He had no trouble unleashing the demon on them.

But these girls, they were innocents, staring at him with their big, wide eyes, pleading for help. "They haven't done anything wrong. They don't deserve any of this."

His uncle stared at him as if he'd grown a horn from the center of his forehead. "After all I've done to help you, now you're going to try to take the moral high ground? You have a job—now do it!"

"No."

Even in the dim light of the parking lot, he could see the vein pulse in his uncle's forehead, the frustration he couldn't contain making the muscles in his jaw pulse. "How can you expect me to protect you when you won't fucking listen?" he asked, his tone that of a parent struggling to keep it together while dealing with an obstinate child. David pinned him with a look full of disgust and disappointment and held out his hand. "Gun."

His thugs exchanged a look, but the AK was handed over without protest. A metallic click pierced the rain, and David took aim.

Bam. The first girl went down, followed by the other four in quick succession.

He swallowed hard and kept his gaze locked on his uncle so he wouldn't have to look at their wide death stares.

"I gave you a place, protection, and even a means to deal with your need to do things no sane man can wrap his head around," David said in a low whisper. "In exchange, you do what I tell you to do, when I tell you to do it. Got it?"

He nodded mutely, swallowing against the acid burning his throat.

"Now get this cleaned up."

The cars disappeared into the rain. As he dragged the limp forms back into the truck, he fought away the memories of Sarah—another girl, another innocent he couldn't save. But he still had Megan. He closed his eyes, called up her image and clung to it.

He moved his mind away from the grisly scene in front of him. Soon all of this would be over, and he would be with his Megan. He would be saved.

—⁂—

Megan sat on Cole's couch, sipping coffee and checking her voice mail as if it were just another February morning, the sun hidden behind bullet-dark clouds as rain smacked against the skylight above her head.

Right, just another Thursday, she thought as she listened to a voice mail from Devany, the second in two days. The meeting with Devany, her mother, her aunt Kathy and the social worker hadn't gone well, and Devany had been inconsolable. And it didn't help that Devany had been put through another round of questioning by the police about Bianca's work at the mission. But Megan had been so distracted she hadn't even called her back.

Okay, *distracted* was a bit of an understatement. She made a mental note to call Devany in a couple hours. The next message was from Nate, who had called yesterday evening when she was still being questioned by Petersen. She hadn't had a chance to check her messages before she'd been otherwise . . . distracted.

As she thought of the man sleeping down the hall— the reason for her distraction—her guilt took on the bitter cast of shame. Nate was so freaking *nice. "Just calling to see how you're doing and let you know I'm here if you want any company."*

Perfectly nice guy out there to lend a comforting shoulder, and she'd spent the better part of the night coming her brains out with a man who two weeks ago she would have sworn up and down she hated with the white-hot intensity of a thousand suns.

Now, as she sat on his couch, her emotions in a hopeless tangle, she knew it wasn't that simple. *It's a thin line between love and hate.* Megan immediately shied away from that thought, not even wanting the L-word to so much as enter her consciousness in relation to Cole.

Yet she couldn't deny the truth, that Cole's appearance in her life had unearthed a whole host of emotions she thought she'd buried, and hatred wasn't even close to the top of the list. She closed her eyes, picturing him as she'd left him. The sheet pulled down to his waist, one muscular leg flung out to the side. His broad, tanned chest dark against the white, rumpled linens. His craggy features were soft with sleep, the dark shadow of beard on his jaw tempting her to trace her finger along the delicious roughness.

It would be so easy to slip between the sheets with him. *He was right here, so close. . . .* The desire to go back down the hall, climb back into bed with him and shut out reality for another precious hour pulled at her until it was like a physical ache.

Her nipples tightened under her sweater, and her thighs squeezed against the knot of desire that pulled tight at just the memory of him inside her.

But their relationship was complicated enough before she'd given in to temptation. Now, thanks to her weakness, things were a whole lot messier.

When they had been together years ago, she'd known sex with Cole would change everything.

How stupid of her not to realize that was still true. After last night, she felt rocked to the core, like she'd been broken apart and put back together with enough cracks in the facade she would never be the same. Left with a need that gnawed at her, a yearning so powerful it threatened to consume her.

But it wasn't just about the sex. Her feelings for Cole would be so much easier to manage if they were all about scratching an itch, finally satisfying her curiosity about what it was like to sleep with him.

What she felt was so much more complicated than that.

Yearning. That's what he made her feel, an emotion so absent from her life for the past three years she'd forgotten what it felt like. The helpless desire for something different, the useless wish that their lives had taken an entirely different direction.

She sank back onto the couch and swallowed back tears as that yearning mingled with the bitterness of guilt. What kind of person was she, sleeping with Cole, wallowing in thoughts of what could have been, while Sean was in prison?

While she was rolling around Cole's king-size mattress, shutting out the rest of the world, Sean was locked in a cell, destined to die in four days if she didn't find some real evidence that someone else was guilty of Evangeline Gordon's murder.

A possibility that was dwindling by the minute as she sat on the couch mooning over Cole. She needed to focus, face reality, and follow every last lead, no matter how tenuous.

Stephanie's death was a morbid indicator that Megan was onto something. Too bad she didn't know what.

She swallowed a sip of coffee, the pain in her throat a stark reminder of her own brush with a violent end. She shivered a little, wondering if the police had picked up Jack yet, or if they even took her suspicions seriously.

She heard a door open and heavy footsteps on the hard-wood floor. She quickly dialed Devany's number, using the phone call as an excuse not to face Cole head-on just yet. The call went to voice mail. "Hey, Dev, it's Megan. Sorry I didn't get back to you yesterday." A pair of large, tanned feet appeared in her view. Megan tried to ignore them but found her gaze drawn involuntarily up. "I know you're angry but..."

She completely lost her train of thought as her eyes were dragged up a pair of strong legs covered in green plaid flannel, past the substantial bulge in his groin, giving way to a symphony of tawny skin sliding over six-pack abs and powerful pecs. Her brain froze as Cole's body called to her, tempting her to lean just a few inches forward and run her tongue along the grooves of his abs, trace the silky line of hair that disappeared beneath the waistband of his pants. She would take him in her mouth, run her tongue around the thick head of his cock, savor the hot, salty taste of his arousal....

"Who are you talking to?" Cole's voice was neutral, but the molten look in his eyes told her he could read her mind as if it were a billboard.

It was enough to jerk her out of her sensual haze. She rose to her feet and brushed past Cole on her way to the kitchen, trying and failing to ignore the sleep-warmed scent of his skin as she passed. She kept her gaze forward as she strove to put as much distance between them as possible. "Anyway," she said into her phone, fumbling to reclaim the thread of her message, "you don't need to worry about the cops. They're going to protect you. As for your mom, it's going to work itself out."

"Good mor—" Cole started, cutting off when Megan raised a silencing hand. "What, no good morning kiss, no thanks for the amazing sex? I feel so used."

Megan's fingers tightened around her phone, not wanting him to see that it was taking all of her restraint not to throw herself into his arms.

He shook his head and followed her into the kitchen. He poured himself a cup of coffee, ignoring her as he gathered bread and eggs for breakfast. Desperate to get some distance between them, Megan retreated to the adjoining family room and curled up on the couch. She shoved aside the pinch of shame at blowing him off as she responded to Nate's message. More guilt there as she tapped out a quick text. *Thanks for ur call. Sorry I've been MIA. Too much going on with Sean and work!*

The text was a cop-out, but she didn't have the energy right now to risk talking to Nate, knowing what he wanted from her when she'd just left Cole's bed.

She closed her eyes, bracing herself to face reality in the form of six-foot-three inches, two hundred twenty or so pounds of half-naked male whose irritation she could sense from across the room.

He'd turned on the radio, and she could hear the clank of utensils against the pan mixed with the voice of the newscaster. She snuck a look at him in the kitchen. She could see the thick slabs of muscle shifting under the skin of his back as he worked at the stove. Her fingers tingled at the remembered feel of smooth, sweat-slicked skin as he moved over her....

She shoved herself up from the couch, afraid if she stayed a second longer she'd spend the next twenty-four hours back in bed with him instead of doing whatever she could to help Sean. "I'm going to take a shower—"

He caught her by the arm before she'd taken two steps. "Have some breakfast first."

"I'm not hungry," she said, and tried to pull her arm from his grasp. At that moment, her stomach rumbled, foiling her attempt to get away.

He gently steered her to the table. "Fighting crime burns calories, and you haven't been taking care of yourself." He guided her to the chair and pushed a plate of eggs and toast dripping with butter in front of her. "Come on, I scrambled them with cheese, just how you like them."

Megan froze with her fork in her hand, afraid she was going to burst into tears. Why was it so easy for him to work past her defenses even when she was telling herself to be careful? To not fall for the lure of depending on him again, for anything, because he'd shown her how easy it was for him to turn his back on her.

But right now all she could think about was that they could have had a thousand mornings like this, sitting across the table from each other, if things hadn't gone so horribly wrong.

"Did you ever wonder what might have happened if—" It was only Cole's stare, freezing her midsentence, that made her realize she'd asked the question out loud.

"If I hadn't arrested Sean?" he finished.

Heat seared her cheeks and she fixed her eyes on her half-eaten eggs. "Never mind—it's a stupid question and this isn't the time."

"No," he said.

Megan's stomach bottomed out and she wanted the floor to open up and swallow her. She closed her eyes, wishing he would disappear instead of sliding his hand across the table to cover hers.

"I never let myself think about it because it hurts too much," he continued in a rough voice. "I knew it was over, and the only way I knew how to deal with it was to shove what I felt for you away and pretend it didn't matter."

Shock washed through her, and she opened her eyes to meet his fierce stare. His fingers curled tighter over hers.

"You're a really good actor, because I genuinely thought you couldn't care less about me."

Cole squeezed his eyes shut as though in pain. "It kills me that I made you feel that way." His phone rang, and he cursed softly under his breath. "It's Petersen. I need to take it."

Megan nodded, still reeling, trying to figure out what it meant. Trying to convince herself that whether or not he had actually cared about her didn't matter. It didn't change how he'd treated her after Sean's arrest.

And it didn't mean he wasn't capable of doing it again.

Yet as she thought of the weight of his hand on hers, the

look of dark regret in his eyes, everything he'd risked for her in the past week, it was becoming harder and harder to hold his past mistakes against him.

"Really? Within the next forty-eight hours? No shit." A pause. "No, I understand you can't. I appreciate you giving me this much."

The snippet of conversation dragged Megan back to reality. There was a murderer to catch. Now wasn't the time to navel gaze and reevaluate her twisted knot of a relationship with Cole.

Another pause and then he chuckled softly. "I can't make any promises, but I'll do my best. Thanks for the update."

"What did she say? Did they find Jack?"

"Brooks's alibi checks out," Cole said as he wandered back into the kitchen.

"Let me guess, he was at the club when it happened, and Talia Vega is the one covering for him." There was something about that woman, a coating of dishonesty that clung to her like a bad smell. Many had cast off Megan's assessment of Talia as the by-product of bitterness against the woman who'd been a key witness for the prosecution in Sean's trial. But Megan knew there was more to it; she had always felt Talia knew something more than the story she'd told on the stand. Megan wouldn't put it past Talia to cover for the man who had murdered Stephanie and attacked her and Cole.

Cole gave a soft chuckle and set his phone on the table. "Nope, turns out when Jack's not working security at Club One, he teaches martial arts down at the Southwest Community Center. While we were at the Hillside Motel fighting off the bad guy, Jack was teaching Tae Kwon Do to a bunch of five-year-olds."

Megan shook her head. "Are the parents trying to scare their kids to death?"

Cole shrugged. "From what Petersen told me, aside from a scrape with the Portland PD a couple years ago—he beat the crap out of some guy but was never charged—Brooks has been clean since he left the military two years ago."

So despite the hostile vibe Megan picked up whenever she was around the former Green Beret, it looked like her suspect pool for the Slasher had just shrunk by one.

Megan was still processing that when Cole threw out another stunner. "They're also working a solid lead on the guy from the hotel room and expect to make an arrest in the next couple of days."

"Who?"

Cole looked at her as though she'd lost her mind. "You really think she's going to tell *me* that?"

Megan's face heated, her stomach churning at the memory of Petersen's accusations. "They think they've found the Slasher?" Megan's heart skipped a beat at the thought.

"We'll see," Cole said as he got up and crossed to the kitchen to pour himself another cup of coffee. "The MO is nothing like his recent kills. None of the degree of ritual or preparation. Of course, if he knew you were coming, he knew he didn't have time for all that."

Megan shivered, the small hairs at the back of her neck standing on end at the memory of the killer's voice. He *had* been watching. He *had* known.

"But based on the preliminary examination," Cole continued, "the knife he sliced me with is similar to, if not the same as, the one used on the Slasher victims."

"I hope they get him," Megan said, but she could tell by Cole's raised eyebrow that he'd picked up on her lack of conviction.

Of course she wanted the killer caught. Whoever had brutalized those women was a monster, not to mention Megan would live in constant fear until he was caught, constantly looking over her shoulder, waiting for a stalking killer to emerge from the shadows.

But with no information linking the Slasher murders to Sean's case, Megan and her brother would be stuck exactly where they were right now. And if Megan couldn't find anything, the police and the prosecution weren't going to go digging around looking for a connection to a case they considered not just closed, but also nailed shut.

She began pacing across the living room, wracking her brain as to where to start. "The other victims," Megan said abruptly, "did you find out if there were any more cases where they found evidence of a video recording?"

Cole shook his head. "If there was, it didn't make it into the report. Devany's eye witness account is the first we've heard that he might be filming himself."

Megan grabbed her laptop from her bag, set it on Cole's coffee table, and powered it on. "He might have posted it," Megan said, almost to herself. "Do you know if they're looking at anything like snuff film sites?"

Cole nodded. "Tasso had a team of people combing the Web, looking to see if videos of the victims showed up. As of two days ago, they hadn't found anything."

Megan typed the phrase *snuff film* into her search engine, her stomach falling as hundreds of thousands of results popped up. She felt the couch cushions shift as Cole moved from the armchair to sit next to her. She clicked on a link for seeherscream.com.

"You don't want to see this," Cole said, reaching out and flipping her laptop closed before the page could load. "The FBI has an entire team of people looking at this and tracking down whoever is behind the Web site. What makes you think you'll find anything they can't?"

"They're only looking for videos of the Slasher's known victims," she protested. "What if there's a video of Evangeline's murder too? No one else even knows to look for it."

Cole rubbed his eyes with the thumb and forefinger of his right hand. "Megan, you're going to drive yourself crazy—"

"Too late for that," she snapped. "Sean's going to walk into the execution chamber in four days if I don't do anything. Without something tangible, he won't file another appeal. I know it looks like I'm grasping at straws— believe me, I know how hopeless this probably is, but what else can I do, Cole?"

Cole sat back against the cushions, wincing a little as his knife wound pulled. "Hell, you could come on my boat, let me take you out to the San Juans for the next month or so, pretend nothing else exists."

Though his tone was almost joking, the look in his eyes stopped her heart in her chest. She knew what was shining in those night-dark eyes, knew it because she felt it, too, growing harder to resist every second she spent in his presence.

I never let myself think about it because it hurt too much.

He felt it, too, the need, the yearning for something, anything to grant him the power to go back and change everything, to go back to the time before they fell apart and make sure it never happened at all.

Tearing her gaze away from his was like ripping a scab off a fresh wound.

For a brief second, she let herself entertain the fantasy of disappearing with him and shutting out everything but the two of them.

It was so tempting.

In the next instant, the fact that she'd so much as entertained the thought made guilt burn through the fantasy like acid. "Cole, you know that could never happen."

"Of course not. But is it so crazy for me to want to take you away, keep you from getting hurt any more than you already have been?" He reached out and threaded his fingers through hers, and Megan resisted the urge to lean into his strong, bare shoulder.

But she couldn't keep herself from squeezing his hand. "Then help me. You're a detective. Assume there is a connection between the murders. Tell me how you would start."

———※———

Megan was killing him. Cole tried to steel himself against the pleading in her big green eyes, the clutch of her much smaller hand in his. He wanted to order her to forget about it, then fling her over his shoulder and carry her off somewhere he knew she would stay safe.

But he was as helpless against that look as he'd been when she'd stormed into his office, asking for something, anything, to help exonerate her brother. The only time he'd resisted that plea was the night of Sean's arrest, and it had haunted him ever since.

He didn't doubt Sean's guilt this morning any more than he did that night; he was still convinced beyond a doubt that Megan was doing nothing but torturing herself. And yet he finally realized this was the only way for her to get through this tragedy.

He'd spent the last three years wishing she could accept the truth and move on, make peace with what had happened so she could get on with her life. But he finally understood that there would be no peace, no moving on, until she exhausted all options, until she did everything within her reach to prove Sean's innocence. If she was ever going to get over this—and frankly Cole had serious doubts that she ever would—it would only be if she knew in her soul that she'd tried absolutely everything, left no stone unturned in her quest to save her brother.

Cole didn't have much—hell, any—faith that he could save Sean from the needle, and despite Megan's belief in her brother's innocence, he wasn't sure Sean deserved to be rescued. Yet he couldn't deny the feeling gnawing at him, the hunch that, although all the facts about Sean's case appeared to be right in front of them, in black and white, he couldn't completely rule out Megan's notion that maybe they didn't have all of the answers.

"I'd start with the basics," Cole said. "Throw out everything you think you know from Sean's case, and find out everything that was going on in Evangeline Gordon's life at the time of her murder, see if there's anything that connects her to the other victims."

"I've tried that," Megan said impatiently. "I've asked everyone involved in the case, repeatedly."

Cole shook his head and pulled the laptop from her onto his lap. "You've been making a pest of yourself playing amateur sleuth," he said as he brought up a Web browser. "Now, if it were me, and I weren't suspended"— he couldn't quite keep the trace of acid from the word— "I'd run all of the names through our system to see if anything comes up. But without that"—he typed *Evangeline Gordon* into the search engine—"you'd be surprised how much information ends up on the regular old Internet."

"I've already run searches on Evangeline and anything related to the other cases, and there's never anything new."

Cole clicked on a link to a popular social networking site. Megan peered over his shoulder and shook her head. "That's been up since before Sean's trial. It's a memorial page on FacePlace, set up by Evangeline Gordon's college boyfriend." Megan's mouth pulled tight when she saw a post that read, *Finally the monster will die,* and another, *My sweet Evangeline will finally be at peace.*

"Looks like he's been posting a lot more since Sean's execution date was set," she said, snatching her laptop from Cole.

She scrolled through pages of comments vilifying her brother and grew visibly more upset with every post.

Cole reached to take the laptop back. "You don't need to read this. Why don't you let me—"

"No," Megan said firmly. "I want to see what he's saying." She finished reading the written comments and went on to the photo album, swallowing convulsively as photo after photo showed a beautiful, vivacious young woman wrapped in the arms of her ex-boyfriend, who obviously adored her. "These are all old." Her brows knit into a frown. "But these weren't posted the last time I visited." The new album was already several weeks old. Megan clicked through the first few, then froze. She leaned forward, squinting at the screen. "Holy shit," she breathed, pointing at the screen, "that's Bianca."

Cole leaned over her shoulder to look, his coffee cup nearly slipping from his grip as recognition hit him full force.

Sure enough, there was a picture of Evangeline Gordon, arms flung high above her head as she danced. And there, a few inches away, only half illuminated by the glow of the flash, was the Slasher's last confirmed victim.

Chapter 16

Craig Baranski, Evangeline Gordon's college boyfriend, lived two and a half hours southeast of Seattle in Naches, Washington, a small town on the edge of the Snoqualmie National Forest.

Megan was full of manic speculations about Craig and what the pictures of Evangeline and Bianca signified, but Cole's answers were frustratingly terse. He was closed up tight, back to full-on cop mode as he did his own mental churning over the significance of the pictures.

Megan tried to follow his lead, but after the first hour, she was sure that if Cole gave her one more "hard to tell," with that inscrutable look on his face, she was going to punch him in the mouth.

Still, she was grateful for Cole's steady presence beside her. As they approached the door to the sporting goods store where Baranski worked, Megan braced herself to face Craig again. Her memory of him was still vivid. He and Evangeline had broken up before her murder, but the wiry, serious-looking young man had been in the gallery every single day staring at Sean with eyes that blazed with the fury of hell from behind the lenses of his dark-framed glasses. The first time Megan crossed his path, he'd spit at her feet. During the trial, he'd been stonily silent, the only evidence of his grief the tears rolling down his cheeks as Evangeline's death was recounted in gruesome detail.

And judging from his recent comments, his hatred of Sean and Sean's devoted sister hadn't lost any of its intensity.

Megan's likely poor reception was the main reason they hadn't called ahead of time. That and the fact that Cole wanted a cold read, wanted to see Craig's raw reaction to their questions before he had a chance to prepare himself.

She steeled herself as she reached for the door handle, drawing strength from the warmth of Cole's hand at her back. "You don't have to do this," Cole said quietly, his hand staying the door. "You can wait in the car."

"Are you high? Of course I do. And I know you won't let anything happen to me."

Shocking how good it felt to say that, even better to believe it. In this, at least, she could depend on Cole to have her back. She knew under his calm exterior that he was as curious as she was to know how neither the prosecuting attorney nor Sean's defense team had ever unearthed those pictures.

A little bell tinkled over the door as Megan pushed it open. "Be right with you," called a voice. At this hour on a weekday, the place was empty. Megan did a slow scan of the store, taking in the array of fishing, backpacking, and hunting equipment. She walked slowly to the front of the store, her gaze drawn to the glass case under the cash register.

"Pretty easy for him to get his hands on a hunting knife," she noted.

"Hmm." Cole leaned over her shoulder for a closer look, and she felt a curl of heat at the subtle press of him against her back, the clean scent of his shampoo and shaving cream that teased her. "Evangeline was killed with Sean's knife. Even he admitted to that."

That's all it took for the warmth to drain away. Before she could respond, a man appeared in the doorway.

"How can I—" The man's voice stopped cold as his blue eyes locked onto Megan's face. His friendly smile fled, and hot color surged across pale cheekbones. "What the hell are you doing here?"

Craig's eyes blazed with anger so fierce she was afraid he was going to grab one of the hunting rifles from the rack and start shooting. Cole positioned himself in front of Megan and raised his hand. "You may not remember me. Detective Cole Williams."

Craig nodded. "You're the one who arrested that fucker," he said with a quick nod before he turned his fury back on Megan. "But what are you doing here with *her*?"

"We saw your memorial page, Craig," Megan began.

"You can't make me take it down," Craig said. "It's not libel if it's true."

"That's not why we're here," Cole said, his voice firm and steady. "There are pictures of Evangeline and another woman. Her name is Bianca, and there's a picture of her in the album you posted a few weeks ago."

Craig shook his head. "I don't know who you're talking about, and I don't have to answer your questions. Unless you have a warrant or some official reason for being here, you have to leave."

"Bianca is dead, Craig," Cole snapped. "She was found

last week in an abandoned trailer, raped, mutilated, and her throat sliced open."

Somehow Cole's almost emotionless delivery made the facts that much more chilling. "We're just trying to understand how she ended up there."

Craig's Adam's apple bobbed up and down above the collar of his flannel shirt. He walked over to the door, flipped over the CLOSED sign, and turned to face them, his expression anguished. "Show me which girl."

Megan's stomach knotted as they followed Craig to the back, where he had a desktop computer hooked up to a large monitor. He took a seat in the desk chair and clicked on the album Cole indicated. "Why did it take so long to post these pictures? It looks like everything else went up a while ago."

Craig's voice shook. "I found these on an old data card that had gotten shoved to the back of my desk drawer. They were the last ones I had of her. I thought I'd lost them."

Cole quickly selected the three photos that provided glimpses of Bianca dancing with Evangeline. "Her," Cole said, pointing to the dark-haired woman, her face partially cast in shadow, her arms raised above Evangeline's head as she danced up behind her. "Her name was Bianca Delagrossa, but if you met her, you might have known her as Bibi."

Craig swallowed hard. "And she's dead?"

"Yes. Murdered. Did you know her?"

Craig slumped in the chair, his face falling forward into his hands as he muttered, "Oh, Evie, Evie. I told her to stay away from that place, those people."

Goose bumps broke out on Megan's skin as her gaze

met Cole's over the top of Craig's head. "What are you talking about, Craig?" Cole said.

Craig sat back in the chair, took off his glasses, and rubbed his eyes. "If she had just come home, like we planned, none of it ever would have happened." He shook his head. "But she wouldn't listen to me. I told her moving up there was a bad idea. We were supposed to come back here after graduation and get married, but out of nowhere she said she was moving to Seattle." He paused, his eyes going red when he stared at the screen. "I didn't know that other girl. She was just someone Evie liked to party with. I took that picture the last time I went up to visit her, right before..."

"What was she doing that upset you?" Cole probed.

Craig shook his head. "She never told me for sure. I just knew she was going out a lot, working and partying at that club."

"Club One," Megan broke in.

Craig nodded. "She worked there as a waitress, with that woman, from the trial."

"Talia Vega?" Cole asked.

Craig nodded. "She said was doing some modeling on the side, but she never showed me any pictures."

Megan bet the only modeling Evangeline had done was on a certain Web site.

"There was something else going on there. She kept talking about moving into another part of the club's business where she could make a lot more money. But she couldn't do it with me hanging around."

Megan thought of the blonde, Stephanie, working the guy in the VIP room, escorting him out the back to be whisked away to who knows where. "How do you think they were making the extra money, Craig?"

Craig's expression closed like a door had slammed shut. "She never said."

"But you have a pretty damn good idea, don't you?" Megan pressed. "Why didn't you tell the police about your suspicions? If you really thought she was getting involved in something like that, why not say something?" Megan said, her voice rising in frustration.

"And let the press paint her as some kind of whore? Let your brother's scum-sucking lawyer somehow make it seem like Evangeline deserved what happened to her?" Craig's face turned purple with rage, and a vein throbbed in his forehead. "That monster butchered her. The police had all the witnesses, all the information they needed to prove it. I wasn't about to let her name get dragged through shit."

His accusations hit her like blows, but Megan forced herself to brush them aside. After all this time, she should be used to it, hearing what people believed about Sean, but every time, it singed her like a brand. "Or maybe you were trying to cover your own ass. Maybe you were jealous, because Evangeline was seeing my brother. Maybe you even thought he was a john, that she was letting him fuck her for money after shutting you out. You kill her and frame him; now you're going after the women who you blame for pulling her into this—"

"Shut up!" He was up and out of the chair and had Megan slammed up against the wall before she had a chance to breathe. Cole was on him a second later, hooking his arms through Craig's and pressing his hands against the back of Craig's head. "I loved her!" Craig shouted, struggling against Cole's hold. "I never would have hurt her. I tried to get her to come home."

"You touch her again, and I will snap your arm," Cole said, and shoved Craig back into the desk chair.

Craig shot her a glare but didn't make another move.

"Now, other than Talia Vega and Bianca, did you ever meet any other people she worked with? Do you know if they actually solicited clients while they were working at the club?" Cole asked, easing his hold on Craig a degree as the anger seemed to drain out of the other man.

Craig shook his head. "I only visited her a couple of times before she was killed. She never told me what was going on. It was all stuff I inferred. I overheard a couple of phone conversations, found a lot of cash around her apartment. She said she was just making good tips."

Megan swallowed back a surge of bile. Had Sean seriously stumbled into some kind of secret, high-end prostitution ring? None of this made any sense.

Cole released Craig, who rolled his neck and pinned Megan with a hate-filled glare. "So what, now are you going to the press, talk about how Evangeline was a slut, tell the world she was asking for it in a last-ditch effort to save your brother?"

"I'll do whatever it takes," Megan said grimly as she turned and walked out of the back room.

Craig's venomous voice followed her through the store. "It doesn't matter. You can't save him, just like no one could save Evangeline from that animal!"

Rage twisted with determination as she stormed through the front door. She could hear Cole's footsteps thundering behind her. Now she not only had Club One connecting the two latest victims to Evangeline, but they also had proof of a personal connection between Bianca and Evangeline. She prayed they were actually on to something, prayed the information wasn't too little, too late.

She slid into the passenger seat of Cole's Jeep. One thing she was sure of. "I want to talk to Talia Vega," she said. "I have a lot of questions for that bitch, and I'm not going to stop till she answers every last one."

———

Talia unlocked the door to her office at Club One, shed her coat, and walked numbly to the private adjoining bathroom she'd had put in when she was promoted to manager. It was still early, not even four yet, but she couldn't bear to go home after the afternoon she'd had. Couldn't pollute the white-picket-fence innocence of the house she shared with her sister Rosario, the house that helped Talia pretend, for the few precious hours that she spent there a day, that she was normal, upstanding, worthy of a lovely, quiet house in a lovely, quiet neighborhood a universe away from the place she and Rosario had been born into.

So she came here, to her private oasis of creamy marble and brushed-nickel fixtures. The bathroom featured a state-of-the-art, multiple-jet shower that doubled as a steam room, something Talia appreciated mightily after long nights on her feet, catering to the club's customers' every need.

Not every need. Some things you save just for him.

The ugly thought brought a bitter taste to her tongue as she turned on the faucets to the hottest setting and stripped off her clothes. Tight red dress, black lace bra, matching thong panties, and garter belt hit the floor, followed by black fishnet stockings. He'd been very specific about her outfit today when he'd summoned her. Every once in a while, he liked to send her a reminder of what her place was and what would happen to her if she did anything to try to change that.

Like she had any illusions left.

She could try to whitewash it all she wanted. Girlfriend, mistress, paramour, if you wanted to go really retro. It didn't matter that she'd once been in love with him and thought he'd loved her back. It didn't matter that he'd never actually given her cash outright.

They both knew what she'd become.

She stepped under the scalding spray, completely immune to the opulent luxury surrounding her. She scrubbed at her skin with a bar of lavender-scented, French-milled soap, desperate to rid herself of the sins of the day, knowing that even if she fried off the top layer of her skin with acid, his scent, the feel of his hands, had permeated down to her bones.

You're only doing what's necessary. You can't beat yourself up for that.

That had been her mantra for too long, and while it never served to entirely clear her conscience, at least it kept her from becoming paralyzed with guilt and fear over the web of dark sins and darker secrets her life had become.

But lately it had become harder, and with the latest murders, it was almost impossible to keep up the facade.

It's not like you know anything for sure.

Right, the same feeble excuse she'd been feeding herself for three years, ever since she'd let them convince her to tell part of the truth about Sean Flynn and his relationship with Evangeline Gordon. She'd never lied outright, she'd consoled herself. There had been nothing she'd said on the stand that wasn't true.

But the other stuff...the things she suspected but didn't know for sure. All she knew was that if she voiced her suspicions to anyone, she would end up like Evangeline, or Bianca, or Stephanie, or worse.

Which wouldn't be such a terrible fate, she thought as she turned off the faucets and wrapped herself in a blanket-sized bath towel, if there was only herself to consider. She'd thought of it often, especially in the last few weeks as it all ate away at her. The guilt of standing by, saying nothing as girls were butchered, one after the other, for the sins of wanting more or, even worse, wanting out. She was paranoid from being watched constantly, her every move tracked to make sure she didn't make a single step out of line.

She didn't kid herself. She knew every inch of the club; even her supposedly private office and bathroom were littered with hidden cameras, providing a constant feed to the old man and whoever he was using to do his dirty work. Jack Brooks, the security specialist who'd been forced on her a few months ago, was probably in on it, too, and had no doubt jacked off endlessly watching her wet and naked in the shower.

That was why David had called her over today, the second time in as many weeks. He'd seen Megan Flynn and her cop watchdog sniffing around the club, had seen her talking to Stephanie and wanted to give Talia a warning not to get any ideas.

It was enough to have made her consider taking herself out, or letting herself be taken out, dozens of times. Hell, maybe she could even do some good in the process, put someone on the right track for once as they tried to figure out who was killing these girls.

But she couldn't leave Rosario. Talia knew exactly what they would do to her baby sister if she stepped out of line, and she couldn't let that happen. Her sweet, beautiful sister who was actually going to make something of herself. If Talia had to sacrifice her morals, her conscience, her soul to make that happen, so be it.

Talia wiped away the steam on the mirror and resisted the urge to look away from her reflection. She barely recognized herself without the full face of war paint. Without the added enhancement of foundation, blush, and concealer, she looked as exhausted as she felt, her olive complexion taking on a sallow cast, dark circles ringing her eyes. Her mouth looked fuller and softer without its heavy crimson stain.

With her hair tumbling damply over her shoulders and her eyes void of liner or mascara, she looked younger, more vulnerable. More like the girl she used to be before she'd been taken in by David Maxwell's ruggedly handsome face and charismatic charm.

That stupid, naïve girl who believed in true love and happily ever after. She'd fallen for David like a ton of bricks and got caught up in foolish dreams of life with a man who would pamper her like a princess, let her know every day that she was cherished and adored.

Right. She'd felt adored for all of about three months before it became clear what her place really was. Rich man's mistress. Kept woman. Plaything. By then it was too late; she knew too much, yet not enough. And his reach was too great for her or her baby sister to ever get away.

She had accepted the fact that she wouldn't just have to compromise, that she would have to sacrifice. And some of those sacrifices would devour her from the inside little by little, piece by piece, until soon there would be nothing left.

Only two more years. Two more years and Rosario will be eighteen, off to college and off on her own. Talia would send her far away, with enough money to set her up for school and anything else she wanted to do.

Far away from here, away from the reach of both the foster system or anyone who might seek to hurt her, Rosario would be free. And so would Talia.

Even if freedom came in the form of a body bag.

She shook herself out of her funk and summoned up the protective numbness that had served her so well over the years. She'd gotten so good at feeling nothing that she could give a heroin junkie a run for their money in shutting out the pain. She started to reach for her makeup case, then paused. She had plenty of time before anyone showed up, plenty of time before she had to become the beautiful, coldhearted dragon lady her staff had all come to know and love. She dropped the towel and pulled on a set of sweats she kept in her office.

She regretted it five minutes later when a knock sounded at her door. Without waiting for her to answer, Jack shoved the door open. He was dressed in all black, as usual, looking big and fierce as he planted himself just inside her doorway. He was exactly the kind of security David Maxwell liked to hire: ex-military, physically imposing, and willing to operate in a moral gray area whenever necessary. A description that seemed to fit Jack to a T and made Talia nervous every time she got in the same room with him.

It it were up to her, she would have never hired him, but it wasn't like she'd had a choice. Even though David had hidden his involvement in Club One under layers of dummy corporations, there was no argument about who called the shots.

When Jack had been referred by the private security firm underwritten by yet another one of David's phantom companies, Talia knew she had little choice but to hire him. Though she suspected he'd been sent over to keep an eye on her as much as on the club's patrons.

All she knew was that she caught him watching her all the time, his steely blue gaze seeming to pierce through the layers of makeup and designer clothes to see too much.

She sat as tall as she could and glared at him from behind her desk. "Who the hell do you think you are, barging in here?" She hated that he didn't even flinch, envied the way he walked into a room with quiet authority and seemed to own it.

"I caught these two lurking out front. They say they need to talk to you."

Talia's indignant facade cracked when she saw Megan Flynn and Cole Williams in the doorway behind Jack. "Get them the hell out of here," she said tiredly, pulling her gaze back to her computer screen like there wasn't a knot twisting in her gut. Like she wasn't fully aware that every word, every look, every twitch was being recorded, would be evaluated, to make sure she stayed in line.

She darted a look at Jack, standing like a sentinel, not moving a muscle as Megan and Cole stepped inside. "Seriously, Jack, I want them out." She stood, then came around the desk. "I swear to God, if you two don't stop showing up here like a bad smell, I'm going to have you charged with harassment."

"Shut up, Talia," Megan said. "We saw the pictures. We talked to Evangeline Gordon's ex-boyfriend. We know she and Bianca knew each other, and we know you were involved in helping them both move to the other side of the business."

It struck her like a fist to the gut, both that they'd made the connection between her, Evangeline, and Bianca, and the accusation that she had somehow been responsible for getting them involved. Even though Talia existed only on the periphery, she knew it was a world she'd never wish on another human being, no matter how glamorous it seemed from the outside.

This is how it starts, the sweater unraveling. They'd kept it secret for so long, but now the dots were starting to be connected, and pretty soon it was all going to blow up in their faces. David Maxwell, the scarred creep he called a son, and God knew who else because Talia didn't kid herself that it stopped with just them.

Talia pulled her face into its customary cold mask, careful to give away none of the turmoil churning inside of her. "I don't know what you want from me, but I have no idea what you're talking about."

"I know you're hiding something about Evangeline and her relationship with my brother!" Megan yelled.

"You can cut the shit, Talia."

Though Jack's voice wasn't much louder than a whisper, the harshness of his tone stopped Megan's tirade in its tracks. Talia's gaze snapped to his face, and she found herself mesmerized by those ice-blue eyes, staring at her, through her, seeing *everything*.

"No one's watching now," he said, his tone softening a degree. "You're safe."

—⁓—

Megan was stunned by the sudden change in the usually ultracomposed, practically impervious Talia. Her appearance—no makeup, baggy sweats that gave no hint to the kind of body that made men stare and women bleed green with envy—was jarring enough. The look aroused sympathy for the woman whose testimony had helped land Sean on death row.

For a split second, that cold-bitch mask had cracked, revealing fear, hope, disbelief, a woman who had a glimpse of freedom and was desperate to reach for it. "How?"

Jack shook his head. "The how isn't important. But I took care of it yesterday, after the blonde turned up dead and you were attacked," he said, nodding at Megan.

If he was irritated at her role in having him questioned as a suspect, it didn't show. Then again, nothing much seemed to show on Brooks at all except for a whole lot of scary.

"Stephanie," Talia said in a choked voice, her shoulders slumping. "Her name was Stephanie." She turned to face Megan, her dark eyes full of anger and regret. "And she was killed because they saw her talking to you."

"Who saw her?" Cole broke in. "What was she going to tell Megan?"

Talia shook her head, the cold, closed mask once again in place. "I'm sorry. I have nothing more to say."

Megan could see she was scared, but any sympathy she might have felt evaporated in a wave of angry frustration. "Oh, but you had plenty to say at Sean's trial, when you lied about him and his involvement with Evangeline Gordon."

"I never lied," Talia snapped, her mouth pulled tight as she struggled to keep her lips from trembling. "I never said anything that wasn't true. Evangeline left with your brother that night, and she ended up dead in his house."

"You claimed Sean was stalking her."

Talia looked away and shrugged. "Maybe that was an exaggeration, but not much."

Megan's hand curled into a fist and every sinew in her body tensed. Sensing she was about to lose it, Cole wrapped his hand around her upper arm in a gentle but inescapable grip.

"Your exaggeration put my brother on death row where he's going to be killed in four days."

Talia stared at Megan, her fathomless dark eyes shining with tears. "I'm sorry," she said in a low, choked voice, "but we all do what we have to do to protect the people we love."

Megan exchanged a look with Cole. On the way over here, Megan and Cole had used their contacts in Social Services to dig up more details on Talia and her younger sister, Rosario. It wasn't in Megan's nature to fight dirty, but if it helped Sean, she'd go straight for Talia's underbelly and not stop until she got what she wanted. "This is about Rosario, right? You got custody of her after the trial."

Talia's eyes widened and her breath hitched.

"I talked to my friends in Social Services and found out you fought for three years to get custody, and then suddenly, miraculously, you were granted guardianship. Amazing how that happened."

Talia licked her bare lips. "Amazing."

"You know, it doesn't sound like you have the best home environment to raise a teenager. Working all these late hours, possible involvement in prostitution and who knows what else?"

"I'm not involved in prostitution," Talia said.

"I find that hard to believe, but even if you're not, you know what's going on here, and you know why those women were killed. You may have friends who helped you get custody, but your caseworker is a pretty good friend of mine. It wouldn't take more than a phone call for me to make life a lot more difficult for you and Rosario."

"Don't." Talia's impervious facade cracked wide open. "You can't take her away from me."

"Then talk to us," Cole said. "Talk to the police."

Talia sank down on the couch across from her desk. A sound ripped out of her chest, a combination of a laugh and a sob. "If they find out I'm talking to the cops, what they do to me, and what they do to Rosario, will be way worse than her going back into foster care."

"We can put you both in protective custody," Cole said, "even get you into witness protection if that's what it takes."

"Don't you get it?" Talia said. "They have eyes everywhere." She looked up at the ceiling of her office and gestured with her hands. "They have people on the police force, in the court system. They will know, and they will find me, no matter what you can promise. How do you think they've gone this long with no one catching on?"

"Who is *they*?" Megan demanded. "And what exactly are they involved in?"

Talia snapped her lips closed and shook her head. "I'm sorry. Use whatever pull you have in Social Services. Do whatever you're going to do."

Megan swallowed back a scream of rage. Talia was closed up like a vault, and if the investigation continued, she'd have to give up something to the cops. But not in time for Sean.

Cole knelt on the floor in front of Talia. "Sean Flynn is going to die, and you might have information that could save his life. Can you really live with that on your conscience?"

Talia lifted her desolate gaze to his. "I was already damned a long time ago, Detective. But I'll do whatever it takes to keep my sister safe."

On another occasion Megan would have admired Talia's devotion. Right now, however, she was darting her gaze around Talia's office, looking for bamboo shoots to shove under the other woman's fingernails to get her to talk before it was too late.

"I can help get Rosario somewhere safe." Jack stepped forward from where he'd been standing sentry by the door.

"How?" Talia said, her voice dripping with skepticism.

"A good friend of mine, my former commanding officer, has a security firm outside of San Francisco. One of the best in the country. It will be handled outside of the system, completely under the radar."

"Why the hell should I trust you?" Talia said. "What's your angle?"

Jack shook his head and ran a hand through his short, dark hair. "I don't have an angle."

Talia gave a sharp laugh. "Everyone has an angle."

Jack shook his head. "I came to work here because the money is good, and if I kept my head down and did my job, there would be bigger opportunities down the line. I figured it was none of my business if girls wanted to set up meets here to go make a little extra cash. But what's happening here...I can't stand by and do nothing."

"So, what, you suddenly grew a conscience and want to play hero?"

Jack shrugged. "You need help, and I'm offering."

Talia eyed him suspiciously, as though she couldn't imagine anyone offering help without an ulterior motive. "Maybe this is all a big trap. You're probably lying about the cameras, aren't you, and this is all some fucked-up test to see if I'll talk or not. I'm not talking," she yelled up at the ceiling. "I'm not saying anything and I better get credit for that."

Cole and Jack exchanged raised-eyebrow glances that speculated on Talia's mental state.

"You don't have a choice, and you know it," Jack said. "You're getting in deeper by the second, and no matter how much you say you're already damned, it's eating you alive to stand by and do nothing for girls like Bianca and Stephanie." Jack pulled Talia to standing and bent so his face was mere inches from hers. "And you know they're never, ever going to let you—or Rosario—go free." His low, menacing whisper sent a chill down Megan's spine and had Talia swallowing convulsively. "This is your best opportunity. Take it."

Cole jumped in. "I can set up a meeting for you, away from police headquarters, with someone I can guarantee is clean. You can give your statement and we'll make sure you're protected."

Talia snorted at that.

Cole held up a hand. "If, as you say, there are people on the inside, then you're right—it won't be completely without risk to you. But we'll do everything we can to make sure you're safe."

Talia shook her head, and Megan's stomach sank. Then Talia shocked her with her next words. "When I know that Rosario is safe"—she slanted a wary look up at Jack before looking to Cole—"I'll tell you whatever you want to know."

———⁓———

Sean did another slow turn around the yard, then stopped, closed his eyes, and tilted his face to the sky. Drizzle fell on his cheeks, and he took a deep inhale of cold, wet air. Alone in his cell, he kept in almost constant motion, the frenzy of activity the only thing that could keep him from hitting the wall going ninety.

He couldn't fuck this up. He had to keep it together till the end, not let on how close he was to the breaking point.

God forbid the state of Washington killed a crazy guy.

This single hour a day was the closest he got to stillness. Air. Rain. Sky. He drank it in, filled himself with it. The only sensations he let himself feel anymore, the only things that could quiet his racing mind.

The hours were dwindling. Part of him was sad at the thought of never feeling rain on his face again.

Most of him was eager for the day he wouldn't need this pitiful hour in the yard to survive the other twenty-three hours a day. Soon he wouldn't need anything.

The thought made him smile.

"Yard in."

Sean's stomach sank at the signal that time was up.

"Maybe you didn't hear me? I said yard in!"

His shoulders tensed at the guard's voice. He stood stock still, willing himself to relax, scrambling for the peace that had filled him just seconds ago.

Another guard might have cut Sean a little slack, had a little sympathy. But Riley was a mean cocksucker who got off on throwing his weight around.

"Give me a minute."

"Get your ass over here."

Black rage welled up, thick like tar, choking him. Sean struggled to block it down with each deliberately slow step across the yard. He was so sick of fat little turds like Riley directing every detail of his life. When he showered. When he ate the slop from the kitchens. When he could replace the dog-eared books and magazines he'd already memorized.

Not too much longer now. One last deep breath of fresh air before he stepped inside. His stomach revolted at the stink of bodies covered by a thin veil of Lysol. He started to shake. Couldn't make his feet move.

Oh shit, he had to pull it together.

"Move!" The shove barely budged him.

A blow to his ribs with a baton made him gasp for air. He looked up and saw Riley's smug face before the baton came down again, cracking against Sean's forearm. Riley, with his fat, smirking face and beady rat's eyes was getting off on beating him down.

Something snapped. Sean knew he shouldn't fight back but couldn't stop his fist from crashing into Riley's face. Flesh tore and teeth crunched. He grabbed Riley by the shoulders and flung him against the wall. The satisfaction was so great at first he didn't hear the thundering of footsteps down the corridor or feel the blows on his back, arms, legs.

He registered a baton swinging toward his face, too late to duck. *Crack!* Pain like a lightning bolt shot from his cheekbone into his skull. Another baton hit his head with a hollow thunk, and Sean fell to his knees. He tried to guard his face with his hands, but three guards shoved his face into the concrete, wrenched his arms behind his back, and cuffed him.

Even then Sean didn't stop struggling. He was like a wolf in a trap, the primitive beast taking over even when he knew it was useless to fight.

Chapter 17

W here are we going?" Megan asked as Cole pulled away from the curb.

"I told you, we're going to talk to someone we can trust with Talia's information. If what she says is true, I can't be a hundred percent sure about anyone."

"Who is it?" Megan asked for the hundredth time since Cole had gotten off the phone. "Why won't you tell me who we're going to talk to?"

Cole's hands tightened around the steering wheel as he guided the Jeep onto the freeway on-ramp heading north. He hadn't told Megan because he knew her reaction wouldn't be good. The animosity Megan had toward Talia Vega was nothing compared to the white-hot hatred she felt for Deputy Prosecuting Attorney Krista Slater. The woman had been relentless in her quest to get Sean convicted, vocal in her determination to settle for nothing less than the death penalty.

Though the case had been led by District Attorney Benson, Slater had been the driving force in painting Sean Flynn as a conscienceless monster who had murdered Evangeline Gordon in a drug-fueled rage. The case had made Slater's career and cemented her reputation as a hard-nosed, pull-no-punches prosecutor.

Though he didn't know her well socially—no one did, considering the woman practically lived at her desk—he liked working with her. She was ambitious but shared his appetite for justice. When others played politics, grew cynical, or compromised heavily in order to keep a high conviction rate, Slater maintained the same dedication she'd had when she'd first joined the PA's office. Cole knew that when she was assigned to his cases, as long as his evidence was solid and clean, she'd do her damnedest to make sure the perp wasn't able to plea down to a sentence that amounted to a slap on the wrist.

She was also fanatical about making sure she had every shred of information relevant to the case and the suspect. He knew she wouldn't shy away from truth, no matter how damaging it might prove.

Though he trusted his partner, he knew Petersen would feel obligated to go to Lieutenant Chin and Agent Tasso with any information relevant to the Slasher case. And until he knew for sure who this mysterious "they" Talia was referring to and what their reach was, he didn't want to risk the information getting into the wrong hands.

"I still don't understand why you couldn't set this up over the phone," Megan said. She was shifting in her seat, a ball of nervous energy. "We're wasting time with this. We shouldn't have let Talia out of our sight, and I still don't trust Jack. They're playing us—"

Cole reached over and gave her thigh a warning squeeze. "They're not playing us."

"How do you know?"

Cole brushed his thumb over the top of her tight quad, as much to savor the feel of her under his hand as to soothe the tension radiating from the muscle. "I've been at this for a long time, and I've gotten pretty good about knowing when someone is lying. Brooks is solid, and he'll make sure Talia plays along."

She shook her head. "There's something going on with him. He knows something about what's happening there and he's not willing to talk."

"He's worked there only a few months," Cole said. "He may suspect something, but only Talia knows how Evangeline Gordon's murder plays into this. We need to make sure she cooperates."

"By leaving before she tells us anything?"

"Trust me on this. She's scared, and she needs time to get her shit sorted out. She's not going to talk to anyone until her sister is secure, and that's going to take some time. And in the meantime, I need to handle this meeting in person."

Megan emitted an exasperated sound and turned her face toward the window. She was in constant motion, fidgeting, jiggling her leg, but she didn't remove his hand from her thigh. He let it rest there, pretending for a few seconds that they were like any other normal couple cruising down the highway, on their way home, on their way out to dinner, on their way out of town. Anywhere but on some desperate bid to see if there was any way to stop a man's execution when he had no desire to stop it himself.

Cole pulled up in front of a small ranch-style home. The garage was closed but the front window glowed with light. He got out and Megan did the same, shooting him a questioning look as she shut the door.

He pulled Megan into his arms and gave her a quick, hard squeeze. "Promise me," he whispered against the top of her head, "you'll keep a hold of yourself and let me do the talking."

Megan stepped back with a miffed sound and followed him up the walk.

The door flew open at the first knock. Slater stood in the doorway, hands on her hips, chin tilted back. "This better be damn good, Williams. I have to prepare for court tomorrow and shouldn't be out of the office at all—" Her mouth snapped shut when she caught sight of Megan, half hidden behind him.

Megan's eyes narrowed into a feral glare. "Her? You're coming to her with this?"

Slater's already determined chin jutted out a few more notches. "Please tell me that cryptic phone call was not about Sean Flynn's case."

Megan's hands balled into fists, but to her credit she didn't launch herself at Slater. Instead she wheeled around and took two steps down the walk before Cole's hand shot out to grab her. "We found some new information connecting Evangeline Gordon with the Slasher's most recent victim."

Slater's arched brows snapped together over the bridge of her nose. "I'm listening."

Cole drew Megan closer and gave her a warning look as Slater ushered them inside. He started by telling her about Stephanie's murder while waiting to meet Megan and Megan's subsequent attack. He then gave her a rundown on Megan's theory about the video camera, the possibility the medical examiner had misinterpreted Evangeline Gordon's knife wounds, and the speculation that Evangeline, Bianca, and Stephanie had been involved in a high-end prostitution ring somehow connected to Club One.

"Let me get this straight. You want me to reopen the

Flynn case based on the possibility that the Slasher is an ambidextrous psychopath capable of framing Sean Flynn for murdering a woman who may or may not have been a prostitute?"

"That and because Talia Vega has additional information regarding both cases."

Slater grabbed her briefcase and tucked a strand of hair behind her ear. "Which she's already told Special Agent Tasso, right?"

Cole shook his head. "She's afraid she and her sister will be in danger if it's discovered she talked to the police."

"Discovered by who? The Slasher?"

Cole couldn't suppress a grimace. "Among others. She seemed to think he has contacts within the force. But she won't say anything until her sister is secure, and then only to someone I guaranteed she can trust. That's where you come in."

"I'm flattered by your high regard for me, Cole, but I'm not sure I understand what it is you want from me."

Megan started to open her mouth and Cole shot her a warning look. "Take her statement, find out what she knows. And then you decide what to do with it."

He could see she was intrigued, could see the glint in her eyes as her mind snapped closed on the idea that something might have been missed in the investigation—or worse, that someone had deliberately misled them. Still, she wasn't convinced. "I don't like going behind Tasso's back on this. The feds could really screw things for me down the road."

"My brother is going to die in four days if we don't do something," Megan said. "I know you think he's guilty, but are you *sure*?"

Slater's mouth pulled into a tight line, and Cole could see the same doubt that was gnawing away at him settle in. She looked at Cole, her gaze coolly assessing. "What do you think, Cole? Do you think there's a connection?"

He blew out a breath, Megan's stare burning him like a laser as she waited for his answer. He wasn't sold on Sean Flynn's innocence, not by a long shot. But that didn't banish the gnawing feeling that important details were missing. "Between what we learned from Craig Baranski and Vega's admission that she didn't reveal everything, I'm getting a bad feeling someone didn't do all of their homework before sentencing Sean Flynn to death."

"I'll try to ignore that dig," Slater said, then gave a short nod. "Fine. Set up a meeting with Vega and I'll talk to her." She accepted Sean's case file from Cole, which included the new information about Craig Baranski, his FacePlace page, and copies of the photos of Evangeline with Bianca. Slater opened the folder and flipped through the first few pages. "Even if I do want to get involved, there's no guarantee Benson will let me reopen the case. If you want to buy your brother some more time, you better convince him to file another appeal."

Megan didn't bother to say good-bye to Krista before slamming out the front door. Cole thanked Krista and caught up with Megan halfway down the driveway. Her shoulders were stiff as she took out her phone and dialed. "I need to speak to the warden." She was silent a few seconds. "This is Megan Flynn, Sean Flynn's sister. I want to put in a request for a visit this week."

Cole looked over at Megan's sharp gasp. In the gray afternoon light, her skin was chalk-white as she listened to the warden. "I see," she whispered, and hung up. "Sean got in a fight with one of the guards. The only person he's allowed to see is his attorney."

"It's going to be okay—"

"It's not going to be okay, Cole! I need to talk to him and tell him what's happening before it's too late. And what if he's hurt? They wouldn't tell me anything."

"It's going to be okay," Cole repeated, firmer, as he guided her to his car. "I'll take care of it."

—⁓—

Krista closed the door behind Cole and Megan and shook her head. She might have thought this was a sick joke, but Williams wasn't exactly known for his sense of humor. She had always liked him and the way he worked. His cases were rock solid, the evidence clean and everything done by the book. If he thought there was something more to Sean Flynn's case, some key piece of information Talia Vega could provide, she couldn't in good conscience dismiss him out of hand. Even if it was possible he was thinking harder with his little head than his big head.

Krista would have liked nothing more than to blow Cole off as horny at best and delusional at worst. Despite her conviction that they'd convicted the right man, it wasn't an easy thing to know she'd helped sentence a man to death.

She already had trouble shutting her brain down enough to sleep at night. The last thing she needed was to add doubt to the equation.

She wanted nothing more than to push it aside, but she trusted Cole and his instincts as a cop. She'd never forgive herself if she didn't at least humor him, talk to Talia Vega and review the case with the new information in mind. She sat down at her kitchen table, flipped open the folder, and started skimming the familiar contents.

Crime scene photos. Witness statements. Court transcripts. It was all here, in black and white. Every shred of evidence, down to the fingerprints on the knife pointing to Sean Flynn.

She picked up a page of Talia Vega's testimony, and as she did so, a photo slid out onto the floor. It was a picture of Flynn, decked out in his full army dress uniform. With his dark green eyes, chiseled features, and dark hair clipped close to his skull, he looked like a hero. The exact kind of man you wanted on the front lines protecting truth, justice, the American way.

He didn't look like a cold-blooded murderer.

Yet she'd never doubted they'd nailed the right man. And there was nothing in the evidence to make them think otherwise.

A perfect case, gift wrapped and handed to them. So perfect that Detective Suarez, who'd taken over as lead investigator after Williams was off the case, had never seriously pursued any other suspects.

Too perfect?

What if Williams was right? What if Talia Vega hadn't told them the whole story? What if there was a connection between Evangeline Gordon and the Slasher's other victims?

Coincidence. A connection doesn't make Sean Flynn any less guilty.

But what harm could come from taking a second look?

—⁓—

The streetlamps cast an eerie glow through the fog as she and Cole pulled up in front of the Walls. It was after midnight, but Megan was keyed up even after the long drive. Cole parked across the street from the entrance gate and pulled out his phone. "We're here."

On impulse, Megan leaned over from the driver's seat and gave Cole a quick hug. "Thank you. Thank you so much for this." She had no idea what kind of favor the head guard owed Cole; all she knew was that he was cashing it in for her. And for Sean. "I still don't totally understand why you're doing all of this for me."

She could just barely make out Cole's rueful smile in the shadows. "Because I didn't before."

A man appeared at the gate and motioned to them before Megan could get her brain wrapped around that.

"Let's go," Cole said.

Megan got out of the car, shivering a little as she followed Cole. Cole and the man who introduced himself only as Joe shook hands.

"Thanks for doing this," Cole said as Joe led them between two buildings of the compound. Megan had never been to this part of the prison before.

"Anytime."

"We'll go in through the infirmary."

"Stay close," Cole said, and wrapped his hand around her arm.

Megan didn't need to be told twice. Joe led them through a maze of dim, silent hallways, around corners and through reinforced steel doors. At the end of a long corridor, Joe opened a door that led to a covered passageway connecting the medical wing with the IMU where death row inmates were held.

The passage opened up to a cavernous two-story room with cells lining the top floor. In the silence, Megan could hear deep breathing, snores, the sounds of bodies shifting in sleep.

Joe led them through the common area and out toward the visiting area. "You can wait here." He ushered them into a small room containing a table and two chairs.

Minutes later, Megan heard the metallic clank of handcuffs as Joe led Sean into the room.

She burst into tears. His face was mottled with bruises. His right cheekbone was purple and swollen, and he had a line of stitches over his right eyebrow.

Megan flung herself at him and wrapped her arms around him. "Oh God, it's so good to see you." It took her several seconds to realize Sean was flinching away.

"What are you doing here?"

Her stomach dropped. He didn't sound happy to see her.

"And what the fuck is he doing here?" Sean asked, his angry stare locked on Cole.

"He's helping me," Megan said, and reached out to put a reassuring hand on Sean's arm. He jerked away and she felt like she'd been kicked in the stomach. "What happened?" She reached a hand toward his face but dropped it before she touched him.

"I lost it on a guard and got the shit beat out of me," he said coldly. He turned again to Cole. "Why the hell am I being dragged out of my cell in the middle of the night? I don't want her to see me like this."

She winced at his tone. Sean didn't want to see her again before he died. Period. He'd made that clear.

"I needed to see you and make sure you were okay, and try to convince you to call Brockner to file an appeal first thing tomorrow," Megan said.

Sean shook his head. His dark brows drew into a frown as he shook his head. "I'm not doing that. I don't know what the cop's part is in all of this, but unless you've found the real killer and enough evidence to back it up and get me out of here, I don't want any part of it. I'm done with this."

Something in Megan snapped. "You're done? *You're* done? You think you can just say you're done and I'm going to say, 'Okay, Sean,' and slink off into the corner to cry?" she shouted, shoving him at a chair, ignoring his wince of pain. She sat down in the chair across from him. "I almost got killed trying to find information that will save your ass." She tugged at the collar of her shirt, exposing her bruises to the harsh fluorescent lights. Since yesterday afternoon, they'd darkened to a lurid purple. "I've done everything I can possibly think of to help you in the last three years, so the least you can do is give me the goddamned time of day before you let them kill you."

Sean's complexion went pale under his own bruises.

He listened silently, the grooves on either side of his mouth deepening as she detailed everything they'd discovered. Every once in a while Cole would remind her of a detail or tell her to clarify a piece of information, which she would relay to Sean. By the time she finished, Sean was sitting back in his chair, his manacled wrists resting on the table, his stare moving right past her to a point about a thousand miles in the distance.

Finally his focus turned back on her, and her stomach sank at the grim resolve etched into his face. "It's not enough. Just a few random bits of information that may or may not connect the victims, but there's nothing that will get me out of here."

"We just need more time," Megan said, wishing she could grab Sean by the hair and beat some sense into him. "It doesn't look like much now, but if we keep looking—"

Sean's laugh echoed through the room like a gunshot. "Right. More time for you to follow leads that go nowhere, getting yourself hurt, possibly killed in the process, while I'm rotting away in this hole waiting for a fucking miracle that's never going to come. Look at me, Megan." He gestured at his brutalized face. "I'm gonna be dead soon no matter what. They don't need to strap me to a gurney to kill me."

This wasn't the way this was supposed to go. He was supposed to believe in her, in the possibility that she would uncover the truth, but he had to give her more time. Why was she the only one who believed, who had to carry the crushing weight of hope on her shoulders when everyone else had given up? She was staggering, suffocating under it.

How easy it would be to let it go, let it crash to the earth and take her with it, drag her down to a place where she could finally stop fighting.

Cole came up behind her and gave her shoulder a quick squeeze.

It was enough. Enough to remind her that she wasn't alone in this. Cole didn't share her unwavering faith, but he was here; he was searching for answers alongside her, willing to consider the possibility of an answer that didn't lead to her brother's guilt.

The burden lightened and she felt steely determination

take root in her spine. "It's not just me looking at this, Sean. Cole has been helping me, and earlier today we took everything we found to DPA Slater—"

Sean's snort cut her off. "Krista Fucking Slater? If she uses that information for anything at all, it will be to make sure they give me an extra dose of Pentathol just to make sure I'm extra dead."

"Krista's got more integrity than anyone in that office," Cole said.

Sean snorted. "Like that's saying something."

"Having Krista on our side lends a lot more credibility to our theory," Cole said quietly.

More credible than the sister of a convicted murderer and the cop who was sleeping with her, Megan knew. "Cole's right. He trusts her, and so do I," she said, not even realizing it until she said it out loud. As much as she wanted to hate Slater and believe she'd use any ammunition to feed Sean to the wolves, Megan could sense a core of honesty in the woman. Slater had gone after Sean because she'd believed they had the right man. Though Megan resented the woman's zeal for nailing her brother to the wall, she knew Slater wouldn't have gone after Sean if she'd had any doubt he was guilty.

Now Megan hoped Slater would go after the truth with similar dedication.

Sean was silent as he absorbed that.

"This isn't just me running down shadows, Sean. Slater's looking at your case. Talia's going to tell us what she knows about Evangeline and everything else. But none of it will matter if you don't do something to stop yourself from getting killed."

Chapter 18

Cole watched as Megan stood and walked over to Sean and wrapped her arms around him. "Please call Brockner. Please buy us a little more time," she whispered.

Sean took a deep, shuddering breath and buried his head in Megan's shoulder. He didn't make any promises.

Megan straightened and said, "I guess we should go."

Sean sat motionless in the chair, his head bent as though he couldn't bear to look at her. He looked beaten down in a way that had nothing to do with the bruises mottling his face. The years in custody had whittled Sean's body down to muscle and bone. His skin was tight over sharp cheekbones and the blunt edge of his chin. Under the short sleeves of his prison jumpsuit, his biceps bulged like softballs under his skin, his arms practically an anatomy lesson of tendons, muscle, and veins pushing through skin gone pale from lack of sun.

"Wait," Sean said. "I want to talk to you." He lifted his head to look at Cole. "Alone." Even as Sean sat, motionless, Cole could sense the energy humming through his body.

"I can't—" Joe started.

"It's fine," Cole cut him off. "I'll be fine."

"If you get hurt or killed—"

"He won't kill him," Megan snapped. "You better not kill him," she said to Sean.

Sean just held up his cuffed hands. "Couldn't if I wanted to."

Cole wasn't so sure, but it was a risk he needed to take. "We're good."

Joe didn't look sure either, but he escorted Megan out and locked the door behind him.

"What the fuck do you think you're doing with my sister, Williams?"

Cole had felt this coming and was ready when Sean leaped out of the chair like a mountain lion. Even cuffed, Sean had him slammed against the wall, fists digging into Cole's throat.

Cole gave him a sharp jab in the ribs. Sean dropped like a rock and gasped in pain. "I'm trying to keep her safe."

"How?" Sean gasped. "By leading her on, giving her false hope, pretending to help her with my case so you can get close enough to fuck her?"

Cole hid a grimace. While he liked to think his intentions were noble, Sean's comment pricked at his conscience. "Megan was putting herself in danger, tracking down leads she had no business chasing. I was afraid someone was going to hurt her, and I was right."

"What exactly happened?" Sean asked as he slumped back into a chair.

Cole took the seat across from him. As he explained how he'd found Megan in that hotel room, the masked man's fingers squeezing her windpipe, the feral rage that had overwhelmed him at the scene surged forth once again, along with the sick fear of seeing Megan hurt, nearly dying in front of him.

He could see his rage mirrored in Sean, whose knuckles were stark white as his fists clenched. There was something else in Sean's gaze, beyond the rage. Helplessness, and the despair that went with it. The sick sense of futility that came from knowing someone you loved suffered and having no ability whatsoever to help them.

Cole could relate. He'd felt it when Kelly was killed and the years passed with no more clues to the identity of her killer. And he'd felt it that night when he'd arrested Sean, and again at Sean's sentencing hearing, when he'd watched Megan shatter with grief and had not been able to do anything to ease her pain.

"So you saved her from that fucker," Sean said. "I owe you for that. But you have to stop her. She's going to get killed, and we both know she's not going to find anything."

"Don't be so sure of that."

Sean's swollen lips curled into a sneer. "Don't tell me you've taken up her cause. You think I'm innocent now?"

"I'm not a hundred percent sure you're guilty."

"Better than nothing." Sean fixed his unwavering stare on Cole. "I didn't kill that woman."

Something shifted in Cole's gut at the look on Sean's face, something that had nagged at him from the very beginning. Cole had learned a lot about human nature in his years on the force. He had honed those instincts, developing his expertise as an interrogator, and he prided himself on being able to spot a liar a mile away. And his gut insisted that Sean Flynn wasn't lying to him now.

Yet three years ago, when he'd arrested and interrogated Sean, Cole had been one hundred percent sure Sean was lying through his teeth when he said he didn't kill Evangeline, and they had the incontrovertible evidence to back it up. When he'd finally gotten Sean to admit that it was possible that he had killed Evangeline and not remembered it, Cole had treated it as a confession.

Now, staring across the table at Sean, Cole couldn't shake the sick feeling that maybe he'd been more wrong about Sean than he'd ever been about anything.

What had changed? Was he so far gone under Megan's spell that he could no longer trust his instincts?

Or was he finally seeing through to the truth after all this time?

What he and Megan had discovered called everything about Sean's case into question. "You were the only one there that night."

Sean shook his head. "I kept saying I thought I remembered someone there."

"Right, someone whose face you never saw, whose voice you never heard, who left no trace of himself in your house."

Sean gave a mirthless laugh. "Yeah. The guy everyone decided was actually just me and that I was hallucinating or having some kind of psychotic break or some shit."

At the time Cole had accepted the explanation. Now he wondered if there had been another man, one they'd never bothered to look for.

Jesus, what if Sean had been telling the truth the whole time?

To hell with it. He couldn't change the past, but he could sure as shit do everything in his power to uncover the truth, no matter where it led. "Tell me everything you remember about the guy."

Confusion flickered in Sean's eyes. "I don't remember anything. That's the fucking problem."

"Try." Cole had spent years guiding suspects and witnesses, helping them conjure the smallest of details they didn't even realize were filed away in their brains. "Close your eyes. Try to remember something, a sound, a smell, a feeling."

"Is this some fucking joke? I'm days away from the needle and now you're going to try to get me to remember?"

"Listen, asshole," Cole said through clenched teeth, "I'm here because I care about your sister and I'd rather cut off my left nut than see her hurt. The *only* thing that can make her happy right now is for us to find some proof of your innocence so we can get you out of this shithole, so for her sake, fucking humor me, okay?"

Sean's eyebrows rose and Cole saw a hint of grudging admiration in his eyes. "Just your left nut, eh? You telling me my sister's not worth the whole package?" But he closed his eyes for several seconds, his face screwing into a frown as he focused his attention inward. "He was big," Sean said. "Strong. I think I remember him moving me." His eyes squeezed harder. "I think he had something on his arm." His eyes flew open and he held out his own left arm, staring down at the tattoo on his biceps with a look of disgust. "Shit. I am crazy."

"No, you're not. The man who attacked Megan—it was dark, but she thought she saw a tattoo on his arm."

Sean's eyes narrowed. "You're serious?"

Cole nodded.

"So he's military, maybe Special Forces, like me."

"Maybe." He wasn't ready to say for sure, but he could no longer rule out the possibility out of hand. "Any ideas?"

Sean shook his head. "Lots of guys get inked. Damn near everyone in my Ranger class got one of these," he said, pointing to his tattoo.

"Any idea who might want to hurt Evangeline? And why would they want to frame you?"

"If I knew, I wouldn't be sitting here," Sean said, his shoulders slumped in defeat.

"You need to call your attorney."

"Can you guarantee I'm going to get out?"

"I can't guarantee anything, except that if you don't file an appeal you'll be dead and I won't give a shit either way what we find."

"Maybe it's better that way."

"Better for who? Not Megan."

"Really? You think it's better for her to get her hopes up all over again, only to be smacked down? You think it's better for her to almost get herself killed trying to save her convict brother?"

Cole let out a weary sigh as he heard his own sentiments echoed back at him. "It doesn't matter if you push for an execution date and go through with it, Sean. That's not going to stop her. She has no doubt you're innocent. She's not going to give up even if you do."

"She always was stubborn," Sean said with a shake of his head.

"So you're going to give her a little more time?"

"I'll think about it. But I can promise you this: If you hurt my sister any worse than she has been, I'll fucking come back from the grave to haunt you."

—⁓—

"We have to get him out of there. I can't let him die in there like a beaten dog." Megan scrubbed at her eyes as she watched Joe lead Sean back to his cell.

Cole felt an answering tug in his chest and gently took her arm as they waited for Joe to return and lead them out the way they came.

He was grateful when she fell asleep a few miles into their drive. He kept his gaze glued to the highway as his brain slowly sifted through the past forty-eight hours. In one bucket were facts, things they knew for certain about all the victims and all the cases. In another were the new pieces of information that raised more questions than they answered.

Questions that cast a serious shadow over those so-called facts.

He'd be doing Megan and Sean—hell, even himself— a serious wrong if he didn't step back and reexamine everything he thought he knew about the case.

Megan didn't rouse until they'd reached the outskirts of the city. He didn't realize she was awake until he started to pass her exit. "Wait," she said around a yawn. "I need to go to my place."

"It's not safe."

"We don't need to stay long, but I need to get more clean underwear. I packed only one pair."

"Fine, but I get to pick it out."

She let out a muffled chuckle. "Pig."

It felt good to hear her laugh after the night they'd had.

A winter storm had blown in off the coast, soaking the ground and whipping branches around. In the time it took them to sprint from his Jeep to her door, they were drenched. They were in and out of her place in five minutes. Megan didn't let him pick out her underwear, but the glimpse he got was enough to get him as hard as a spike thinking about getting her in—and out of—the bits of silk and lace.

Even so, he was determined to play the gentleman, for what was left of tonight anyway. Their visit with Sean had put her through the ringer. The last thing she needed or wanted was him going after her like a Neanderthal.

He parked the Jeep in his garage and ushered Megan through the door before setting his alarm code. "You can have the bed," he said, and tossed his keys on the table. His dick twitched in protest, and he knew he wouldn't get much sleep.

It was bad enough before when he could only imagine how it felt to bury himself deep inside of her. Now that he knew . . . sleeping under the same roof as Megan and being unable to touch her was going to be fucking torture.

Sean Flynn's face flashed in his mind. *Suck it up, asshole. Could be worse. You could be on death row trying to decide whether to go ahead and end it all or sign up for another stretch of spending twenty-three hours a day alone in an eighty-one-square-foot cell.*

That thought alone kept him from trying for a repeat performance of last night. That and Sean's jab about Cole's motivations for staying close to Megan. He wanted her safe, sure, but it was a rush being close to her again. At the heart of it, Sean was right. Cole was a selfish prick, taking advantage of her in her weakest state. He'd take any piece of her he could get, for as long as she'd let him, and so what if they had no future?

Cole would get over that when the time came. He would have no choice.

"Are you doing okay?" He tugged at his collar, over-heated even though his house was cold. A sheen of sweat coated skin that felt two sizes too small. "Are you hungry or anything?"

Megan shook her head and leaned against the kitchen counter. Cole looked away, trying not to imagine how she'd looked last night, naked, legs spread as she guided him inside.

She unraveled her braid and ran her fingers through the strands, filling the air with the scent of her shampoo. "I just wish Sean would have a little more faith in me. In us."

The sadness in her voice ripped him out of the fantasy. He knew it was a bad idea, but with her chewing on her plump lower lip and looking at him with sad green eyes, he couldn't keep from taking her in his arms. God, it felt so good, the way she melted into him.

"We're close to something," Megan said as she leaned into his chest. "I can feel it. All we need is a little more time."

Cole started to get stuck on that "we" thing, then found himself fully distracted at the feel of her hand sliding up his back.

He tried to stick his butt out so she wouldn't feel him hard as a club against her stomach.

Get a goddamn grip. You're acting like you haven't gotten laid in months, instead of hours.

And that was the problem, wasn't it? He'd had sex with Megan less than twenty-four hours ago, and instead of satisfying the craving, scratching the itch, it was like a junkie's first hit of meth. Now all he could think about was having more. More of her skin under his fingers and tongue. More of her, tight and wet, stretching for the invasion of his cock.

Pull it together. He'd promised himself he wouldn't try anything tonight.

He took a deep breath, trying to calm himself down, but couldn't stop his hand from stroking the silky length of her hair. He wanted to wrap his fist in it to hold her in place for his kiss, then guide her head slowly down to kiss his chest, his stomach.

He coughed to cover the groan as she hugged him tighter.

"Are you okay?" Her question was muffled against his chest.

"Yeah," he said. "Just tired." *Just dying to know how it would feel to have your lips around my cock.* He wished he could escape, go out for air, a drink, anything to give himself a little space to get himself under control.

He gave her a hard squeeze and forced himself to step away. "You must be exhausted."

She shook her head and wrinkled her nose in that way he'd always found too damn cute. "I am, but I'm feeling kind of wired." She stared at him thoughtfully for a moment. "Are you sure you're okay? You look a little... strange."

"I'm fine." As fine as he could be with all of the blood in his body pulsing in his groin.

She smiled tiredly up at him. "Thank you again for getting me in to see Sean. For everything you've done in the last few days."

It was all he could do not to jerk her back into his arms and tell her exactly how he'd like to be thanked.

"I've been alone with this for so long. You have no idea how good it feels to have someone I can count on."

Cole's breath caught in his chest as she slid her hands up his chest and rose on her tiptoes to plant a kiss on his chin. He willed himself to accept the gesture for what it was, a kiss of gratitude, not a sign she wanted a repeat performance of last night. He'd seen the look on her face this morning. He didn't want to put that look of guilty shame back on her face.

The press of her mouth was like a brand against the skin of his jaw. Her hand slid higher and her fingers grazed the bare skin of his neck, sending a jolt of heat straight to his cock.

In the next breath, her lips slid one inch up and to the right until they covered his. Cole groaned and slanted his mouth over hers. His hands slid around her back, pulling her close. The hot slide of her tongue against his, the soft press of her tits against his chest. And, Christ, her hot palms sliding up under the hem of his shirt, scorching the skin of his chest and back. It was nearly enough to make him spontaneously combust right then and there.

"You don't really want this, Megan." He tore his mouth from hers and struggled for breath.

"Don't tell me what I want." She yanked his shirt up his chest. Her head bent and he felt the hot slide of her tongue against his abs and nearly crumpled to his knees.

"You don't owe me this."

"I'm not doing this out of gratitude, Cole." She straightened and slid her hands down over his ass to pull him close. "I'm doing this because I want you." She rubbed her stomach against the hard ridge of his cock straining behind his zipper.

"You're going through an emotional time. You're not thinking straight."

She whipped her long-sleeve shirt over her head, slipped off her bra, and stood in front of him, all smooth pale skin and tight pink nipples. "That didn't stop you last night. Don't tell me you're going all noble on me."

"I was going to try." For her sake. Shit, for both their sakes, because God knew he was getting sucked in deeper with every second he spent with this woman.

He didn't know if he grabbed her or if she grabbed him, but suddenly their arms were tangled around each other, their kisses fierce and frantic.

"Don't," Megan said in a frantic whisper. "I don't want to think about anything tonight except how much I want you." She kissed him again. "I need you, Cole."

The words sent the final, crushing blow to any noble restraint he might have had. *I need you.* Christ, he couldn't imagine anything sweeter coming from her lips. Except...

I love you.

Don't even go there.

Between the two of them, they got his shirt off and Cole managed to steer them down the hall to his bedroom. But as soon as the backs of her knees hit the mattress, Megan halted him. "Shower," she said, breathless. "I can't stand the idea of being with you with the stink of that place on me."

Sean's face flashed in Cole's brain at the reminder, and for a split second the sting of guilt threatened to burst his lust-fueled high. But then Megan kicked off her boots and tugged her jeans down her legs. As he watched, she turned her back to him and hooked her thumbs in the waistband of her panties. She gave him a naughty look over her shoulder and slid them down, revealing the pale, luscious curve of her ass to his hot gaze.

The scrap of silk and lace slid down her sleekly muscled thighs and slim calves, and then the only thing covering her was the curtain of dark, silky waves tumbling nearly to her waist.

She cocked a dark eyebrow at his hands, frozen on his own waistband as he drank her in. "So, are you going to join me or what?"

Cole snapped into action, kicking off his shoes, shucking his jeans, boxers, and socks in one long tug, and followed her into his bathroom. She stood with her back to him, slightly bent as she adjusted the water temperature, offering a mouthwatering, unimpeded view of her ass and thighs. The little space at the top gave him the sweetest glimpse of her sex, as pink and luscious as her pretty pink mouth. His mouth watered at the thought of kissing her there.

Last night he'd been in such a hurry, desperate to get inside her before he lost control. Tonight he was going to explore every inch, not stop until he knew her body as well as he knew his own.

. He pressed himself against her from behind, rubbing his dick against the silky curve of her ass as his hands slid around front to play with her nipples. He nipped at her shoulder, loving the little sounds she made as he pinched and rolled her nipples between his fingers. Steam billowed around them as Megan swept back the shower curtain and beckoned him inside. Water cascaded down their bodies as he pressed her back against the tiles and grabbed a bar of soap.

She sucked hungrily at his lips and tongue as he covered her skin in rich lather. He kneaded her breasts, loving the look of his tanned hand as it swallowed up her pale curves.

Her nipples were hard, begging to be pinched by his fingers, sucked into his mouth. He bent his head, drew one firmly between his lips, tasting salty-sweet flesh and the remnants of soap. Her cry echoed off the tiles as he sucked hard, first at one breast, then the other. His cock bobbed between them, slipping against the soap-slicked skin of her stomach.

He straightened and grabbed the bar of soap again, working up a fresh lather as he ran his hand up and down her back and lower, over the plump swell of her ass, down her thighs, up in between. At his urging, her legs parted, and he ran his palm up the inside of one inner thigh, almost but not quite touching her sex as he went down the other side. Teasing, stroking, alternating kissing her mouth and sucking her tits until she was breathing hard, her hips rocking with every stroke as she urged his hand farther between her legs.

Cole wasn't the only one doing the teasing. Megan grabbed the soap from him and ran the bar over his back, chest, ass, thighs. Then it was just her hands, sliding over his skin, her mouth chasing rivulets of water with her tongue as they skated down his stomach. She ran her hands over his butt, down his abs, her fingers tracing the dark line of hair leading down from his navel. Her tongue slid into his mouth as she slid her palm between his legs, grazing, teasing, but not quite touching the heavy sac pulled tight against his body.

One last kiss and she paused, reached for the bottle of shampoo and handed it to him. "Wash my hair," she ordered. Eyes closed, she tipped her head back under the spray. She was gorgeous, her hair slicked back and throwing her delicate features into stark relief, her eyelashes thick, dark shadows on her cheekbones. He lathered her hair, drinking in every sweet inch of her, savoring the heavy weight of her hair in his hands, her wet skin against his as he pulled her close.

He tipped her head back under the water, and her hands came up to help rinse out the shampoo. With her back arched and her arms raised, her breasts tilted to the ceiling. Drops of water slid down her throat and chest, catching on the dark pink tips of her nipples until he couldn't stop himself from flicking his tongue out to catch one. She gave a little gasp, and her hands moved from her head to his, her fingers threading through his hair to guide his head up so she could reach his mouth.

He reached behind her and turned off the water, then blindly swept back the curtain. He groped for a towel, his mouth never leaving hers, and clumsily blotted at both their bodies as he guided them out of the tub and into his bedroom. He was drowning in her, her taste, her scent, her feel, and he never wanted to come up for air.

His cock was so hard he felt like he was going to burst out of his skin, but he resisted the primal drive to thrust blindly into her wet heat and finish too soon. He'd gone fast and furious at her the night before, and now he wanted to taste every patch of skin he'd missed.

"Please, Cole," she said as he bent his head to suck at her nipples. "You're driving me crazy."

"Be patient," he said, and sucked her nipple hard. "I've come up with about a hundred different ways to make you

come in the past few years, and tonight I'm hoping to try
at least a dozen."

"I could make some suggestions," she said as he slid
his mouth down the smooth, pale skin of her stomach.

"I think I've got it covered." He planted a kiss right
above the soft tuft of curls at the top of her mound and
sank to his knees beside the bed, shifting her so her knees
rested on his shoulders. The scent of her flooded his
senses, sending a jolt of heat down his spine.

"Oh, I guess you do," she said, and gasped as Cole
planted an openmouthed kiss on the skin of her inner
thigh.

A quiver ran through her as he licked higher, flicking
along the crease where her leg met her body. So close, but
miles from what he wanted.

What she needed.

With her legs hooked over his shoulders and her hips
tilted slightly off the bed, she was open to his gaze. "God,
you're pretty," he murmured, taking a moment to look his
fill. Other than a little modest patch, she was smooth, her
bare sex slick with need. Her clit was a shiny little bud,
firm and ready and begging to be tasted.

He spread her open with his thumbs and bent his head
to feast, licking, sucking, stroking her clit in long slides
and tight little circles until she was running hot and wet
and rocking against his face. "God, you taste so good,"
he groaned, salty sweet and spice all at the same time.
She arched off the bed, her heels digging into his back as
he sucked her into his mouth, stroked her with his tongue.

He licked lower and slid his tongue inside, fucking
her with his tongue as she writhed and moaned. His cock
throbbed, insistent in its need to take his tongue's place.

Cole shoved the demands of his own body aside. Right now it felt too good to satisfy Megan's. Every moan, every sigh, every rush of moisture his lips, tongue, and fingers teased from her body made him feel like a fucking king.

And when he sucked her clit into his mouth and slid one, then two fingers high inside her and felt the rhythmic tightening of her body as she came on an endless wave, he felt like he had just seen the face of God.

He gave her one last, lingering kiss and let her legs slide down his arms as he rose from the floor. His dick was painfully hard, his balls drawn tight against his body, and every nerve ending sizzled with need. He put one knee on the bed and reached for her, but Megan rolled to her knees and wrapped his cock in her warm, firm grip.

Breath hissed between his teeth as she bent her head, and then, oh, Christ, yes, pressed her lips to the swollen head. Cole reached down to brush back her dark curtain of hair so he could see her hot little tongue circle the tip, lick up a drop of precome. He clenched his jaw, willing his orgasm back as she ran her tongue up and down his shaft, licking and squeezing until he was going out of his mind.

"Megan, God, you're driving me crazy. Jesus, please," he muttered, not sure what he was begging for, his universe shrinking until all he knew was her mouth and hands on his cock and the arousal heating to a nearly painful pitch.

She sucked him into her mouth, and he let out a shout, feeling the pressure build at the base of his spine as she took him as deep as he could go. Christ, he'd spent hours fantasizing about this, but nothing he could imagine ever came close. His imagination couldn't possibly touch the reality of Megan taking his cock in her mouth like she was starving for the taste of him, the little sounds she made in her throat as she sucked him off, her silky hair slipping through his fingers, the clean scents of soap and shampoo mixing with the musk of sex.

Another pump of her hand almost sent him over the edge, and he reluctantly pulled her head up. As unbelievably good as it felt, he didn't want to come this way. He wanted to come inside her, buried deep, feeling her take everything he had.

The need to have her, claim her, rose in his blood, primal and savage. He rolled her to her front and pulled her onto her knees. She was so beautiful, the curve of her spine, the silky smooth skin of her back. Her round ass tilted up, the wet, pink folds of her sex beckoning him in.

He wrapped one hand around her hip and the other around his cock and guided himself to her entrance. He squeezed inside, watching his cock disappear into her heat, the pleasure so keen he thought the top of his head might blow off.

She was wet, but so tight. He forced himself not to shove into her full force. But Megan was watching him over her shoulder, her eyes dark and mysterious, her mouth red and swollen. "Please," she moaned, rocking her ass back against him, taking him deeper with every stroke. "I need you, need you..."

Her breath exploded on a high sound of pleasure as he shoved into her full length, pulled almost all the way out and pushed all the way back inside. She spread her knees wide and rocked back to meet the surge of his hips, her moans growing louder with every stroke.

He could feel her tight and pulsing around his cock,

could see the muscles in her back tighten with pleasure. She was so close and so was he, his orgasm bearing down on him with the force of a freight train as he struggled to hold out a few seconds longer.

He reached around and found the firm swell of her clit, their moans mingling as her muscles clenched around him. His fingers slipped and slid against her in concert with his thrusts, heightening her pleasure as he strove to hold his at bay.

"That's it," he whispered as she stiffened against him, every muscle in her body tensing. "I want to feel you come, Megan. I want to make you feel so good. . . ."

Her cries echoed through the room as she shook with release around him, her sex kneading and squeezing him like a tight, wet fist. He jerked and pulsed inside her, turning inside out, coming with such force his vision darkened and he was afraid he might pass out.

He fell forward on her, barely catching himself before he crushed her. He rolled her to her back and looked into her dazed green eyes, wanting to say something but afraid he'd burst into tears if he opened his mouth. God, he'd never felt anything like he felt right now, the desperation to keep her close, keep her safe, a compulsion no amount of sex could ever take the edge off of.

She cradled his cheek in her hand and pressed her lips to his in a kiss full of lazy satisfaction and pure, unadulterated affection.

Cole felt the impact like a hydrogen bomb going off in his chest.

Jesus, I love her.

He swallowed past the softball-size lump in his throat and pressed his lips harder against Megan's to mask the slight tremble in his. He pulled her tight against him, skin to skin as he swept his tongue in her mouth, tasting her in lazy strokes. Relishing every detail of lying naked next to the woman he . . . loved.

He'd tried to hold it at bay, tried to chalk it up to unsatisfied lust, unresolved guilt over how he'd treated her after Sean's arrest. Told himself what he felt for her couldn't possibly run that deep.

But he couldn't run from it anymore, couldn't deny what he'd known practically from their first date. He'd tried to deny it then, had denied it for the past three years even as she haunted his days and nights.

Maybe there was a way. What if by some miracle they managed to uncover evidence that would exonerate Sean? Would that be enough for Megan to give them a second chance?

Don't even go there, he told himself even as he pulled Megan tighter. He was a realist, and the reality was there was almost zero chance of him and Megan working out.

Recognizing his emotions had long since crossed the line from attraction to crazy, balls-out in love with her didn't change anything.

He'd get over it, he told himself as he ran his hand down the smooth bare skin of her back, squeezed the lush curve of her hip.

It might take him a little while, but he'd get over it. He'd gotten over his share of heartache, and knowing whatever he had with Megan would end sooner rather than later would be enough to stave off total annihilation.

Right. Because you had such an easy time getting her out of your head the last time around.

Cole ignored the voice and pulled Megan closer,

determined to savor every second he did have with her. It would be enough. It had to be.

—⁓—

Rain ran down his face, soaking him to the skin, but its frigid bite did nothing to cool the rage swelling inside him. He wanted to scream at what he saw through the slats of the blinds. His Megan, splayed out like a whore, letting that disgusting cop fuck her. Putting her filthy mouth on his cock, letting him put his mouth between her legs. Her face flushed, mouth open, making disgusting sounds he could hear through the glass.

Soiling her. *Ruining her.* Ruining everything.

You were supposed to save me.

He should have known the second he snuck into her apartment and found her bed empty. Should have known when that guard dog of a cop had followed her in.

He was so naïve, convinced that she was good, that she was pure. His Megan would never give herself to another man, especially not to the cop who had arrested her beloved brother. He should have known. He should have kept a closer watch on her like he did all the other whores.

But he'd trusted. Blindly. Stupidly.

His hand formed into a fist to punch through the window. He was going to slaughter them both. Tie her down and fuck her until she screamed and force Williams to watch. He'd cut her throat, cut off Williams's balls and let them watch each other bleed to death.

His hand slid to the knife tucked in his waistband.

NO! The voice penetrated the red haze saturating his

mind like blood spray. He forced himself to look away from their sweaty, tangled bodies.

He pulled out the knife and ran it across his own wrist. Focus on the pain, the warmth of the blood dripping into his glove. The beast in him roared, struggling to break free, but he beat it back. He couldn't lose control, not yet.

His sharp breaths slowed.

His mind cleared.

He would kill her, but not yet. Not in a fit of blind rage. For her, he would do something special. A date with the Monster.

——

I did it again. Megan waited for the guilt to hit her, to urge her to pull herself out of that bed and out of his arms. But even as the outside world threatened to creep in, it was too good, too perfect, his arms around her, the shift and flex of his muscular body moving against hers.

His kiss was sweet, tender, only hinting at the fierce lust that had overtaken them only minutes before. His huge hands were so gentle on her skin, caressing, squeezing, like he was trying to memorize every inch of her.

Nothing had changed. Sean was still in prison, waiting to be executed. The real killer was still out there, lurking. Ready to kill Megan to keep his secret safe.

Yet everything had changed. Talia Vega was ready to give a statement. Krista Slater was taking a closer look at Sean's case to see if it could be connected to the Slasher murders.

And Cole had been by her side every step of the way. He'd been reluctant at first, but now Megan couldn't question his commitment to uncovering the truth.

His commitment to her.

The knowledge sent a rush of warmth through her as she savored the taste of him on her tongue, the feel of his hair-roughened skin against hers, and oh, the slide of his lips against her nipples, so gentle, like he could tell how sensitive they were after two orgasms. It was crazy how safe, how whole she felt with him, and she wanted to will the rest of the world away so she would never have to leave this bed, never have to leave his arms.

She couldn't, of course, but for the first time in what felt like a century, the real world held hope. There was finally a real chance Sean could go free.

And maybe, just maybe, there was a real chance for Megan and Cole. Because even though common sense said they were still doomed, the thought of letting him go made her heart feel as if it were being sliced open with a straight razor.

Oh God, I love him. She'd tried to keep it buried, but it had been there the whole time, simmering along with the anger, hurt, and resentment that had kept it hidden.

Now it burst to the surface, undeniable in its force.

There's no guarantee Cole feels the same.

Just because he was helping her didn't mean he loved her back. Guilt was a powerful motivator, and God knew she'd misread Cole's feelings before.

Megan burst into tears. Cole stiffened, then wrapped his arms tighter against her. "Shhh," he whispered. "It's going to be okay, Megan. Don't worry. Sean's going to file the appeal. Talia's meeting with Krista. You'll have more time."

Megan sobbed harder as she realized she hadn't been thinking of her brother and his pending execution but of her selfish love for Cole and the inevitable heartbreak that loomed on the horizon.

"It's going to be okay," he whispered. "No matter what, I'm with you. I know you don't trust me after what happened last time, how I treated you after Sean was arrested. I let you down, let you think I didn't care for you, but it's not true." The words came out in a rush, as though he wanted to get it all out before he thought too hard about it.

Megan's heart stuttered, than started to beat so heavily she could feel it in the tips of her fingers. "Then why did you say those things?"

"I didn't, at least not the way they were quoted by the reporter."

"You never tried to correct him." She buried her head against his chest, afraid to look at his face, afraid to hope he meant what she thought he might.

Her head rose and fell with his heavy sigh. "I thought it would be better for you to hate me, less complicated." He made a sound that was half chuckle, half sigh. "I was an idiot." He reached down and cupped her cheek, urging her to meet his eyes. "I want to make sure you understand I"—he hesitated, swallowing hard—"cared for you. Very much. And I still do. You can trust me, Megan. I'm not going to let you down again."

There were so many things she wanted to say, questions she wanted to ask, but she couldn't force them past the lump burning in her throat. She lifted her mouth to his, greedily drinking the kisses he rained on her lips and cheeks. Stealing their warmth and hoarding it away. Trying to shove away the knowledge that even with Cole by her side, they weren't even close to being out of the woods.

—∿—

"Can you translate this into English?" Krista said, glancing from the report to the white-coated lab geek looking up at her expectantly from his chair. She rubbed her eyes and stifled a yawn. It was six-fifteen and she wasn't firing on all cylinders yet.

Tucker was the only one in the lab at this hour, wide awake and on the job for two hours already. Krista was banking on getting out before anyone else came in.

Tucker quirked an eyebrow over his wire-frame glasses. "How about you tell me what you're doing in here at the crack of dawn asking me to run unauthorized tests."

Krista shot him a withering glare. "How about I don't tell anyone about the time I came in and found you surfing bigblackasses-dot-com?"

Tucker blushed so hard his bald spot turned pink. He took the report from her and laid it on the desk next to the baggie containing the knife Sean Flynn used to kill Evangeline Gordon. "His prints and her blood are all over it, just like the original report said. But right here, and here"—his finger indicated two spots on the knife, one on the hilt and one on the blade—"there was something else. Latex powder residue."

"Could it have been contaminated during testing?"

Tucker scrunched his nose. "It's possible I suppose, but for that amount to get on the knife, someone would have had to handle it pretty rough."

Krista was starting to feel a little sick. "No one noticed it in the initial report?"

Tucker shook his head. "It would be hard to miss if it was there."

She pulled the original report from the case file. "Where's the tech who did the initial analysis?"

"Ortiz? He left over a year ago. Moved to somewhere in California, I think."

Krista nodded absently and shoved the old report, Tucker's new analysis, and the bagged knife into her briefcase.

She left Tucker with a curt "thanks" and tried to tell herself it was probably nothing. Either the powder had gotten on the blade during testing or Ortiz just hadn't noticed it.

First Talia Vega coming forward with new information, and now this. Not matter how hard she tried, Krista couldn't shake the sinking feeling that something about Sean Flynn's case was starting to stink.

Chapter 19

He took a quick look around and darted across the street to Talia Vega's house. It was still dark, and the rain was coming down in sheets, but he still risked encountering an early morning runner or someone getting a head start on work. He was late, later than he'd wanted to be. He clamped down on the agitation. It had taken longer than he'd wanted to get everything ready. He needed to stay in control if he wanted to succeed.

The early hour and nasty weather were working in his favor, so he could slip, unnoticed, around the back of her house. A trip to the fuse box disabled the security system, and he had the bolt lock on Talia's back door picked in seconds.

He crept through the kitchen, barely breathing as he entered the living room. He slipped a pair of night-vision goggles on to navigate the inky darkness of her living room. The sound of heavy breath, the shift of a heavy body on the couch. He turned and saw Brooks's huge body on Talia's couch.

He'd expected the whore to share her bed with him. What a pleasant surprise not to have to take the other man's sloppy seconds.

He moved carefully through the darkness as he snuck up on Brooks. He leaned over the end of the couch and moved his hand down.

Brooks's hand shot up, knocking his hand away as he rolled to the floor. He jumped to his feet, hands up, poised to fight. "Who's here?" Brooks whispered.

He could see Brooks's wide eyes through the NVGs as the big man tried to focus. He charged, and Brooks saw him too late. The needle sank into Brooks's neck, and within seconds the man slumped to the floor as the phenobarbital went to work. He gave the man a quick frisk, removed a Glock from Brooks's waistband and tucked it into his own.

There was a creak of floorboards coming from the hall off the living room.

"Jack? Is everything okay?"

His breath caught and his body went tight with anticipation. He could hear her padding down the hall. Closer... closer.

He covered her mouth and yanked her to his chest. "You thought you could get away with it, didn't you, little cunt. You know what happens to the ones who talk."

She was squirming, little mewling sounds coming from behind his hand. His cock was rock hard. He shoved her against the wall, made sure she felt him bulging against his fly. "Feel that? It's all for you. I've been wanting to do you from the first time I saw you, but the old man wouldn't let me touch his special pet."

She made a choking sound and tried to shrink from him.

"I can't wait for you and Megan to see what I have planned for you." His balls tightened when he thought of

the fear that would mask their faces as they saw exactly
what would happen to them before they died. They'd see
their blood, hear the screams as he cut them, hear them
beg as he shoved his dick into their unwilling bodies.
Knowing they would share the same fate.

Stupid bitch, thinking she'd get away with this.

Stupid idiots, thinking they could control him. They
thought they could control him, keep him in check by
throwing him a tasty little morsel every now and then.

They had no idea the damage he was capable of when
he didn't get what he wanted.

He dropped her to the floor, went back to Brooks's
slumped form, and grabbed him by the hair. He pulled out
his knife and felt the skin of the man's neck give against
the blade. His muscles tightened in anticipation of delivering the killing blow.

No.

This wasn't necessary. Brooks hadn't seen him, would
never be able to identify him. And even if Brooks could,
by the time the drugs got out of his system enough for him
to make sense, Megan and Talia would have suffered the
heat of his revenge, and he would be long gone.

He started to leave Brooks where he lay, facedown on
the floor. *Think, idiot.* Once they heard Talia had missed
her little meeting, they'd come looking. It wouldn't do for
them to find Brooks unconscious, all but announcing that
Talia had been kidnapped.

There was an SUV parked next to Talia's sedan that
he assumed belonged to Brooks. He stuffed Brooks and
Talia in the back and covered them with a blanket.

He drove away from the city, up a narrow winding
road littered with tree limbs blown down by the storm. A

fire road split off to the right, and he turned, guiding the car over the dirt road peppered with potholes full of rain. He stopped when the fire road got too narrow, about two miles from the main road.

He pulled Brooks from the trunk, took his phone, wallet, and shoes before dragging him a hundred yards off the road into the woods. He shuddered in the damp frigid air of the February morning. He didn't have the drive to kill Brooks himself, but there was no guarantee the man would survive the morning. In a cold, wet rain like this, hypothermia could set in in a matter of minutes, and that was if a man was active. The dose he'd given Brooks would leave him inert for at least four hours.

He started to walk away, then went back to Brooks's prone body. He lifted Brooks by the hair and pulled out his knife, delivering a deep slice that bisected the skin over Brooks's cheekbone.

A little souvenir, if the other man survived the morning. A reminder of what happened when he tried to play hero.

The way the blood pooled under his cheek to mix with the rain and mud made him smile.

He climbed back in the SUV and continued up the hill several miles swerving to avoid tree limbs blown down by the storm. Finally he turned down a driveway. The house wasn't much to look at. The paint had been peeling and the steps had been broken when he'd bought it years ago. But it was far from the neighbors and private. More private than his condo downtown could ever be.

A stairway led from the outside of the house, down to the one room he'd bothered to work on. He dragged Talia through the heavy steel door, down a short hall, and into the finished basement.

When he'd bought the house, he'd known instantly this would be a perfect screening room for his own personal projects. A fifty-two-inch plasma TV dominated one wall, hooked up to a state-of-the-art surround-sound system. A hard drive on the shelf held hours of his favorite films. The walls were thickly padded, soundproofed by an acoustics expert who built recording studios. When he watched his own productions, he liked it loud, and he considered himself a courteous neighbor.

Beyond the screening room was another room, one he'd dug out and framed himself. The construction was crude, but it had been the perfect retreat, until today.

The demon roared again and he shoved the rage back. He couldn't think about it now. Soon, soon. The betraying bitch would be here soon, and he could spill her blood on what should have been an altar of love.

He wiped a shaky hand down his face and laid Talia down on the couch. Maybe he could wake her up, take the edge off....

No. He wanted to do Talia when he had time to linger. Time to do it right.

And she was still too out of it. He wanted her fully conscious, fully aware of what was happening to her. Wanted her to understand with her last breath that no whore was going to fuck up his plans and get away with it.

He wanted Megan to hear her screams fade as the blood poured from her neck.

Talia slumped on the couch across from the TV. The dose he'd given her should keep her out for several hours, but he bound her wrists and ankles with plastic zip ties just to be sure. He didn't bother with a gag. Nothing could penetrate the soundproof walls.

He stroked the smooth, buttery skin of her cheek. He could already see it yielding to his knife. "Enjoy your rest, Talia. You're going to need it."

—⁓—

Megan awoke in tangle of bedsheets. She was disoriented, not quite sure at first where she was and why she was naked.

Then she heard Cole's voice next to her, felt his bulk shift as he pushed himself up to sit against the pillows. Despite everything, she felt a sudden rush of warmth, savored the feel of how right it was to wake up next to him after a night in his bed.

And still burning this morning was that faint glow of hope, which had slowly come to life over the past few days, clawing its way through the darkness, becoming stronger with every hour she and Cole spent working on Sean's case.

Hope that the end of the nightmare really was in sight. Hope that Sean really would be set free. Hope that maybe, by some miracle, she and Cole could come out of this and still have a fighting chance.

"That doesn't sound good." Cole was on the phone, his tone grim.

Megan struggled to hold on to the flicker of optimism.

"No, I have no idea where either of them would go."

He listened for a minute, and Megan leaned in, but she couldn't hear anything on the other side of the conversation.

"Right. I'll call you if I hear anything." He set the phone down and ran a hand through sleep-disheveled hair.

He looked over and saw that Megan was awake. "Hey." His grim expression softened a bit as he leaned over and pressed a quick kiss to her mouth.

Megan kissed him back, holding the real world at bay for a few more seconds. Judging from the look on Cole's face, reality was about to intrude, big-time.

"That was Slater," he said, rolling to his feet to pad naked over to his dresser. He pulled on a pair of boxers and a T-shirt and tossed another one to Megan.

"What did she say?" Megan caught the shirt and slipped it on before scooting out of bed.

"Talia missed their appointment," he said.

"That's not until…Jesus Christ, it's already after eleven," Megan said, shocked when she looked at the clock on Cole's nightstand. She shouldn't be surprised, considering when she and Cole had gone to bed. "What happened?"

"Krista waited at her house for over an hour, and Talia and Jack never showed. Never called her either and she can't reach either of them."

The faint glow of hope was extinguished. "Their meeting was at nine. Why didn't she call us earlier?" Megan said as she followed Cole to the kitchen.

"Court." He grabbed a bag of coffee and filled the carafe of water. The gurgling of the machine filled the kitchen in seconds. "She couldn't call till she had a break."

Megan grabbed her phone from her purse and sank into a kitchen chair, her stomach churning. "This is a disaster. We have to find Talia. Without her we don't have anything." She scrolled through her missed calls. Nate had called twice, but there was nothing from Sean's attorney.

"That's not completely true," Cole said as he poured two mugs of coffee. He put milk and sugar into one and set it in front of Megan. "Slater had a lab tech run an analysis on Sean's knife. They found traces of latex residue."

The mug froze halfway to Megan's mouth. "That was never in any of the reports."

"The tech who did the original analysis didn't include it. It could have happened during analysis or—"

"Or it could have happened if the murderer was wearing latex gloves," Megan said. "We need to call Brockner and talk to Slater about filing a motion—"

Cole held up his hand, shaking his head in a way that made Megan's stomach sink all over again. "She already told Brockner, and he's going to do what he can, but it's still going to be almost impossible for him to file an appeal without Sean's consent. And a questionable lab report isn't going to be enough for Krista to move to reopen the case. She has to have Talia's statement, and even then—"

"Then why are we doing nothing when she's already been missing for hours? We have to find her!" Megan's cup clattered into the sink.

"Wait." Cole stopped her as she made for the bedroom to find the rest of her clothes. "There's something else. The police arrested Jimmy Caparulo earlier this morning. They think he's the Slasher."

—⁂—

It was time. Long past, and she still hadn't emerged from the cop's house. Slut. Acting to the world like she was on some crusade to save her brother, and instead she was fucking the cop who had put Sean in jail.

They'd gone at it for hours. He'd left, disgusted, before they were even finished.

Was she fucking the cop even now? She hadn't bothered to return his calls. His temper strung tighter with every minute that passed.

He didn't risk getting out of his car to look. In the dark of early morning, he could stay hidden, but the houses were close together and with the storm blowing, neighbors had stayed home from work. Several were even out in their yards, clearing leaves from drains and warily watching the heavy limbs swaying in the wind.

It was hard to resist the voice saying to hell with the neighbors, to hell with being seen. His life was over anyway. What did he care? He could get in there, kill them both, torture them, and no one would find them until it was too late.

But it would be so much better to wait. He needed her to come to him. Because if he had to take her from the cop, the cop would end up dead.

And he needed Cole to live. For a long, long time. Tortured by the knowledge of Megan's death and how she'd suffered. Tortured by the knowledge he'd arrested the wrong man, leaving the real killer free to kill and kill and kill.

He knew it was the right plan, but he was running out of patience.

Time to bring Megan out of hiding. He knew the perfect bait.

—⁓—

"Get me the lights this time, okay? The reds shred my throat." Dev dug a ten-dollar bill out of her pocket and gave it to Amber.

Amber shrugged. "Jesse smokes the reds, but I'll get

the lights if there's enough left over." She ducked in the convenience store before Dev could say anything. It sucked being fourteen and looking her age, at the mercy of everyone else for something as dumb as cigarettes. She pulled the half pack she'd swiped from Aunt Kathy from her coat pocket and lit up. Her lungs seized at the first inhale and she started to choke.

"Fucking menthols," she wheezed. No wonder they'd been buried in the kitchen junk drawer. Her mom must have left them when she'd visited a couple days ago.

"You know you shouldn't be doing that, right?"

Dev straightened abruptly at the male voice speaking so close.

She looked up warily, eyes narrowing as she recognized the blond hair and the toothpaste-commercial smile. "It's not like it's weed."

"Devany, right?"

Dev nodded and took another deep inhale, managing not to choke this time.

"I'm—"

"I remember you. You're Megan's friend Nate." She gave him a half smile. He was hot, she supposed, in a totally straight, preppy kind of way. She could see why some women might go for him.

He smiled back, but it didn't quite reach his eyes. He was looking at her a little too hard.

"Yeah. Have you talked to her lately? I really need to see her, and I can't seem to get in touch."

Devany blew a cloud of smoke in his face. His nostrils flared, but he didn't flinch.

"I really need to get in touch with her," he repeated.

"Why?"

"It's between me and Megan." His voice was sharp.

So he was pissed at Megan about something. Dev wasn't about to help him track Megan down, not with that kind of attitude. "I'm not her social planner," Dev said, cocking a hip as she took another drag.

She hid a smirk as his mouth tightened into a white line. She'd been walking the straight and narrow so long, she'd forgotten how fun it was to fuck with people. And she was getting a weird vibe from Nate, like he was a little too intense about getting ahold of Megan. Something in her gut told her she needed to stall him long enough to give Megan a heads-up.

She flicked her bangs off her forehead and hit him with a smile. "I'm just messing with you. I'm supposed to meet her at home around lunchtime."

"Good. I can give you a ride." He reached for her arm.

Crap. She should have seen that coming. She was getting soft, too comfortable living with Aunt Kathy, leaving her slow on her feet. She backed up a step. "My friend gave me a ride here. I'll meet you back there." She'd wait till he left for their empty trailer and call Megan to warn her.

"I insist." He wrapped his arm around her upper arm.

"Just let me tell my friend." She tried to get Amber's attention, but she was too busy trying to convince the clerk to sell her cigarettes without an ID.

She didn't make a scene as he guided her across the street. He was setting off her Spidey sense, but she was pretty sure he wasn't going to do anything. Not in broad daylight anyway. Once she got him back to the trailer, she could keep him occupied, buy Megan an hour or two before she got the slip on Nate and could call Megan to warn her that Nate was pissed at her about something. Megan could decide for herself if she wanted to see him.

Not that Dev expected Megan to refuse. Megan was way too nice. She saw the good side in everyone. No way could she see past the good looks, expensive clothes, and too-nice attitude to recognize that he might not be such a nice guy underneath it all.

Lucky for her she had Devany to look out for her.

—⁓—

Megan's gasp of shock reverberated through the kitchen. "They think Jimmy's the Slasher? Why?"

"They found text messages from him on Stephanie's phone, and when they searched his place, they found the knife, bindings, video equipment, everything."

"That doesn't make sense," Megan said, shaking her head. "Jimmy isn't like that—"

"He's been arrested for assault, not including what he did to you."

"I've known him for most of my life. I think I'd sense it if he was a cold-blooded killer."

Damn Megan and her soft heart, always wanting to believe the best about people even when the cold, hard truth was staring her in the face. "The evidence is pretty damn convincing."

"Evidence can be planted, Cole. You know that as well as I do."

"Come on, Megan, that stuff only happens on cop shows."

She shook her head. "Before their fight, Jimmy was Sean's closest friend. There's no way he would frame Sean for murder. He wouldn't have killed Evangeline—"

"He didn't," Cole said softly.

She cocked her head to the side like she hadn't heard him correctly. "But if Jimmy's the Slasher and the Slasher killed Evangeline Gordon..."

Cole shook his head. "Jimmy's alibi for the night Evangeline was murdered checked out, remember?"

Megan shook her head again, grasping. "Someone lied for him, then. We'll talk to whoever was covering for him."

Cole put his hands on her shoulders, steadying her. "Jimmy was picked up for a DUI the night of the murder, remember? He spent the night in lockup when his aunt couldn't come up with the money that night."

All of the color washed out of Megan's face. "Oh God, I forgot. So many details..." Her voice trailed off. "This doesn't make any sense. The Slasher killed those women and he killed Evangeline—"

Cole blew out a frustrated breath. "That was never a foregone conclusion."

Megan froze, her eyes narrowed on his face. "You still believe Sean did it?" Her lips barely moved as she whispered the question.

"Don't put words in my mouth," he snapped. "I believe there's a connection between the victims we didn't see until now, but if Jimmy was in jail the night she was murdered..."

Megan shook her head, her lips moving. No sound, but Cole could see her mouth form *no, no, no* over and over.

He curved his hand around her back. "It's going to be okay."

"No, it's not," Megan yelled. "This has to be a setup. Don't you see?" There was a wild look in her eye he didn't like.

"You have to look at the facts, Megan," he said, hoping logic would pull her back from the edge. "The evidence against Jimmy Caparulo is hitting hard. We have to consider—"

"The *facts*," Megan practically spat. "Always with the facts, never willing to believe anything unless it smacks you in the face. You never believed in any of this, did you?"

Cole's jaw clenched as he absorbed the insult. He pulled his arm from her as though stung, then turned and walked down the hallway to his bedroom before he said something he regretted.

She trailed him down the hall. "You can't give up on this now, not when we're so close."

Cole's patience snapped. "How the hell can you accuse me of giving up, not believing in you, after the shit you've put me through?" he said as he jerked on a pair of jeans and a sweatshirt. "My career is in the shitter. I even took a goddamned knife for you. I know I can never make up for what happened to Sean, but Jesus Christ, doesn't that count for something?"

Her face went chalk-white, and he could see her throat working convulsively. Her hand went up imploringly. "You're right. That was totally unfair. What you've done for me, you have no idea—" A sob choked off whatever she was going to say next.

He caught her as she launched herself at him, his heart squeezing at how she felt somehow smaller, frailer in his arms.

"This can't be it, Cole. I refuse to believe we've been chasing down the wrong person all this time."

Cole stayed silent. She wouldn't hear any arguments right now.

She pulled out of his arms and started to pace. "Think, Cole. The Slasher was meticulous. It was right there in the files. He thought through everything and never left a trace. Jimmy has a documented drinking problem. He'd been arrested for assault. That's not a guy with the kind of discipline to pull this off."

"If that's true, it will come out in the investigation."

She stopped and looked at him with huge, pleading eyes. "What if it's not in time to help Sean? What am I going to do?"

God, he hated seeing her like this, her face pinched with strain when less than twelve hours ago it had glowed with the first rays of hope. "Look, I'll do everything I can—"

His phone rang and he cursed when he saw Lieutenant Chin's number on the display. He had no desire to get his ass chewed, but his chances of getting more information about Caparulo's arrest were better if he tried to play along.

"Petersen tells me you've been doing some investigating on the side."

Shit. "That's correct, sir. I was following some leads that connected the Slasher case with Sean Flynn's case."

"Petersen says you may have actually come up with something useful. I need you to come down to the station to make a statement."

"I'd be happy to give Olivia my statement over the phone, sir, but I'm in the middle of something right now—"

"I didn't make myself clear. You need to make your statement in person, and bring with you any materials pertinent to the case."

"Sir, now that you have the suspect in custody, nothing I have is urgent in nature. If we could put this off until tomorrow, or even later this evening?" *After I find out what the hell happened to our key witness . . .*

"Tasso wants your badge for leaking information. I put my ass on the line for you, and you're goddamn lucky you got off with just a suspension. But if you don't have your ass down here in twenty minutes, consider your suspension permanent."

———m———

Dev dropped her wet coat on the floor of the trailer and walked to the refrigerator to grab herself a Coke. "You want one?" she said over her shoulder to Nate, who followed her in and carefully hung his wet coat on the peg by the door. "We have beer, too, or something stronger." She flashed him what she hoped passed for a flirty smile, calling herself a hundred kinds of moron for letting him get her back here alone.

No big deal. She'd gotten herself out of plenty of jams. She could get away from him, no problem.

"I don't drink alcohol," he said as he took a seat on the edge of the worn couch. "But I will have some water."

She could feel his eyes on her as she filled a glass. Her hands were shaking, making the ice clink against the glass.

She perched on the couch next to him and lit up a cigarette.

"Your parents know you smoke?"

"I don't live with my parents. And my aunt smokes so much she doesn't know the difference." She tried to keep her fingers steady as she flicked ashes into a half-full ash-tray. "Does it bother you? Let me guess, you don't like the taste when you kiss a girl." She waited for him to blush and look away. Old guys didn't know what to do when jailbait like her pretended to hit on them.

But he didn't blush or stammer or any of that.

Her skin crawled as he looked her up and down, taking in her skintight jeans and the tight T-shirt under her coat that showed off her B-cups and a three-inch strip of her bare stomach. His gaze moved back to her face, and what she saw in his eyes scared her, even worse than Davos had scared her the other night when he'd pinned her on the bed and shoved his hand up her skirt.

It wasn't the lust—she was used to that. It was the split second of something she'd seen in other eyes.

Dev's blood chilled as she realized she may have seriously underestimated how big of a creep Nate really was.

If this guy jumped, she needed to be ready to bolt.

He drank the water in three gulps and set the glass down on the coffee table. "What time did you say Megan was supposed to meet you here?"

"She should be here soon. Why, am I boring you?"

"Not at all." There was a dead look in his eyes, and Dev knew in that instant he didn't believe her story about meeting Megan here.

She didn't have to fake her shiver. "It's freezing in here. I'm gonna go get a sweatshirt."

She could hear her heartbeat thudding in her ears as she ducked into her room. She yanked a hoodie over her head, then took her cell out of her pocket, swearing when the low battery notice flashed.

Shit. She'd just have to sneak to a friend's and call

Megan from there. She climbed on her bed and slid the window open, freezing at the squeal of metal on metal. No footsteps, so she opened it the rest of the way. Icy rain hit her in the face and wind blew her hair back, but she was grateful for the storm as it muffled the clatter of the screen falling to the ground as she popped it out.

She heaved herself up with her hands and pushed her head and shoulders through the window and braced herself to hit the mud.

She cried out as hard hands seized her hips and dragged her back through the window. Her sweatshirt rode up and her hips and ribs scraped against the hard metal edge of the window frame.

"I don't think so, little girl."

Her scream was lost to the howl of wind as Nate flipped her onto her back and pinned her to her bed. One big hand covered her mouth; the other wrapped around her throat. Dev bucked against his weight, but he was too big, too strong. *No, no, no!* She screamed against his hand, but all that came out were muffled whimpers.

Tears streamed down as she stared up into his face. He was freakishly calm as he looked down at her.

He removed the hand from her throat, and before she could even breathe, she felt the cold sting of a knife against her neck. "Now, you are going to call Megan and get her over here, or I will hurt you. Are we clear?"

Chapter 20

Dev's mind raced as Nate bound her hands and feet and dragged her to the kitchen. She needed to get out of this, needed to somehow warn Megan before it was too late.

She filled her lungs, hoping a five-alarm scream in the middle of the day would rouse a neighbor.

"Don't even think about it."

The scream died in a whimper of pain as Nate tugged her sweatshirt up and slid the knife along her waist. "That's just the beginning." He pulled a bandana out of his pocket, wadded it up, and shoved it in her mouth. A second bandana was tied around that.

"Or maybe you like being cut?" he said, tracing the knife along the back of her hand but not hard enough to slice through the skin. "Maybe you'd like a moon and stars in your skin, like your friend Bianca."

Oh God. He'd killed Bianca. He was the one who had raped and tortured her and filmed the whole thing.

A swell of nausea pushed up her throat, and she was afraid she was going to choke on her own vomit. That might be a better way to go.

"No? Then you better help me if you don't want to end up exactly like her."

He left her on the floor by the couch while he went to the kitchen to retrieve the phone. He dialed and held it up to her ear and tugged the gag away. "When Megan answers, you know what to do."

"Hello? Dev? Is that you?"

"Megan, don't—" The phone crashed to the floor and the knife sliced her forearm.

"You bitch. Don't try anything. You have no idea how bad it will get for you if you try to fuck with me."

She shook her head. "I won't let you hurt her." Megan was the only one who cared about her. Dev couldn't let him hurt her like he'd hurt those other women. "You can do whatever you want to me, but I won't do it. I won't—"

They froze at the sound of a car door slamming in front of the trailer. Dev tried to scream, but Nate shoved the gag back in her mouth and slammed her head against the floor so hard her vision swam.

Footsteps on the metal stairs, the click of someone trying the door latch. Nate ducked behind the door just as it swung open.

Dev's stomach sank when she saw her mother's thin frame enter. She looked from side to side, small, birdlike movements, checking to make sure the house was empty. *God, Mom, why did you have to pick today to come raid Aunt Kathy's cash jar?* Dev tried to yell, warn her.

Her mother's head jerked when she spotted Dev, her eyes widening with confusion, then fear as she took in the fact that Dev was bound and gagged on the floor of the trailer. "Dev, honey, oh my God." She started toward her, hands outstretched.

Nate's hand snaked out and covered her mother's face, so fast she couldn't even scream. He lifted her mother off the floor and shoved the knife against her neck. "Either you call Megan, Dev, or I'll cut her fucking head off."

Dev shook her head reflexively, then screamed against the gag as the knife slashed across her mother's cheek, leaving a gaping slash behind. He held the tip of the knife under her mother's left eye. "Next I'll pop it out like a grape."

Her mother was moaning against Nate's hand, frozen in terror.

"And then I'll skin her like a rabbit before I cut her throat, all while you watch. Is that what you want?"

Dev shook her head and sobbed. She didn't want him to hurt Megan. And she was angry, so angry at her mother for everything, but right now all she could remember was the pink bike her mom had bought her for her sixth birthday and the way she used to make Dev strawberry pancakes in the shape of hearts every Saturday. The whispered I-love-yous and desperate hugs when she was taken away.

She couldn't. She couldn't.

"Will you call Megan?"

Dev nodded. She waited as Nate bound and gagged her mother. When he went to retrieve the phone from where it had rolled under the couch, Dev inched her way over to her mother and burrowed against her, whimpering like a puppy.

Nate jerked her up, dialed the phone, and pressed it against her ear. "Don't do anything stupid," he said as he pulled the gag from her mouth once again.

Dev shook her head.

—⁓—

"They want me to go down to the station."

Megan's chest filled with dread as she took in Cole's

expression, that awful, carefully blank cop face he put on when there was bad news to be delivered. "Shouldn't we go find Talia? She's the only one who really knows what's going on."

This whole thing with Jimmy was just a setup. The real killer was still out there no matter the evidence they had against Jimmy. Megan knew it; she could *feel* it in her very bones. But unless they found Talia, no one would ever believe her. It would be dismissed as just another one of her desperate theories.

Cole ran a tired hand down his face. "Look, if I go in, I can get more information about the evidence they have against Caparulo. If I play by their rules, I have a better chance of staying in the loop."

Though he didn't say it, there was something else going on. "And you'll have a chance of keeping your badge."

"There's that too."

Funny how his admission didn't fill her with rage or a sense of betrayal. For three years, she hadn't been able to forgive him for turning his back on her in favor of his job. But now, all she felt was a horrible sense of inevitability. That despite how hard she'd fought, despite everything he'd done to help her, none of it really mattered.

In the end, Sean was going to die. "I understand."

"When I get down there, I'll tell them to put out an APB on Talia. As soon as I tell them what we've found out, and when Slater talks to them—"

"But Slater's not going to do anything without talking to Talia." She was surprised at how calm and matter-of-fact her voice sounded. Almost like Cole in his full-on Robo-cop mode.

From the near panicked look in his eyes, it was almost as though they had switched places. A muscle throbbed in his jaw. "I'm going to do everything I can. I promise—"

Megan's phone rang, cutting off her reply, and she swore under her breath when she saw Dev's number. She couldn't ignore it. "Hello?" No answer. "Dev? Is that you?" She thought she heard a muffled noise; then the line went dead. She tried to call back, but the line was busy. She pushed aside the ripple of concern and turned back to Cole. "I understand, Cole. You've done a lot to help me, and I'll always be grateful for that."

His dark brows pulled together. "Why are you talking like we're never going to see each other again?"

"I didn't mean it like that," she said. Or did she? Because really, despite everything between them, where could they go from here? How could she ever be happy with Cole, knowing she'd failed Sean? "It's okay," she repeated. "You do what you have to do. Just take me back to my car, and I'll go look for Talia—" She stopped as her phone rang. Devany again. "Hello?" she said tiredly.

"Megan? Can you come over, please?"

"Dev, what's wrong? It sounds like you've been crying." She followed Cole down the hall, through the kitchen, and into his attached garage.

"It's—" Suddenly Dev's voice was muffled like she was putting her hand over the phone. "It's my mom," Dev said. "She came over and—" Dev broke into sobs. "You have to come over, right now!"

God, she thought wearily, *why now?* "Dev, this isn't a good time. I can come this afternoon—"

"No!" she yelled sharply. "It has to be right now."

"If your mom's bugging you, I can call Kathy or your caseworker. Dev, you can always call the police too."

"You said I could count on you when I needed you! You get over here now, or I promise you, Megan, you will never see me again."

Megan's jaw clenched as she sucked a frustrated breath through her teeth. "Fine, I'll be over in ten minutes, but I can't stay."

The line went dead. Megan ground the heels of her hands against her eyes but couldn't hold back the tears of frustration. "I have to go see Dev," she said as Cole followed her into the garage.

—⁂—

"Good girl," Nate said as he hung up the phone.

"What are you going to do now?" Dev whispered.

Nate didn't answer, and Dev's blood curdled when he leaned toward her to lift the gag back over her mouth, that same dead look in his eyes.

Then something in his face changed. His blue eyes widened, his lips parted, and he leaned his face closer to hers.

She froze, holding her breath, trying to shrink away, but there was nowhere to go. The hand around her throat loosened and he brought it to her face. She squeezed her eyes shut and felt his thumb wipe over her eyes. A sob choked in her throat, but instead of trying to dig her eyeballs out, he rested his hand against her cheek and didn't do anything.

She opened her eyes just enough to see, her scalp prickling when she saw him staring at her, smiling.

His lips moved and she thought she heard him whisper a name.

"Sarah."

—〰—

He gazed down at the big eyes staring up at him. He hadn't been able to see her at first, not through the choppy, streaked hair, the heavy eyeliner, and the nose ring. The flirty, slutty attitude he'd have to break her of before it got out of control.

But there, in that split second, he'd gotten close enough to see the milky smoothness of her skin, the light dusting of freckles across her nose. The fear in her wide brown eyes.

The innocence.

Take out the streaks of purple, grow the hair past her shoulders, and change the brown eyes to the color of grass, and Devany was what Sarah would have looked like had she lived three more years.

How could he have not seen it? He swallowed hard, his hand shaking as he brought it up to her cheek. God, he'd been so close, so close to extinguishing that light forever.

It was Megan's fault, that bitch. Making him so angry he'd almost missed her, almost destroyed the one who would save him.

He'd already done damage; he could see it from the fear and the horror in her eyes. She was remembering what he'd done to Bianca, remembering what she'd found in the trailer that night. "I'm sorry. I didn't see it that first night I saw you in the trailer," he said. "You should have never seen that. If I had known you would find me, I would have done it somewhere else."

He leaned down and pressed a kiss to her forehead. "But it's okay, Sarah. Everything will be okay."

———∿∿∿———

"Who's Sarah?" Dev asked in a shaky voice. "What are you going to do to my mom? You're going to let her go, right?"

"Shhh, don't worry about it," he said, the gentleness in his voice creeping her out even more than when he was threatening her.

He put the gag back in place and went back over to her mom. The knife was in his right hand, the blade twisting back and forth as he flipped the handle between his fingers.

Oh God, oh God.

Nate grabbed her mother by her short blond hair and yanked her head back. She and her mother screamed behind their gags.

Nate froze and he turned back to Dev. She felt like her heart was going to explode through her chest.

He walked over to her and lifted her in his arms. She struggled and he squeezed her so hard she couldn't breathe. "I'm not going to hurt you. I'm just taking you somewhere you won't have to see."

He carried her to her bedroom and placed her gently on the bed and even tucked a pillow under her head. "It will be over soon. I promise."

Dev screamed and thrashed against her bonds as he shut the door behind him. She screamed until her throat was raw, but no one heard.

Her screams faded to sobs, and she prayed he wouldn't torture her mother before he killed her.

—✳✳✳—

They drove in silence to Dev's trailer. Megan felt like the world was shifting, crumbling around her. Cole was silent, tension radiating from him. Several times he turned to her to say something, then stopped as though he couldn't quite get the words out.

"Do you want me to go in with you?"

She shook her head. "You have stuff of your own to deal with."

For some reason that seemed to make him angry.

She reached for the door handle. But before she could open the door, he grabbed her shoulders and pressed her back into her seat. "I wish with everything I have that I could wave a magic wand and get your brother out of prison. You know that, right?" He closed his eyes and pressed his forehead against hers. "I would do anything to go back and change everything so we could be together. Like we were supposed to be."

Her breath caught at that, then hitched again as he cradled her cheeks in his hands and caught her mouth in a hard, almost desperate kiss. "I know." But his words, his kiss, couldn't erase the fact that her world was crumbling around her. God, what kind of deluded idiot was she to think she was going to single-handedly save Sean?

Now there wasn't a damn thing either of them could do but wait for his execution. "Sometimes we have to know when to throw in the towel, right?" she said as she reached again for the door.

"Don't say that. There's still time. This isn't over. You can't give up yet," Cole said fiercely.

"Sure," she said as she opened the door. She knew

Cole was right, but she couldn't see past the despair. How many times could she get up and fight after having her hopes smashed to the ground? "Call me if you find out anything new, and I'll do the same."

"We're going to get through this," he said as she started to climb out of the car. "Whatever happens, I'm with you, okay?"

She nodded and heard Cole's whispered curse as she closed the door behind her.

She felt like she was imploding as she heard Cole drive away. *You can't give up yet.* She knew that, knew she needed to focus, first on helping Dev through her latest crisis, then on finding the answers Sean needed before it was too late.

And yet with Talia's disappearance and the police honing in on Jimmy as the Slasher, those answers had never felt more out of reach.

She swallowed back the devastation and forced herself up the steps to Dev's trailer. She knocked, then tried the latch when there was no answer. "Dev, it's me," she said as the door swung open. "You shouldn't leave the door unlocked. . . ."

The smell was the first thing that hit her. Metallic blood and the stench of bodily fluids. She choked on a scream when she saw the crumpled form on the floor surrounded by a thick puddle of blood.

Adrenaline obliterated her exhaustion as fear roared through her.

"Devany!" she screamed, and ran forward to kneel next to the body. Blood soaked her jeans, and it took her several seconds to realize the small body was not Devany, but her mother. She sprang to her feet and called Devany's name, fumbling through her purse to find her cell phone. She stumbled down the hall, phone in hand and heard a thump coming from Dev's bedroom.

She kicked the door open. "Oh, my God." Dev's hands and ankles were bound. "It's going to be okay!" She pushed the 9 on her phone, and Dev started heaving and screaming on the bed.

Megan felt a whisper of movement behind her and turned.

"Nate?" she whispered, confusion morphing to fear when she saw the fury contorting his face.

He moved like a striking snake, wrapping a steely arm around her, his huge hand covering her mouth before she could even draw a breath to scream. Megan struggled with everything she had but was no match for his strength and size.

"I thought you were going to be the one to save me, Megan."

Terror snaked down her spine as she recognized that throaty whisper from the hotel room, the feel of strong fingers crushing her throat. "But you're a whore, just like them. Now you're going to find out what happens when you betray me."

She could hear Dev's terrified screams behind the gag, could see the tears spill from the girl's eyes as she struggled, helpless, against the bonds. Nate's grip grew tighter. An unbearable pressure built behind Megan's eyes, and her head filled with a red, roaring haze.

———— ❧ ————

Cole stopped at a light and slammed his fist against the steering wheel. He felt like he'd just taken a slug to the chest from a sawed-off shotgun.

Jesus, he wished she'd yelled at him, raged at him for leaving her to report to duty instead of helping her finish this.

Anything would be easier to take than that desolate look in her eyes. That hollow, empty look that happened only after a person had lost all hope.

He'd seen it last night in Sean's eyes. He'd never imagined he'd see it in Megan's. It didn't seem possible that she could lose faith so completely, not after she'd fought so hard for so long.

And it was his fault, even if she didn't say it. Cole knew it. His fault for not being able to do enough, for stupidly following his instincts and trusting that Talia would show up as promised and do the right thing.

What the fuck was he doing, heading back to the station as if he was going to pull his career out of the crapper?

Like he really cared anyway.

He didn't, he realized with shock. He didn't give a shit about anything except making things right with Megan, doing whatever he could to wipe that devastated look from her face and get her back to where she'd been just last night.

Happy. Hopeful.

Counting on *him* to help her make this right.

Even if he hadn't been in love with Megan, he would have been compelled to do something before it was too late. Slater was right. Something about Sean's case was starting to stink, and Cole couldn't live with himself if he didn't find out what.

He started to pull a U-turn, then stopped himself. It was better to go look for Talia by himself. Who knew what he would find, who he would encounter? He'd feel better knowing Megan was safe while he was out chasing down the bad guys.

He dialed Megan's number, cursing when he got her voice mail. He didn't leave a message—what he had to say was too important to relay over voice mail.

He tried calling Talia and Jack again, with no luck. In a last-ditch effort, he called Jack's friend who ran the security firm in California. As planned, Danny Taggart and his brother had picked up Rosario last night at the airport, but Danny hadn't heard from Jack since then.

Where the hell were they? He could see Talia getting cold feet and running, but he'd trusted Jack to keep her on a short leash. It didn't seem likely Talia could get the drop on him, not without help anyway.

Then again, she and Brooks could have hightailed it out of here as soon as they got Talia's sister on the plane last night.

He pulled up to Talia's house and gave her front door a cursory knock before slipping around the house and gaining entrance through an unlocked window. Something wasn't right; he could feel it the second his feet touched the floor.

His suspicions were confirmed with a quick inspection of the empty house. Talia's purse, containing her cell phone and her wallet, were on the dresser in her bedroom. In the living room, the coffee table had been kicked over, and the couch looked like it had been through a tornado.

Cole checked the garage. Talia's car was still there. Jack's was nowhere in sight. He pulled out his phone and dialed Petersen.

"Cole, you need to get your ass in here," Petersen said. "Chin is on the warpath—"

"I'm not coming in. I need you to put out an APB on a vehicle for me." He quickly rattled off Jack's information.

"What? Why?"

"I don't have time to go into detail, but I believe Talia Vega and Jack Brooks may have been kidnapped, and they could have been taken in Jack's car—"

"Cole, we have other priorities right now. The Slasher is in custody, and you need to get down here—"

Cole was outside, sprinting to his car. "That's the thing—I don't think Jimmy Caparulo is your guy."

He climbed in the Jeep and took off for Talia's house. By the time he arrived, the storm was overwhelming the drains, and Talia's street was beginning to flood. He carefully guided his Jeep through the rising waters." "What time did you arrest him yesterday?"

"Around ten-thirty. What you mean you don't think he's our guy? You haven't seen the evidence."

"What was he doing before ten-thirty?" If Jimmy really was the Slasher, he may have had time to take out Talia and Jack. It wasn't likely, but Jimmy was tough, former Special Forces. It was possible he could have gotten the jump on Jack and snatched Talia.

"Come down here and ask him yourself," Petersen snapped. "I'm serious, Cole. I will kick your ass if I have to find another partner."

Cole hung up. Petersen was right—if he really wanted to figure out Jimmy Caparulo, he needed to talk to the man himself. But if he went to the station, he'd never get out of there. Talking to Jimmy wasn't an option.

He swore. He didn't like this feeling of flailing around in the dark. All his cases were puzzles, but this one felt like it was missing too many pieces to ever come together.

He drove, listening to the rhythmic *thwap* of the windshield wipers.

He called up Jimmy's address on his phone. It was a long shot, but under the circumstances, it was the only move he could come up with.

—◊—

Megan came to as strong arms lifted her from the back of a vehicle and hoisted her over a broad shoulder. A quick twitch of her arms and legs told her that her hands and feet were bound tight.

"Why are you doing this?" she croaked, wincing as even the short question seared her throat. When he didn't answer, she tried yelling for help, but nothing emerged but a pitiful rasp.

"You know why." A car she didn't recognize was parked in a garage behind a small house, away from the road. Rain pelted her as he carried her several feet before setting her next to a door on the side of the house that led to a cellar. "I thought you were different. I thought you were like Sarah."

"I don't know who Sarah is, Nate, but I promise you I am different. I'm your friend. I care about you. If you just untie me, we can talk about it—" She gasped, the breath knocked out of her as he slammed her head against the wall.

"You're a fucking whore, soiling your body to get what you want. I thought you were good, like her."

"I am good, Nate," she sobbed hysterically, wondering how someone so perfect-looking could hide such evil. Now with his face contorted in rage and the manic light in his eyes, it seemed impossible that she had ever thought him handsome, that she had turned to him for help, trusted him as a friend.

As she struggled through her panic to find the words that might convince him to let her go, she wanted to vomit at the memory of him touching her.

"I saw you with him!" Nate screamed, saliva flying from his mouth as his hand cracked hard against her cheek. "After the way he treated you, you let that cop put his hands on you, let him fuck you." He shook his head and stepped back, and Megan slumped to the floor, her vision swimming.

"I told myself you were good, that you'd learned, that you'd never let him touch you again, but you goddamn cunt, you let him use you all over again. You're nothing but a whore, just like her."

He moved then, and that was when she saw the figure slumped on a leather couch. Talia.

She didn't stir. Megan's gaze darted frantically around the sparsely furnished room, taking in the barren walls covered, oddly, in some kind of thick fabric. The small speakers mounted in the ceiling. The enormous plasma-screen television mounted on the wall across from the couch.

"Where's Devany?" she asked, frantic. "What did you do to her?"

"The girl will be taken care of."

"If you hurt her, I'll fucking kill you—"

His hand cracked across her face again. "I have the knife. That means I make the threats, not you."

She barely breathed as Nate pulled something from his pocket and ducked through an opening in the wall near the TV. "Talia! Talia, wake up," she whispered as she tried to roll toward the other woman. Maybe if she could get close, they could untie each other.

"She can't help you." Nate's laugh froze her blood in her veins.

She watched in horror as he drew a knife from his waistband, its lethally sharp blade catching the light as he hefted it in his left hand. Custom made, favored by troops who served in the Special Forces. Nearly identical to Sean's, which had been used to kill Evangeline.

He knelt over Talia and the knife slashed forward.

"No!" Megan screamed, but Nate was cutting the flex ties around Talia's wrists and ankles. Next went the clothes, the sound of the fabric splitting under the knife sending a ripple of fear through her.

He shoved something under Talia's nose and her head snapped back, the whites of her eyes showing as she struggled to open them.

"Wake up, bitch," Nate snapped, waving the packet under her nose again. "I want you awake for this."

—⁓—

The scratchy sound of tiny feet sent a wave of nausea through Dev's body. She heard muffled voices outside, then silence. Something skittered over her feet.

Oh God, she was alone in a pitch-black pantry full of mice, and Nate was taking Megan somewhere else in the house. To kill her. She didn't try to kid herself that there would be any other outcome. Dev started to cry again, thinking of her mom. She hadn't been able to stop herself from looking when Nate had taken her from the trailer.

Blood, so much blood. The slice across her throat gaping, just like Bianca. Nate was going to do that to Megan, maybe worse, if she didn't do something. And she was next.

She drew her hands up and tugged at her gag. When she got it free, she screamed and yelled as loud as she could. But the house was far from the road, isolated in the woods. Her throat was raw, and still no one came.

"You motherfucker!" she yelled into the darkness. "You son-of-a-bitch cocksucker! I'm not gonna let you kill me! I'm not gonna let you kill me!"

Her bound feet flailed, kicking at the walls like she would break them down. Boxes fell from the shelves, and a can of something thudded painfully on her chest, but she didn't stop. A jar smashed near her head and she froze.

She turned to her side, glass slicing her fingers as she grasped in the dark. Her cupped hands closed over a big shard.

She pushed herself to a seated position and wedged the glass between her clenched knees. It took a few tries and several more painful slices to her hand, but she managed to find the right angle. Her panting echoed in the dark as she frantically sawed the plastic tie against the sharp edge of the glass.

The tie split with a faint pop. Her hands were slick with blood, and she fumbled with the glass, but she managed to saw through the ties around her ankles. She shoved to her feet and flailed her hands until she found the doorknob. She turned and pushed, but the dirtbag had locked her in.

Frustration roared through her and she threw herself against the door, sobbing as she bounced back into the darkness. Her foot lashed out, hitting the door with enough impact to rattle it on its hinges. Again, again, again, but she was too small, too weak....

Crack! Dev's sneakered foot went through the bottom of the door. She fell on her ass with a yell of surprise. She yanked her foot free and kicked again, over and over until the hole was big enough for her to slide through.

She squirmed through like an eel, barely feeling the scrape of splintered wood along her stomach. Her bloody hands left prints on the linoleum as she pulled herself out. She was sprinting for the door before her feet were even under her.

Chapter 21

Jimmy Caparulo lived with his aunt in a tidy moss-green house in the Crown Hill neighborhood of Seattle.

"Just a moment," a voice called when he knocked.

It seemed to take forever for the slow footsteps to reach the door.

Deep lines carved Angela Giovanni's wan face, and Cole immediately saw why it had taken her so long to reach the door. Her clothes hung off her frail frame, and small plastic tubes emerged from her nostrils. The tubes led to a small oxygen canister that she cradled in her left arm.

Her eyes were sunken and ringed with dark circles as she looked up at him. "Can I help you?"

He quickly introduced himself. "Can I ask you a few questions about Jimmy?" Cole asked, pitching his voice to be heard over the pounding rain.

She gave him a wary look and started to close the door. "Anything you want to know, you ask his lawyer."

"I'm trying to help."

"Are you the cops?"

Cole pondered his answer. "Not at the moment. I'm trying to help out a friend of Jimmy's—Megan Flynn. You know her, right?"

Angela eyed him for a few more seconds and shrugged. "Might as well come in from the rain."

Cole went inside and waved off her offer of coffee. "I don't mean to be rude, but I'm a little short on time. The police arrested Jimmy here last night. Is that correct?"

"Yes. They came right before ten. Jimmy was in his room, and I had just sat down to watch the news." She pressed her lips tight. "Jimmy's had a hard time, but I know him, and I know he didn't do what they're accusing him of. He's taken care of me—his sick aunt!—for over three years, ever since he got out of the army. You think a young man who is so loyal would hurt women the way they said he did?"

Cole shook his head. "I couldn't say, ma'am."

Her mouth pulled tight. "The police said they found a knife and all kinds of camera equipment in there, but I never saw anything like that."

"What was Jimmy doing last night before he was arrested? Did he go out at all?"

She shook her head. "Not at all. In fact, he'd barely been out for almost a week. Comes right home after work and gets on his computer."

"You're sure?"

"Yes, I'm sure. I was here all day. He came home at six, had supper, made sure I was settled in front of the TV, and then he excused himself."

Cole's doubts about Jimmy's innocence faded another degree. No way he could have taken Talia and Jack without a hovering mama like Angela noticing. "Do you have any idea who he might have been talking to? Anyone who would have a reason to blame him for this?"

She shook her head and blinked back tears. "He hasn't talked much. He's been upset with me."

"You had a fight?"

"It was the stupidest thing," Angela replied, shrugging her thin shoulders in bewilderment. "A friend from his army days came by to see him. Jimmy wasn't home, so I offered him a cup of coffee. But when Jimmy came home, he was furious, ranting and raving. He's never talked to me that way! But he kept going on about how I never should have let this man into the house. Oh, and when he found out he was a computer guy and that I asked him to fix the computer cable in Jimmy's room, you would have thought—"

The skin prickled on the back of Cole's neck. "What's the friend's name?"

"Nate, Nate Brewster. Nicest young man, and so handsome. He and Jimmy got to be friends in the army. I never knew they had a falling-out. . . ."

Cole didn't hear her over the alarms shrieking in his head. Nate, who had taken off after Sean's arrest and come back to Seattle about a year ago, right when the murders started.

Nate, the computer consultant, who could have easily built and managed an exclusive escort site and had access to Club One's networks and security cameras.

A friend of both Sean and Jimmy, with access and opportunity to frame both men.

But why?

Cole shook his head. The why didn't matter right now. He had to find Talia and warn Megan.

He cut off Angela with a terse "thanks" and headed for the door.

"Wait," she called to him as he sprinted to his car. "What about Jimmy?"

"I know he didn't do it," Cole called over his shoulder. "I promise the truth will come out soon enough."

He drove as fast as the weather would allow back to Dev's trailer, his knees buckling at what he discovered. A woman dead, her throat cut on the floor.

Megan and Devany nowhere to be found.

—⁂—

Devany ran back in what she thought was the way Nate had come, but it was hard to tell since she'd been on the floor of the car during the trip. She ran for what felt like forever before she hit another house. She banged on the front door, sobbing with frustration when no one answered. There was no one at the next house either, or the next, and she was starting to wonder if the whole fucking neighborhood was deserted when she caught a flash of headlights through the sheets of rain.

She ran into the road, waving her hands until the minivan screeched to a stop. The window rolled down and a woman leaned out to yell, "Are you crazy? I could have killed you—"

Dev ran around to the woman, whose expression softened a little when she got a closer look at Dev.

"What are you doing out in this, dressed like that? You'll catch your death if a tree doesn't come crashing down on you first."

"I need to borrow your phone. It's an emergency!" Dev's hands came up to grip the door. The woman gasped when she saw the deep cuts welling with blood.

"There's a guy, he has my friend, and I really need to call the cops."

"I don't get cell coverage up here."

"Then dammit, give me a ride to a real fucking phone!"

The woman's face paled and she glanced behind her. Dev followed her gaze and saw two boys strapped to car seats in the back. "Mommy, she said *fuck*," said the older one.

"I know, Wyatt," the woman said through clenched teeth.

"Please, lady," Dev said, her teeth chattering as the cold finally caught up with her. "Just take me to a gas station or something." She pitched her voice lower so the little kids wouldn't hear her. "He's going to hurt my friend. Please help me."

The woman closed her eyes and gave a quick nod. Dev dashed around to the passenger side and climbed in. They drove down the road another mile or so before the minivan had to stop for a fallen tree.

"Can't you go around it?"

"There's a market just up ahead, at the junction of this road and Forest Drive." The woman leaned over Dev and opened her door. Dev took the hint and hopped out with a muttered "thanks." She picked her way over the tree, cursing when she slipped on the wet bark and skinned her knee.

The little market was right where the woman said, and the guy working the register took pity on her and pointed her to the phone in the back. She dialed 911 with shaking hands.

"Thank you for calling the King County central dispatch. To reach the fire department, press one. To reach the sheriff, press two."

A fucking voice mail menu?! Dev punched two. *"Emergency services are experiencing a high volume of calls. Please hold…"*

"I don't have time to fucking hold!" Dev slammed the phone down and swallowed back angry tears. What the hell was she supposed to do?

Duh. She dialed, picturing the card Cole Williams had given her the night of Bianca's murder, thanking whatever powers had blessed her with a freakishly good memory for numbers. She bounced on her toes as the phone rang, praying he could get here before it was too late.

—⁓—

Megan watched as Talia blinked foggily for a few seconds; then, as she became aware of her surroundings and her nudity, she let out a high, frantic scream. Megan joined in, Talia's hysteria feeding her own, until it seemed impossible that someone wouldn't hear them.

Nate laughed as Talia launched herself clumsily off the couch, her legs buckling as the effect of whatever he'd drugged her with maintained its hold.

"Scream as loud as you want. No one can hear you except for me." He dragged Talia to the middle of the floor, positioning her on a beige rug that Megan just now realized was covered with heavy plastic.

He grabbed Megan from the floor and shoved her onto the couch. "I want to make sure you can see everything."

He pulled out a remote and pointed it at the TV. Megan swallowed back a rush of nausea, fully expecting to see Talia's image on the screen as the naked woman tried to crawl away, only to fall flat on her stomach as her legs and arms collapsed under her weight.

From the corner of her eye, Megan was aware of Nate stripping off his shirt. The smell of a match striking and burning tobacco stung her nose. She gasped as Nate turned, and she saw his naked torso for the first time. He had a tattoo on his upper right biceps, just like Sean, Jack, and Jimmy Caparulo.

But Nate's ink didn't stop there. "You like it?" He smiled and spread his arms wide. On his right arm was the head of a snake, fangs bared, the rest of its gold and black scaled body coiling up his arm, down his back, and around his torso. He flexed his muscles and Megan stared, transfixed, as the snake undulated around his body.

On his chest was a bloody heart with a knife through it, with tear-shaped drops of blood dripping out of it, all the way down the left side of his chest and abdomen. "One drop for every kill," Nate said.

There were dozens.

"She was one of my favorites, though." He pointed at the TV.

"Oh my God." There, in full color, was Evangeline Gordon, naked, on her knees, her blue eyes wide with terror, her screams muffled around the gag stuffed down her throat. Megan recognized the familiar furniture of Sean's living room. She watched in horrified fascination as Nate appeared on-screen and mugged sickeningly for the camera. His image blurred as he approached the camera, which was abruptly wrenched to the right.

Nate laughed at Megan's audible gasp at the image of Sean, slumped against the wall, completely unconscious.

Oh God, oh God. Megan had always wondered if

something like this had happened, but she'd never envisioned this kind of horror.

"Sorry you have to miss all this, buddy, but you'll see soon enough what happens to people who fuck with me."

On-screen, the camera swung back to Evangeline, her screams getting more frantic behind the gag as Nate's hulking form came into the frame. Without warning, he pressed the lit cigarette into the skin of Evangeline's buttock.

Megan's attention snapped back to the room at Talia's animal cry of pain, the smell of burning flesh making Megan gag.

"Stop!" she screamed as Nate hefted the knife.

His hand moved, blindingly fast, and a red stripe welled across Talia's back as she arched and screamed in pain.

"Please stop hurting her!" Megan cried. "You don't need to do this. Let her go."

"You have no idea what I need." He shifted the knife to his right hand and made another cut, creating a bloody X that covered Talia's back from hip to shoulder in each direction. He leaned down until his mouth was at Talia's ear. "What made you think you could talk and get away with it? No one else ever has." Talia's spine arched as Nate traced a bloody line along the skin of her inner arm.

From the speakers, Evangeline's screams grew louder. Megan squeezed her eyes shut against the violation replaying on the screen, against the horror happening in this very room.

"No!" Nate was screaming in her ear, yanking her head up. "Open your eyes and watch, you bitch, or I'll make it even worse for both of you."

She opened her eyes just in time to see Nate flip Evangeline Gordon to her back and tease her with his knife before delivering the killing blow.

A choked sob ripped from Megan's chest, and she snapped her focus back to Talia, who was on the floor, her eyes locked on Megan's, pleading, as though Megan could somehow get them out of this.

"I did all of this for you," Nate said with a savage yank of Megan's hair. The cold bite of his blade pressed against her throat. The slightest movement would draw blood.

"I did everything, set it all up so perfectly, so we could be together. Sean tried to keep me away from you, and he lived to regret it. They tried to keep me away from you." His hand ran down the side of her almost tenderly. "And you don't even care. You ruined everything."

The blade sank into the tender skin just under her ear. "You're going to watch every second so you see exactly what I did for you. So you can understand what you're going to suffer for failing me."

He released Megan and stripped off the rest of his clothes. Completely nude, except for the tattoos that continued down the lower half of his body, he was even more terrifying.

He pounced on Talia like a hyena taking down a wounded deer and flipped her to her back. His blade flashed and Talia's screams filled the room.

The screams filled Megan's head, tore from her throat, the scents of blood and fear choking her as she succumbed to the living nightmare unfolding in front of her.

⁓

Cole screeched to a halt in front of Nate Brewster's building. He'd left a message for Petersen but didn't have much faith she would follow up on his findings. Not that he could blame her. They had a suspect in hand and a load of damning evidence. It didn't make sense to chase down a less likely suspect based on little more than a hunch.

Cole might have felt that way himself, if he weren't stone-cold sure Nate had taken Talia, Devany, and the woman he loved. *Please, God, let her be alive.*

Cole couldn't even contemplate the alternative.

He scanned the directory, saw Nate's name, and rang the buzzer. Shocker, no one answered. He didn't have to wait long before another tenant came into the entryway, shaking rain off her trench coat as she slid her key into the lock. She didn't even give him a second look as he slipped into the building behind her.

So much for a secure building.

He knocked on the door. No answer. He gave the door a quick once-over. Strong, but not steel core. He drew his gun as a precaution, angled his body, and delivered a hard kick, just under the dead bolt. Another kick, and the sound of splintering wood echoed through the hall as the door swung open.

"Hey, what are you doing?" A guy with heavy-framed glasses and a goatee had opened his door two doors down. "I'm gonna call the cops!"

"I am the cops," Cole said as he shoved inside Nate's apartment. He did a quick sweep, though every instinct screamed the place was empty. What had he expected? That Nate would suddenly change his MO and bring Megan and Talia back to his condo?

He pawed through Nate's desk, through his bedside table, looking for something, anything to give a clue as to where he might have taken them. He'd killed in abandoned homes around the city, with no evident pattern in how he chose the locations for his kills.

Fuck. He dialed Petersen. "I need you to look something up for me," he said as soon as she answered. "Find out if Nate Brewster has any property besides his primary residence." He hung up before she could utter a sound.

He could hear voices outside, neighbors wondering what to do about the maniac who had just kicked down the door. Time for Cole to get out before the police made it here.

He sped away from the building and parked two blocks over, banging his head against the steering wheel.

Nate had Megan. She'd been gone for over an hour. Plenty of time to hurt her, to kill her. His eyes stung and he wracked his brain, coming up dry. He swallowed against the lump in his throat. He'd done this. He'd left her alone, and now she was going to be killed—if she wasn't dead already.

His phone rang, a number he didn't recognize on the display. Cole answered, his voice choked.

"Detective Williams? It's Devany Sinclair."

Cole almost lost it. "Where are you? Where's Megan?"

"I'm at the Pick n' Save store in— Where the hell am I?" Cole heard a muffled voice answer in the background. "I'm in Coal Creek." Cole knew the area, a town southeast of Seattle. Most days it took about twenty minutes to get there, but that was without a storm blowing trees down every other block. "But that guy Nate—Megan's friend— he still has her. He killed my mom." Cole heard her voice rise in hysteria. "He killed her and now he's going to kill Megan, too, if you don't help her."

"Where's the house? Tell me the address."

"I don't know," she sobbed. "I know it's on 168 south-east, but I don't know the number. I can show you—"

"Stay where you are." Cole put the Jeep in gear and floored it. "Keep trying nine-one-one and I'll be there in fifteen minutes."

———————

At some point Megan's screams faded to whimpers. Deafening sounds of horror filled the room from the blaring speakers as Nate showed them one sickening video after another of him and his victims.

But he hadn't raped Talia—not yet anyway. In fact, his penis hung flaccid between his legs as he loaded up a new video. He left Talia prone, silent on the floor. Her dark eyes were slitted open, staring and empty like she'd escaped to a faraway place only she could reach, away from the horror of what was happening.

Megan wanted to join her, but she was acutely aware of every noise, every image, the metallic smell of blood, the acrid sweat hanging in the air. Nate didn't have to tell her to watch—she couldn't look away, couldn't shut it out as every sickening detail was branded into her brain. The small part of her brain capable of logical analysis noted that he was taking an abnormally long time making his kill.

He was drawing it out, making them both suffer. A sick part of her wanted to scream at him to do it already, get it over with and put them all out of their misery. In a flash of clarity, she understood, on some primitive level, why Sean had chosen the path he did.

But while they were alive, there was still some chance someone would find them.

But how? The only person who knew they were with Nate was Devany, and she...

Megan bit back a sob. He was going to kill Devany, too, and she couldn't do anything to stop it. Cole had no idea where she was.

Oh God, Cole, is this how it really ends for me? For us? For Sean?

She scanned the room, searching desperately for something, anything, she or Talia could use as a weapon. But the more she struggled against the flex ties binding her hands and ankles, the deeper they cut into her skin.

She tried to catch Talia's eye again, but the other woman was gone. Not dead, not yet, but definitely someplace other than the room.

Her fear increased as Nate loaded another video, this one of an exotically beautiful woman in her early twenties. Nate stared, fixated, at the screen, absently running his thumb over the blade of his knife. The woman smiled uncertainly at the camera as Nate said something off-screen that Megan couldn't quite make out.

Whatever he said replaced the woman's ingratiating smile with a look of terror, a look that said the woman had seen the face of death and knew it was coming for her.

Nate let out a frustrated curse. Megan's attention snapped to him, and she realized with horrified disgust that he was masturbating. Or trying to. Tugging and jerking brutally at his penis, he couldn't get it up.

Relief that she and Talia wouldn't be raped shot through her.

It lasted a mere second before Nate turned his terrifying anger on Megan.

"I did everything for you, and now you're taking it all away," he raged.

Megan tried to scramble away as he lunged at her, but with her bound hands and feet, she only managed to fling herself to the floor, where she heaved herself like a spastic inchworm toward the narrow hall that branched from the right side of the room.

He caught her by the hair and twisted her around with such force she thought her neck would snap. With her face now level with his groin, she lunged without thinking, teeth snapping, but he caught her with an open handed blow that sent pain exploding across her cheekbone. She would have fallen had he not still had his fist twisted in her hair.

Another blow split her lip, and his knee to her ribs made the oxygen spew from her lungs in a rush. A loud buzzing sounded in her ears and a red fog clouded her vision.

—✦—

Cole turned up Stonegate Road in Coal Creek, a twisting road that wound up a hillside and was lined with dozens of large properties. He blew past an emergency crew that tried to flag him down and continued up the road. He'd lost cell coverage a mile back. No way to try 911, no way to find out if Petersen had gotten anywhere. He was on his own.

The dread grew stronger with every passing minute. Nate had taken her more than an hour ago. He had no idea how long Nate kept his victims alive after he first took them. Days? Hours?

Minutes?

How long would he torture her? Cole tried but couldn't stop thinking about the other victims. Jesus, was Megan at that very second screaming in pain, begging Nate to end it so she could stop hurting?

Cole swallowed back a surge of bile. *Focus.* He couldn't afford to dwell on the worst-case scenario if he wanted to have a chance in hell of saving her.

Megan was alive. He was going to find her.

He nearly missed the turnoff to the convenience store where Dev was waiting. The Jeep fishtailed as he swung it through the turn and into the store's tiny parking lot. He bounded up the stairs of the building and found Dev inside, behind the counter huddled on a stool in a sweatshirt that was two sizes too big for her.

She jumped to her feet. "Took you long enough."

"Just let me use your goddamn phone," a male voice boomed from the back of the store.

"Let's go," Dev said, heading for the door. "A crazy guy just burst in here."

A chubby teenager rounded the corner. "Dude, find a pay phone. I'm gonna call the cops."

A large, barefoot man followed close behind. He was soaked from head to toe, dressed only in a thin T-shirt and cargo pants. "I don't have any money," the man said in a strained voice. "Don't make me kick your ass—"

"Jack?"

The man's dark head whipped around. Jack's face was almost gray, his lips blue.

"What the fuck are you doing here?" Cole asked.

Jack shook his head. "Fuck if I know. All I know is I woke up about half an hour ago, facedown in the woods." A shudder racked his large frame.

Cole didn't know how long he'd been out in the rain, but it was long enough for Jack to get good and cold. "Let's go."

"Wait, you know him?" Dev asked as Cole herded her to the car.

Cole nodded and they all scrambled into the Jeep. He cranked the heat and peeled out of the parking lot in a spray of gravel. He filled Jack in on the details as they sped up the road.

"Son of a bitch got right by me," Jack said tightly, his hands shaking as he held them up in front of the vent. "Must have dosed me with something strong. All I know is I woke up facedown in the mud, no shoes, no money, no gun, no idea how I got there."

Jack still looked foggy from both the cold and the drugs, shaking his head every so often as though to clear the cobwebs. He flexed his fingers in the hot air pouring from the dashboard and winced as his skin started to pink up.

"How much farther?" Cole asked Dev.

"Not too far." She stared intently out the back passenger window. A few more minutes passed. "There it is. On the right, past the boulder."

They parked on the side of the road. "Do you have any idea where in the house he took them?"

"Not in the house," Dev said. "He put me in the kitchen, but then he went outside and didn't come back in."

So they were looking for a shed or a garage or something. "You two wait here," Cole told them.

"No fucking way," Jack said. "You'll need backup."

"You're half hypothermic and coming off whatever he hit you with. Besides, you need to get her out of here," Cole said, nodding toward Dev.

"You have to save Megan," Dev said. "Don't worry about me."

Jack's jaw tightened and his shoulders went back. "I'm fine," he said. His face was still ashen, but the shaking had lessened in the warmth of the car. "I fucked this up and let him take Talia. Let me help." The look in his eyes said he was coming with Cole whether he liked it or not. Cole was pretty sure he could take him, but he didn't have time to waste fighting.

Cole caved. He turned to Jack. "If you fall on your drugged ass, you're on your own."

"Do you know how to drive?" he asked Dev.

Dev nodded. "If Jack isn't back here in five minutes, take the car back to the store. Find out where the nearest sheriff's station is and send them here with the paramedics."

They cut through the wooded area on the neighbor's lot in case Nate was keeping watch. Creeping between the trees, they sidled up to the detached garage. Cole heard nothing. They entered through an unlocked door. Nothing but a black SUV was parked inside.

"Motherfucker stole my car," Jack muttered.

The guy was tough. Cole had to give him that. Jack's jaw clenched against the shudders as the icy rain pounded down on them, and he hardly winced as his bare feet crunched against the wet gravel of the driveway.

There were no other structures on the property that they could see. Despite what Dev had told them, Cole picked the lock on the back door and they ducked inside the house. A quick search of the rooms revealed nothing.

"They have to be somewhere close," Cole said, trying to clear his mind of the panic so he could think. "Dev said she didn't hear a car."

Jack's gaze swept the room, locking on an old-fashioned metal floor vent. "There's a heat vent, but I didn't see a furnace anywhere up here."

The garage was detached. That meant the heating system had to be in a basement or crawl space.

But there was no way in from inside. They dashed outside and walked the perimeter of the house, eyes trained on the siding, careful to miss nothing as they searched for another entrance to the cellar. As they started down the south side of the house, Cole saw it.

Partially hidden by two green plastic garbage bins was a set of weathered wood doors, barely the height of the garbage cans, like it was built to hold them once the trash had been picked up. Cole yanked the doors open and ducked in. He descended a short staircase that led to the basement door.

Unlike the flimsy, easy-to-pick front door, this door was steel core, rigged with an electronic keypad that activated three heavy-weight dead bolts that kept the thing locked.

Cole pulled out his Glock and took aim at the door.

"No!" Jack deflected the gun with a sharp chop of his arm. "It won't penetrate the locks and will only let him know that we're here."

"How the fuck do we get in there, then?"

Jack squatted down next to the keypad and tilted his head, studying.

"What?" Cole snapped.

"I've worked with a system like this before," Jack said. "I'm pretty sure there's a way to override it."

"So do it."

"Give me a minute," Jack snapped, rubbing at his temples. "I have to be careful. If I do it wrong, it will set off an alarm." Jack nodded to himself, straightened, and started to trot back up the stairs.

"Where the fuck are you going?"

"I need to get something out of my car," Jack called down.

He was back in seconds with a small tool set. He pulled out a Phillips-head screwdriver and tried to raise it to the keypad, but his hand was shaking too bad to fit the driver with the screw head.

Cole snatched it from his hand and knelt down. "Talk me through it."

———

Megan tried to shrink back but there was nowhere to go. The room blurred around her, and she fell to her back, Nate straddling her chest. Her blood froze in her veins when she saw the blade flash in his hand once again.

Megan heard a feral cry that didn't even sound human. The knife stopped its deadly path as Nate was jerked to the side by the black cord digging into his neck. *Talia!*

Fear and rage twisted her beautiful face as her slender arms flexed and strained, knocking Nate off balance enough for Megan to wiggle out from under him and land a kick to his chest with her bound feet. She kicked again at his hand but couldn't dislodge the knife.

Nate roared and thrashed around like a wounded bear. He reached one hand behind him and yanked Talia over his shoulder, throwing her to the floor in front of him. Her scream cut short as her back met the ground, and Megan watched, as it though were happening in slow motion, Nate bury his knife in Talia's stomach. He yanked the blade out, and blood bubbled from the wound, soaking her abdomen and the hands clutching it.

He grabbed Megan by her bound wrists and dragged her across the room, through the crude door cut into the wall, and into another room. Light from the other room barely trickled in. She could smell dirt and damp. A sharp click and the room was flooded with the light of a single hanging bulb. The room was little more than a cave in the ground with a dirt floor.

He yanked her up by her hair. "Do you see? Do you see how much you were loved?"

It took her eyes a second to focus, but what she saw made her breath freeze in her chest. The only finished wall in the room was covered with pictures.

Of her.

He'd put up pictures of her from the paper, from Sean's trial. There was even a picture of her and Sean, fishing poles in hand, taken before their parents died.

It had been on Sean's mantel.

Nate pulled her onto a crudely built wooden platform in front of the wall, set like an altar in front of the pictures. He shoved her face against the wall, and she realized the photos weren't just of her. Some were of another girl, pictures ranging from infancy to about twelve years old.

The girl had dark brown hair and big green eyes. It was like looking at pictures of herself as a girl.

"I loved you so much," he whispered, his hand tightening in her hair. "I did everything for you. Did you even know how many times I saved you?"

There were other newspaper clippings, headlines screaming BOY, 14, KILLS IN SELF-DEFENSE AFTER MAN KILLS MOTHER AND SISTER.

Her heart dipped to her stomach. She could only catch a few words of the articles, but the headlines—and the pictures—told her enough of the story. The girl who looked so much like Megan must have been Nate's sister.

Sarah.

She scrambled to find a way to pull him back from the edge and buy herself a little more time. "I know, Nate. I know what you did for me, how much you love me," she said in a shaky whisper. "I love you too." She reached out her bound hands and made herself touch him. "Please don't hurt me anymore, and I promise I'll love you and stay with you forever."

He made a sound that was almost like a sob. "I want to believe you. I wanted you to be the one to save me. But it's not you." His hand reached out and stroked her hair.

"I don't want you to be alone."

His tender smile made the nausea coil in her stomach. "You don't have to worry. I found someone new."

"Who?"

"Her." He sounded euphoric as he pointed to the photo right in the center of the collage.

Megan wanted to howl in protest. She recognized the ponytailed, freckled ten-year-old immediately. Before she'd streaked her hair purple, pierced her nose, and started caking on the eyeliner, Devany could have been Megan's little sister. Other than the brown eyes, she could have been Sarah's twin. Nate had stolen the picture from Dev's trailer.

"I should have known that first night I saw her that it was her all along." His mouth pulled into a sneer. "Not a slut like you."

He pushed her down to the platform and the knife came down. He slipped it up under the hem of her shirt, and she waited for its cold sting against her belly. She started to scream, then realized he was cutting her shirt off. Her heart lodged in her throat as her bra followed, and then she was naked from the waist up, the tip of his knife tracing the soft undercurve of her breast.

"Please, please don't," she whispered through swollen, bloody lips. "Please leave Devany alone."

But he didn't seem to hear her. "You are so beautiful, so beautiful." He circled the knife around her nipple, almost like a caress. Then his blue eyes narrowed on her face. "But not innocent. Not like her. I would have worshipped you, and this is the thanks I get. I should have known you were nothing like Sarah. I should have seen you were a whore." He raised the knife, and Megan turned her head to the side, knowing in her gut this was it.

No more playing, no more taunting.

"You were supposed to set me free," he whispered.

She felt the muscles of his arm shift as he raised the knife higher.

The room exploded in noise as a deafening cacophony assaulted her ears. Startled, Nate loosened his grasp on her and she flung herself away.

"No!" he screamed, and launched himself at her, knocking her to her back.

Megan shoved her hands up, felt the knife bite into her

palms. Through the wail of the alarm, she heard a shout but didn't dare look away as she managed to bring her knees up against Nate's stomach. She shoved hard and he rolled to the side, bringing her with him.

A gunshot blasted, and a spray of dirt hit her face. She needed to get out of the way. She kicked, bucked, squirmed, but couldn't break his hold. Nate rolled to his knees and jerked her up in front of him, using her body as a shield, the blade of his knife pressed against her jugular.

The alarm cut out, leaving eerie silence in its wake.

"Let her go," Cole said, his voice calm, his gun perfectly steady as he held it on Nate.

The hot sting of the knife made Megan gasp.

"I don't think so," Nate said with a laugh that was like an icy finger down her spine. "I think it would be much more fun to kill her while you watch."

Megan tracked the bead of sweat trickling from Cole's hairline, its path mirroring the warm tickle of blood sliding down her throat. "Let her go, and you'll have a chance. You kill her, you die too."

"I think your suffering will be worth it."

Megan shrank back into Nate's chest as the pressure against her neck increased. *Don't look,* she wanted to shout to Cole. *Don't watch.* But she couldn't make her mouth move.

"Look," Cole said, holding his gun out to the side. "I'll put down my gun. I'll let you walk out of here. Just let her go." He dropped the gun to the ground and held up his hands, a naked plea in his eyes.

She could feel Nate's arm tensing, the muscles bunching. Megan squeezed her eyes shut.

There was a scuffle and a shout from the other room. "Oh my God! Is she dead? Where's Megan?"

Devany. No! Megan didn't want Devany to see this anymore than she wanted Cole to.

The girl appeared in the doorway and froze when she saw the scene laid out in front of her. "No." She swallowed hard. "Don't. Please don't. Not Megan too."

Megan felt the tension in Nate's arm ease almost infinitesimally.

"Sarah? Sarah, you need to go. You shouldn't watch—"

"Let her go!" Dev screamed.

Nate's hold slackened another degree. He still had his fist in her hair and his forearm locked around her, but maybe he was distracted just enough....

Megan threw herself to the side, felt the cold pain of the knife slicing into her shoulder as she went down. Cole was a blur of motion as he dove to the side.

Gunshots thundered and Megan felt the hot spray as blood and flesh exploded from Nate's chest.

Another shot, and Nate fell to the side, half of his face blown away.

Then strong arms were around her, holding her tight as the bindings on her hands and legs were cut.

"Cole." He was cradling her face in his hands, his eyes frantic as he ran his hands over every inch of her. He pressed a frantic kiss on her mouth, hurting her bruised lips, but Megan didn't mind; she was too overwhelmed with being safe and alive and in his arms to care.

His lips were moving against her mouth and cheeks, but she couldn't make out more than a low murmur. Then she could hear him, but it sounded like she was underwater. "Thank God, thank God," he said.

She wanted to ask him a thousand questions, like how he knew how to find her, but all she could do was cling to him as if he were a lifeline and bury her face in his neck. "Devany?"

"I'm here," the girl sobbed, ducking under Cole's arm to glue herself to Megan's side. "Are you okay? Please tell me you're okay."

"I'll be fine," she said.

Dev sniffed and pulled away. "I'll go wait for the ambulance and show them where to go."

A lump settled in Megan's throat as she watched Devany walk away, her back so straight as she tried to hold the day's events at bay.

Cole settled her more firmly against him, and she winced as the movement jostled her hands. The cuts on her hands and the slice in her shoulder started to throb, but she knew she was lucky to escape mostly unharmed. Dread settled in her stomach. Talia hadn't been nearly so lucky. "Is Talia…"

Cole's mouth pulled tight and he shook his head. "She's lost a lot of blood. But the paramedics are on their way." He looked down at her and his expression went soft, almost tender. "I was so afraid I lost you," he said. "I was so fucking scared."

"Me too," she croaked.

He let out a hoarse sound, part laugh, part sob. "Jesus, I love you," he said. "I love you so much. We're going to make everything right, and I'm with you every step."

"I love you too," she whispered, and the world seemed to go fuzzy around the edges. "I love you too." Then, as she nestled her head against Cole's heartbeat, she remembered something she needed to tell him, something important. "Video." She pushed the word between her swollen lips, her hand gesturing clumsily to the TV. "The video for Sean before it's too late."

Chapter 22

The news of Nate Brewster's death hit the media within two hours. The story of how the Seattle Slasher had recorded his murders and the speculation that he'd framed Sean Flynn for the murder of Evangeline Gordon had the press practically wetting their pants in excitement.

Carl Grayson opened the door to his stepfather's office. The man who had married his mother fifteen years ago called himself David Maxwell, but Carl knew that name was an invention, a new identity to hide the past he'd left behind in some dusty town in the eastern part of the state.

The past he'd invited in when he reached out to help his sick fuck of a nephew had come back to haunt him in a big way.

Now David's powerful shoulders slumped as he stared out the wall of glass at a view that included the Space Needle.

"You took care of it?" he said without turning.

"Yes," Carl said. "As far as anyone is concerned, Nate was acting entirely on his own." He'd done a clean sweep of both Nate's properties, leaving behind the relevant videos, as well as interesting finds like passports for both Nate and Megan Flynn under false names. "I've been assured that any official investigation into the murders ends with him." No one who had any say in the matter would allow an inquiry to move forward. Not if they wanted to avoid total and absolute ruin.

His stepfather nodded shortly. "What about Talia?"

"Still missing," Carl said grimly. She'd disappeared without a trace from the hospital where she'd received treatment for her knife wound. "Rosario is gone too."

"How?" David raged. "How the fuck could they just disappear like vapor?"

Carl shrugged. "They probably had help. But we haven't been able to find a trail."

"For her sake, she better hope it stays that way," David said bitterly. "I never thought..." He trailed off, shaking his head.

"I don't know why you're surprised. She's no better than a whore." A feminine voice cut through the office like a blade.

"Mother," Carl cautioned.

His mother rolled her eyes. "Serves you right. You got careless, letting him run wild like that. You should have taken care of him years ago."

Carl couldn't agree more.

"It's over now," David said. "Nate's dead, and it's over."

Carl shook his head at the grief in the older man's voice. He never understood his stepfather's commitment to the sicko, his compulsion to protect Nate. So what if David was the only family Nate had left after his mother and sister had been killed? Nate put them all at risk with his behavior. But David had refused to see it, convinced they could channel Nate's urges to serve the organization.

But Carl had known from the beginning that Nate was flawed to the core, that his appetite, his sickness, was beyond their control, regardless of how they tried to manage and channel it.

Nate had been a vicious dog, one who couldn't be muzzled or contained. He'd needed to be put down.

Carl's only regret about Nate's death was that it hadn't happened sooner.

Now there was nothing to connect the prostitution ring or the murders to them.

Except for Talia Vega, who knew damn well what would be waiting for her if she ever dared to breathe a word.

—✧—

"You've got a visitor, Flynn."

Sean rolled to face the door when he heard the voice calling through the cuff port in his door.

Lights-out had been two hours ago—a relative term since the single overhead light in his cell was never actually turned off.

He wondered if it was Megan. She'd been in two days ago along with Brockner. Sean's brain was still in a twist from what he'd learned about Nate. It still didn't seem real that the man Sean once considered a good friend could be such a monster. The story Megan told seemed too ridiculous to be real, but he still hadn't recovered from the sight of her bruised face and bandaged hands.

Because of a man Sean had brought into their lives. He wished he could dig Nate Brewster up and kill him all over again.

In the last forty-eight hours, he'd experienced every emotion from grief to anger to guilt.

Most importantly, he'd felt the cautious burn of hope. They had evidence now that Sean didn't kill Evangeline; that was the important part. After three years, the truth had finally come out, and Sean was going to get another chance. Soon he'd be free on bail, and if things went the way Megan and Brockner promised they would, soon Sean would be free for good.

Sean cuffed up as ordered and followed Joe, one of the head guards, down the dark corridors of the prisons to the same common room where Megan and Cole Williams had paid their midnight visit a little less than a week ago.

Sean's lip curled, half smile, half sneer, when he saw the woman seated at one of the tables. "Ms. Slater. Didn't expect to see you."

Her pale blond hair was pulled into a tight ponytail, and she didn't have on a lick of makeup. But with her big blue eyes and perfectly sculpted features, she was one of the most beautiful women he'd ever laid eyes on. The kind of woman who made his hands itch to mess her up a little.

Not that Sean would ever try. After what she'd put him through, Sean knew better than to tangle with Deputy Prosecuting Attorney Krista Slater.

Sean took a seat at the table across from her while Joe hovered a few feet behind him. He rested his cuffed wrists on the table with a thunk.

She tried but couldn't quite hide her flinch. "I wanted to apologize in person, for everything you've been through."

Sean kept himself perfectly still, careful not to let her see the rage and resentment simmering under his skin. He raised his shackled hands. "You think that makes up for this?"

"Of course not."

Sean could see the pulse beating in the delicate skin of her throat, could smell the scent of her perfume getting stronger as her body temperature increased.

She licked her lips, drawing his attention to the plump curve. He felt a faint warmth low in his gut. It had been so long since he'd felt anything close to that, it took him several seconds to recognize it as the beginning of sexual arousal.

He jerked a little in surprise and chalked it up to the fact that it had been three years since he'd been in the same room with any woman other than his sister. Stood to reason his dick wouldn't be very discriminating. There was no other excuse for feeling even a hint of attraction for this woman.

He dragged his eyes from her mouth. Her cheeks were flushed, like she knew what he was thinking.

Throughout the trial and the months leading up to it, he'd never seen Krista lose her composure. Now she shifted nervously in her seat, and when she spoke, there was a little shake in her voice. "I'm going to make sure you're exonerated," she said. "When we go in front of the judge, I'm going to file a motion to drop all charges against you. With the video evidence and what Nate did to Megan, I can't imagine a reason the judge would deny it."

Hope blazed a little brighter. He was careful not to let her see it. "You expect me to thank you?"

Her blue eyes were full of remorse, and she looked away from his hard stare. "Not at all. I just wanted you to know where I stood. I made a huge mistake and I'm going to fix it." Her slender shoulders shrugged. "I didn't want you to worry. Felt like the least I could do."

He didn't like feeling gratitude toward her, but it felt good to know he was one step closer to having this nightmare end. "I'll sleep better."

"Good." She gave him a small smile that faded quickly when he didn't return it. "I'll see you next week in court." She nodded at Joe to signal the meeting was over. "And after that, you'll never have to see me again."

———~m~———

Two Months Later

Megan shoved her makeup kit into her suitcase and ran down her checklist one more time to make sure she had everything she needed for her weekend away with Cole. Her stomach fluttered in anticipation of three uninterrupted days at a secluded cabin in the San Juans. Their time together had been limited in the last couple of months as Megan focused on helping Sean adjust to life on the outside, and Cole dove headfirst back into work.

And even though Sean had sworn up and down he didn't have a problem with Megan's relationship with Cole—Cole had saved Megan's life, for God's sake, and had gone above and beyond to make sure Sean was exonerated for the murder of Evangeline Gordon—Megan still couldn't shake off the twinge of guilt over being so over-the-moon happily in love with Cole when Sean was still struggling.

She grabbed her bag and walked out to the kitchen where she found Sean drinking coffee, one hip cocked against the counter. He smelled faintly of sweat and damp spring air. Every morning he went out for at least an hour-long run, rain or shine. After three years of spending almost all of his time inside, he couldn't get enough fresh air and open sky.

A cool spring breeze rose goose bumps on her skin, but she didn't close the window over the kitchen sink. Sean couldn't tolerate being in any enclosed space without having a door or window open, another aftereffect of prison. In the two months since Sean's release, Megan's heating bills had doubled, and she'd taken to wearing full-body fleece, but it was a minuscule price to pay compared to having her brother back.

"So you're all packed," Sean said, nodding at her suitcase.

"You're sure you're okay with this? I feel bad leaving you alone."

"I'll be fine," he said, managing to scrub most of the irritation from his voice.

She knew he was getting tired of her hovering, but it was hard for her not to. Though he did his best to paste on a happy face for her, she knew he was having a hard time adjusting to life on the outside.

"You'll call if you need anything?"

Sean dumped what was left of his coffee in the sink and grabbed her in a quick hug. "I'll be fine. Don't waste your weekend worrying about me, okay?"

How was she supposed to not worry when the brother she'd grown up with, the outgoing guy who was always ready with a laugh and who made friends everywhere he went, seemed to have disappeared?

She'd been so focused on getting him out of prison

that she hadn't considered that he might emerge a different person than she'd known. But every now and then, a glimpse of him would poke through the silent, brooding surface, and Megan knew that if she was there for him and kept chipping away, the old Sean would eventually bust free.

In the meantime, it didn't seem fair that she go skipping merrily into her future with Cole when Sean was having a rough time.

"Maybe Cole and I should wait, slow things down until you're more settled—"

"Don't." Sean cut her off with a wave of his big hand. "Get that look off your face. Don't you dare feel guilty for getting on with your life, not after everything you've done for me."

"You would have done the same for me," she said stubbornly.

"And I will have nightmares the rest of my life because of what you went through for me."

"I wouldn't do anything different."

He took a deep breath. When he spoke again, his voice was softer. "I know." A slight smile softened the grim lines of his face. "But listen to me. I want you to go away this weekend. I know you've missed him because you've been too busy hovering around, coddling me—"

"It's not like it's a burden!"

Sean held up his hand. "I know, and I love you for it. But it's enough, Megan. I want you to be in love and be happy. I want you to live your life, okay?" He paused. "And I need to start living mine."

Something in his voice made her uneasy.

"So I won't be here when you get back."

"Wait, what?" Megan shook her head to clear it. "Where are you going?"

"I'm going to move up to Dad's cabin."

"Sean, that thing is falling down."

"It will be a good project for me to rebuild it. I'll have room to build a workshop and everything."

"Look, if this is about me and Cole—"

"It has nothing to do with that. Jesus! I brought a man who tried to kill you into our lives!" He paused and took a deep breath. When he spoke, his voice was gentle. "After all that, I think that gives you a free pass to date whoever you want to."

"Was that supposed to be funny?" She leveled a hard look at him. "We talked about this. I thought the plan was for you to look for a place nearby and find work until your settlement comes through. I just set up two more job interviews for you."

"I don't want you to think I'm ungrateful—I'm not. I'm more grateful than I can say for what you and Cole did to get me out, but me living here…it's not working. I need some time alone to figure some stuff out." He chuckled softly to himself. "And, yeah, I get the irony of a guy who just spent two years in solitary needing time alone."

Megan laughed too. "I hate the thought of not seeing you every day," she said, "but I get it." After what he'd been through, Sean had to figure out how he fit back into the world. Contrary to her hopes, Sean couldn't just step back into his life where he'd left it.

"It's not a bad drive, and you won't have to talk to me through Plexiglas."

"Smart-ass," she laughed, even as her eyes stung with tears. "I'll really miss you."

"And I'll miss you."

He crossed to her and gathered her into a fierce bear hug. Megan buried her face against his chest, wishing she could wave a magic wand and make everything in his life be okay. She had been able to get Sean out of prison, but now that he was out, he had to find his own path.

And she had to follow hers.

Heavy footsteps sounded on the stairs, followed by a knock on the door. "That's my ride," Megan said, stepping out of Sean's embrace.

Joy seared through her as she opened the door to Cole's wide smile. But the smile and the wicked glint in his eyes morphed into concern when he saw Megan's face. "Is everything okay? Did something happen?"

Any doubts Megan might have had about Cole's devotion to her would have been obliterated by the way he cradled her cheek, the almost frantic look in his eyes at her distress.

"It's fine," Megan said. "Sean and I were just having a talk."

He shot a look at Sean over her shoulder. "Do we need to cancel?" Cole couldn't quite mask the resignation in his tone. He'd been patient these last two months, understanding Megan's need to take it slow and ease Sean into the idea that she and Cole were in it for the long haul. But it was clear the lack of time—and especially Megan's firm policy of no overnighters—was beginning to wear on him.

As they were on her. She couldn't stop her smile when Sean snapped, "God, will you two stop worrying about me? Jesus, man, get her out of here and show her a good time already." He gave them a wave and retreated to the bathroom.

Cole pulled her into his arms as soon as the door clicked shut. "Hey," he whispered, covering her lips in a kiss that sent sparks sizzling across her skin.

"Hey, yourself." She wrapped her arms around his waist and felt her whole body sigh.

"So is everything okay? Why do you look sad?" His dark eyes were full of love and concern.

"Sean's moving away, up to our dad's old cabin in the mountains. I understand why he needs to get away, but... I wish he'd stay close."

Cole stiffened and his hand froze on her back. "Is he moving because of us?"

Megan shook her head. "He says it's not, and I believe him." She raised her hand to stroke Cole's cheek. "He wants this for me. He knows we love each other, and he wants me to be happy."

"Would you still be here if he'd said different?" He let out a low curse as soon as the words left his mouth. "Forget I asked that."

Megan's heart swelled a little. It seemed impossible that Cole, who came off as so cool, could feel an iota of insecurity about her feelings. "Sean's my brother. I love him, and I want him to be happy, but you're the one I'm supposed to be with. You're the one I want to have a life with." It was time to let the past go and step into her future. With Cole.

Cole kissed her, slow and deep. "You know, even if you didn't feel that way, I love you so much I'd probably spend the rest of my life sniffing around, begging for whatever scraps of affection you'd be willing to toss me."

A grin pulled at her lips. It was still so amazing, unbelievable, that he was here, with her, and they were really getting a second chance. "Lucky you, you get the whole thing."

He kissed her again, hard, and when he lifted his head, his eyes were suspiciously shiny. "The luckiest man on the planet, and don't you think for a second that I don't know it."

Sean Flynn never counted on his past
coming back to haunt him...
until *she* showed up on his doorstep.

Please turn this page
for a preview of

Hide from Evil

Available in November 2011.

Y ou ready to go?"

Krista Slater looked up and nodded at King County Prosecuting Attorney Mark Benson, who stood in the doorway of her office, briefcase in hand and an over-stuffed accordion folder under his arm. She gathered the notes she'd made on the witness statements she'd taken in the last month, trying to summon up that hungry feeling that used to overtake her every time she prepared for court.

But that last court date with Sean Flynn had extinguished the fire in her belly. When you mistakenly put a man on death row, nothing, not even the sight of him walking out of the courtroom as a free man, could ever make up for the years of his life that had been stolen.

It didn't matter that the evidence had been compelling. It didn't matter that Nate Brewster had done a masterful job of framing Sean and taken them all for a ride. Nothing could erase the fact that Krista had failed. Miserably. And Sean Flynn had suffered hugely for it, as had the dozens of other women tortured and killed by Brewster, aka the Seattle Slasher.

That knowledge, not to mention the hollow look in

Sean Flynn's eyes even as he was granted his freedom, had taken the killer instinct that she'd built her reputation on and replaced it with guilt and, worse, doubt. Doubt in her own abilities, doubt in the system.

Come on, Slater, eye of the tiger, she told herself as she shoved her files into her briefcase. She needed to be on her A-game today. No room for self-doubt or mistakes, not when they were facing off against a slick fish like Roman Karev and his team of five-hundred-dollar-an-hour attorneys. Karev, a restaurant owner with known ties to the Russian mob, was accused of murdering a local businessman and his wife.

Today was the pretrial hearing, and while she was damn sure their case was rock solid, she knew any mistake, any slipup, could and would be used to get crucial pieces of evidence thrown out. She couldn't afford to be distracted by anything, especially not—

The phone on Krista's desk buzzed, and she pushed the button on the intercom. "What is it, Lisa?"

Her paralegal's voice sounded on the speakerphone. "Ms. Slater, I have a phone call for you. He won't say who he is, only that he was told to call you."

As casually as she could, Krista punched Lisa off speakerphone and picked up the handset. She shot Mark an apologetic look, praying her elevated pulse rate and the twist of anticipation in her belly didn't show in her face. "I have to take this."

Benson looked pointedly at his watch. "We need to be there in ten minutes, and I need to go over some last-minute details."

"Two minutes, I promise." Krista ignored Benson's glare. "Put him through." She glanced up, stifling a grimace when it became clear Benson had no intention of leaving.

Krista swiveled her chair, turning her back to Benson, a thousand questions racing through her mind in the seconds it took for Lisa to put the call through.

"Is this Krista Slater?" asked a hoarse male voice.

"That's me," she said. "Who's this?"

"This is Jimmy, Jimmy Caparulo."

"I'm so glad to hear from you. I've been waiting for you to call."

"Uh, yeah," the man replied, his confusion at Krista's borderline flirtatious tone evident.

Her heart thudded against her ribs. Jimmy Caparulo, the man Brewster had tried to frame as the Slasher before he'd been caught and killed. "I'm really glad you called," Krista said again. "My friend mentioned you might be in touch."

The "friend" was private investigator Stew Kowalski, who Krista knew through his work on several cases with the prosecuting attorney's office. But this time Stew wasn't working in any official capacity, so she was careful not to mention him by name in front of Benson.

Krista had hired Stew a couple of months ago to look deeper into the Brewster case. Even though there was no doubt Brewster was guilty of killing many women, including Evangeline Gordon, some things about him just weren't adding up. Too many gaps of information, too many things screaming at her that what happened to those women didn't begin and end with Brewster.

But everyone, from the FBI agent in charge of Brewster's case to Krista's own boss, seemed content to let it go. The Slasher had been caught; they had incontrovertible proof in the form of videos that he'd killed more than six victims—including Stephanie York, who he strangled in a hotel room, and Evangeline Gordon, Sean Flynn's alleged victim.

Sean Flynn had been exonerated, freed, and generously compensated, and now everyone seemed content to put the entire embarrassing episode behind them.

Except for Krista, who couldn't let it go. When it became clear there was no way to keep the investigation active, she hired Stew on her own dime to find out the real story behind Brewster and the prostitution ring he'd run out of one of Seattle's most exclusive nightclubs.

"I told Stew I would talk to only you. I know the way you helped Sean. You were one I could trust," Jimmy said, his words coming out in a rush.

"I wish you'd called sooner." Krista injected a pouty note in her voice and snuck a glance at Benson. His expression was one of disbelief.

"I knew they would hurt my aunt if I said anything," Jimmy continued, unable to stop himself now that the words had started. "But now Nate's dead and she's gone too. I can't keep it in anymore. I should have said something sooner. I should have helped Sean—"

Krista cut him off before he got rolling. She couldn't completely focus with Benson glaring daggers like that, and she didn't want to miss a word. "I really want to talk to you more, but this isn't the best time. Can I call you later, or better yet, why don't we go out?"

"Go out? Yeah, this will be better in person. Where do you live?"

"Wow, you don't waste any time!" she said with a little

laugh. "How about we at least meet for a drink before you invite yourself over."

"What the hell are you doing?" Benson whispered harshly. "We have to leave, now!"

Krista held up a finger and grabbed a pen as Jimmy rattled off a coffee place near his mother's house. "Tonight at eight. It's a date," she said before she hung up.

She gathered her things, avoiding Benson's eyes as she braced herself for the ass-chewing that would begin in five, four, three, two . . .

"What the hell are you thinking?" Benson said, his footsteps echoing off the hard floors of the corridor that connected their office wing to the courthouse. "Ten minutes before we face off against Karev is not the time for a personal call."

Krista bit back a smart-ass response. As relieved as she was that Benson had bought her performance, it galled her that he really thought, after working with her for over seven years, that she was that much of an idiot. Still, he'd be furious if he knew she was investigating Brewster after he'd told her to drop it. "I know, and I'm sorry. But I made a commitment to myself to give a little more balance to my personal life, and my friend has been trying to connect me with this guy for months now, and I've been really excited to meet with him."

At least that part was true. She'd always suspected Jimmy Caparulo knew more about Brewster than he'd let on, but even when Brewster had tried to set Jimmy up as the Slasher, Jimmy wouldn't say a word other than they'd become close friends in the army but had lost touch over the years. Nothing new, nothing Jimmy's aunt, who Jimmy had cared for during the last years of her life, couldn't tell them.

But now...

I knew they would kill my aunt if I said anything.

Her heart skipped a beat. *They.* So she was right. Nate Brewster hadn't been working alone.

It looked like Jimmy had something to say after all. It took all of her restraint not to rub it in Benson's face, but she needed to play her cards close to the vest until she had something concrete to go on.

Then all bets were off.

Benson paused and stayed Krista with a hand on her arm. "I know the last few months have been hard on you, and I know it's hard to drive forward after a mistake like that."

"A *mistake*? Mark, what happened to Sean Flynn was a catastrophe. And we were the engineers."

Mark's mouth flattened into a thin line. "We did the best we could with the evidence we were given. No prosecutor would have acted any differently."

Krista couldn't shrug it off so easily. "We didn't have to go for the death penalty."

Mark rubbed his thumb over the crease between his brows. "Mistakes were made. It's going to happen. You have to get over it."

Krista swallowed hard. Get over it? How could she get over it when all she saw when she closed her eyes was Sean Flynn's haunted gaze across the table in that prison visitation room? They'd put that look in his eyes, sentencing him to death row, where he'd spent two years alone in his cell, an existence so miserable Sean had chosen to waive all appeals and let himself be killed rather than fight.

"You've lost that fire, that passion that got you to where you are, and where I know you want to go," Benson said.

Oh, the fire was back, all right, but it had nothing to do with climbing the ladder or advancing her career.

"This is a big deal," Benson continued, "being part of the Karev case, and I put you on it because I know you're the best. This is your chance—our chance—to put the whole Sean Flynn disaster behind us and get this office's reputation back on track."

"And I appreciate that," Krista said, knowing that was the only acceptable response. But there was a knot of dread that had settled in her belly shortly after Cole Williams had asked her to reexamine Sean Flynn's case so many months ago. It had expanded in size every day as she became more convinced that while she'd spent her years in this office committed to justice, the people around her had much more selfish motivations.

She hated to believe that Mark, her mentor, who had hired her straight out of law school, cared about nothing but bolstering the reputation of "the office" and positioning himself for the next election. But with rumors swirling that he had his sights on the governor's office, it was getting harder to ignore the feeling that this man she'd looked up to as a second father was not nearly as noble as she'd believed.

Krista wasn't naïve. She knew a guy like Benson didn't make it to where he was without playing politics. But lately the bitter taste had gotten stronger in her mouth, the compromises Benson made harder and harder to swallow, his ability to shrug off what happened to Sean and move on incomprehensible.

. . .

Six hours later, Krista's gut was still churning as she entered the coffee shop where she was supposed to meet Jimmy Caparulo.

She ordered a latte and forced herself to stop brooding over today's failure and instead focus on how she was going to salvage the case.

Jimmy was late, so she pulled out the case files to review while she waited. Her irritation escalated as eight turned into eight-thirty, then eight forty-five. Finally nine o'clock passed and still no sign of Jimmy Caparulo.

Two phone calls at the number he'd given her dumped straight into voice mail, and her texts went unanswered.

She swore under her breath as she looked up Jimmy's address from the report Stew had given her. Jimmy was not the most stable person in the world, with documented PTSD and a history of alcohol and drug abuse. Most likely he went on a bender and either forgot about their meeting or passed out before he could meet her.

Which also made whatever information he provided less than reliable, she reminded herself as she walked the short distance to the house where Jimmy lived with his mother.

Still, it was a start, and maybe if it wasn't all bona fide, he'd give her something—

Her inner monologue stopped short as she registered the flashing blue and yellow lights in the driveway halfway down the block. She bit back a curse when she saw it was Jimmy's house.

As she got closer, she could hear the voices popping over the radios and the murmurs of the small crowd gathered on the small front lawn.

A woman was sobbing incoherently against the shoulder of another woman. "It was awful, so awful. Thank God Angie wasn't here to see it."

Krista recognized one of the uniforms controlling the perimeter. "Roberts! What happened in there?"

Roberts looked at her in confusion. "What are you doing here?"

"I was supposed to meet with Jimmy Caparulo about an hour ago," Krista admitted. So much for keeping their meeting secret until she'd built up her case, but with her number popping up all over his cell phone in the last hour, there was no way to keep a lid on it. "When he didn't show, I decided to come by."

Roberts let out a mirthless laugh. "Guess he was too busy blowing his brains out to keep your date."

Krista's stomach bottomed out at the news. "He killed himself?"

"They're not gonna call it right now, but from where I'm standing, there isn't much question he ate the business end of his Glock."

She swallowed back a surge of bile. "Who found him?"

"Neighbor," Roberts said, inclining his head in the direction of the sobbing woman. "She found him about fifteen minutes ago and called it in."

"How'd she get in the house?"

"She has a key. She was a friend of Jimmy's aunt, and since she died a couple weeks ago, neighbors have been taking turns bringing him dinner. Came over to deliver a plate of enchiladas and got one hell of a surprise."

"Neighbors didn't hear anything?" The houses on Caparulo's street were close together. "Seems like someone would have heard a gunshot."

"It's an older neighborhood," Roberts said, and as

Krista took a closer look at the crowd milling on the lawn, she saw a lot of white hair and hunched backs. "The lady next door says she might have heard it, but at the time she thought it was the TV."

"She say what time?"

"About seven-thirty."

Krista pulled her wool coat tighter around herself. All that time she had been waiting for Jimmy at the coffee shop, and he was already dead.

And he just happened to kill himself on the day he was supposed to meet me.

A shiver that had nothing to do with the damp spring night slithered down her spine. "Okay if I go inside?"

Roberts frowned. "The ME's still in there, and they haven't even moved him yet—"

Krista cut him off with a wave of her hand. "I've seen worse."

Yet Krista could see a thousand bloody crime scenes and nothing could ever prepare her for the smell. She was brutally reminded of that the second she stepped into the small, one-story house. She flashed her ID at a uniform and didn't bother to ask where Jimmy was.

It was all too easy to follow the odor of violent death. Sickly sweet, metallic blood and excrement mixed with an indescribable stink, like she could smell the body already rotting though he'd been dead for less than two hours.

She followed the smell and sounds of activity down a short hallway, past a bathroom on the left and through the second door on the right. Like a homing beacon, her gaze skipped right to the headboard of the double bed and the wall above. A wall that was painted white but now displayed a splatter of blood punctuated with the occasional pieces of gray brain.

Despite the cavalier attitude she'd shown Roberts, Krista's knees went a little wobbly and her vision started to tunnel. She leaned carefully against the doorjamb and took a deep, quiet breath as she kept an iron-clawed grip on her composure. She'd worked for the prosecuting attorney's office for seven years, dealt with some of the bloodiest crime scenes imaginable, and had never shown even a hint of weakness. She wasn't about to start now.

She forced herself to look at the scene analytically. She knew the crime scene guys would do a thorough investigation, but she wanted to take her own look around and see if there was anything going on here that would indicate it was anything other than a gory suicide scene.

Jimmy was flopped back on the bed, his booted feet resting on the floor, knees bent over the edge of the mattress. His right hand was flung out to the side, and there was a chalk mark on the bed to indicate where the gun had fallen.

Flashbulbs popped as the techs took pictures of the scene, and she recognized Medina from the coroner's office leaning over Jimmy's body. She greeted him and immediately regretted it when he straightened up, giving her a good look at Jimmy's face—what was left of it anyway. Her stomach lurched and she pinned her stare to a blank spot on the wall until she was sure she wasn't going to hurl up the coffee she'd drank.

"This guy wasn't screwing around," Medina said as he snapped off his gloves and dropped them into a biowaste container. "We'll need ballistics to confirm it, but judging from the way it took off half of his skullcap, Mr. Caparulo used a hollow point, which expanded on impact."

"Roberts said the Glock was registered to him."

Medina nodded. "I guess so—that's for these guys to figure out." He gestured at the crime scene techs.

"You're sure he did it himself?"

Medina frowned like the question confused him. "I need to do a full postmortem, and the forensics will have to confirm it, but he has powder residue on his hands."

A cold breeze wafted through the room, providing momentary relief from the suffocating stench. The shade flapped against the window frame. "The window's open." Krista lifted the shade and saw the screen was still in place. She turned to one of the techs, an Asian woman wearing wire-frame glasses who dusting Jimmy's desk for fingerprints. "Was it like that when you got here?"

"I'm not sure. You'll have to ask whoever was first on the scene."

Krista started to ask who that was when her gaze snagged on a silver-framed photo on Jimmy's desk. She recognized Jimmy Caparulo, dressed in army fatigues. He looked younger, smiling into the camera with his arms slung over the shoulders of the two other men in the photo. Her breath caught as she recognized the other two.

Flanking Jimmy on the left, looking like a fallen angel with his dark hair and piercing eyes, was the man whose face had haunted her, waking and sleeping, from the day she'd watched him walk out of the courtroom a free man.

But the man in the picture wasn't the Sean Flynn she knew. Gone were the deep, grim lines in his cheeks, the tight mouth, the eyes dark with anger.

In the picture was a Sean Krista had never seen. Eyes sparking with humor, mouth wide open and laughing, his teeth bright white in contrast to his sunbaked skin.

So happy and gorgeous it was hard to believe she'd ever believed him a murderer.

And on Jimmy's right, Nate Brewster, the epitome of an American hero, his blond-hair, blue-eyed perfection hiding the well of evil at the root of his soul. Evil that had ruined the lives of the men who had considered him a friend.

Now Jimmy was dead, just as he had been about to tell her secrets that Brewster had killed to keep.

Despite Medina's assessment, Krista knew in her gut it was no coincidence. "Make sure you check the window outside for signs of forced entry," she said to the tech dusting for fingerprints, who looked confused by the order but nodded in agreement.

Who else could be hurt by the information Jimmy had? What were they missing?

Before she could ponder the question further, her phone rang. When she recognized Stew's number, she ducked out of the bedroom and into the bathroom across the hall, closing the door before she picked up.

"Jimmy Caparulo's dead," she said.

"I know," Stew said. "They're speculating he killed himself after the trauma of being framed for the Slasher murders."

"Conveniently on the same night he was going to meet me," Krista said. "I don't care how the ruling ends up. I don't think this was a suicide."

"I'll look into it. But that's not why I called you. I think I found something."

"Yeah?"

"I've been tracking Brewster's financials, and I think I've found something. Something big."

THE DISH

Where authors give you the inside scoop!

♥ ♥ ♥ ♥ ♥ ♥ ♥ ♥ ♥ ♥ ♥ ♥ ♥ ♥ ♥

From the desk of Jami Alden

Dear Reader,

Whenever I start a new project, people inevitably ask me, "what's it about?" With BEG FOR MERCY, my answer seemed simple. This book is about Megan Flynn's desperate quest to get her wrongfully convicted brother off death row before he's executed. It's about a woman who is so determined she'll risk anything: her heart, when she begs Detective Cole Williams, the man who broke her heart when he arrested her brother, for help as she tracks down the real killer. And her life, when she herself becomes the target of a brutal killer's twisted desires.

But as I got further into Megan and Cole's journey, I realized that's *not* really what this book is about. Scratch beneath the surface, and you'll see that this book is really about faith. Not necessarily the religious kind, but the kind of faith you have in the people you love. It's also about the faith you have in yourself, in your gut, your instincts—whatever you want to call it. It's about listening to yourself and the truth that you cannot deny, even when the rest of the world tries to convince you that you're wrong.

No matter the evidence that points to her brother's guilt, Megan knows, deep down in her core, that her brother is not capable of the kind of brutal murder for which he was convicted. Nothing will convince her otherwise, her belief in her brother's innocence and faith in his true nature is absolutely unshakeable.

It's so strong that it can even convince a skeptic like by the book, just the facts ma'am detective like Cole Williams to put aside everything he thinks he knows about this case. It will drive him to risk a career that means everything to him in order to help the woman he loves.

Megan and Cole's journey to happily ever after isn't an easy one, but nothing worth having comes easily. I hope you enjoy their story, and as you read, ask yourself, how deep is your faith in yourself and the people around you? How far would you go for someone you love?

Enjoy!

Jami Alden

www.jamialden.com
www.facebook.com/jamialden
twitter @jamialden

♥ ♥ ♥ ♥ ♥ ♥ ♥ ♥ ♥ ♥ ♥ ♥ ♥ ♥

From the desk of Carolyn Jewel

Dear Reader,

Paisley Nichols, the heroine of MY DANGEROUS PLEASURE, is living her dream. She owns a bakery in San Francisco's financial district, and she's making a go of it. It's hard work and long hours, but she loves what she does. I had some real-life inspiration for her character. When I was a kid, my mother baked from scratch; bread, cinnamon rolls and delicious cookies, which my siblings and I took for granted. It wasn't until much later in life that I realized that not every mother baked like that. Now I bake goodies for my son, and if I have to taste test what I bake, well, that's a sacrifice I'm willing to make.

My youngest brother worked as a pastry chef for a while (he now does catering on the side) and there was a time when he was training when he'd drive up from Santa Barbara where he lived, spend the weekend at our house, bake up a storm, and leave us with a refrigerator full of whatever he was practicing at the time; crème brûlée, chocolate soufflé, chocolate mousse, and what have you. When he got married, the restaurant threw a party for him, and if you've never been around a slew of professional chefs, let me tell you, you are missing out on great food and lots of fun.

With my brother as an example, I got more ambitious

with my own baking. He taught me that quality ingredients make an enormous difference in the outcome, but there are also any number of little tips and tricks that get left out of many recipes that can transform a dessert from great to amazing or from decent looking to professional looking. For example, when making pie crust, use ice water, not room temperature water. Not even the *Joy of Cooking* mentions that crucial fact. Suddenly, my pie crusts were a success! I've also picked up and shared lots of recipes and tips from people on Twitter (I'm @cjewel).

Lest you think my story is nothing but sweetness and 70% (or higher) pure cocoa chocolate, Iskander, the demon hero of MY DANGEROUS PLEASURE, has a very dark side to him. He's been tasked with keeping Paisley safe from the mage who's stalking her, and when she develops some unusual magical abilities, his job gets even more difficult. There are people after them both, and they aren't very nice. But in between the enslaved demons and magic-using humans chasing them, Paisley and Iskander do find the time and place to indulge themselves with delicious sweets and each other.

Enjoy!

Carolyn Jewel

♥ ♥ ♥ ♥ ♥ ♥ ♥ ♥ ♥ ♥ ♥ ♥ ♥ ♥

From the desk of Laurel McKee

Dear Reader,

I have a confession to make—I am totally addicted to dark, brooding, tortured heroes with complicated pasts! I blame *Jane Eyre*. This is still one of my all-time favorite books, and I first came across it when I was ten or eleven years old. It was a battered, old paperback copy from a box of books from a garage sale, and I stayed up all night reading it. I was shocked by the wife in the attic! And when I had finished, I started reading it all over again. I then snatched up every Gothic romance I could find. I guess I've never gotten over the "Mr. Rochester thing."

When I started writing the second book in The Daughters of Erin series, DUCHESS OF SIN, I had planned for Sir Grant Dunmore to be part of a love triangle in the story, who would probably die in the end. But as I wrote his scenes, he showed me that he was much more complicated than that. His scenes with Caroline seemed to take on a life of their own, and I wanted to find out more about him. I wanted to see what would happen between Grant and Caroline and where their unexpected attraction would take them. The answer became LADY OF SEDUCTION. And their passion for each other caused a *lot* of trouble for them, and fun for me!

I've loved spending time with the Blacknall sisters and their heroes, and I'm sorry to say good-bye to them in this book. But I'm very happy they've all found their happily-ever-afters. For excerpts, behind-the-book information on the history of this era, and some fun extras, you can visit my website at http://laurelmckee.net.

And if you'd like to put together your own Irish feast, here is a recipe for one of my favorite dishes—Shepherd's Pie! (The first two books featured Irish Soda Bread and Sticky Toffee Pudding, all great when served with a Guinness . . .)

Ingredients

- 1½ lbs ground round beef
- 1 onion chopped
- 1–2 cups vegetables—chopped carrots, corn, peas
- 1½–2 lbs potatoes (3 big ones)
- 8 tablespoons butter (1 stick)
- ½ cup beef broth
- 1 teaspoon Worcestershire sauce
- Salt, pepper, other seasonings of choice

1 Peel and quarter potatoes, boil in salted water until tender (about 20 minutes).
2 While the potatoes are cooking, melt 4 tablespoons butter (½ a stick) in large frying pan.
3 Sauté onions in butter until tender over medium heat (10 mins). If you are adding vegetables, add them according to cooking time. Put any carrots in with the onions. Add corn or peas either at the end of the cooking of the onions, or after the meat has initially cooked.

4 Add ground beef and sauté until no longer pink. Add salt and pepper. Add Worcestershire sauce. Add half a cup of beef broth and cook, uncovered, over low heat for 10 minutes, adding more beef broth as necessary to keep moist.

5 Mash potatoes in bowl with remainder of butter, season to taste.

6 Place beef and onions in baking dish. Distribute mashed potatoes on top. Rough up with a fork so that there are peaks that will brown nicely. You can use the fork to make some designs in the potatoes as well.

7 Cook in 400 degree oven until bubbling and brown (about 30 minutes). Broil for last few minutes if necessary to brown.

Serves four.

Enjoy!

Linnel McKee

♥ ♥ ♥ ♥ ♥ ♥ ♥ ♥ ♥ ♥ ♥ ♥ ♥ ♥ ♥

From the desk of Katie Lane

Dear Reader,

There's something about a bad boy that's irresistible, something about a man who lives on the edge and plays by his own rules. And whether it was the time you caught the teenage rebel checking you out in your new

Christmas sweater—or the time the tatted biker sent you a blatantly sexual look as he cruised by on his custom bike—a run-in with a bad boy is like taking a ride on the world's biggest roller coaster; long after the ride's over, you're still shaky, breathless, and begging for more.

No doubt a portion of the blame lies with our mothers. (It's so easy to blame Mom.) Maternal warnings always include the things that turn out to be the most fun—wild parties, fast cars, and naughty boys. (All of which got me in plenty of trouble.) But I think most of our infatuation has to do with our desire to take a break from being the perfect daughter, the hard-working employee, the dependable wife, and the super mom. For one brief moment, we want to release our inner bad girl and jerk up that sweater Aunt Sally gave us and flash some cleavage. Or hop on that throbbing piece of machinery and take a ride on the wild side.

Even if it's only in our fantasies—or possibly a steamy romance novel—we want to throw caution to the wind and fearlessly proclaim . . .

MAKE MINE A BAD BOY!

Katie Lane

www.katielanebooks.com